W9-BUA-116

Praise for *Motorcycles & Sweetgrass*

NATIONAL BESTSELLER

"A near-perfect debut, a masterful mythic-comedy balancing contemporary issues and realities with magic and history in a First Nations community in Ontario. . . . A broad, bawdy, raucous, deeply felt and utterly involving narrative, a genuine pleasure to read."   Robert J Wiersema, *Edmonton Journal*

"Drew Hayden Taylor has woven an epic tale of magic, mystery and charm for the world to discover in *Motorcycles & Sweetgrass*. This is a novel to savor. A complete delight!"
Richard Van Camp, author of
The Moon of Letting Go and *The Lesser Blessed*

"*Motorcycles & Sweetgrass* may be concerned with aboriginal community politics, identity, mythology and intergenerational legacies, but it reads like a romp. . . . The book's real strength is its underlying account of a community struggling to weave an increasingly abstract traditional past with some kind of meaningful future."   *Toronto Star*

"Drew Hayden Taylor's got no qualms about poking fun at his Native roots, and that's what makes *Motorcycles & Sweetgrass* such a pleasure. It's playful yet soulful, with a narrative that keeps those pages turning."   *NOW* (Toronto)

"*Motorcycles & Sweetgrass* is a cultural blend of legend, magic and modern community life. . . . Taylor's humour is farcical as he gently prods at the silliness, the politicking of modern day life, the structures imposed by a government far from the reserve."

The Halifax Chronicle-Herald

"Fast-paced, uproariously funny and genuinely thrilling, *Motorcycles & Sweetgrass* is an epic tale told with an admirable simplicity of language and tone. It is also the best book—so far—from Drew Hayden Taylor, who remains one of Canada's finest and funniest writers."

Ian Ferguson, author of *Village of the Small Houses*

MOTORCYCLES

&

Sweetgrass

—~ A NOVEL ~—

Drew Hayden
TAYLOR

VINTAGE
CANADA

VINTAGE CANADA EDITION, 2011

Copyright © 2010 Drew Hayden Taylor

All rights reserved under International and Pan-American Copyright Conventions. No part of this book may be reproduced in any form or by any electronic or mechanical means, including information storage and retrieval systems, without permission in writing from the publisher, except by a reviewer, who may quote brief passages in a review.

Published in Canada by Vintage Canada, a division of Random House of Canada Limited, Toronto, in 2011. Originally published in hardcover in Canada by Alfred A. Knopf Canada, a division of Random House of Canada Limited, in 2010. Distributed by Random House of Canada Limited.

Vintage Canada with colophon is a registered trademark.

www.randomhouse.ca

Library and Archives Canada Cataloguing in Publication

Taylor, Drew Hayden, 1962–
Motorcycles & sweetgrass / Drew Hayden Taylor.

ISBN 978-0-307-39806-2

I. Title. II. Title: Motorcycles and sweetgrass.

PS8589.A885M68 2011   C813'.54   C2010-903829-0

Design by Kelly Hill

Printed and bound in the United States of America

12 14 16 18 20 19 17 15 13

101 THINGS TO DO WITH AN INDIAN CHIEF

~ DISCLAIMER ~

The author has never been nor probably ever will be in the employ of the Indian Motorcycle Company. While confessing to *being* an "Indian" (the feathered, not the dot kind), the author reluctantly admits it is unlikely he will ever *own* an Indian (the internal combustion variety, the feathered or the dot kind).

This book is dedicated to the memory of my mother, Fritzie Taylor, who always had time for my stories.

"Heart breaker, Soul shaker.
I've been told about you.
Steam roller, midnight stroller.
What they been sayin' must be true . . .
Now you're messin' with a son of a bitch."

"Hair of the Dog,"
Nazareth

Hey, wanna hear a good story? Supposedly it's a true one. It's a long story but it goes something like this . . .

Somewhere out there, on a Reserve that is closer than you think but still a bit too far to walk to, lived a young Ojibway boy. Though this is not his story, he is part of it.

As all good tales do, this one begins far in the past, but not so far back that you would have forgotten about it.

There was much too much splashing on the lake. It was inconsiderate and downright unfriendly. The minnows were not happy. Same with the perch, the rockfish, and especially the lone sunfish that called the water near the two sunken cedar trees his home. The other fish were just passing through, but for the sunfish this was a serious intrusion of privacy. Those creatures from above the waterline had been there all afternoon creating havoc. And the sunfish hated havoc. It was counter-productive to a sunfish's life.

For unfathomable reasons, these large, rude, scaleless air-breathing things had jumped off *his* half-buried trees, creating a lingering cloud of silt. The other fish had left, looking for quieter spots to contemplate the age-old aquatic question, whether the lake was half full, or half empty. But this was the sunfish's home, and he watched from a distance as the creatures splashed and dove as if they owned the place. There was nothing he could do. He was just a sunfish and they were people. And occasionally, people ate sunfish. It's hard to lodge a complaint given that balance of power.

Besides, there was something familiar about the man. The sunfish was sure he had come across him, but where, the sunfish couldn't say.

The woman, barely into the second half of her teens, swam naked through the water. As the man, a tad older but also naked, watched her, he thought about who had made this creature. Certain cultures believed the Creator made man in His own image—but the Anishnawbe language was not hung up on gender. If the Creator had made this woman in Her own image She was an astonishingly beautiful five-foot-six, lean, Anishnawbe woman. The dappled sunlight, the smell of pine and cedar, the tingling feel of the cool clear lake. It doesn't get much better than this, he thought. And he'd been around. Wherever around was, he'd been there. Twice. And had long ago lost the T-shirt.

The two had been there all afternoon, and if either could have had their way, they would have been there forever. But that was not to be.

"What are you thinking?" came the female voice across the water, speaking in an ancient language.

He just smiled.

"No. Tell me. What are you thinking?"

The man pondered for a moment, but, just as he was about to speak, he dove into the water quick as a dragonfly. Treading water, hair spread, she scanned the surface of the lake in all directions. Becoming anxious, she called out to him. "Stop that. Come back." But the only response was a nearby loon's call. She began to panic.

No one could hold their breath that long. Out of the corner of her eye she saw a hawk make its way across the sky. The loon, mirroring her concern, called again.

"Hey!" she yelled, and then, "Hey, where . . . ?" Suddenly she was gone. Silence returned, and the hawk eyed the bubbles rising to the surface.

Two human bodies came crashing through the surface, gasping for air, and then exploding with laughter.

"I scared you, didn't I?" the man asked roguishly. The light cutting through the forest canopy dappled on the man's face and danced in his brown eyes.

The girl, wiping the hair back from her face, muttered, "I hate it when you do things like that. What are you, half fish?"

"On occasion."

The girl back-paddled a metre or so away from the man. "Say you're sorry."

"What?"

"Say you're sorry. Now."

The man was perplexed. "Or what?"

"Oh, nothing. I just want you to say you're sorry."

"All right, if it will make you happy. I am sorry. I am so sorry." The man was now yelling. "I AM SO INCREDIBLY SORRY! How's that?" His voice echoed across the water and back again, gradually growing more distant. "Hear that? That makes me three times as sorry."

The girl smiled. "Thank you. It's not often you find a man who takes orders so easily."

Swimming closer, the man rolled over onto his back. "You'll find I'm a little different from most men . . . You know, this is how sea otters eat. They put clams and crabs and things like that on their stomach, and crack them open with a rock, using their bellies like a big wooden kitchen table."

"What are sea otters?"

"Oh, they live way out west, in the ocean. You know what an ocean is?" The girl nodded. "They are kind of like the otters around here, only different. And have funny moustaches."

"Otters have moustaches? Like White people?" The girl watched the man float lazily around her. "You're lying. You have to be. The things you've told me. But I love your story about squirrels that can fly. You've travelled a lot, haven't you?"

"A bit. Here and there, and they don't fly, silly, they glide."

"This is going to be my first trip anywhere. I've never been more than a few hours' walk from home," she said.

The man started treading. His eyes forced their way into hers. "Then don't go."

The girl looked away. "I don't have a choice."

"Everybody has a choice."

The secluded bay grew a little chillier and the girl trembled in the water. "You don't know White people. They don't take no for an answer. My parents tried but . . ."

The man wasn't listening. "There's supposed to be a thunderstorm tomorrow. A big one."

"There is? How do you know?"

"I just do. I know how much you love thunderstorms, with the lightning criss-crossing the sky, and the booming thunder shaking the cups in your mother's cupboard."

"It's like the sky is waking everybody up."

"Well, this one is supposed to be the biggest of the summer."

"How do you . . ."

"I just do. I had to call in a few favours, though. There's that place up at the top of Bear Hill, where we can sit and watch. The lightning will leave us alone. We have an agreement, the lightning and I."

"Don't be silly."

He took her hand. "I'm not being silly. We can sit there all night, watching it. It will be our storm."

The girl struggled to answer the man. "I can't. You know that."

The man, now silent and brooding, looked away. His eyes were on the far shore, and yet they weren't. "If you loved me . . ."

"I do, but . . ."

Now the girl was getting anxious. This was not how she wanted to spend their final day together. Tomorrow she would be sent away to be educated in one of those big places White people liked to build. Older than most of the local kids sent off, she'd managed to remain hidden from the White man's so-called education. But her father had died, and her mother had seven other kids to feed, and she worked all the time. So, being the oldest, she was a prime candidate for the school. The local on-Reserve school had taught her to read and speak English. But it could only take kids so far, which is why the Canadian government had built these other schools where their welfare would be better maintained than on a Reserve.

Manifest Destiny, as the White people to the south believed, dictated that this little Anishnawbe girl be removed from her home and sent away to be taught about the Battle of Hastings, dangling participles, and how to draw a pie chart. For a year or two anyway. Starting tomorrow. And this man, who'd come into her life a few months ago, was about to be left behind.

"It's your new boyfriend, isn't it. What do women see in him?" the man asked.

"He's not my new boyfriend. He's just some guy. Don't be angry. With me or him."

The man was silent. Then he hauled himself out of the water and sat on the log running perpendicular to the shore. He looked troubled, and frustrated.

The girl continued. "Everybody says he's great, and really smart. He can do all sorts of fancy tricks and things."

"So can I."

Slowly, the girl swam toward the man. She reached out and caressed his leg, trying to restore his playful mood. "I know. But this guy has lots and lots of friends in high places, all over the world. He's one of the reasons we're being sent off to this place. Everybody talks about him."

Growing glummer, the man moved his leg away from the young girl's caresses.

"Everybody used to talk about me. Now they talk about him. I don't understand. What's he got that I don't. He's so depressing. What's his name again?"

" . . . Jesus."

"What kind of name is that?" The man shook his head.

"He comes from far away and he's very nice. You should meet him."

The man had been hearing of this guy for quite some time. He kept getting more and more popular, and the man couldn't figure out why.

"I don't play well with other children," he countered.

"Don't be like that—"

"I thought you'd stay here. With me. But you don't care. Nobody cares. Choose that guy then. I don't care."

Once again, the man dove deep into the water, a fair distance from the girl. Far beneath the surface, the sunfish saw him disappear into the weeds, swimming like he'd been born under water.

"Don't go!" cried the girl as she swam to the spot where the man had disappeared.

This time, he didn't reappear. The girl dove under the water, her eyes frantically searching for him. Finally, her lungs bursting, she crawled ashore.

"Come back! Don't leave!" The girl cried out and her voice bounced across the lake, only to echo back. "I don't want to go . . ." She wiped her eyes.

The next day the girl went to school.

And the man . . . now that's an interesting story too. But later.

ONE

The first day she arrived she knew she wouldn't like it. The place was cold and drafty. The clothes they made her wear were hot and itchy. They didn't fit well at all, and all the girls had to wear the exact same thing. The boys, situated at the opposite end of the building, were not allowed to talk to the girls. Brothers weren't allowed to interact with sisters, cousins and so on. Only the People in Black, otherwise known as the Nuns and the Priests, were allowed to talk to each other. To the young girl, these people had nothing interesting to say. And what they did say was usually not very nice. And what they did was sometimes even worse.

Those with darker skin who were not yet adults and free of this mandatory education called it the Angry Place. Still, she put up with it. It had taken a long time to get here and she instinctively knew it would take her a much longer time to get home. Wherever that was—she had no idea if it was north, south, east or west. It was just far away. As soon as she arrived, she was told stories of one of the girls trying to run away. She wasn't the type to break the rules like that. Instead, she decided to deal with the present by concentrating on the past and the future: remembering the family she had just left, and imagining the family that she would someday have.

Sister Agnes had christened the girl Lillian. As soon as she had arrived, they told her that her Anishnawbe name was not to be uttered anymore. Her old name became her secret that she kept close to her—so close, she would seldom speak it aloud. Her grandmother had given it to her a decade and a half ago. In this place, words other than English or Latin were unchristian and those who used them were punished severely. So, she became Lillian.

The girl worked hard to learn their language better. She was an average student, but critical, often wondering to herself why she should care about a train leaving Toronto, travelling at eighty kilometres an hour. She outwardly learned to respect this place— but was suspicious of it. An incident just before bed on her second day there had planted that seed. In fact, it made her doubt the whole enterprise. She and Betty, a newly made friend, had discovered that their mothers had the same name—and they had found this hilarious, falling into an uncontrollable fit of the giggles. Out of nowhere, Sister Agnes appeared. She scolded, "Stop that this second."

The girls looked at each other, uncertain. Betty, who had always kept on the sister's good side, asked meekly, "What is it, Sister?"

"Stop that laughing—it is rude and not acceptable in a house of God such as this."

This, of course, made the girls laugh all the harder. What kind of a place was this? Not a day, or more like it, an hour went by at home when Lillian didn't hear her mother break into loud guffaws. It was what Lillian loved best about her. Oftentimes (more often than not) these White people made no sense at all.

———

"Did you hear about Sam?" whispered Rose, one night, about a year after Lillian had arrived. Rose was the only one of them who had managed to pick up a smattering of Latin during the many church services they were forced to attend. As a result, most considered her the People in Black's pet. All the girls were kneeling by their cots saying their prayers. In an attempt to curry favour with her fellow inmates—though she maintained that she didn't know that much Latin—Rose would often tell them what was going on.

"No," said Lillian. "What about Sam?" Sam Aandeg was from her community, one of the only familiar faces here, though they spoke only about once a month. She was related to Sam through her mother's first cousin—and he had a rebellious streak. When he arrived he'd bitten a Nun attempting to shave his head. That was seven years ago, and time and repeated punishments had not managed to subdue him.

"He's in trouble again!"

"Why?" Lillian asked, kneeling by the cot next to Rose's.

The girl whispered, "The usual. Being mouthy. He's in the shed. And Father McKenzie won't let him leave until he can memorize all the monologues in that stupid play. He'll probably be there overnight."

"Again!" she said. Lillian had taken to caring for her wayward cousin, knowing his nature was instinctively to wade against the current of any river. But one did not wade against the current of the Angry Place. "Well, it's a good thing the mosquitoes are gone," she told Rose. "Like sitting in that shed is going to change anything. He should know better." Secretly, though, she admired his resistance. Indian boys and girls who misbehaved spent a lot of time in the shed, Sam more than most. Some people might not see the connection between placing defenceless children in confined spaces for prolonged periods of time and any particular passages in the Bible. Perhaps the People in Black reasoned that Christ had spent those couple of weeks in the desert, trying to figure things out and come up with a life plan. It had worked for Him. It should, in theory, work for these savages too. It was, they believed, a win-win situation.

So there sat Sam, a copy of a four-hundred-year-old play, which he struggled to read, on his lap. For most of the day in October, the shed was way too dark to read in. Still, boredom made unwitting readers of the most stubborn students. On clear nights when the moon was waxing, a narrow diagonal strip of light fell across the dirt floor. If the resourceful penitent placed the book just right, he could sometimes make out passages in the moonlight.

Memorizing sections of this play was no problem. He came by it naturally. Though consensus in the big brick building was that Sam was unintelligent and a problem student/child/Indian, he was actually very smart. And he wilfully refused to give Father McKenzie and the rest the satisfaction of knowing this. "To be or not to be, that is the question," he read aloud.

Sam liked this question. He, and practically every student in the building, could understand the quandary. Many wrestled with it every day. Some won. Some lost—but there were always more arriving to fill their places.

It was too cold to sleep, and the growling from his stomach kept him awake. Gradually he dragged the book across the dirt floor, struggling to read in the shifting patterns of moonlight.

His lone voice broke the silence. One line, after the monologue in Act I, Scene iv, caught his eye. "'Something is rotten in the state of Denmark.'"

Boy, he thought, I don't know what or where the hell this

Denmark is but it can't smell nearly as bad as this place. Denmark would have to be an improvement.

"Sam! Wake up! Sam Aandeg! Hurry and wake up!"

Amazingly, Sam had managed to fall asleep sometime before dawn, worn down by the cold and strain of trying to read in the darkness. The book had been his pillow. It was a few moments before he could manage a response to his cousin's tense knocking on the shed's splintered wall.

"What!" he snapped groggily. He tried to unroll from a fetal position, but couldn't. Waking up in this place was painful. He longed for his bed back home.

"It's me, Lillian. You okay?"

All he could make out was one brown eye peering through a gap, and a bit of the plain grey dress she, like all the girls, wore.

"I hate that name. You're not Lillian."

By now, he had managed to move to his hands and knees, and he stretched like a cat.

"Don't be like that. I can't stay long. Here, I brought you something to eat."

"I'm not hungry." They both knew that was a lie. "What . . . what did you bring?"

Near the bottom of the rear wall of the shed, about a foot of one plank was missing, broken off when a shovel had once been carelessly tossed into the back. Through it, she passed a wrapped-up packet, and Sam groaned in pain as he reached for it.

"It's just some toast and jam. That's all I could sneak out."

Trying not to look ungrateful, he took the offering and slowly opened it. He was an angry boy, and life was unfair, and a large part of him wanted to piss off the entire world. But there was still enough of the little boy from the Otter Lake Reserve to know right from wrong. And to be gracious when someone was being kind.

"Thank you" he managed to mumble. Trying to show some restraint, he ate the toast as slowly as possible.

"You shouldn't be here. They'll catch you and you'll be on the inside looking out, like me." He watched as his cousin looked around warily.

"I just wanted to make sure you were okay."

"I'm cold. I'm hungry. I'm mad. But I'm okay."

All of this was spoken in Anishnawbe, the forbidden language. Sam revelled in it, but Lillian switched quickly back to English. It was bad enough that she was here now, but if anyone overheard them, who knew what they would be in for.

"Why do you always get yourself in trouble like this?" whispered Lillian. Licking his fingers of the last remnants of jam, Sam just shrugged. "I can't keep sneaking around in the middle of the night to bring you food. If either of us gets caught . . . And someday, you'll get yourself into so much trouble that they'll send you away and I won't be able to help at all. You should just do what they say. It's less trouble."

"I don't care about trouble, I just want to get back home. This place is no good. I'm going to run away," he answered in Anishnawbe.

Lillian shook her head. "You'll get yourself killed. You don't even know which way home is. Remember Daniel River and James Magood." They were both silent for the moment.

"I'm not them. I know where home is. I saw it in that book. I saw the river and the islands. I'm sure that's them. And I know the bush." Sam paused for a moment. "Wanna come?" From somewhere near the kitchen, they both heard some of the kids yelling as they played a quick game of soccer before classes. "No, huh?" Lillian leaned against the shed, making it squeak. "You like it here, don't you."

"No. Not really."

"Then why don't you want to go home?"

Sam could see her hair squeezing between two of the boards as she rested her head against the shed. "I'm older than you, Sam, so you listen to me."

"Only by three years."

"That doesn't matter. I get to go home next year. And I like learning. I like knowing there's so much out there. I'm still trying to figure things out. Remember that map they showed us of the world? My grandmother used to tell me all of us were sitting on the back of a Giant Turtle. That's what we were taught. I didn't see any turtle there, Sam. It's a big . . . they call it a continent. There're lots of them."

"I'll find you a turtle if you want one so badly."

"I thought the world was full of magic. I don't think it is. Maybe once it was. Not any more."

"What are you so depressed about? I'm the one in the shed."

"And I kind of like this Jesus guy they talk about all the time," she said.

"You like a White guy?"

"They say he's Jewish, and that's not the same."

"Looks White to me."

Silence surrounded them, and Lillian looked behind her to make sure she hadn't been discovered. Her life up until then had been divided into White people and her people. "I think they are White too—but a girl here told me that it has something to do with their dicks. And pigs. I think."

"Dicks and pigs? They're weird. That guy Shylock is a Jew— and he was mean. Fine, then. I'll go home alone."

Lillian turned and looked at him once more, one eye peering through a separation in the slats. "I really wish you wouldn't."

"I'm not staying here. I won't stay here."

"Sam, please be careful. This place is no good, I know. But if you just pretend, it's so much easier. Don't make such a fuss."

"But it's different for me than you—that priest . . ."

"Oh, Sam, he's just a big bully. He can only hurt you if you let him. Don't you remember what you promised your folks? That friend of your mom's—you said you wouldn't end up like her. Nothing is worth that."

"But I can't stay here—I just can't."

"Sam, that guy's just mean. But at least he's teaching you all about Shakespeare. You told me you loved that stuff. You're so smart." She had slipped into Anishnawbe without realizing, until her tongue tripped on that old writer's name. She checked herself—if she wasn't careful she might be keeping her cousin company in the shed some time soon.

For the first time, their eyes locked. "What, what is it Sam?"

But he couldn't tell her what it was; he hardly knew what it was himself. "Goodbye, then, Mizhakwan . . ."

She glowed inside—he had said her name aloud in the forbidden language. And she knew that he was right. The best thing was for him to get away any way he could—and she should help him too. But these people had eyes in the back of their heads. Both of them would be punished. She looked around and walked stealthily away.

She was so confused. It was possible to be right and wrong at the same time. This place was challenging everything she had ever known before. But at least she was learning more than she ever learned back home.

TWO

It was hard to tell which hurt worse, his stomach, his head, his elbow—or his pride.

He had once more forgotten to turn off the single light bulb that burned over his bed. Light bulbs cost money and he was one of those people whose other needs took priority over being well lit. In fact, he once spent a whole season in the dark. Except he couldn't recollect whether it was a physical or spiritual darkness. It didn't matter. Dark was dark, and both involved walking into walls.

Except this morning. He arose in the bright mid-morning light. His foot slid onto the cigarette-scarred floor, knocking over some empty bottles. He started the day as he did every morning—with a deep breath and a vague understanding that the way he was living was wrong. But like the nausea in his stomach and the pounding in his head, the feeling would go away. There was an underlying fear that one day it would not go away. But he would worry about that tomorrow. Today he had woken up, and that was something, at least.

Now came the next step. Getting to his feet. A much more complex and difficult manoeuvre than most would expect. Immediately he found himself leaning for support on the sink next to his bed, his elbow throbbing from some recent impact. He let the water run, hoping against experience the water would get cold enough to numb his elbow. But it never got hot enough when he needed it to, either. Instead, he stared into the mirror. His face had changed so much over the years, he always startled himself.

"Good morning," the old man said to himself, barely recognizing his own voice. He didn't find many occasions to talk in this life, other than for panhandling and buying vast amounts of alcohol. On top of that he now spoke only in English. His former life had been tucked away in some dark recess of his mind. Hidden from reality with a security door protected by an eighty-proof lock.

The water, dripping from the semi-clogged sink onto his untrimmed toenails, made the reality of the room and his life all the more apparent. The sink had been partially plugged since he'd found himself here but a lack of both competent landlords and initiative on his part had left it unrepaired. So, his feet were wet, but he had survived far worse. He turned off the tap and dipped his hands into the full sink, then wet his face and hair. The shock of the water always brought him to the teetering edge of his past life. The knob on that locked door in his mind momentarily rattled. But the closer he got to where the water took him, the more he remembered, and the more he turned away. This time was no different.

His hair and face still dripping, he walked to his lone window and looked out. Outside he saw concrete and telephone poles. Mail and newspaper boxes. Cars. And the odd half-dead tree rising out of the sidewalk. As he stared off into this world he'd surrendered to, he was barely conscious of the cockroach that approached his wet feet, drawn to the water. The cockroach and the man had been roommates for the past couple of months. Sensing a bond with the man, a fellow reject relegated to existing on the fringes of society, doing what it could to survive, the cock-roach didn't fear him.

The old man, on the other hand, felt differently. He viewed the cockroach as just another immigrant from some far-off land, staking a claim to Native land, pestering him. Just another example of immigration gone wild. Same with those damn pigeons and doves. Who asked them to come to this country anyways?

The antennae of the cockroach gently touched and probed the man's feet, but due to the calluses, scars and bad circulation, the man was unaware of the cockroach's friendly intentions until it crawled over his toes. The result being a loud scream, a kick of his foot, a flying insect, and an old man falling backwards onto his ass. There the old man sat, even more aware that this was not the path the Creator had chosen for him. The man had chosen it for himself. Once more he stared out the window onto a world he hadn't created and didn't belong to, noticing a car that was driving by. On its rear-view mirror hung a dreamcatcher. On its back bumper was a sticker that said: THIS IS FIRST NATIONS COUNTRY.

Something loud and anxious started beating behind his mind's locked door. Curious, he crawled to his knees, momen-tarily intrigued by what was struggling to get free. He leaned out of the open window, trying to get a better look. The car stopped next to a roti shop across the road. Out got a woman, obviously Native—the eyes, the skin colour and the turquoise jewellery gave her away—and extremely pretty. In her hand she carried a cloth bag that from the man's window appeared to be filled with clothes. The woman entered the dry cleaner next to the roti shop. Through the large storefront window, the man watched her pull from the bag two sweaters, a skirt and a large blanket sporting a Native design. She seemed to be on familiar terms with the Asian man behind the counter.

Something continued to stir deep in the man. Something familiar, yet it had not reared its head in a very long time. The woman was pretty, that was obvious. He watched her as she took her receipt and exited the building. Taking a chance for the first time in a long time, the old man waved to the woman, his arm swinging wildly out the window.

"Hey, you—up here! Hi! Hello!" He had no idea why he was doing this, but something inside made him.

It took a moment before the woman located where the voice was coming from and concluded that it was directed at her. She glanced at the ground floor of the old man's building, and followed his voice up to the third floor.

Excited that she was looking at him, he continued gesticulating and calling. "Hello! Hello! Up here! Yeah, me!" A sliver of light spilled out from underneath that locked door, and the man spoke a lone word.

"Ahneen!"

Where that had come from, he wasn't sure. But he couldn't hold it back. He yelled it a second time, then a third, but then the expression on the woman's face silenced him, and the light from the locked door disappeared. He'd seen the expression before, a thousand times. It was a combination of disgust, pity and embarrassment. It stung the old man, the remnants of his pride struggling to come out of its coma. Hurt, the old man mustered his strength and responded in the only manner he could.

"Fuck you!"

As it turned out, he had summoned up a little too much strength. The virulence of the "f" and "ck" sound was more than his worn teeth and gums could stand, and as those two words went sailing out of his mouth, so did his right bicuspid. Out over the sidewalk and landing four feet from the woman. Looking shocked and more than a little repelled, the woman got back into her car and drove off, leaving her dirty laundry and the crazy letch in the window behind.

The old man, equally shocked but for different reasons, watched her leave. So this is what he'd become. Once a mighty battler of monsters, creator of creatures, teacher of tales and both chief troublemaker and champion of Canada's Native people, he was now . . . pathetic. He sat back down on his ass, not really knowing what to do or feel. And though he'd gotten up just ten minutes before, he fell back onto the floor.

He lay there for hours, fading in and out of consciousness, bits and pieces of past lives trying to claw their way to the surface. Wendigos, his long-dead mother. Women and men he'd known, fought and loved. Hunting deer. Buffalo. Whales. Creation. More memories than a hundred people could possibly have, yet they were all his. He just lay there, as his past ran over him, like pages from his life randomly flipping by.

Then, from the recesses of his damaged mind, she appeared. The face that had once stopped him from wandering the country, the body that had made him forget all the others (at that time anyway) and the smile that had made him hold his breath. He had known from the moment he met her, so long ago, that he could never be the man she wanted, needed or deserved, but so long as he could fake it, he had figured they would both be happy. She must be old now, he thought. Like him. Well, hopefully not like him. His eyes popped open. He hadn't allowed himself to see her face for decades. Why now? he thought. He propped himself on his elbows, perplexed. He shook his head, trying to remove the cobwebs from his mind. This was more than a flashback. It was more than an idle memory. This—she—was real. For some reason, he looked out the window again, this time to the horizon, his eyes gazing to the far north where he had once roamed the forest, and had swum in the lakes. Something was calling to him.

Once more he managed to achieve a standing position. Like a compass, his attention never wavered from the north. A dozen or more seconds passed as he debated his options. Glancing back over his shoulder he saw again his reflection in the mirror. This time he wasn't surprised. This time he felt the beginnings of a new confidence. Having a purpose could do that to a man. Turning to face the mirror, looking deep into his bloodshot eyes, he shook his head.

"That . . . will not do," he said to the reflection, knowing he now had an appointment to keep.

But first, he vomited.

THREE

Virgil was concerned, but didn't want to be. Everybody was rushing about, talking in hushed tones, looking downward in a respectful manner. It was true that his grandmother was dying, though nobody would admit it in exactly those words. His entire family had spent the past two weeks hovering about her house, bringing in food, taking out dishes of half-eaten casseroles, all frustrated by their inability to do anything to help Lillian Benojee.

Virgil loved his grandmother. But he was one of eighteen grandchildren and never quite knew were he stood on the totem pole of her affection. One grandchild, about ten years older than him, was well on his way to becoming a successful lawyer. Two others had started up a popular restaurant in a nearby town, providing Nouveau Native cuisine to all the American tourists. Kelly, another cousin who was only five days younger than him, had won some speech contest or something, and had just gotten back from Ottawa where she'd met the prime minister. And then there was Virgil. And there was nothing particularly bad about the boy, but neither was there anything notable about him. He wasn't as good as some, nor was he as bad as Chucky or Duanne, whose names were frequently found on the police flyer. Virgil was just a grade-seven student who acknowledged that vanilla ice cream, ginger ale and bad sitcoms were the highlights of his existence. The bell curve was invented for boys like him.

Oh yes, except that most bell-curve graphs don't include a mother named Maggie Second who happened to be the chief of the First Nations community known as Otter Lake. Virgil's father, dead from a boating accident three years ago, had been chief before her. Seeing how hard his mother worked, and how miserable the work made her, he was grateful that chiefdom, as applied under the Indian Act, was not dynasty-oriented.

Sitting on his grandmother's deck overlooking Otter Lake and oblivious to the warm spring air, he watched the comings and goings of his grandmother's house through the big see-through sliding doors. Food being put out, people eating, occasionally somebody going into his grandmother's bedroom. It had pretty well been the same since she collapsed. At the moment, there were about a dozen people in the living room, getting in one another's way.

Then he saw Dakota, yet another of Lillian's descendants, who was exactly two months older than him. She opened the door and let herself out onto the deck, and she was carrying something. Dakota had two brothers and a sister, named Cheyenne, Sioux and Cree. Dakota always believed the naming of her and her siblings said more about her embarrassing parents than it did about any of them. Especially since *their* names were Fred and Betty.

"Didn't see you at school yesterday."

"Wasn't there."

"I kind of put two and two together. Here—you don't come inside any more," she said, sitting in the chair beside Virgil and placing two bowls on the deck table between them. "So I thought you might be hungry." She slid one bowl across the table toward Virgil.

There was a reason she was his favourite cousin. Virgil sniffed the bowl. "More corn soup?"

"My English teacher calls it 'the Native chicken soup.'"

"What does that mean?"

Dakota shrugged. "I don't know. I think it's a Jewish joke or something, 'cause he's Jewish."

Virgil picked the bowl up and began to slurp away, his spoon spilling more than it carried to his mouth.

"Did Aunt Julia bring this?" he asked.

"Yep, a whole big pot. How did you know?"

Virgil shrugged. "She always puts too much salt in it."

Dakota slurped her soup too, seeming to enjoy the salty flavour. She paused long enough to say, "Yeah, but you're eating it. And it's supposed to be salty."

The two ate in silence for a while, watching the activities in the house through the large plate of glass like it was a huge television with the sound turned down.

"Are you gonna go in and see her?" asked Dakota.

"Grandma? I wanna but . . ."

"But you're kinda scared. Right?"

Virgil nodded and went back to his soup. He *was* scared. He'd never seen anybody real sick and close to death before, and even though this was his grandmother, he wasn't sure if he was up to it. His father's casket had been closed.

"I was too. She's okay. Smiled, and even told me a joke."

They both smiled, remembering Lillian Benojee's silly jokes.

"The one about Native vegetarians?"

Dakota nodded. "Yep, that one. Heard it a dozen times but she still makes me laugh." She put her now-empty bowl down on the table and got comfortable in the deck chair. "Haven't seen your mother here today. She coming?"

For the second time, Virgil shrugged. "Don't know. Band Office business, as usual. Said she'd try, but who knows."

To Virgil, "Band Office business" was a four-letter word. Last week it was a meeting of chiefs in Halifax, tomorrow it would be a conference with the Grand Chief of the Assembly of First Nations in Ottawa, and next week something about those negotiations with local municipal governments over that boring land thing. It was always something, and usually it had nothing to do with him. He was a latch-key kid with no latch. Or key, as most homes in the village were kept unlocked.

"I'm bored," he said in a monotone voice as he fit his empty plastic bowl neatly into Dakota's.

Somewhere far to the south, other people were bored too. On the side of a lonely country highway north of a great lake and south of the Canadian Shield, Bruce Scott sat patiently, surrounded by his economic bread-and-butter: about a half-dozen handmade birdfeeders and bird baths. His car was neatly parked on a little driveway entrance to a field. He'd been here every weekend, and a few days midweek when the weather permitted, for the past month, same as with the year before. His wife made the feeders and baths, and she couldn't find anybody else to sell them, so he did this himself, half out of love and half out of necessity. Bruce would sit there in a lawn chair for about eight hours or so at a stretch, reading book after book, listening to his oldies radio station, generally feeling at peace with the world. On a good week-end he'd sell maybe three, making a cool tax-free ninety dollars.

It was a hot day, for May, and though he wore a hat and sometimes brought a large umbrella for shade, he was tanned a nice dark roast-turkey brown, which was odd for somebody of Scottish descent. Today was no different than yesterday, or the day before. Around him, the spring insects buzzed the way they only buzz on really hot days. Bruce took his final Diet Pepsi from the cooler and opened it, enjoying the satisfying hiss of released carbonated air. Holding its cool surface to his forehead, he gazed down the road. About two hundred kilometres in that southerly direction was the big city. That's where all the tourists came from—good or bad. On a day like this, all their windows would be rolled up, air conditioning going strong, and they'd be reluctant to pull over and exit the artificial environment of their cars into this sweltering atmosphere.

The pavement of the highway shimmered in the unusual spring heat, waves rising from it and creating what appeared to be either wet spots or black ice on top. A mirage, he knew. He kept watching, especially the part where the road dropped about twenty-five feet into a bit of a valley and then rose again.

"What the hell . . ."

Rising suddenly from the little valley in the road was a vague figure. It was difficult to see properly, with the heat radiating off asphalt. What was surprising was that although Bruce had been watching, he hadn't seen the figure coming. It was as if it had just appeared on this side of the little valley.

Maybe, Bruce Scott thought, I've been sitting out here too long.

As the figure drew closer, gradually emerging from the wavy lines, Bruce was able to make out more details. The figure was riding a large red motorcycle. An old one too, it appeared. And it was wearing black leather and a dark helmet with an equally dark visor. Now Bruce could hear the distinctive sound of the engine. As it approached him, it slowed down, and Bruce got a good look at what was moving north. It looked back.

This wasn't something you saw every day.

"Nice bike," Bruce Scott muttered to himself, but his voice was lost in the sound of the already departing vehicle.

Elizabeth and Ann Kappele were twins. They lived with their parents in a small nesting of houses and businesses just outside the Otter Lake Reserve. Most people in the county called the smattering of homes Roadside. Barely seven years of age, Elizabeth and Ann were happy to be out of school and were enjoying the spring day. That consisted of throwing a big blue ball back and forth, singing "Ring of Fire" at the top of their lungs. Johnny Cash was practically the only music their father let in the house. Maybe some Randy Travis, the occasional Garth Brooks, but deep in his heart, Daniel Kappele felt there was no music like the old music.

"Higher!" squealed Ann, caught up in the moment of ball frenzy.

Elizabeth threw the blue ball high over Ann's head, half by accident and half on purpose. Twins are like that. Ann turned and chased after the ball that bounced along the driveway and was rapidly rolling toward the highway and, across the road, the Setting Sun Motel. It was the Kappele family's financially dubious business. Both Ann and Elizabeth had long ago been taught the dangers of living so close to a busy road, so Ann instinctively slowed to a walk and looked both ways as she prepared to cross the road in search of her ball. It had come to a rest halfway across the pavement, just past the parallel yellow lines.

Darting out, Ann grabbed the ball and was about to turn back when she noticed something hazy in the distance. And she heard something too. A far-off buzz that grew into a deep growling coming from somewhere up the road. Puzzled, she watched for a few seconds, her eyes squinting in effort.

"Ann, get off the road. You know what daddy says! You shouldn't be standing there! Throw me the ball." Elizabeth, even at her age, felt waiting was for people who had nothing more important to do. Frustrated and worried, she ran to Ann's side and grabbed the ball roughly. "If you're not gonna throw it, then I will!" she shouted.

But then, she too saw what was coming. It was a motorcycle. Both had seen plenty in their day, their father had even owned one a few years ago, but this one seemed different. It had a different design to it, sounded different and had a rider who was definitely different in the way the helmet was designed, and the way the motorcyclist's head cocked like a bird when the machine slowed to a stop a few feet from the girls. One black boot slid off the pedal and touched the ground, a bright blue handkerchief tied just above the knee.

The Kappele twins could see themselves reflected in the dark visor with the odd markings on the side. For a moment, neither party moved, and then Elizabeth dropped the ball. It bounced once and rolled forward, coming to rest at the rider's boot.

Slowly, the rider reached down, picked it up and tossed it back to the girls. As the ball arced in the air, the rider suddenly gunned the throttle of the bike, making it roar loudly. Scared, the girls turned and ran, disappearing up the driveway, leaving little trails of dust and a bouncing blue ball in their wake.

Just as quickly, the rider and the motorcycle were gone, leaving a trail of burning rubber and exhaust that drifted across the driveway of the Setting Sun Motel.

The sign at the side of the road said, WELCOME TO OTTER LAKE: HOME OF THE ANISHNAWBE—PEOPLE OF THE LAND, and on top of it, to the left, sat a large black crow. The crow was not perched there as a political statement or social commentary, since it was a creature of the air. It too was just bored. The roadkill had been good this week and his tummy was full. So it sat there, watching the world go by . . .

On any given day, dozens of cars would zoom past, along with a lot of trucks, several minivans and the occasional RV. The crow had seen them all. He wasn't expecting anything much different today. Then, from around the bend, came a motorcycle. And a figure on top of it, his outfit as black as the crow himself. The vehicle slowed, and finally stopped directly in front of the sign. Though it was impossible to tell what was happening beneath the helmet, the rider seemed to be reading the sign. There was even a slight nod. The crow couldn't help feeling there was something very different about this creature, especially when it finished reading the sign and looked up at him.

The crow had seen lots of these two-legged creatures look at him, usually when he was ripping through their garbage, or cawing loudly early in the morning. But this time it was different. Even though the rider's eyes were hidden, the crow could feel its piercing gaze. The rider lifted its helmet a few inches until only its mouth was visible. And from that mouth came a loud caw. Not a human imitating a crow, but what seemed to the crow an authentic *crow* caw. The crow had been around for a few years and knew the difference. Crows do communicate, in their own way, and "I'm back" is what the crow heard.

The crow, having had enough of this weird business, decided to put a few treetops between himself and this creature. So it took to the air. Whoever or whatever it was that might be "back," the crow didn't want to stick around to watch.

The rider returned the helmet to its shoulders, and watched the bird disappear over the deciduous forest next to the highway. Crows never had much intestinal fortitude, the rider thought. Must be all that roadkill they eat.

The rider revved the engine and continued on the journey. Its destination was fast approaching.

Across most of the world—except those urban centres where they are more reviled than rats—raccoons are known as cute and clever creatures. Less well known is the fact they possess long memories. Memories of a multi-generational length. The woods around Otter Lake held many raccoons. On that bright Saturday afternoon, at least a dozen or so were casually foraging along the side of the road. Most should have been sleeping in a hollow log or hole in the ground because they were nocturnal animals, but today was different. Something special was happening. Though it was hard to say how or why, it's safe to say they were waiting, as they had been waiting for a very long time. And rumour had it, their waiting was soon to be over.

Under most circumstances, the roar of a motorcycle would have startled them and made them scatter. But not this time. It was like they were expecting it, and its rider. One by one, they watched the figure on the motorcycle whiz pass. Their little fingers twitched, their eyes sparkled.

It was him. And he was back.

This was good. In this part of the country, revenge was furry and wore a bandit's mask.

They were affectionately called the Otter Lake Debating Society. They met practically every day on Judas James's front porch. There, Judas James, Marty Yaahah, Gene Macdougal and Michael Mukwa held court, along with a case or two of beer, discussing the events of the day or week. Great philosophical issues were bandied about with enthusiasm. There were frequent associate members that occasionally joined in the discussions, but these four individuals were the core members of the society. They were a mainstay of the community, seldom moving from the porch, seldom without a beer in their hands, debating late into the night. All were well into their forties in both age and belt size. As the society members spent their days in debate, village cars would drive by, honking their encouragement of such cerebral endeavours.

Today, the heated topic revolved around which of the *Gilligan's Island* girls was the sexiest: Mary Ann or Ginger. They were almost coming to blows over this one. Judas and Marty were definitely Mary Ann fans. In their own lives both had married the "pretty girl next door," while Michael Mukwa was waiting for a Movie Star to enter his life. Faith has often been described as belief without proof, and Michael had a lot of faith this would happen eventually. Gene, as usual, bucked the trend and voted for Mrs. Howell. The discussion moved into its fourth hour and second case of beer with little hope that a consensus would be achieved, and the debate expanded to include similar comparisons, like the blonde chick from *I Dream of Jeannie* versus the blonde chick from *Bewitched*: who was cuter and who was more powerful? Suddenly finger-pointing and yelling had to cease because of another noise.

"Judas, I think your furnace is acting up again." Gene's comment prompted more argument, this time about the noise, until the source of the growing racket stopped in front of the headquarters of the Otter Lake Debating Society.

The members stared at the figure on the motorcycle. The figure turned its head to look back at them. It was a stalemate.

"Judas, do you know him? Her? Is that a guy or a girl?" said Gene under his breath.

Judas just shook his head.

Then, as if finished taking stock of the group, the figure on the machine moved on. Everybody on the veranda that day was pretty sure nobody in the village had a motorcycle, let alone one like that. And nobody dressed like this newcomer, for sure. And there was something else . . . something they couldn't really put their finger on. The rider was new here, yet in a way they couldn't explain, he also wasn't. Maybe it had something to do with that odd design on his helmet. From where they were sitting, it almost looked like some sort of bird. It was all so . . . complex.

The Otter Lake Debating Society, for the first time in a long time, was struck silent.

— FOUR —

Maggie's 2002 Chrysler pulled up into her mother's driveway. It had been a long day of work already, and it was only two-thirty, and it was a Saturday. There was still so much to do. The Otter Lake First Nation had recently bought a huge chunk of land adjacent to the Reserve, and this had introduced a whole whack of problems into Maggie's political life, which far too often drifted into her personal life.

First of all, the paperwork involved with turning the newly acquired parcel of land into Reserve land was enough to make the most die-hard civil servant cringe. There were three levels of government—four if you included the Reserve—that had to sign off on it. And of course, the idea of Native people getting more land was an absurd concept to most non-Natives. Five hundred years of colonization had told them you took land away from Native people, you didn't let them buy it back. As a result, the local municipality was fighting tooth and nail to block the purchase. If it was transferred over to Otter Lake, and therefore into federal jurisdiction, it would mean a loss of revenue on three hundred acres of taxable municipal land. This loss made the local municipal powers very uncomfortable. So this left Maggie juggling the local reeve, MPP and MP. She'd rather be juggling flaming chainsaws.

But ironically, that was the easy part. To her, as chief, White politicians, while having the potential to be devious, self-serving and a general pain in the ass, were less stressful than the over twelve hundred people she represented, most of whom she was related to, all tugging at her pant legs with suggestions about what to do with the new land. Three hundred acres was an almost twenty-percent increase in the size of the community. Every member of the band had an opinion on the purpose and destiny of that land. And they all had a very strong need to share their opinions with her, whether she wanted to hear them or not. Her husband had been chief, but ever since he passed away, Maggie had felt obligated to see to it that the things he had started were finished—so she ran and was acclaimed in a sympathy vote. They had fought a lot during the last few months of their marriage and occasionally, on days like this, she couldn't help wondering if this inherited responsibility had been her husband's lasting revenge.

She was thirty-five years old. She had started out her money-making career babysitting, and twenty years later, little had changed. As sad as it was, her mother's illness was a welcome respite from her duties. A love of the land, which had once united Aboriginal people, was now tearing them apart.

Add to that all the land analysis, economic assessments, viability studies and other assorted bureaucracy Maggie was forced to deal with and she now more than ever wished she'd finished that degree in forestry. Right now, she could be up on a fire watchtower, peacefully alone, wishing she could order a pizza.

On top of everything else, her mother was ill. It never rained but it poured. It never poured but it was a deluge. Maggie felt soaking wet. Noah never put up with this much rain, she thought. And at least he had a boat.

Sitting on the right side of the house, Maggie saw Virgil on the steps of the wraparound deck. "Hey, honey!" She waved. Virgil had been a lot quieter these days and she didn't know if it was because she worked so much or because his grandmother was ill. At least he was here, not sitting by the train tracks that ran parallel to the western boundary of the Reserve. She knew that sometimes he would go there and wait for the trains to pass. And watch. She knew boys could be solitary creatures, especially at this age. Still, Maggie couldn't help worrying.

"Hey, Mom" was his response, and he waved back.

Dakota was with him, and Maggie was pleased. She liked Dakota, and except for the fact they were first cousins, in a different reality they might have made a good pair. But in a year or two when the hormones really kicked into full gear, they would probably drift apart.

"You're late. You said you were gonna be here an hour ago."

"I know. Sorry. Work. How is your grandma?"

As usual, Virgil shrugged. He was very good at it.

"Hey, Dakota, your parents here?" asked Maggie.

The girl shook her head. "They left, maybe forty minutes ago or something. My dad was hoping to see you here. He has something he wants to tell you, I think."

An opinion on what to do with the land, Maggie was sure. In the last two months she'd heard every suggestion, from a campground, to a water slide, to an industrial park. What Dakota's dad, Fred, envisioned, she could only guess.

"Well, he knows where to find me."

Just then, the glass door opened and Maggie's brother Willie popped his head out. "Maggie, good. Mom's been asking about you. She wants to see you. I'll tell her you're here."

Maggie nodded and started toward the door. "Have you been in to see her yet?" she asked Virgil.

"Not yet."

"Well, you better. Soon." Maggie slid the glass patio door open and entered, closing it behind her.

Once in the kitchen, she was met by the aroma of half a dozen casseroles, several roast chickens, moose stews, chicken stews, salads and freshly baked bread. She could hardly miss seeing all the food scattered and piled haphazardly across the kitchen. Maggie hadn't eaten since breakfast, but lunch would have to wait until after she saw her mother. Both kids watched Maggie through the transparent doors as she made her way past a handful of relatives, nodding and exchanging brief acknowledgments. Willie was waiting by their mother's bedroom door, slowly opening it for her. With a sisterly touch on his arm, Maggie walked past him and entered.

Inside Maggie was surrounded by everything that was Lillian Benojee. Pictures of her father and other members of her family, flowers, various biblical quotes hanging on all four walls, an armchair and rocking chair, and an ancient wrought-iron bed covered in quilts. In that bed was Lillian Benojee, mother of nine children, of which eight had survived. Eighteen grandchildren and one great grandchild. Seventy-six years of life could be seen in her eyes.

Looking at her resting peacefully in the bed, Maggie smiled, remembering all the times her mother had terrified her as a little girl. Her mother had seemed larger than life. Here lay a woman under covers that looked too heavy for her frail body. Already Maggie missed her mother.

"Mom, I'm here."

Slowly, with effort, Lillian opened her eyes. Over the past eight decades those eyes had watched the world and had seen a lot, both good and bad. Finally they focused on her daughter, and she smiled.

"There you are, I thought maybe you found another mother to make wait. You know, I ain't got too much time left. Making me wait is a luxury you won't have much longer," she said in Anishnawbe, the language of her people. She spoke it like all the old-timers did, with strength and confidence, not hesitantly and softly like the youngsters who took the language in university, if they took it at all.

Maggie smiled, as she always did around her mother. She responded, also in Anishnawbe, but with not quite the same command. Still, she was more accomplished with her Native tongue than most of the community. If nothing else, that was the legacy Lillian and her husband, may his soul rest in peace, would leave behind. All their kids spoke the language—some better than others, but at least they spoke it. And in this day and age, that was their little miracle.

"I stopped to get a haircut."

Her mother laughed. Of all her children, perhaps this one had inherited Lillian's humour.

"How are you feeling?" Maggie asked.

"I'm dying. How am I supposed to feel? I've been lying here for two weeks. Doing nothing, just looking at the wallpaper and talking to people who are afraid to say anything worthwhile to me because they think it will be the end of me. That's how I feel. How do *you* feel?"

Even near death, she had an opinion, Maggie thought.

"Do you want anything to eat? Your kitchen is full of food."

Lillian was silent for a moment, thinking. "Got any wild meat?"

"I think maybe there's a moose stew out there. Want some?"

"Nah, nobody knows how to cook decent moose any more. They put all those strange spices in it. Never mind. I'd rather go see my Maker with a pleasant memory of how moose *should* taste than what somebody has out there. I mean, who puts garlic in moose stew?"

Maggie sat on the edge of her mother's bed. "My goodness, you're in a mean mood. That time of the month again?"

Once again, Lillian laughed, or tried to.

High above Lillian's wrought-iron bed frame hung a picture of a penitent Christ, clasped in prayer. Right beside it was an elaborate dreamcatcher, with several pictures of grandchildren attached. Both moved slightly as Maggie's added weight gently knocked the bed against the wall. For a moment she thought one or the other was going to fall.

"You know, that dreamcatcher is supposed to go in your window, or so they say."

"They say a lot of things, but that's my dreamcatcher and I'll put it where I want."

Maggie continued to gaze at the Christ figure and the dreamcatcher, marvelling that they seemed at home side by side on her mother's wall. A sudden thump came from the floor.

"What was that?" asked Maggie.

Rolling over with difficulty, Lillian reached over the side of the bed. "That was probably my bible. I was reading it when I fell asleep. Can you see it?"

The big black book was lying open on the ground, open to the pages listing all the birth dates of Lillian's children, their weights and godparents. Gently, Maggie picked it up and leafed through the pages.

"Got it. I still can't believe I was ten pounds, four ounces. I was a fat little baby."

"Not like your brother Tim. He was eleven pounds, thirteen ounces. Just about killed me. I never forgave him for that."

"You and your big, fat babies. What were you reading?"

"Genesis. Right back to the beginning. It's a good old-fashioned story. I like that. 'In the beginning . . . ' Good way to start a story."

"I don't think I ever asked you this, Mom, but how much of these stories do you actually believe?"

Lillian held out her hand, indicating that she wanted the book. Closing it, Maggie passed it to her waiting hands. The book, large and heavy, almost slipped from Lillian's weakened grip, but she held on and let it rest on her stomach as she opened it to Genesis.

"Enough, I guess. I remember when I was young, I was taught that we all lived on the back of a Giant Turtle. Didn't much believe that then or now. Then I was taught this stuff. The earth was created in seven days. Heck, it took the Band Council here two years just to pass a membership code. I read somewhere that most religions have pretty much the same message, they just use different books. I believe enough in this book to know what's right and what's wrong. What's good and what's bad."

Wrapped around one of the iron posts was an old dry sweetgrass braid. Maggie picked it up and inhaled its still fragrant aroma. She was smiling to herself.

"What you smiling about?"

"What about all that residential school stuff? What about Sammy Aandeg? Look at what the Bible did to him."

"No, the Bible didn't do that. Men did. Don't confuse the two. The other side of the track has its flaws too, Maggie. Remember your old buddy Jimmy."

Lillian was talking about Jimmy Pine, a supposed medicine man who made a regular practice of claiming to treat women traditionally—usually White women interested in Native spirituality, who didn't know any better—through the use of his pecker. Maggie had gone to school with him.

"I guess you're right." Maggie replaced the sweetgrass braid.

"Has Wayne come yet?"

Maggie looked out the window next to her mother's bed. Across the lake she could see a small island. On that island lived her youngest brother, perhaps the most eccentric member of the family. "No, not yet, Mom." In her heart, she doubted Wayne would make an appearance in this house, in this room.

"He'll come. Sometimes I look out that window and think I can see him."

"Maybe ... maybe he's busy or something."

"Does he know? About me?"

"I told him. About a week ago, I went over."

Lillian was quiet for a moment, and the next few seconds slipped by unbroken.

Maggie added, "You know how much he likes to be alone."

Ever the pragmatist, Lillian yawned and said, "Well, he's his own man. He can make his own decisions."

Maggie, like everyone else in the family and practically the whole village, knew Wayne had been and still was Lillian's favourite, though her mother would deny it. Maybe all that attention had spoiled him, they said. Still, he was way over there across the water, and Lillian and the family were here. And as always, Lillian the mother was willing to forgive him his peculiarities. Maggie tried not to let her anger over the flagrant injustice of the situation creep into the room. She had thought she got over that in her twenties.

Luckily, just then the sound of Virgil's and Dakota's voices darted into the room through her open window, strong and vibrant with youth, and once more Lillian smiled.

"That Virgil?"

"Yeah, he's outside. I think he's afraid to come in. He doesn't want to see you like this."

Lillian nodded. "Can't say that I blame him. I remember when my grandfather was dying, my parents made me go in to say good-bye. Cancer just about ate up the old man. He was scary to look at, especially to an eight-year-old. Maybe it's just as well you don't force Virgil. Let him come of his own accord. Besides, I ain't much to look at. He'll remember me his own way."

Maggie nodded solemnly.

"He still skipping school?"

"I think so. I have a meeting with his teacher in a couple of days to talk about it."

"Why do you think he does it? I mean, skipping school? He's a bright boy."

Maggie had thought long and hard about that. Her son would not go to school, no matter how many times she drove him there, threatened him, begged him and once even tried to bribe him. "I don't know. I've asked him, and he just shrugs."

"That's not good."

"I know, Mom," answered a frustrated Maggie.

"Funny, huh? Way back in my time kids skipped school for different reasons than they do today. They ran away. Kids and schools, the constant battle."

A silence settled between the two women. A comfortable silence born of familiarity and of love. Only the ticking of a clock marked the passing time. Finally, the old woman spoke.

"I've been thinking a lot lately."

Maggie sighed, as she always sighed when her mother bothered to think and share her thoughts. "About what? What a terrible place the world is today? How sad it is most of our people don't speak Anishnawbe? That *Three's Company* is still cancelled? About me? About Virgil skipping school? What this time?"

"Yes, all of those things. So sad. I loved that show. That Jack was such a trickster. But you and all this work you're doing. It's too much. I never liked you being chief. You should be chief of your own home, not Otter Lake. Virgil needs you at home. Maybe that's why."

"I know, Mom, you say this every week. I'm doing what I can, okay? Ever since Clifford died . . ."

Lillian looked at her. "Yes?"

"Never mind."

"Always never mind with you. I do mind. So your husband died. Mine died too. People die. People are born. That is the circle of life." Lillian took another deep breath. "You're not happy. Virgil's not happy. The village is not happy. That's all I'm saying."

"And what would you have me do?"

"Well, nobody should be happy all the time. But nobody should be miserable all the time either."

"What does that mean?"

"It means exactly what it means. You, Virgil, and this whole community. I know people around here are giving you some grief." Lillian turned her head into the pillow, her eyes closed. "Sometimes when something's wrong with the soup, to make it better you got to add something nobody is expecting."

"Like garlic to moose stew?"

"Different type of soup. You'll see."

"What do you mean, I'll see?"

There was a definite sparkle in her eyes, reminiscent of one you would see in a teenager's. "I just wanted you to know, I think something's gonna happen. Should be interesting." Then she mysteriously stopped, still sporting a small, satisfied, if a little impish, toothless grin.

Immediately Maggie became suspicious. "What? What did you do?"

"Noth . . . ing."

"Mamma, you did something. What? And how could you do anything—you've been in this bed for over two weeks? What are you up to?"

Lillian looked out the window. "I called someone. I think this place, and especially you, my lovely daughter, need some magic in your life. So does your son."

"Magic? What are you talking about? And who did you call?"

"You don't know him. I'm not sure if he's still around. I hope he is. I hope he heard me."

"*Who?*" Maggie was getting concerned. Her mother must be confused.

"Never mind. You wouldn't understand. It's an Anishnawbe thing."

"Mom, *I'm* Anishnawbe. We all are."

Lillian put her hand on Maggie's shoulder. "No child, you're what they call nowadays a First Nations. They don't necessarily mean the same thing."

Willie was finishing his second bowl of moose stew when Maggie emerged from Lillian's room. He had sampled a little of everything, but in his opinion, this was the best. The garlic added a nice touch. He noticed that Maggie looked bewildered.

"Hey, Willie, did Mom call anybody or mail anything recently?"

Willie thought for a moment before shaking his head. "Nope. Who would she call? Everybody she knows has been through here."

"That's what I thought," Maggie said, frowning, forgetting how hungry she was. Instead, she went to the washroom.

It was there, while washing her hands, that she first heard the sound. It seemed vaguely familiar, yet still foreign. Drying her hands, she quickly left the bathroom and saw that everybody in the house was looking out the front window. At what, she couldn't quite make out exactly, but she could see that it was red, and it made a lot of noise.

Then she realized that it was a motorcycle.

Virgil had a much better view of the motorcycle that was coming up his grandmother's dirt driveway. An old one, by the looks of it, but in immaculate condition. It glistened in the sunlight as it stopped by the side door. Like most boys his age, Virgil had more than a passing interest in gas-powered vehicles, especially anything that could be classified as "cool." And this scarlet vision before him put the word *cool* to shame. It was red with white trim, old-fashioned headlights, a black solo seat complete with fringes made from what appeared to be black leather, and larger-than-normal wheel fenders. Hanging from the end of each handlebar was a feather, but each was different. The feather on the right looked like it had come from an eagle. But the one hanging from the left was darker, smaller, shinier.

On the side of the bike was a stylized head of an Indian with an elongated headdress. Underneath the emblem was written

INDIAN MOTORCYCLE. It wasn't just cool, it was cool squared, maybe even cubed.

Virgil barely noticed the person riding the bike, until the rider stood up. He had a tall, lean frame, and was dressed all in dark leather, except for one blue bandana tied around his left thigh. The helmet ... it was so unusual. The design on it looked like a screaming bird of some sort. A starling or crow or something.

Who was this man? Nobody in his family was cool enough to know a guy like this, Virgil thought.

The rider lowered the kickstand and slid off the motorcycle with practised ease. Clearly here with a purpose, and taking the steps two at a time, he was in the house before Virgil or Dakota could move. Their eyes returned to the bike, sitting there in the driveway, small puffs of exhaust still leaking out of the rear pipe.

Inside, not stopping or even slowing down, the man, still wearing his helmet, walked past all the startled relatives, heading directly toward Lillian Benojee's door like he'd been here a thousand times before.

Willie and his brother Tim had other ideas. Planting themselves in front of the bedroom, they blocked the stranger's path.

Willie was the first to speak. "Who the hell are you?"

"This is our mother's house." Tim had the tendency to state the obvious. "What do you want?"

The man in black just stood there for a few seconds. He was taller than the two brothers by about four inches, but substantially leaner. The way his helmet kept turning, it was obvious that he was looking back and forth between the two men.

"Well . . . ?" asked Willie.

Once more, the stranger did not move.

"Hey Maggie, what should we do?" It was Tim asking his sister, and the community's chief.

Before the equally curious Maggie could respond, the man in black raised both gloved hands until they were at the Benojee brothers' ear level. The brothers instantly stiffened, wondering if they were in for a fight. Others in the room backed off to a safe distance or stepped forward a foot or two to assist their kin. Maggie rested her hand on the phone, ready to call Larry and Audrey, the two village cops, if necessary.

The mystery man's gloved hands hung there for a time, as if he were a faith healer about to make them walk or see again. Each brother eyed them with trepidation. Suddenly the rider grabbed an earlobe on each of them and squeezed. Though quite burly, the brothers yelped and went instantly to their knees, as if they were children caught doing something they shouldn't. Slowly but firmly, the stranger led them away from the door and sat them on two chairs parallel to the table. He gave each ear one final squeeze, eliciting a squeal from the brothers, before returning to Lillian's door and knocking.

Several other family members rushed, too late, to the men's aid.

A weak voice came from behind the door. "Come in." The pressure of the knock had forced the door to open.

No one moved for several seconds, until once more Lillian's strained voice was heard. "Well, is anybody out there? I haven't got all day. I'm dying, you know."

The man disappeared into the old woman's room, closing the door behind him.

Willie and Tim and a number of other relatives gathered outside Lillian's bedroom, unsure how to proceed.

"Should we go in?"

"Who the fuck was that?"

"We should go in."

"Should I call the police?"

"Tim, why don't you go in?"

"Somebody do something!"

In the end, nobody did anything.

Maggie was mystified as to how this six-foot-two-inch, black-leather-wearing motorcyclist with social interaction issues knew her mother. Part of her wanted to tell her brothers to go in and throw out whoever the hell that was. There were certain social graces to visiting a stranger's house. You didn't just barge into places like you owned them and manhandle people. But another part of Maggie, she didn't know from where or from what, told her not to worry.

Maybe that was the Anishnawbe side of her.

The stranger stood in front of the door, unmoving. Lillian lay in her bed, also unmoving. The only sound was the ancient clock ticking the seconds away as the two surveyed each other. Instinctively, she reached over to the bedside table and put in her false teeth.

"You ain't one of my kids. Or my grandkids. Or any niece or nephew. Or cousin. And I don't know a lot of White people who dress like that, Black or Chinese either. So I'm guessing we've never met. So I'm guessing you must be lost," she said in English, with an accent.

For the first time, the man under the helmet and leather communicated. He shook his shiny black helmeted head once.

"You gonna take that silly thing off and talk to me, or we gonna be in here all day staring at each other?"

The helmet tilted back ever so slightly, giving the impression that the man might have been laughing. Then, slowly, he took off his leather gloves. The skin underneath appeared to belong to a White man, or possibly a pale Asian. From the neck down, they all look alike, Lillian believed. The man flexed his fingers for a second, then grasped his helmet with both hands. Lillian watched, curious but patient. It took a moment or two for the constricting helmet to give, then he slowly lifted it off his head.

His hair was past his shoulders, a sandy-blond colour, like freshly baked bannock. His eyes were blue as the lake outside her window. And his face . . . Caucasian, young—maybe twenty-five or a young thirty—and handsome, with a strong chin and masculine nose. This man was definitely in the wrong house.

"I can breathe again," he said. He scratched just above his left ear, then tried to put his hair back in some semblance of order. "I hate helmet head, don't you?"

"Young man, are you selling something?" she asked in English.

"Nope," he replied. He put the helmet down on a large mirrored dresser, and approached Lillian, stopping beside her bed. "I've come to say goodbye."

"Are you going someplace?"

"No, more like coming back. It's been a while since I was last here." The man gazed out the window, and saw a dock, the boats and, off in the distance, a float plane. "It's changed a lot. And so have you."

Comprehension flooded the mind of the old woman. She knew who he was. It was him. He'd come.

"Gigii bidgoshin!" she said.

"Poochgo nigiibizhaa," he answered, saying, yes, he had had to come.

"I didn't think . . . Where have you been?"

For a moment, he hesitated. "I've . . . I was sick for a while."

Lillian reached up and touched the man's face, his hair, as if trying to find somebody else in there. "We've all been sick. And this, all this? What's up with this?"

For the first time, the young man smiled. And it was a familiar smile. "Different times, different faces. I am nothing if not adaptable. Do you like?"

She shook her head. "Never liked blonds."

A loud interrupting knock was heard at the door. "Mom, you okay?" It was Willie.

Lillian answered quickly. "Yes. Go away."

"All that brood out there yours?" asked the man.

She nodded. "Most of them."

"You've been busy."

"Had to do something. Baking pies gets kind of boring after a while."

"I suppose it does. I guess you can't go swimming forever," he added, sadly. "How was that school of yours?"

"Educational, in more ways than one." Over his shoulder, Lillian could see the helmet resting on the small table. She pointed at it. "Your helmet, that thing you painted on it. It's hard to tell, the way it's drawn, but that's a raven, isn't it?"

The man was surprised. "Yeah. How would you know?"

Smiling, she leaned back in her bed, her head almost disappearing into the pillow. "I used to get around. Read a lot. That's West Coast art, ain't it? Believe it or not, I've even seen a sea otter!" She sighed. The clock seemed to tick louder. "So what happens now?"

"What always happens."

"I suppose. Why should I be any different, huh?" She saw him pick up a photograph from her dresser, one of her at a much younger age. "You came all this way to say goodbye?"

He nodded. "You called. I came." Looking at the disease-ravaged woman in front of him, the man could still see the pretty young girl he'd once known.

She hesitated, then asked, "Tell me the truth, do you hate me? For going away?"

The man put the picture down and once again looked out the window. "No. That was a very long time ago. And you called me back . . . from where I was. I guess that's fair."

"And here I am, leaving you again." The man did not respond. "Neither time did I have a choice. Tell me, what will you do when . . . when I go?"

The man turned from the window and faced her again. "I will do what my nature will tell me to do. That's all any of us can do. I know that's not what your boyfriend believes, but . . ."

Lillian put up her hand, cutting him off. "Oh, don't start that again. Please. I am so sick of that argument. He's not my boyfriend. He's just a good person with a lot of good things to say. You really need to get a better grasp of this whole situation. There was room for the both of you. Quit being a child and give him a chance."

"I don't think we hang out in the same bars."

Both fell into a silence.

Finally, the man said, "I am what I am. You of all people should know that."

Her face softened. "I know. You're right. That's part of your charm." He smiled, and she smiled back. "It's so good to see you again. Blond hair, blue eyes or not. I missed you. I think we all missed you. You shouldn't go away like that."

"A person's gotta feel wanted."

Lillian shook his head. "A person's gotta *make* himself be wanted. And you were always wanted. By me and everyone."

"It didn't feel like it."

"Did you come back all this way to bitch?"

"I came back because you called me."

"You didn't have to come back. I didn't think you would."

"Of course I had to come back. You're the last person who really believes in me. As a person. After you . . ." He shrugged. "Besides, sounds like you're the one doing all the bitching."

"Yeah, well, what are you gonna do about it, Mr. Blond Hair?" Gritting her false teeth, she grabbed a small throw pillow lying on the bed and tried to toss it at him. But the ravages of time and sickness, combined with the law of gravity, resulted in the pillow merely rolling off the bed onto the floor.

The man picked it up and held it. "Nice try. I remember when you could skip a stone clear across the river."

"That was a long time and a lot of stones ago."

"I suppose. Still, it's nice to see that determination in your eyes. The furnace may have some wear and tear but the fire still burns hot."

Her breath was now growing wheezy. "I bet you say that to all the old dying women."

Kneeling, the man took Lillian's hand. "No, just the pretty ones."

"What's going to happen? To me? Now?"

With what strength she had left, she squeezed the man's fingers. He caressed the top of her withered hand in response.

"Like I said, what always happens."

Her voice was now barely a whisper. "No more riddles, please."

"In all my time on this land, I have learned there are three constants in this universe: getting fat, mosquitoes and saying goodbye," he replied, his voice low. "I think even your buddy Jesus would agree with that one."

"My daughter . . ."

"Yes?"

Lillian closed her eyes, summoning effort to speak. "She's not doing very well. Too busy. This community. Too busy. Everybody wants something from her. She thinks life is in that Band Office building. It isn't. Killed her husband practically. And my son. My grandson. They need to believe . . ."

"I have no idea where you're going with this."

"You . . ."

"Yes, me?"

"After I'm . . . after . . . I want . . . I want you to . . ." She was rapidly losing her ability to talk.

The man leaned closer. "What? What do you want?"

The old woman reached up and grabbed the back of his blond head, gripping as tightly as her frail muscles would allow. "A favour . . . no, two favours . . . okay . . . promise me . . . please . . ."

He put his ear by her mouth and heard her dying requests.

From outside, Virgil and Dakota had seen the man enter through the side door, and watched him barge into their grandmother's room. They had watched the family fight in whispers about what to do, and shuffle around her door like bees around a rotten apple. Being thirteen, they were intensely curious about what was happening in there. Virgil's grandmother's bedroom window was situated at the edge of the deck, and could be peeked into with a little effort.

"I wonder what's going on in there," said Dakota.

"Let's find out," said Virgil.

Dakota nervously looked at the window. "Should we?"

Virgil nodded. "Yes, we should. Come on."

Conspiratorially, they made their way to the edge of the deck, directly under the window. It was Virgil who took the first peek. What he saw inside would shock and puzzle him till the end of his days.

His dying grandmother, matriarch of the Benojee clan and widow of Leonard Benojee, was locked in a passionate embrace with the motorcyclist. The man's long blond hair was obscuring what was happening, but Virgil was sure, positive in fact, that the man was kissing his grandmother, and quite passionately too. It was the kind of kiss you see only in movies and on television, the eyes-closed, toe-curling kind.

This was not the grandmother Virgil was used to.

"What's happening in there? What do you see?" Dakota was trying to push Virgil aside, eager to peek.

Unwilling to move, Virgil continued to peer through the window, unsure of what he was witnessing.

Lillian's window was open, and as she often did when annoyed, Dakota raised her voice to an almost whining pitch. Her voice floated through the mosquito screen, across Lillian's room and into the man's ear. Still deep in the kiss, he opened his eyes, and his expression registered that he saw Virgil's face at the window. The man raised an eyebrow, and Virgil quickly retreated, his heart beating loudly.

"What? What did you see?"

Virgil flattened himself against the side of the house in case the man looked out the window for him. He urged Dakota to be quiet, and dragged her against the wall too.

"What? What? Tell me!"

"Shhhh."

They both stood there, quiet, until they heard Lillian's door open and close, and the sound of the man's boots fading down the hallway.

"Come on, Virgil. Tell me what you saw!"

Not knowing how to tell his cousin what he'd seen without sounding crazy, he just said, "Nothing."

FIVE

Three days later they buried Lillian Benojee beside her long-departed husband, Leonard. The whole village turned out for the ceremony. The church was filled to capacity. You don't live for almost eight decades without making a lot of friends, or conversely, a lot of enemies. Lillian had definitely been the "friends" type. After the service, it seemed the whole community moved in a surge toward the graveyard, following the hearse. Maggie walked with Virgil and the rest of the family. Several hundred others followed respectfully behind.

Sammy Aandeg was there too, dressed in what could have been a thirty-year-old black suit. One that hadn't been worn in thirty years. Ten years of living at the residential school, plus over half a century of living with the effects of that school and finding new ways to damage his body hadn't left much of the young, defiant boy that Lillian had once known. Instead, there shuffled an old, broken-down man who reeked of alcohol, of urine and of just about every unpleasant smell a human body could emit or absorb. And yet, somehow he'd managed to throw himself together and make it to this funeral.

Some people might point to Sammy as an example of what happened to the children that had been sent away to such schools, and had never really come home because they suffered from a form of shell-shock. Other less-sympathetic folks merely pointed to him as a crazy old drunk. Luckily, he didn't care. He just mumbled to himself, rubbing the fingers of his right hand together non-stop.

The mourners hung their heads as the priest said his comforting, priestly things. Some remembered Lillian as the source of their life. Others thought they should have stopped by to visit more often. Still others regarded the funeral as symbolizing the passing of a generation, of a library of culture and of an Aboriginal lifestyle rapidly becoming extinct. All were saddened by the death of a good person. There were so few of those special people still left in the world.

The entire Otter Lake Debating Society was there. Lillian was Marty's aunt and Gene's second cousin, as the complex family trees of Reserve members intertwined. "She once told me I was her favourite nephew," said Marty, though everybody knew Lillian had said that to all her nieces and nephews at one point or another.

"When my son died, she stayed with me. For two days. I never forgot that," Marissa Crazytrain told Maggie. Marissa had no close relatives, so when the tragedy occurred she had few shoulders to cry on. Except for Lillian. The very thought of losing one of her sons had sent a chill down Lillian's spine, so she showed up on Marissa's doorstep and cared for her until she was strong enough to be by herself. She even organized most of the child's funeral. Maggie remembered that now, wishing she'd been around to help in Lillian's time of need, instead of on her honeymoon.

The testimonies dragged on, but Virgil was too distracted to listen. He'd never worked up the nerve to go in and see his grandmother, especially after what he'd observed through the window. The stranger had left immediately after that, in the same abrupt manner in which he had arrived. Virgil and Dakota, peeking around the corner from the safety of the deck, had watched him with eager intensity.

As the stranger straddled his bike, helmet in hand, he glanced toward the corner of the house, where they were hiding. A small smile crept onto his handsome face, and he cocked the same eyebrow as before.

"See you around," he said. Then he put his helmet over his head and kick-started his bike. It roared to life and took the blond man down the driveway and out of what had started out as a boring afternoon.

Who was he? the boy wondered. He and Dakota discussed that very question for the rest of the day, but Dakota's primary contribution to solving the mystery of the motorcyclist consisted of repeating, "He's cute," which Virgil found of little use.

Inside the house, everybody was buzzing over the appearance of this man, and his actions. They asked Lillian, but she just smiled enigmatically.

"That would be spoiling the surprise," she managed to say. And then she added one final word: "Magic."

Later that night, as she slept, her spirit and her body became two separate things. And the world moved on.

And now everybody was saying goodbye. Maggie had known her mother was dying, but she still wasn't prepared. They had had one more brief conversation before her end came, and what saddened Maggie was that it was entirely inconsequential. Virgil was growing up quickly and needed bigger clothes. Lillian had urged her daughter to buy him clothes that were a size or two bigger—that way they would fit longer, as all mothers knew. But Virgil hated baggy clothes, how he always felt lost in them.

Maggie would tease him that he'd never make it as a hip hop star, and Virgil would fake a laugh.

"He's my son and I know what he likes."

"What he likes and what he needs can be two different things."

Maggie now regretted having such a confrontational discussion with Lillian, so soon before ... She should have just said yes and then gone ahead and bought Virgil an extra-large everything. That was the kind of relationship the two of them had, and Maggie accepted that on an intellectual level, as she was sure Lillian had. But funerals and dead mothers are not intellectual exercises. So Maggie was awash in regret, sadness and more than a little bit of guilt.

She could tell Virgil was deep in his own thoughts and she squeezed his hand reassuringly. The boy looked up at his mother and returned a sad smile. Both were aware that behind them and to the right stood a tombstone bearing the words CLIFFORD SECOND—beloved husband and father, with some dates carved below. During the ceremony Virgil had been glancing at it surreptitiously. And so had Maggie. Both dutifully made pilgrimages to it every year on the anniversary of Clifford's death, and on Graveyard Day, when local custom dictated that close relatives place fresh flowers on the graves of loved ones.

Virgil had loved his father, as all sons should. Maggie had loved her husband ... for the first few years anyway. Half a decade into their marriage the Clifford Second she had married had become the Clifford Second she was *married to*. The Band Office had become more of a home to him than the home the three of them shared. He had dreams for the community and the Anishnawbe nation, but not so many for his family.

Then came the accident. A simple fishing trip with tragic results. Tim, Maggie's brother, had been out with him. A sunken tree stump and a motorboat at full throttle in the fading evening light had combined, with devastating consequences. Tim had swum to shore on a nearby island, but Clifford had gone down with the boat. The result was a spring funeral.

Maggie had mourned, as had Virgil. But in many ways, Clifford had not been part of their lives for much longer after his death. Their normal routine had resumed only a month or two after his funeral. And for reasons neither could explain, Maggie and Virgil both felt guilty for carrying on so easily without him. As a result, Maggie had hated the Band Office and everything it stood for: the responsibilities that had taken her husband away from her, but also management by the three colonizing levels of government, paperwork that would cripple a small South American government and the challenge of dealing with the wishes of individuals within a disparate community.

Not twelve feet away, Clifford Second lay buried, possibly laughing at her in some ectoplasmic way. *See! Now you're chief! Now you know what I had to go through! I bet you're sorry now!*

Virgil was having different memories. He had heard the news of his father's death early one morning, and a succession of aunts and uncles had hugged him in sympathy. Yet, he hadn't known what to feel. Of course he was sad and depressed that his father had died, but there was none of the wailing or thrashing about that he had learned to expect from movies and television. He just felt . . . numb. For the last third of his life, Clifford had been somebody he'd seen at breakfast and then just before bed. Occasionally, the peace was punctuated by arguments between his parents.

Twice a year now he came to pay respects to his dead father. Meanwhile, he saw his mother being drawn into the same lifestyle that had engulfed his dad. And this made him apprehensive.

Thoughts of his father were still in his head when Virgil saw, parked casually on the road running parallel to the graveyard, a familiar red-and-white vintage motorcycle. Leaning against it was the blond stranger. Maggie noticed something had caught her son's attention, and turned to look as well. "Mom . . ." Virgil began.

"I see him, honey."

"Did anybody ever find out who he was?"

Maggie, still studying the man, shook her head. "No."

"I wonder how grandma knew him."

The stranger seemed to be staring straight at her, she thought. "It seems Grandma had a much more interesting life than we thought. Now, shh, listen to Father Sauvé."

Maggie forced her attention back to the service, but it was a little more difficult for Virgil. He noticed that across from him, Dakota too had spotted the stranger. Everyone else seemed too engrossed in the funeral to raise their heads.

Across the fence separating the graveyard from the land of the living, the man leaned against his motorcycle, watching the proceedings. His expression did not reveal his thoughts. He recognized some of the people he'd seen briefly in Lillian's kitchen, including Lillian's daughter. He was sure it was her. She was an apple fallen from the Benojee tree. Lillian's beauty was too strong to be diluted by someone else's DNA. He'd also seen a family photo hanging on Lillian's wall and that woman had been in it . . . along with the boy. He knew the boy had peeked in the window and realized what he'd seen must have confused him.

The man had to decide what to do now. He had crawled out of his self-imposed purgatory to say goodbye to Lillian. Now what? Go back into what had been his life (if it could be called that) again? The idea did not thrill him. Take his new motorcycle and ride off into the sunset? No, too melodramatic, and eventually he would hit an ocean, no matter what direction he went. Settle down, set up shop somewhere and learn to live a middle-class Canadian life, go from being an Anishnawbe to an Anish-snob? That was not in his nature.

There was also, of course, Lillian's last request. It was complicated, but most things with women were, he thought. Still, it might be fun. Could be interesting too. And he had all the time in the world. For someone like him, fun and interesting trumped most things.

Once more his attention turned to Lillian's beautiful daughter. He'd only glimpsed her back at the house. Tallish, long dark-brown hair, the cutest little pug nose, and just the right amount of curves to make her alluring. Well, that was something to keep him busy, he thought. It had been a while since he'd enjoyed the company of a pretty woman . . . hell, any woman . . . and it was always best to start off by setting attainable goals. Now he had a purpose, and he was happy.

Virgil could see the man watching them and smiling. And for some reason this made him uncomfortable. Though he didn't know why, he took a step closer to his mother.

But, the man thought, first things first. His eyes wandered over to Sammy Aandeg, standing by himself. The man knew Sammy's type; even from here he could practically feel the alcohol and anguish steaming off him. After all, he'd been there himself not that long ago. And this man could be put to good use. They spoke the same language, in more ways than one.

Not more than seven kilometres away, across the lake, a thin man named Wayne sat on the shores of a small island. The water lapped at his bare ankles. He was looking toward the mainland. Wayne wished he could be over there, saying goodbye to his mother. He had almost gone to the funeral, but something had prevented him. He didn't like strangers, and even though he probably knew every single person at the funeral, they were still strangers to him. In many ways, he felt a stranger to himself. Unconsciously he picked up stones in the water using only his toes, tossed them into the air, and caught them with his hands.

He sat watching the sun shine down on Otter Lake. He had been mourning the passing of his mother in his own way, as tradition dictated. And when the time was right, he would go to where her body had been placed, and say goodbye. Until that time, he would sit here and brood. Over the years he had gotten pretty good at it. He had received the message Willie had left him, and understood what Maggie had told him over a week ago. Part of him felt bad about not going immediately to his mother's side, but in his mind, there had been no need. Lillian knew he loved her and treasured her. Watching her die in that painful way wouldn't have changed anything. As for the rest of the family, they considered him the weird brother, he knew, as did most of the community. Even the really weird people in Otter Lake thought he was weird. And that didn't exactly make him feel sociable.

Idly, he grabbed another smooth rock from just below the waterline, this time with his hand. After weighing it, he threw it and watched it skim across the surface of the lake, just as his mother had taught him. By the eleventh skim he had lost interest and was again looking toward the mainland.

Though his thoughts were of his mother, this was just the latest in a series of events that seemed to be testing him. He had lived on this island for four years: training, practising and developing his art. But admittedly, he got kind of lonely. And what exactly was he practising and training for? Originally this had been a great idea, refining his philosophy and technique with isolation, as had all the great martial artists. But the enthusiasm that had led him to this monastic existence was beginning to wear thin. He missed showers. He missed television. He missed the scent of perfume lingering on the neck of a woman. He missed ordering pizza.

Maybe I *am* weird, he thought.

SIX

The funeral reception was held at the community centre. Virgil watched everybody milling about eating sandwiches made, for the most part, of white bread, butter, baloney and processed cheese. He knew the traditional soup and chili would be served later, but a quick shot of carbohydrates was what was needed to take people's minds off the solemnity of the day. He was off with his cousins of the same age, talking about the stranger. Everybody had seen him ride in but nobody had seen him ride out. Three days had passed since his first appearance and Reena Aandeg, Sammy's niece, who lived along the main road near the highway, swore up and down that neither she nor her family saw him leave.

"Then he's still here on the Reserve somewhere," reasoned Virgil.

"Where would a guy like that stay? It would be kind of hard for him to hide," said Dakota. "I wonder if he gives rides on that motorcycle. That would be so cool."

To Virgil, she sounded like a silly girl. You didn't go for rides with strangers on motorcycles. Everybody knew that.

"What if he's a mass murderer or a rapist?" he said.

Dakota shook her head. "I doubt it. He has kind eyes."

"Oh yeah," agreed Jamie, a cousin of both Dakota and Virgil.

"It's always in their eyes. I read somewhere that eyes are the window to the soul."

"His are blue! Really blue! So blue" gushed Dakota.

"Wow!"

Speaking of eyes, Virgil was busy rolling his. At least he didn't have to try to get out of going to school today. He knew that was an incredibly inappropriate thought to have at his grandmother's funeral, but even more so when he could see his mother dealing with band politics across the room. She couldn't even take a day off for her mother's funeral. That was really inappropriate.

Sitting at a scarred wooden table, trying to enjoy the blandness of the sandwiches, Maggie recognized that her momentary respite from Reserve political intrigue was drawing to an end.

"Maggie, I know this isn't the right place to discuss this but I need to talk to you." It was Anthony Gimau, a big man with even bigger opinions. Back in the sixties when he was growing up, he'd wanted to be a radical, anything to shake up the system. Being Native automatically gave him ammunition to be an annoying gadfly. Therefore everything "White" was evil, except of course his Jimmy 4-by-4, which he adored, almost as much as he adored his wife, Klara, who was German. In his personal philosophy, there was a yin and yang kind of thing to people who orbited the Native community. There were the "wannabes"; people who were, for one reason or another, fascinated with Native culture and *wanted to be* Native. These types generally annoyed most Native people, including other wannabes. But that was the yin. The yang, Anthony believed, was the "shouldabeens"; those who were unfortunate enough not to be Native but who *should have been* Native. His wife, Klara, though born and raised in Jena, Germany, was a shouldabeen.

In his earlier years, Anthony used to sport a Mohawk haircut as a statement, but as time passed, his male-pattern baldness reduced him to shaving only the sides of his head, and leaving a one-and-a-half-inch strip of hair on the very back of his head as a somewhat diminished political statement. Somehow, he blamed White people for that too.

"What is it, Tony? I'm not in the mood to discuss anything."

"I know, I know," he said, nodding, then swallowing. "However . . ."

Maggie shook her head. "No however. Tony, we just buried my mother. Now is not the time."

Tony's eyes brightened. "I know. I know. When then?"

Maggie knew she'd walked into a trap. He wanted to talk about the plans for the new land they'd bought, and now he'd cornered her into setting a specific time and place. Everybody in the room had an opinion and was dying to share it with Maggie. Tony had just beaten them to it.

Sighing, Maggie said, "I don't know. Day after tomorrow. Eleven o'clock. How's that? Can I finish my sandwich now?"

"Yes, yes, of course. My thoughts are with you and your family. But wait 'til you hear what I have to say!" Anthony trotted off in search of some traditional corn soup or sauerkraut. Maggie sighed, dropping her unappealing sandwich onto the plate. Her husband was dead, her son was retreating into himself and the acquisition of all this new land was proving to be the hottest political potato the community had seen in a long while.

Maybe she should have cut Clifford more slack, back when he was chief. He had been dealing with the Royal Commission on Aboriginal Peoples, affectionately known as the RCAP, an attempt by the federal government to address many of the problems being complained about by Canada's Native population. And it took years. Clifford had spent many nights in Ottawa, and many more nights at the Band Office or on the phone. In her imagination, Maggie began to imagine the RCAP as a woman, her husband's mistress. A big fat woman, a selfish one, always wanting more. She promised so much, but in the end, she delivered so little. Every night Clifford would come to bed with Maggie, but he was always thinking about "her," the other woman, the RCAP. And now the legacy of that relationship was Maggie's cross to bear.

Some wanted the three hundred acres used for new housing. Others felt the time was right to install a water filtration plant, which in turn could mean somebody (quite probably the woman who had made the suggestion) could open up a laundromat, and all those who either didn't have or couldn't afford a washer/dryer wouldn't have to drive forty minutes into town and stand around for two hours waiting for their clothes to be cleaned. And they could stop worrying about their town dying off like what happened in that Walkerton place. There were proposals for a golf course or a casino. Of course it wasn't solely Maggie's decision; there was the Band Council to go through, as well as a bunch of committees and boards to deal with. White people may have invented bureaucracy, but their relationship with the Department of Indian Affairs had taught the First Nations people of Canada how to excel at and, in their own way, indigenize it. All land utilization ideas and economic development schemes started their journey on Maggie's desk. And she was getting tired of it.

All around her the community swirled and flowed, everyone except Tony caught up in mourning. She thought of her family, brothers, sisters, uncles, aunts and cousins. She couldn't comprehend how families with only one or two kids functioned.

Maybe that was why Maggie was such a good chief. She had been forged within the anarchy and chaos of a large family. Each brother and sister had made her stronger, both by love and by torment.

The chair beside her scraped on the tile floor. "I don't suppose anybody has seen Wayne?" said Diane, Maggie's eldest sister. Wayne was Maggie's youngest brother, three years younger than her, the youngest of the Benojee brood.

"You know he won't be here. He'll probably come tonight when nobody's around."

"Or when the moon's full." Diane, her plate a mound of triangular white sandwiches, began to feast. "Willie dropped by his island a few days ago. Couldn't find him, so he left a note. Geez, you'd think he'd be here."

"You know Wayne. He's got his own way of dealing with life." Maggie couldn't help noticing the pile of processed food on her sister's plate. This was not the diet the doctor had prescribed for her diabetic sister.

Diane noticed the look and scowled. "Don't you dare give me that—there are no calories, sugars and starches at funeral receptions. You know that." To illustrate her point, she stuffed a whole sandwich in her mouth, and grinned.

Maggie couldn't help but smile back. As for her younger brother, it wasn't uncommon for Wayne to go missing for weeks, even months at a time. An isolationist and contemporary Native—*mystic*, for lack of a better term—Wayne led a strange and separate life and there were always rumours about what he did over on his island. People fishing just offshore of his island would occasionally hear strange yells. Family, when visiting, said the place looked like a primitive gym, with homemade punching bags constructed from canvas and stuffed with leaves and sand.

Her brother rarely came to the mainland, and if he did, it was usually for supplies and to visit his mother. Though he was the youngest, he spoke the best Anishnawbe—like his mother, strong and without hesitation.

And then, of course, there was the famous rumour, the stuff of legends. Supposedly a few years ago, some rowdy boaters had landed on the shores of what had once been called Western Island, but was now more frequently known as Wayne's Island, intent on building the world's biggest bonfire. They started foraging for wood, and soon discovered the island was occupied. According to the story, Wayne disagreed with their starting a fire, and his disagreement was strong and severe. Exchanged words and issued threats developed into an altercation. Five drunk White guys against one lone Indian. This had the makings of a pretty good civil rights case.

The next morning their boat was found drifting a kilometre offshore of the island. Inside that boat were many bruises, one dislocated elbow, numerous lacerations, seven cracked ribs, four black eyes and at least a dozen missing teeth. The White men said everything was a blur. One guy mentioned a crazy Ninja Indian on the mysterious island, but the others shushed him up, embarrassed.

"Mom?" Virgil was standing beside her.

"Yes, honey."

"I'm gonna go now. Okay?"

"Did you have something to eat?"

He nodded. "Three sandwiches, one apple, a grape juice and some cookies. Okay?"

"I guess so. Where're you going?"

"Dunno. Probably home."

"Tired?" she asked.

"A little."

Behind Virgil, she could see Duanne DeBois hovering, waiting for his chance to speak with her. God only knew what he wanted to do with the land.

"Well, go get some rest. Hopefully I'll be home in a few hours and will make you a real dinner. Something with vitamins and fibre maybe. Sound good?"

For a moment, Maggie saw the saddest smile on his face. She realized she'd said this before. Many times. And she'd often failed to keep her promise.

"Sure," Virgil said, and then quickly left. Maggie watched him walk through the hall doors.

"Maggie, good to see you. You got a second?" said Duanne DeBois as he sat down beside her and opened a colourful flow chart.

SEVEN

About half an hour later, Virgil was walking toward the railroad tracks that ran through the Reserve's northern border. He had lied to his mother once again, only because he knew that she wouldn't understand and that it might start an argument neither of them wanted. Virgil knew he was running late and he had increased his pace. About twice a day, a passenger train would speed through the forested hills as if afraid to stop—rumour had it there were Indians about. Frequently, Virgil would be sitting there on a large flat-topped rock set about ten feet back from the tracks, watching the train thunder past on its way to wherever it was going. He'd done some research on the computer and most of the trains were heading to Toronto, or out of Toronto, several hours to the south. He would catch a glimpse of faces in those windows, some looking out at him, others engrossed in a book or laptop. Where were all these people going? Who were they? What did they do?

Virgil had never been on a train and his dream, mundane as it might seem to others, was to book himself a ride when he got older. Those trains reminded him that there were places to go, beyond the Reserve. The next train was due by in about six minutes, though the exact time was always a rough estimate, with VIA Rail's record. The engineer had seen him sitting there so often, it had become his habit to blow the train's horn as he went by. It was a loud noise, one that Virgil had become used to and enjoyed. It was an acknowledgment of his existence by somebody other than his family. At least some things in this world could be counted on.

Virgil often came here instead of the classroom. He knew that his skipping school upset his mother, and perhaps somewhere down the line he would pay for it, but right now, he didn't care. Maybe he should be more like Dakota. She went to school religiously and took to each subject like a kitten to a ball of string. But school was almost out for summer anyway, weakening his educational resolve.

Today had been a long and sad day and he was glad to get away. The tree branches grabbed at his black jeans and black shirt—perfect funeral attire—but he ignored them. He knew the large limestone rock that sat three metres to the left of the train tracks was just up ahead. There he could ponder the mysteries of the universe, or think about absolutely nothing. Both were equally enjoyable. He emerged just west of the rock, where the bush was the thinnest, and walked along the railroad ties. He didn't know why he was feeling so solitary these days. He'd heard people say stuff about his turning into a typical moody teenager. Great, now he was becoming a cliché.

His flat-topped rock was surrounded by a small field of sweetgrass. That's how he'd found it. His grandmother had taken him out one day when he was small to teach him how to pick sweetgrass, and she'd told him this was the best spot. Maggie had come with them once, but usually only Lillian bothered to gather, dry and braid the wild grass. "I used to do this with my grandparents," she'd often tell the bored Virgil. Though he found the smell pleasant, he had never tried to pick it himself. He knew it was one of the four sacred herbs, the others being cedar, sage and, the most important, tobacco. Soon, though, it had become too difficult for Lillian to make the tiring journey through the woods, and it was left to the boy. Only now he came for the train, not the sweetgrass.

Sitting on his rock was the blond stranger, watching him approach, as if he was waiting for him. Virgil stopped on the railroad tracks, unsure what to do. The motorcyclist leisurely lay back on the boulder, and yawned as the boy approached. Virgil could hear the creaking of the man's leather garments.

"Hey, what's up, little man?"

It was a casual greeting for such a startling encounter. Virgil didn't think anybody knew about his precious rock. He didn't know how to respond. Instead he just stood there, in the middle of the tracks.

"Beautiful spot, don't you think? It's a wonder they haven't put condominiums up yet." The motorcyclist stretched out on the rock as if it were a bed. He seemed quite at home, staring up at the blue sky spotted with wispy clouds. "Have fun at the funeral?"

At first Virgil didn't respond, but then he thought about the man's question. "That's stupid. Nobody has fun at a funeral."

"My mistake."

The stranger looked at the boy. "You know, that may not be the safest place to stand. You might want to move off to the side. I know every man walks his own path, but sometimes a little advice from a stranger can save your life."

A little embarrassed, Virgil moved to the shoulder of dark gravel opposite the black-clad man.

"Here, I made you something." The man held out a perfectly braided length of sweetgrass. "I haven't made one of these in years. Just smell that. Now that's Anishnawbe."

Virgil didn't move. He did, however, notice the pile of freshly picked sweetgrass drying on the rock beside the stranger.

"They do speak English here, don't they?"

Virgil swallowed hard before answering. "Yeah. Who the hell are you?"

This seemed to amuse the man on the rock. "Oh my, now there's a direct question. Geez, where to begin. Who the hell am I? Well, I guess I could start with a name. That's always a good beginning. You can call me ... John." John put the sweetgrass braid down on a corner of the rock.

"John ...?"

The man looked up. "I suppose now you will want a last name too. As if one name isn't good enough. I remember when all you needed was one good name to get you through life. But not anymore. Okay then, my name is John ... Tanner. John Tanner. Yep, that's me. Happy?"

John Tanner. Such an innocuous name for such an unusual individual.

"And as is the custom, I assume at some point you will tell me your name?"

Virgil hesitated. He and every kid in North America had been warned through school and the mass media not to tell strangers too much about themselves. But this was no ordinary stranger.

"Virgil Second."

"Is that like Henry the Eighth?" The man laughed at his own joke.

Virgil scowled. He'd heard that joke, or a variation on it, too many times in his life. "What are you doing here?" he asked instead.

"Why do you want to know?" said the man, suddenly engrossed in braiding another strand of sweetgrass.

"You were at my grandmother's."

"That I was. So were you," the man replied, intricately weaving the three strands together. They represented the mind, body and spirit, and how strong these elements could be when properly balanced.

Off in the distance, the train could be heard, its lonesome horn announcing its approach.

"The great iron horse approaches," said the man, in his best Hollywood Indian voice. "Boy, I remember when I first saw one of those things, just about scared the shit out of me."

Again, Virgil didn't know what to say. The man seemed to concentrate for a second before letting out the mournful sound of a train whistle. It sounded . . . like an actual train whistle, the kind he'd heard hundreds of times.

"Did you like that?" asked the man.

Then he took a deep breath and let loose the plaintive cry of a wolf revealing its heart to the moon. It was startling in its authenticity.

"How can you do that?" asked the astonished boy.

"Can I help it if I'm multilingual?"

Next, the call of a loon came from the White man's mouth. It was note perfect.

"A little something I picked up on my travels. Maybe I'll teach you sometime. That woman at your grandmother's house, and with you at the graveyard, I take it that was your mother?"

The new braid finished, the man reached down and retied the blue bandana around his ankle.

"Why?"

"She's pretty."

This puzzled Virgil. His mom pretty? Moms weren't supposed to be pretty. Especially to strangers in black leather. Especially to a stranger he'd seen kissing his grandmother. A stranger who had been sitting out here in the middle of the woods braiding sweetgrass and waiting for him, it seemed. The boy was growing increasingly uncomfortable.

"What do you want?"

The man sat up on the rock, giving Virgil his full attention. "Me?"

Virgil nodded.

"Well, that's a tough one. Admittedly that took me a while to figure out, especially after your grandmother died. You see, I haven't had much to do lately. A little of this and that. More that than this. Years ago I fell victim to what's called T & A, you may be familiar with it. They are the two greatest enemies of a person's self-esteem. Tedium and alienation. That put me out of the loop for a long time. You see, I knew your grandmother way, way, way before you were born." The White man's blue eyes danced. "That was the last time I felt good. I want that feeling again. I'm hoping it runs in the family, if you know what I mean."

Virgil did not know what he meant. "Why are you telling me this?"

"I thought maybe you could help. Or at least, stay out of my way."

If Virgil was puzzled before, he was really puzzled now.

"Me? Why would you want *me* to stay out of your way? And how am I supposed to help you?"

"I'm glad you asked, because I did promise your grandmother I would let you know what I was up to. She was quite fond of you, you know. You should have come to say goodbye to her. Like I did."

The young boy's heart tightened with disgust.

"Still, a promise is a promise. I made your grandmother two promises, and both involve you."

"Me?"

"You."

"What . . . what . . . did you promise her?" If there was such a thing as a weirdness indicator, Virgil was sure the needle was dangerously into the red.

The man slid off the rock and stood up. "Well, you see, there are some things that have to be done. I haven't done this kind of stuff in a while, but I want . . ."

The rest of what the man had to say was drowned out by the roar of the train. The ground shook beneath their feet. The wind buffeted them. And the noise of the engine, the passenger cars on the metal tracks and the blowing horn overpowered all other sounds. The man's mouth continued to move.

Just as suddenly, the train was gone, and the motorcyclist finally finished what he was saying. " . . . and so you're either part of the problem or part of the solution, young man. So there. The choice is yours. Otherwise, tikwamshin!" With that, he gave the boy a polite bow. "I'm glad we got that out of the way. I feel better, don't you?"

"But . . ." said Virgil, having no idea what the man was talking about.

"Sorry, I don't do Q and A's. Anyway, time to be going. And, Virgil, if I were you, I wouldn't hang around out here by yourself too much. Never know what freaks and desperate types you might run into." Brushing the twigs and dried grass from his pants, John Tanner disappeared into the woods.

Virgil, still overcome with surprise, simply watched him go. What had he said? Tik . . . something? What did that mean?

Lying on the flat rock were seven braided strands of sweetgrass.

— EIGHT —

Chief Maggie Second was so tired she was afraid she'd drive off the road. Two days had passed since the funeral, and she'd been forced to jump right back into the thick of band affairs. She was just driving back from meeting with the MP for the municipality. The local county authorities continued to be upset over all the confusion in Otter Lake regarding the land acquisitions. Local non-Native residents had gotten wind of the purchase and were concerned that the Native people were trying to buy back all the land the non-Natives' ancestors went to so much trouble to appropriate. Native people with additional land—that could not be a good thing. And there was good money to be made in using the land for cottages. After five hundred years of European settlement, all they had to show for it were cottages lining every lakefront, complete with noisy Jet Skis.

The whole land deal was almost complete, but there were still i's to dot and t's to cross. To create extra roadblocks, the local municipality was demanding more studies to find out if Otter Lake had the capability to administer and properly use the additional land. Things like water resource reports and road access issues, among others. A set of high-tension power lines ran over one small section. What would happen if they went down and had to be repaired? Who had jurisdiction?

The previous owners, three families whose total property had comprised the three hundred acres, had not been grilled so severely. In fact, one family, the Fifes, who lived primarily in Toronto and had never actually set foot on the land (it had been left to them in a will) had sold it without a second thought. None of their portion was lakefront, and it was only a couple of dozen acres, so not worth getting hot and bothered over. The Goodman family had a cottage on Otter Lake, one that had been in the family for generations. It looked like a sixty-year-old cottage; the Goodman family were not known for their maintenance capabilities. They purchased another, more modern cottage on a nearby lake with the profits from the sale. The third participant in the sale, Michael Bain, lived adjacent to the land. He was a local farmer who occasionally used the area as a woodlot. Being a third-generation NDP supporter, he felt it was his civic duty to help Canada's Indigenous people assert themselves culturally, spiritually and, of course, financially. So he eagerly sought to participate in their geographical expansion onto their once rightful land, while making a tidy sum.

Maggie found it odd that such a peaceful chunk of land could be causing such an uproar. Just yesterday she'd spent an hour on the property, lying on the hood of her Chrysler, listening. That was all. Just listening to the sounds of the deep forest. She heard birds and insects. Saw a porcupine. Four raccoons passed by, remarkably close, intent on where they were going. This was what her life had come to, hiding in the woods. Her mother had never wanted her to become chief. Lillian had felt that Maggie, of all her children, hadn't yet found her place in the universe. Even weird Wayne was doing his own thing. Lillian's peculiar blend of Christianity and traditional beliefs had eventually made her happy. "But you," she had said to Maggie. "You're too much like I was.

You need something you're not expecting. Babysitting twelve hundred people is not it."

Still, Maggie felt she was a good chief. This was now her second term, and other than the chaos of this particular land issue, she felt confident she wasn't letting the people down. Land . . . no issue affected Native peoples and non-Native peoples so strongly and yet so differently. On the one hand, White people thought land was there to be owned and utilized. Something needed to be done with it. Otherwise it was wasted. This was even in the Bible, where God gave man dominion over Nature. Native people, on the other hand, saw themselves as being part of Nature. It was a big huge intertwining web. You could no more own the land under your feet than you could the sky over your head, though it was no secret White people were already working on that too.

But colonization had a nasty tendency to work its way into the DNA, the beliefs and philosophies and the very ways of life of the people being colonized. Nowadays, some of the people on Maggie's Reserve, other than having a good tan, were indistinguishable from White people.

Lillian, however, had been what could be called an old-fashioned Indian, and she had taught her family respect for this land. Maggie had thought of that as she lay on her car, thinking about her departed mother, her rebellious but lovable son and the rest of her family. Maggie could have stayed on that hood all day contentedly pondering life, but damn her work ethic! There was still a lot to deal with.

Today, once again, she was driving alongside the controversial land. Maggie was growing to like this side road. It was thick with trees and, depending on the season, interlaced with snowmobile and ATV trails. Personally, she wished it could remain the way it was, semi-wild. It would remind them all of the way the land used to be, its simplicity.

Blasting from her speakers and keeping her company was music from Maggie's well-worn Nirvana tape.

Maggie was deep in thought when it happened. A sudden noise made her jump, and her car swerved to the left. Reacting quickly, she applied pressure to the brake, forcing the car over to the right shoulder and gradually bringing it to a stop, all the while grumbling under her breath. When the Chrysler had come to a stop she stepped out and investigated the trouble.

"Son of a bitch!" As she suspected, it was a flat tire. Her first one in almost fifteen years. And of course it had to be out in the middle of nowhere. Though technically she was only a ten-minute drive from her house, she was in one of the desolate patches of wilderness still to be found in Otter Lake. Maggie knew from experience that she had about as good a chance of finding cell phone reception out here as she had of finding affordable underwear that didn't ride up. Luckily, Maggie had a spare tire in the back. She sighed. As a woman of the new millennium, she was confident she could do anything her brothers could do, and probably better, short of writing her name in the snow, but that didn't mean she had to enjoy it.

Deep in the trunk, under a stained blanket, boxes of files and an old shoe, she managed to find the tire, which felt suspiciously low on air itself. But having no alternative, she hauled it out and began the laborious task of hooking up the jack, and then pumping it until the left side of the car was elevated. She was fiddling with the nuts when she heard the distinctive sound of a motorcycle approaching.

She could tell it was the stranger riding the machine everybody was talking about, evidently still roaring up and down the Reserve roads. She hadn't seen him since the funeral. And here he was, approaching at about sixty kilometres an hour. Maggie wasn't unduly nervous, but she was a lone woman, on a deserted road, with a flat tire. Though she would have denied it, her hand tightened around the tire iron.

The bike slowed to a stop in front of her car. When the stranger took off his helmet, she could see that he was much handsomer than he had appeared across the graveyard. And his eyes were the most perfect shade of blue she'd ever seen. Wrapped around his wrist was a blue bandana.

Sitting astride his machine, he glanced at the tire iron in her hand. "Flat tire?" he said with a smile. "Need some help?"

"No," she answered. "I can handle it."

"I'm sure. Still, I have a way with rusty nuts." He cocked an eyebrow.

Maggie looked down at the tires and noticed that he was right. They were rusted on tight. And like an idiot, she'd elevated the car without loosening them first. Which meant that if she had to fight to loosen the nuts, the car might fall off the jack and injure her or damage the axle or wheel alignment. This, she thought, is what happens when you change a tire only once every fifteen years.

"Damn."

"I'll ask again. Need some help?" The man swung his leg over the fuel tank and stood facing the woman, as he took in the situation with an amused expression.

Maggie's brow creased in frustration. "I suppose you think I'm some sort of damsel in distress that you can save?"

He shook his head. "No, ma'am, I never make assumptions about a woman holding a tire iron. Just trying to be neighbourly. If you wish, I'll keep going. And come next spring, maybe I'll drive back here and gather your bones. Is that okay with you?"

Maggie reasoned out his offer and decided to take a chance. "All right, I suppose it would be okay if you helped."

"Please, your degree of gratitude is overwhelming. I'm blushing." The man got off his motorcycle and removed his leather jacket, revealing a white T-shirt.

Against her will, Maggie found herself smiling. "Sorry, just a little tired and not feeling very social. My name is Maggie Second." She held out her hand.

The man removed the glove from his right hand and shook hers with a firm, though gentle grasp. His hand lingered, Maggie thought, a little too long.

"John. John Richardson. Well, I guess we should lower your car and take care of your rusted nuts."

Maggie laughed. "Well, when you say it like that."

"I'm sure mine are just as rusty. On my bike, I mean. May I?" He took the tire iron from Maggie and kneeled down to begin the task of lowering the car.

Maggie's eyes wandered over to the man's motorcycle. Though she knew little of such machines, she could see it was a superb work of engineering. Almost as beautiful as he was. Then, realizing she'd thought that, Maggie blushed ever so slightly.

"I don't know about that. Your motorcycle looks in awfully good condition. It's . . . beautiful. I've never seen one like it." Maggie felt drawn to the magnificent motorbike, and moved closer to inspect it.

"It's a 1953 Indian Chief motorcycle," John began. "Gorgeous, isn't it? It has an eighty-cubic-inch motor, which in today's metric is 1300cc. Its top cruising speed is over a hundred and forty clicks an hour, and it could cruise all day without a problem. The engine is a forty-two-degree flathead/side-valve unit and no other machine sounds like it. They don't make them anymore, and fewer than eight hundred were ever made. I know it's kind of old, but not everything new and original is better than what came before it. I'll match this baby against a contemporary Triumph or Harley any day of the week. I gather it . . . meets with your approval?"

Maggie stroked the leather seat first, then the handlebars. "Where did you get it?"

"You'd never believe me." Then, through gritted teeth, he said, "Man, these nuts are really on." The first nut gave way just then with a tortured squeal. "That's a good beginning," John said as he tackled the second nut. From across the motorcycle, Maggie could see his muscles straining under his shirt. Almost instantly, the second nut came free as did the third and fourth.

Maggie turned to admire the motorcycle again, and was still running her eyes over its lines when she heard John say, "I could use some help over here." She started and looked over to see him pointing to the spare tire.

"Sorry."

By the time she rolled the tire over to him, John had the flat off. He lifted the new tire up and into place, tightened the nuts and lowered the car again. John stood up, and they both stared at the half-deflated tire.

"When's the last time you had this thing checked?"

Maggie looked at him. "You're supposed to have spare tires checked?"

"In theory."

"God damn it!" Frustrated, Maggie kicked the tire, her fists clenched. "I don't need this. I really don't. I'm getting such a headache. You probably think I'm some ditzy broad who doesn't know a thing about car maintenance."

"Actually, I would say most men wouldn't know to have their spare tire's pressure checked either. I think forgetfulness is not gender-specific, like many acts."

"Like stupidity."

"That too. All right, you've got one blown-out tire, and one almost flat. What are our options?" He looked at her, waiting for an answer.

Maggie thought for a moment. "It's not completely flat. I could drive it into town, to the garage. What do you think?"

John kneeled down to take a closer look at the tire. He shook his head. "I wouldn't advise it. This could go anytime too. That would really fuck up wheel alignment, and your day. Know anybody in the village who might be able to help?"

Maggie nodded. "My brother Tim. He's got a garage in his backyard full of tires and parts. He likes to fiddle with cars. He might have a good spare tire. Or at the very least, he'd take me to get a new one."

"Looks like we have a plan. Tim's it is. I'll take you, but you'll have to sit on the gas tank. Don't worry, I won't let you fall off. You guide, I'll drive." He hopped onto the Indian Chief, and was about to put his helmet on when he noticed Maggie still standing there. "What's wrong?"

Maggie didn't know how to put it into words. It was the idea of riding through downtown Otter Lake, straddling this hard-to-ignore motorcycle, this equally hard-to-ignore gentleman's arms wrapped around her. A chief on a Chief. There was bound to be talk.

And there was something else.

"Who are you?" asked Maggie.

"Me? I'm a friend of your mother's."

"I gathered that, but from where? No offence, but you don't look like her usual bunch of friends."

John smiled. "Let's just say I know a side of your mother that you probably don't. She was a wonderful woman with many incredible traits, and I came to say goodbye to her. That's about it."

"I saw you at the funeral, standing by the road. Why didn't you come to the service, or to the reception?"

He leaned back on his motorcycle, took a deep breath and met Maggie's eyes. "A long time ago, your mother was forced to make a decision. She did, and I harbour no grudge against her, but I don't go where I'm not wanted."

"What do you mean, a long time ago? You're younger than me. This doesn't make sense."

The man's smile came flooding back. "Yeah, I know. Isn't it great? Who needs sense! Hop on. Let's get this puppy rolling." With that, his boot kick-started the Indian Chief and it roared to life. Reaching back, he handed Maggie the spare helmet. He shrugged on his leather jacket again before putting on his helmet. To entice her, he roared his precious machine down the highway a dozen feet or more, then pivoted on his foot a hundred and eighty degrees, wheels squealing in protest, and pulled up to Maggie, where he waited expectantly.

"If your bike isn't built for two people, why do you have an extra helmet?"

"You're not the first damsel in distress I've had to save. Let's just say I like to be prepared."

With the helmet in her hand, the proverbial ball was now in her court. Maggie jammed the helmet on, sat herself on the gas tank and felt one of John's arms quickly encircle her. She liked the feeling of leather and muscle against her back much more than she would have expected. But it also felt a bit naughty. He was, after all, at least ten years younger than she was. Still, it felt good. Her earlier fatigue had mysteriously disappeared.

With a powerful lurch, the machine shot forward down the highway, toward Otter Lake.

People still talk about the day the strange man on the strange bike came riding through the village, with the widowed chief snuggled a little too comfortably into the driver's lap. The patrons at Betty's Takeout almost dropped their fries when the huge red-and-white machine raced past. The employees at the daycare centre almost forgot about the kids playing on the swings. Delia and Charlene, who traded off receptionist duties at the Band Office, almost dropped their coffee and cigarettes. When John and Maggie passed the Otter Lake Debating Society they waved at the assembled panel, who, unsure what else to do, waved back and were momentarily distracted from today's topic.

Of course, the community's reactions paled in comparison to Virgil's when he saw them approaching. Walking casually along the road, a block or so away from the school, serious things were weighing on his mind. It was lunchtime and he was debating whether he should return to school after eating. He had an English class that afternoon and his teacher had been giving him grief for not turning in an assignment. But he had promised his mom he would try harder . . . Maggie, bracing herself on the Chief, was looking the other way, toward the school. Virgil recognized her by the pants she had worn at breakfast, and her favourite black vest with red embroidery. John waved to him, and playfully pointed at the figure nestled much too closely against him. Before Virgil could yell anything, they were gone, heading down Gate Road.

What the hell was his mother doing riding around with that guy? Virgil was standing there, still trying to figure out at exactly what point his reality had shifted, when Dakota pulled up on her bicycle.

"Holy! Virgil, was that . . . ?"

"I . . . I think so," he replied.

They both watched the dust slowly settle on Gate Road.

"Cool," she said. "Think she can get me a ride with him on his bike?"

For reasons not obvious to Dakota, Virgil wasn't listening.

"Wow, your mother is so cool. Mine just watches *North of Sixty* reruns. Come on, let's get to class—we have to dissect a frog, I think."

Unwilling or unable to argue, his mind so filled with that unexpected image of his mother on the motorcycle, he numbly followed his cousin back into the school.

What a day it had been for John. Luckily the flat-tire incident had worked out as he had planned, though it took a while. He had trailed Maggie into town and out again before the tire finally blew. If he ever found himself in such a situation again, he'd make sure to cut deeper into the rubber. At least now he had been able to establish himself as a rescuer, and that was always the first step. He remembered how she'd leaned against him as they drove into town. All in all, things had worked out pretty well. And in the bargain, during a subsequent conversation, he had learned a little more about what made Otter Lake tick.

Now he was standing on a little service road deep in the wooded land recently purchased by the Otter Lake First Nations. Maggie had told him of the divisions and controversy over the purchase. Yet, the land looked the same as any other chunk of land left over from the ice age. John shivered at his memory of the ice age. It was a harsh time, and though he sometimes missed the occasional mastodon steak, he much preferred swimming in temperate waters.

In the woods here were poplar, cedar, pine, the odd maple and oak, and lots of scrub. And as he stood there, he could feel eyes on him. Something out there was watching him, closely. He hadn't spent most of his existence, except for the last few years, living by his wits without getting to know when he was being observed.

John turned around slowly, his eyes trying to pierce the foliage. Then he glanced up, and saw a sizable raccoon perched on a large oak tree branch, looking down at him.

John narrowed his eyes and ground his teeth. He hated raccoons, and they hated him. It was a feud whose beginning had been lost in time and memory. But the hate remained and burned brightly. To his right, he saw another of the creatures, and behind it, four more. He definitely had the size advantage, but they had the numbers. Theirs had long been a stalemate, but that didn't mean the idea of a final settling of scores wasn't on their minds. This time, the ceasefire held, and they stared at each other, lost in their own cruel thoughts.

Then, one by one, the raccoons turned and disappeared into the greenery, leaving the man alone, his fists clenched.

"I hate fucking raccoons."

Somewhere deep in the forest, the raccoons were thinking the same about him.

NINE

That night, for the first time in a week, Maggie had the opportunity to fix Virgil a decent meal. With all the trouble over her flat tire, she had decided the rest of the day was a loss as far as work went, so she headed home to see what she could rustle up for dinner. Sitting on the table in front of her and her son were some Shake'n Bake chicken, corn niblets, mashed potatoes and a salad. For the first time in a long time, Maggie felt happy. She was actually humming to herself.

Virgil, however, was silent. He ate his food haltingly, barely glancing up from his plate.

"So, what did you do today?" she asked, salting her corn. He responded with a Virgil shrug. "That much, huh?" Again he only shrugged. "Want some more potatoes?" He nodded this time and she dished him out a heaping spoonful.

Though he loved Maggie's mashed potatoes, which were becoming a rare treat, today he could barely taste them. His mind was elsewhere.

"Hey, know what happened to me today?" she asked.

For the first time that meal, Virgil's head came up and he looked at his mother. "What?" he asked cautiously.

"I got a ride on a motorcycle! Remember that guy that was at Grandma's house? Well, I got a flat tire out on the back roads, and bang, there he was, out of nowhere. He gave me a lift to Tim's place. He's seems like a really nice guy. Says he knew Grandma some time ago."

A flat tire, she said. That explained some things. "His motorcycle, huh?" Virgil said slowly. "Did you have fun?"

"It was scary at first. I can't remember the last time I was on one of those things. But I just held onto his arms and let him do the driving. Anyway, got the tire fixed almost immediately, thanks to Tim. I was kind of lucky, I suppose. I could still be standing at the side of the roadway back at Hockey Heights."

Virgil could hear the excitement in her voice.

"Can you pass the bread, please?"

Virgil handed her the platter.

"Who is he?" he asked.

"His name is John Richardson. That's about all I know about him, other than that he rides a vintage 1953 Indian Chief motorcycle. When he dropped me off at Tim's, he said he'd see me around, so I guess he's here for a while. Hmm, wonder where he's staying."

Virgil's mind was racing. Richardson? The stranger had told him his name was John Tanner. There was something about the guy . . . something not quite right. Again the image of this man kissing his grandmother so passionately filled his mind, and for a brief moment, he contemplated telling his mother. But somehow, the words just wouldn't form in his mouth, and the moment passed.

"How'd he know Grandma?"

"I asked him that but he didn't really say. Just that they met a long time ago. He was kind of evasive, mysterious about it. Maybe he'll tell us more tomorrow."

"Tomorrow?"

"Yeah, I invited him over for dinner."

Dinner, here, in this house? Virgil wasn't sure that was a good idea. Why had his mother gone and done that?

"You know, to thank him for helping me. If it weren't for him, I could still be up there by the arena, instead of having dinner with you. There might even be ice cream in the freezer." She smiled a happy smile.

Virgil didn't share that smile, though Maggie didn't seem to notice. "There are lots of cars that come through that way. Somebody would have stopped for you eventually," he said.

"Not at that time of the day" was Maggie's response as she dug into her chicken.

Virgil couldn't remember the last time they'd had a non-relative come over for dinner—especially a guy with two different last names. Make that a *good-looking White guy* with two different last names. And a motorcycle.

Virgil ate faster.

It was late into the night and the whole community of Otter Lake was asleep. Except for a certain motorcyclist who was busy fiddling with the uncooperative back door of the church at the centre of the village. He'd been there for about ten minutes, cursing under his breath, trying to pick the lock. He was a man of many talents and this was one of the more recent skills he'd picked up on his travels. Finally, with a slight flick of his wrist and the correct pressure on the lock tumblers, he succeeded. The door swung open, and John entered.

Standing amid the pews, he was surprised by how bright it was inside. Shining in through the big windows was four-fifths of a full moon hanging above the southern horizon, and more light filtered in from a street light on the far side of the road. Making himself comfortable, John sat on a bench three from the front. Above the altar was a large, elaborately carved crucifixion scene, complete with the agonized figure of Christ, nailed for eternity. The statue must have been as big as he was.

"Hello."

John's voice echoed through the empty building. It was like he was in a cave, or in an empty universe. Why he had broken into this church he couldn't really say, other than that he had a need to see this man whom everybody flocked to. The one hanging so high up above everybody else. So there John sat, alone with his thoughts in the semi-darkness, struggling to understand this man's appeal.

In the moonlit air, he could see dust motes floating all around him, like so many dreams. In the wood of the pews and the altar, he could feel the hundreds or thousands of unanswered prayers that stuck to the varnish like dead flies on a windshield. In the bricks of this building he felt great fear, and ironically great love. It didn't make sense to him. But then, this Jesus guy never had made sense. He wished he could meet the man, and see if he was as great as everybody said. But unfortunately, Jesus didn't come around much anymore.

John stared at the elaborate figure on the cross, taking everything in. He counted Jesus' ribs, examined the pained expression on his face, the nails in his hands and feet, the cut in his side, the crown of thorns, all carefully reproduced on this wooden icon. He remembered reading somewhere that there is no record that this Jesus guy ever laughed or even smiled. Jesus sounded boring, in fact, aside from the fact he could do some clever magic tricks. John himself could do a couple of amazing things too, but nobody had ever raised a steeple to him. What did this Jesus have to offer?

Everlasting life? John had been around quite a long time himself and he knew the novelty wore off. And most people led dull lives anyway, so what was the draw? There was that place called Heaven, but it seemed too hard to get into. Too many rules to follow to get them to open the door. Jesus looked to be in so much pain, so sad, so pathetic, so alone. John had been through some tough times of his own, having survived big battles, silly accidents and just bizarre things that had left him pretty screwed up, but he would never have let anybody make a carving of him looking so wounded. So vulnerable. He had way too much pride for that. The more the stranger gazed at the figure on the cross, the less he understood what power Jesus had had over Lillian, and so many others. For several hours John sat there, trying to make sense of all that surrounded him in the church. The dust motes swirled and the moon migrated across the sky, and still John was no closer to understanding. The nails in the man's feet and hands looked particularly nasty. That especially annoyed him.

"You let them do this to you?" John asked aloud. "And your Father . . . He let them do this to you?"

Oddly enough, the two men had much in common, though both would deny it. Each had been born of a human mother, and had had a father with a less-than-corporeal presence in their lives. There was, however, one big difference.

"At least I got the chance to beat the hell out of my father," said John, more to himself.

Realizing he would not find the answers he had come looking for, he decided to call it a night. But before he left, he signed the guest book at the front of the church. *John Prestor.*

———

Something woke Maggie. She looked at her clock: four in the morning. She listened carefully; perhaps she'd heard a squirrel in the attic, or maybe a nearby branch had fallen. But the house and the surrounding woods were quiet. She listened some more, and still heard nothing. For a fleeting second, Maggie thought of the motorcycle.

It had been just over three years since her husband died. And since then, she'd been busy raising Virgil, taking care of her chiefly responsibilities and trying to find her way as a single woman again. She hadn't had a date since his death, nor had she wanted one. But she wasn't thinking of the upcoming evening with John as a date. It was merely a dinner to thank him for his help. The man was among strangers, and he had been a good friend of her mother's, after all. Over dinner she could find out more about how they knew each other. She was sure there was a story there. And it was just a dinner. Virgil would be there. It was just dinner.

Still, John *was* young, incredibly good-looking, muscular, and had that magnificent machine. Maggie knew a lot of girls went for the bad boys (even if they usually married the good ones). But then, the fact John rode a motorcycle didn't necessarily make him a bad boy. That was just a stereotype . . . Here she was, a fully grown woman, lying in bed thinking about this strange man. This is what teenagers do, for Christ's sake, she thought. Something is seriously wrong with me. Still, it had been nice to hold on to his arms, real tight. It had been a long time since she'd been that close to a man, or felt like this. Whatever this was. There was something about the guy . . .

But it was only dinner, she reminded herself. Realizing she wouldn't be able to get back to sleep now, she got up to make some coffee. By the time the sun rose, she'd been through all her dusty,

long-unopened cookbooks, trying to find just the right recipe for
this run-of-the-mill thank-you dinner.

The early morning light found the motorcyclist sitting on a fallen
log to the east of Maggie's house, watching. He'd seen the light
come on in her room an hour ago. From where he sat he had an
excellent view. John, having just come from the church, hadn't
slept all night, but he didn't feel tired. In many ways he had slept
for decades, and besides, the idea of sleeping only reminded him
of passing out, and he'd had enough of that.

The night was a time for thinking, while the daylight hours
were a time for doing. Though he didn't yet know what he was
going to do tomorrow, or the next day. Generally he was a man of
impulse, of improvisation. Planning was for those who feared surprises, but on occasion some advance forethought made things
more amenable to his needs. Over the years he had discovered
that the hard way. So there he was. Why he'd come, the man was
not sure. Was it the secret promise Lillian had extracted from
him, or perhaps something of a more personal nature? Besides
Virgil, Maggie was the only person he knew in the village, and he
would love to know her a lot better. This place called Otter Lake
had changed so much since he'd been here last. This very spot had
once been an open field, with the nearest house half a kilometre
away. Now he could hear a clock radio going off just a dozen or
so metres behind him.

It was still early enough that there might be raccoons about.
That made him uncomfortable. They'd get what they deserved
someday, by every god that was worshipped, but not this morning. He did not want to start something he couldn't finish.

He stood up, stretched toward the rising sun. There were things to be done and places to go. His motorcycle was hidden down by the water, behind a large lilac bush. He made his way along a path that cut through the woods, always conscious of masked faces with beady little eyes following his progress, from the trees, bushes and ditches. The man muttered under his breath all the way back to the Indian Chief.

Every day he was here, there seemed to be more raccoons. They were gathering. This was not good.

— TEN —

Virgil was lying on his rock by the train tracks, deep in thought. The next train was not for another hour and a half. He had promised himself he would miss only the first two classes of the day. After all, he had vowed to his mother he'd try better. Just two classes was at least a beginning.

Luckily, there was no blond man here today. Virgil lay across the rock, as he'd seen John Richardson/Tanner do. The smell of sweetgrass was unusually strong. High above him, the clouds slowly drifted by, not really caring about the problems of an earthbound Anishnawbe kid, just intent on reaching the far horizon. Virgil watched them pass, one by one, against the blue sky. One cloud looked like a fat fish with a big head. Another had a wispiness to it, like a streak left behind by a paintbrush. Next came what appeared to be a horse's head. Then, for a moment, he thought he saw a puffy white image of a man on a motorcycle, but the cloud quickly morphed into something more abstract.

He sat up and took a sip from the ginger ale he had brought, then, without looking, put the can down on the surface of the rock—right on top of a pebble. The can tipped and most of the pop poured out. The boy jumped from the rock, not wanting to get wet. Muttering to himself, he righted the can to save what drink he could.

"Shit! It figures," he said as he grabbed a handful of leaves and tried to brush the sticky liquid off the rock before the local ants, bees and other assorted bugs would home in.

That's when he saw the markings. Something seemed to be carved there, on top of the rock. Clearing the surface of fallen leaves and pebbles, Virgil was surprised to see what appeared to be pictures gouged into the limestone. It took him a moment but he remembered the name of what they reminded him of: *petroglyphs*. And judging by the dust and small chips surrounding the images, their creation was recent.

There were two distinct images. One appeared to be a man riding something—maybe a horse—or sitting on something. The second crude rendering, appearing beside the first, seemed to represent a woman, if those appendages were indeed what the young boy thought they were: boobs. Scrambling around for a better view, Virgil traced the etchings with his fingers.

This rock had been here since the ice age, at least. And he had been its only friend, to the best of his knowledge, for about two years. Except . . . except for John Tanner. Once more studying the first petroglyph, Virgil thought it could easily be a man on a motorcycle. Not the best representation, but it had to be. The motorcyclist had done this. It must have been him. But why? And the other image . . . the stranger had been talking to Virgil about his mother. Could this be his mother? He thought the boobs were exaggerated, but then, he'd never really looked at his mother's . . . Virgil put a stop to that line of thought.

And then Virgil noticed there was another stick figure, a smaller one carved under a small ledge. Just below it, he thought he saw a word scratched into the rock. Virgil thought the word was *tikwamshin*. It sounded and looked Anishnawbe but he couldn't be sure.

Once more, he traced the images with his fingers. The more he looked at them, the more it seemed as if the male figure was beckoning with one arm to the female. The other arm was pointing at yet another image the boy had almost overlooked, carved farther down the rock. It appeared to be that of the sun on the horizon. Did the man who had carved these images want to take the woman away on his motorcycle? Maybe to disappear into the setting or rising sun? Was that his plan?

So that's why the stranger was spending so much time with his mother. It all made sense now. The more he learned about the mysterious man, the more Virgil had a bad feeling about him. And now the stranger was coming over for dinner. Tonight. In Virgil's house. With his mother. There were questions to be answered, and tonight they would be answered. He would see to that.

It was just after one in the afternoon and John was hungry, but he wasn't sure where to go. He pondered this question as he continued to familiarize himself with the local terrain. For the last few days he'd been discreetly—as discreetly as you can be when riding a loud and large motorcycle—mapping the whole area. He always found this to be an excellent survival tactic. Another day or two and he would know the local landscape as well as those born here. Roads, trails, gullies and paths were now a part of his memory. This land, much like Lillian's face, hadn't changed much, just a few lines added here and there.

John was tearing down what was called Charlie's Path when suddenly he saw the raccoon ahead, sniffing a mud puddle in the dirt road. It was difficult to say who was more startled, but John had the definite advantage. He was sitting atop a large, gas-powered, metallic and heavy machine that obeyed his commands. Determining to utilize that edge, he urged the Chief forward at a deathly speed.

The raccoon, having never heard the story of David and Goliath, wondered if she'd eaten her last crayfish. Barrelling down on her was the man all the other raccoons had been obsessed with lately. And it was just her luck to be here alone. The shoulders of the path had been cleared about a metre or two back, meaning she'd have no chance to make it to the safety of the woods in time. So, the young creature did the only thing she could do. She faked him out.

The furry creature dodged to the right, toward a patch of wild raspberry plants, and John augmented his aim to compensate. However, at the last moment, the raccoon stopped, tucked and rolled backward as the motorcycle roared over where she had been scurrying a half-second before. The front tire caught the tip of her tail, tearing out a patch of black and grey hair. By the time John stopped and turned the motorcycle around, the raccoon was already calling him and many of his family members rude names from the bushes.

The raccoon, nursing both her bruised tail and a grudge, worked her way deeper into the woods. The latest skirmish in this ancient feud had ended, but the war was just heating up.

Disappointed, the man left the area. Barely slowing down as he merged onto the main road, John returned to the thought of filling his empty stomach, and decided to ask a resident for recommendations. John pulled up beside a girl, apparently on her way home for lunch.

Dakota jumped at the roar of the engine beside her and then stood rooted to the sidewalk when she realized who it was.

John took his helmet off and gave her his best smile. "Hello there, beautiful. I got a question. Where would a guy like me go to grab something to eat around here? I've got an empty stomach and would love to contribute to the local economy. What fine establishment would you recommend?"

Dakota was stunned. This amazing and mysterious man was talking . . . to her! Asking her something. And more importantly, she had an answer! "Um, um, well, um . . . there's Betty Lou's Take-Out. It's just around that corner and up the road a few blocks."

"Yeah, I've driven by it a few times. I can smell the grease from here. What else is there?"

"That's it." Dakota said, puzzled. There was only one restaurant in the village. Everybody knew that.

The man thought for a moment. He'd been hoping for an alternative, for it seemed to him the diet of the contemporary Aboriginal had changed substantially over the years, and now most First Nations chefs had adopted the adage "When in doubt, deep fry."

"What kind of food does Betty Lou's have?" Unfortunately, his nose had already told him the answer.

"Food. Just food. Nothing fancy. Just food." For the life of her, Dakota couldn't remember anything on the menu.

John looked up the street in the direction the girl had pointed. "Hmm, that way, huh? Looked like you were heading that way too. Wanna ride? You can be my faithful Indian guide. I'll even buy you some fries if you want."

At that moment, Dakota was so thrilled she would have married him, if it were illegal. He was inviting her to ride on his amazingly cool motorcycle. She could get in trouble for this . . . a lot of trouble. If her parents found out they would scream at her about the possibility of him being a kidnapper, a rapist, or a bunch of other horrible things. Still, it was such an amazing bike. And he had such beautiful eyes . . . those piercing blue eyes. But time was wasting.

"Sure!"

Almost leaping onto the gas tank in front of the man, Dakota prepared for the singlemost exciting moment in her life so far. The man put the helmet on her head, tightened the cinch and then said, "By the way, my name is John. John Clayton."

"D-Dakota . . . my name . . ."

"Dakota. I've been there. And I know the Dakota people. But that's such a long story. Let's go."

Placing a muscular arm around her waist, he turned the throttle and the machine set off for Betty Lou's Take-Out. They were there in a scant few minutes, much too soon for Dakota, comfortably nestled between his arms and thighs.

Taking off his helmet and then Dakota's, he surveyed the establishment. A handmade sign confirmed this was indeed Betty Lou's Take-Out.

"So this is the finest restaurant in Otter Lake?" he asked.

"It's the *only* restaurant in Otter Lake."

"Yeah, I figured that, Dakota. Stay here and I'll get your fries." Dutifully, Dakota sat down on a much vandalized picnic table.

It was after the lunch rush, and the place was almost deserted. Most people had eaten by now and were on their way back to work. The noise of the Indian Chief idling outside had announced John's arrival long before he entered the place and began scrutinizing the menu, which offered two possibilities. The first was the Canadian menu with your usual fast-food potentials like hamburgers, hot dogs, fries and BLTs. The other listed Indigenous fast food, such as elk burgers, buffalo stew, Indian tacos and the oddly named Indian steak.

"Interesting. What's Indian steak?" he asked Elvira, who had come out of the kitchen. She had hair like Flo from *Alice*—a Native Flo, mind you.

"You probably wouldn't like it," Elvira said, drying her hands on a stained tea towel. "It's fried baloney on a bun. A local delicacy."

"I could never be that Indian," he muttered to himself as he continued to scan the menu. "How about an Indian taco. I've heard of those. Fried bread, chili, cheese, hot sauce. That sound about right?"

Elvira nodded as she disappeared into the kitchen. "You know your Indian cuisine. One Indian taco coming up."

John called to Elvira, "And a large order of fries too."

"And a large order of fries," she repeated from the back. "You're the guy with the motorcycle, aren't you?" called Elvira.

"What gave me away?" he asked.

She laughed. "The bugs in your teeth. What's your name, and do you want hot sauce on your taco?"

"My name is John. John Frum. And yes, I love hot sauce,."

She propped the swinging door open with her leg so she could make the taco while talking to John. "Frum, huh? Where you from, Frum?" She chuckled to herself. "Ah, you probably get that all the time."

"Nope, that's actually the first time I've heard that, believe it or not. And if I knew where I was from, I would tell you."

The front door opened and a hefty man entered, wearing cut-off track pants, though he probably hadn't run since he was a kid, and a well-worn golf shirt, though he probably hadn't played a round of golf in his life. Elvira emerged from the back to see who it was.

"Hey, Judas."

"Elvira."

She wiped her hands again on the dirty tea towel. "The usual?"

"That's why it's called the 'usual,'" he answered.

He stood beside John, his frame just about taking up the whole counter. He looked over at John and gave a noncommittal nod. John returned the nod.

"I'm Judas. Judas James."

"Hello, Judas. Just call me John. Don't get me wrong, Judas, but that's an odd name. Your parents must have really hated you to name you after him."

The big man shook his head, laughing. "Nah, I'm just the youngest of thirteen. All the other apostles were taken by the time I was born. Twelve boys and one girl in my family."

"What's your sister's name?"

"Mary."

"Of course."

Elvira brought out a Styrofoam container and left it on the counter in front of him. "Just a second," she said to him, taking a large roll of uncut baloney out of the refrigerator. Placing it on the counter, she cut off a slice almost two centimetres thick. Then Elvira took a pair of tongs and grabbed the slab of processed meat. From the counter to the deep fryer it went, Elvira holding it in the boiling oil until it got crispy and brown.

"Ah, the famous Indian steak I've heard so much about," commented John. He stared at the sizzling oil. It was the same fryer that had cooked the bannock in John's taco. And Dakota's fries.

"Something wrong there, handsome?" Elvira said to John as she put the cooked baloney on split pieces of fried bread to cool.

John opted not to answer her question, instead leaving his

money on the counter, and turning to go, holding his lunch at a distance.

"What about your fries?" asked Elvira.

"Give them to the poor," he responded as he left.

Just before the door closed, he heard, "Come back again, John Frum."

Outside, he gave the Styrofoam container to Dakota. "Here. You can have this."

Dakota looked at the sizable box. "This is a lot of fries."

John swung his leg over the Chief and looked at the girl seriously. "If you want my advice, put it down and walk away. There are some things girls shouldn't see. That's one of them. See you later."

And he roared off down the road.

A puzzled Dakota opened the box to discover the Indian taco.

Oh man, I had this for lunch yesterday, she thought.

Suddenly she realized that John Clayton had said he'd see her later. Her! Later! Wow, she thought, what a lunch hour. And to think she'd almost brought her lunch to school today.

ELEVEN

The house smelled like an Italian bistro. Virgil was in the living room trying to watch television, and occasionally he'd hear a plea from his mother to come out and dice an onion, or cut up a green pepper. Virgil couldn't even pronounce what she was making. All the effort his mom was putting into this so-called thank-you dinner was upsetting. She'd never worked this hard for *him*.

In the kitchen, everything was almost ready. Maggie just needed to put the egg noodles into the simmering water and dinner could be served. It seemed the dinner had gotten a little away from her and become quite elaborate. She couldn't remember the last time she'd made a meal like this, but it felt good to be making the effort. She was even wearing clothes that she wore only for special chiefly events.

"Are you getting hungry, my son?" she called to Virgil.

He would have shrugged but shrugging only really worked when another party was in the room.

"Getting there."

"Can you come in and help me with the salad?"

Reluctantly, Virgil went into the kitchen again, to help his mother with a meal he wasn't certain he wanted.

"You cut the cucumber and carrots, and I'll shred the lettuce."

"What is this called again?" he asked looking at the simmering pot.

"I've told you three times. It's a good thing you don't take Italian in school. What time is it? Oh god, hurry, Virgil. Hey, maybe John will take you for a ride on his bike. Would you like that?"

"I don't know." He paused. "You seem awfully excited about this dinner."

"No I don't. It's just a dinner."

Maggie turned on the radio and the music of Nickelback flooded the room.

Virgil, still feeling glum, sliced the cucumber. "Mom, this isn't that meal Dad used to like, is it?"

Maggie looked quickly at Virgil. "No. That was Hungarian. It was called goulash. This is Italian and much different."

"Just wondering," he muttered.

Maggie continued to stare at her son, trying to read her little man.

"I told you, this is just a dinner, Virgil. That's all."

"I know," he said as cheerfully as he could. Then he went back to chopping the cucumber, taking his frustrations out on it. Bits of green skin flew everywhere.

"By the way, I'm going to see your teachers tomorrow. It seems they want to chat with me."

Virgil stiffened, then continued chopping. He opted to remain silent.

"Did you go to school today?"

He nodded, not looking up. He finished with the cucumber and started attacking the carrots.

"The whole day?"

"Pretty much."

"You promised me—"

"I promised you I would try harder."

"You've said that before."

"You've said you'd be home for dinner a lot. Why is it okay for *you* to break promises, and not *me*? Doesn't seem fair."

Maggie knew Virgil was intelligent, despite his aversion to school, but she hated it when he out-reasoned her. Some chief *she* was, bested by a thirteen-year-old boy. "That's different," she countered.

"It's *always* different, Mom."

Maggie was digesting her son's retort when they both heard the distinctive growl of John's motorcycle approaching.

"He's here!" said Maggie. "We'll finish this discussion later."

A quick look in the mirror and a stir of the pot and she was ready to receive her guest.

Virgil dumped the sliced carrots and cucumber in the salad bowl and looked out the window with little enthusiasm. There the man was, in all his glory, getting off his machine. There was a quick knock at the door, and Maggie invited him in.

"I brought some wine, if that's okay. It's from the Okanagan. I hear it's quite good."

If it was possible, John looked better than he had before, Maggie thought. He had dressed up. He was no longer in his leathers, but had managed to fit into some tight black jeans with an exceptionally flattering black shirt, and immaculate cowboy boots. He handed her the bottle.

"I wasn't sure if you drank or not."

Maggie smiled. "I always have room for a nice glass of wine. Would you like a glass?"

He shook his head. "No thanks. I don't drink anymore. But you go right ahead."

Maggie felt a moment of awkwardness. In the Native community the line between those who drank and those who didn't sometimes created a rift on social occasions. But John was White and she hadn't expected that to be a problem tonight.

"Have a glass. Really, I don't mind. I insist."

"You're sure?"

He smiled at her. "One hundred percent. I stand when I pee but that doesn't mean you have to."

Maggie thought about that. "Interesting logic."

"I am nothing if not a man of interesting logic." Then John noticed Virgil standing in the corner, watching him. "And this must be your son. Virgil, I believe? We actually met the other day. Good to see you again." He thrust out his hand. Virgil reluctantly shook it.

"Hi. I'm sorry, what's your name again?" Virgil asked.

John paused, as if sensing a trap, Virgil thought, and glanced at both son and mother. Then he smiled broadly.

"John Richardson . . . Tanner. Yes, I have two last names. I was adopted in my early teens and was given a new name. So I have ID with both names. Sometimes I go by one and sometimes by the other, depending on who I most feel like at the time." The smile disappeared. "Why?" he said, looking directly at Virgil. Virgil shrugged.

"That is very interesting. Adopted, huh?" Maggie said as she tossed the salad.

"Yeah, it was rough but I survived. But been on my own since I can remember. Hmm, smells good. What is it?" He walked over to the stove for a little peek.

"Chicken cacciatore. Hope you like it."

Hovering over the stove, he admired the woman's efforts. "I like it already. As long as it's not deep-fried baloney." Involuntarily, he shuddered.

Maggie rummaged around in a drawer. "I guess you've been to Betty Lou's. Not one of our finer cultural achievements. The hamburgers are pretty good but I would stay away from everything else." Finally finding the corkscrew, she went to work on the wine bottle, but it proved difficult.

"Would you like me to do it?"

"Would you mind?"

John took the bottle and, with barely any effort, released the cork with a loud pop. He handed the bottle back to Maggie. "I'll drink whatever Virgil is drinking."

"Virgil, will you pour two glasses of milk?"

"Um, maybe not. Sorry, but I'm lactose intolerant."

"Would you like a pop? We've got ginger ale, and . . ."

John shook his head. "Borderline diabetic. Sorry. Maybe just coffee if you have it." Luckily, she had made a pot of coffee too.

"Wow, lactose intolerant and diabetic. Sure you're not Native?" asked Maggie.

"Not when I woke up this morning."

They both laughed. The three of them walked into the dining room, where Maggie had set the table. Nothing fancy, just a white tablecloth with candles. Virgil inwardly groaned. They sat down, Maggie at the head of the table and John and Virgil opposite each other.

"Mom?

"Yes, Virgil?"

Virgil looked directly at John when he asked his question. "What does *tikwamshin* mean?"

The guest displayed no reaction. He merely smiled politely.

"*Tikwamshin*? Sounds familiar but, sorry, I don't know. I can ask around for you if you want."

"No thanks. Just wondering."

"Good for you," said John. "Wondering is good. Nothing like a teenaged boy's curiosity." He turned to Maggie. "I'll have my coffee with some non-sugar sweetener, if you have it."

Maggie slid her chair back from the table and went to the kitchen. "I think we have some, somewhere." While her back was to the table, John kicked Virgil in the shin. Virgil yelped.

"Virgil, you okay, son?" Maggie called from the kitchen.

John was looking him in the eyes, as if daring him to say or do anything. Then he mouthed one word: *Behave.*

"Uh, yeah, Mom, just hit my knee against the table leg."

"Well, be careful." She said to John, "I know I have some Sweet 'n' Low somewhere."

"Take your time," said John, still eyeing the boy.

Now it was Virgil's turn to respond. He mouthed, "What do you want?"

"Stuff you're too young to understand," John mouthed back. "This does not concern you. Stay out of my way and quit trying to sandbag me."

"You leave my mother alone," Virgil hissed.

"Or what?"

"Or I'll tell her."

"Tell her what? You know nothing. I know everything. Puts you at kind of a disadvantage."

"Found it!" Maggie called. "You two certainly are quiet."

"Oh, we're okay. We're playing Rock Paper Scissors."

Maggie searched for a decent coffee cup that gave the best impression of their home, and began to pour the coffee. The practically silent conversation continued.

"Why are you doing this? Can't you just leave us alone?"

"What would the fun be in that?"

"My mother isn't *fun!*"

"Kid, leave your mother to me. She's going to be mine. And if you get in the way, there will be problems. And I am very good at dealing with them. So do not become a problem or things could get messy. Very messy."

Virgil gulped.

"She's going to be mine," the man mouthed, with a look of certainty and finality on his face. The memory of the petroglyphs he'd seen earlier that day flooded Virgil's mind. The couple, looking toward the sun on the horizon. All day something about those images had been eating away at him. So, John *did* have plans for his mom. He *was* going to take her. Away from him. Virgil felt a chill. The man smiled.

Maggie returned to the table, balancing a dangerously full mug of coffee. It had a West Coast design on it. "Hope you find it to your liking. Who won the game?"

John smiled. "Me of course, and I'm sure the coffee is fine."

As the man took a sip, Virgil kicked his knee, making him spill coffee onto the white tablecloth.

"Oh my goodness, are you okay?" asked Maggie.

They both tried to wipe up the mess before the stain set in. "Yeah, I'm fine. I am so sorry about that. A sneeze came out of nowhere. I'll buy you a new tablecloth."

"Don't worry about it. I'm sure it will come out."

As Maggie tried to salvage both the tablecloth and the evening, John and Virgil glared at each other. War seemed to follow the man everywhere he went.

———

Sometime later, when dinner was finished and bellies were full, they moved to the living room. "That was an excellent dinner, young lady," offered John, thoughts of deep-fried baloney long since vanished.

Virgil had been silent for most of the evening.

Maggie poured them all tea. "Young lady? I do believe I'm older than you."

"Just by a year or two, I'm sure."

Both adults smiled at the compliment. Virgil didn't. Instead, he sat in the stuffed chair in the corner, quietly studying the man. And his mother's reaction.

"Rule number one, Virgil my man. I find it's a good idea never to argue with women. Especially ones that can cook like that. That cacciatore was fabulous. I love Italian food. In my opinion, it's the best thing Columbus and Cabot brought over." John leaned back on the couch.

"Cabot? John Cabot? Wasn't he English?"

"Nope. He just worked for the English. His real name was Giovanni Caboto from the fabulous city of Venice, Italy. They just anglicized his name when he ended up in England."

Maggie looked surprised. "Virgil, did you know that?"

The boy nodded, answering reluctantly. "We learned it last year in Canadian history."

Back when you went to class, Maggie almost said. Instead she replied, "You should tell me stuff like that. It's interesting. And you, Mr. Richardson-Tanner, what's your background? English too? Irish, or maybe some Scandinavian? That blond hair has to come from somewhere. And those green eyes. Well?"

Virgil leaned forward in his seat. Hadn't Dakota gushed about the man's . . . blue eyes?

John looked directly at the boy as he answered, "Me? You don't want to hear about me. I'm boring," he said coyly, and returned to sipping his tea.

"Do you want me and Virgil to tell you in how many different ways you aren't boring? Come on, give us a little background," Maggie prodded, leaning forward too.

Taking a deep breath, John gave in. "Well, I told you I was adopted. Not much to say about my family, both parents are dead. I've been wandering across this continent for quite some time now, seeing what there is to see, doing what needed to be done. Had a bit of a drinking problem but that's behind me. Now, I'm just trying to find a purpose in life, like anybody else. How's that?"

"It's amazing how you can tell us so much, without really saying anything at all."

John added, "What more is there to say? I met your mother a few years back. Came to say goodbye. Met you two, and the circle continues."

"That's the part I still have trouble figuring out. You knowing my mother and all. How, where, when?"

"If I told you, you wouldn't believe me. But she spoke very highly of you."

Maggie raised her eyebrows. "Me? I kinda always got the impression she was a little disappointed in me. I got the feeling she wanted me to settle down, have a dozen kids and be the great matriarch of the family like she was. I don't think she realized times had changed. Toward the end she kept talking to me about magic. I didn't really understand."

"Oh, I think she realized how times had changed more than you may know. You have to understand, your mother came from a time when people still believed in mystical and magical things. The forest was alive. There were spirits everywhere. I mean, look at the Anishnawbe language itself—the only change in tense is when something is either active or inactive. Basically, alive or not alive. That says it all. Today's world is very different. How active or magical is your Band Office? Not a lot seems alive today to those old-fashioned Indians. I think she wanted you to understand some of what she felt growing up. It made life more interesting, and more Anishnawbe. I think Lillian wanted that for you."

Both Seconds thought about this for a moment.

"That's ... pretty deep. And this was my mother?" said Maggie.

"That was your mother. And she could be very deep."

"How do you know so much about the Anishnawbe language, and us?"

He smiled an enigmatic smile from behind his teacup. "I can't tell you all my secrets. She would say that's part of the magic."

Maggie and John locked eyes.

"Where are you staying?" asked Virgil.

This sudden interruption startled the man. "What?"

"I mean, you've been here almost a week. You must be staying somewhere."

"I ... I'm staying with Sam Aandeg. He's got that big old place down on Deer Bay Road." John drained the last drops of tea from his cup.

Maggie and Virgil looked at each other. They both knew the man, and the place.

"Sam Aandeg? How ... how do you know him?" asked Virgil.

"That would take too long to go into. I just do. Why? Do you know him?"

Both Maggie and Virgil nodded. Then Maggie cleared her throat. "Well, kinda. Everybody knows Sam. I don't know how to say this, but . . ."

Now it was John's turn to lean forward. "Yes?"

Clearly Maggie was uncomfortable with the topic. "Well, um . . . He's . . ."

"Crazy," finished Virgil. "And a drunk."

"Virgil!" exclaimed Maggie. She turned back to John. "That's not exactly how I would put it, but you get the idea. He went to residential school with my mother, but he was there for a much longer time. My mother was fortunate, only two years. Sam wasn't. She used to talk fondly of him, when he was a boy. But since . . ."

"So everybody's written him off. That's so sad," said John.

"He has his parents' house. He's managed to survive, I guess, in his own way. But seriously, John—Sam . . . he's, um . . . he's not quite there, if you know what we mean. He's sort of the bogeyman of the village."

Their guest laughed loudly. "Oh that. I know. He is absolutely weird. Nuts. He's so great. I prefer to say his four-stroke engine is missing two strokes, or he's a few strands short of a full dreamcatcher, but I agree, he's completely, completely insane. But he's better than television. I like people like that. They always give you a new slant on the world and make it so much more interesting."

Again, mother and son glanced at each other, trying to digest this odd reply. The man sitting with them seemed more and more eccentric.

John continued. "Insanity is just a state of mind, after all. You should listen to him talk sometime. It really helps you sort out your priorities."

Maggie was perplexed. "But, John, I thought he spoke only Anishnawbe? How . . . how do you know what he's saying?"

"That was good tea," he said. "No, he, uh . . . speaks English. Just not a lot of it."

Maggie said, "John, Virgil and I both know his family and they've always said that he hasn't spoken a word of English since he got back from residential school almost fifty years ago. He refused to. They would know."

"Oh well, my mistake. It just must have sounded like English. Maybe I was anglicizing him," he said, forcing a laugh. John was talking faster now, and moving. He was up out of the chair and on his way to the door. "Anyway, it's late and I'd better be getting going," he said, putting on his jacket and gloves. Don't want to overstay my welcome. That was an absolutely fabulous dinner. Best I've had in a very, very long time. Virgil, see you later. And, Maggie, you are amazing. Don't let anybody else tell you otherwise. 'Til next time." He took her hand, leaned over and kissed the back of it.

Before Virgil or Maggie could object, John was out the door and leaping onto his motorcycle. In a couple of swift moves, he had his helmet on and his motorcycle engine running. With a wave of his hand and a gunning of the throttle, he was away, leaving behind only exhaust, disturbed gravel and two puzzled Anishnawbes.

"That was a quick exit," commented Virgil.

Maggie nodded. What had started out as a lovely evening had come to an odd close. The food had been surprisingly good for somebody who rarely found the time to cook. The conversation had been funny and enlightening, and the time had seemed to disappear. But the farewell had been accomplished in forty-five seconds or less. The man was nothing if not unpredictable.

"I guess when you gotta go, you gotta go. Want to help me do the dishes?"

"No."

"Too bad. You dry."

As Maggie closed the front door, she began to analyze the way the evening had ended, and what it meant. That's what dishes were for. That's when all her best thinking occurred. She was sure Nietzsche, Plato and Rousseau had all done a lot of dishes in their lives.

John was trying to let the white noise of the engine between his thighs drown out his troubled thoughts, but he wasn't having much luck. As he sped away from the Second house, he wondered if he'd given himself away. He had foolishly said too much, and Maggie had picked up on it. She certainly wasn't stupid. And the boy had been watching him like a hawk too, waiting for him to screw up. He'd tried to bluff his way out but it had been pretty lame. Was he slipping, losing his talents? After all, it had been a while.

He fed the carburetor more gasoline and the bike sped on into the night.

In his hasty departure, John hadn't seen the dozen or so raccoons in the bushes surrounding the house. Now, one chattered and the others nodded their heads in agreement. Things were starting to get interesting.

TWELVE

For Chief Maggie Second, today had been survey day. Technocrats, bureaucrats, politicians and just about everybody loosely affiliated with the three levels of government wanted an accounting of every grain of dirt, every blade of grass, every mosquito on the newly purchased property. So she had spent the morning with the survey crew, asking and answering questions. They had set up their little tripods with their little telescopes, marking things left right and centre, swarming the land like ants on a dead caterpillar. And they were all probably making more per hour than she was.

It was nice to get out of the office, but this all seemed a waste of her time. She didn't understand half the stuff these people were doing. And yet she was there to oversee the work. Once more she marvelled over her ancestors' commitment to the belief that one should not, even cannot, own land. She now wondered if the elders of yore instinctively knew the hassles that owning the land would involve.

Three more people had stopped her that afternoon with an opinion on how the land should be used. Gayle Stone wanted to use it for a theme hotel, catering to Germans (and other interested and well-heeled nationalities) and their hero worship of First Nations. One academic had even coined the term "Indianthusiasm."

There would be trails for horses, workshops for tepee-making (though Anishnawbe people didn't actually use teepees), canoe classes and a bow-and-arrow hunt for buffalo (an animal not domestic to this part of the country). Maggie couldn't begin to list all the things culturally wrong with Gayle's suggestion, but she gamely smiled and listened.

The other two suggestions were a little more uncomfortable. Attawop McFarlane felt the time was right, in these increasingly political and volatile times, to establish a school, or at least a training ground, for protesters. He was sure, dead sure, things were going to get worse with the provincial and federal governments, and that events like those at Oka, Ipperwash and Caledonia were going to become regular occurrences. So logically, there would be a need for experienced and professional protesters. Nothing worse than amateurs running around pointing guns and distributing press releases. Otter Lake could export those trained in blockading roads and handling media relations, and even warriors with a certain amount of paramilitary expertise.

This was when Maggie's migraine began.

Eventually, down the road, Attawop felt they could up the ante. With all the money the institute could bring in, added to the money from the smoke shacks that had been set up recently, and maybe, down the road, a casino or two, Otter Lake could officially secede from Canada. He was already anticipating the need for Otter Lake's own passport, flag, national anthem, etcetera. Maggie had to admire Attawop's enthusiasm, though privately she mourned the direction it took.

The talk with Ted Hunter did not make Maggie's migraine go away. Ted wanted the land to be turned into a gigantic movie studio. With so many television shows and movies about Native people being shot in Canada, it seemed only natural, he said, to build a facility that would cater to that market. Three hundred acres would provide for a lot of studio space, as well as all that natural forest for period productions. For instance, a standard village for all the major tribal affiliations could be constructed in advance: an Iroquois village complete with stockades, a Haida village with totem poles (he hadn't figured out the ocean part yet), a Plains Cree tepee village (the part about the vast empty plains would have to be dealt with at a later date) and so on. It seemed to Maggie that Ted's degree in radio and television broadcasting from a local community college had given him, if nothing else, ambition and incentive.

By the end of the day, Maggie wanted to run screaming out of her office. But that would have been very un-chieflike. So instead, she took two Advil and quietly snuck out the side door to head for Virgil's school for her meeting with his teacher, Ms. Weatherford. Three years of being chief had taught Maggie to read in advance the mood of any meeting she would be going into. The mood of this one did not look good.

"Your son," Ms. Weatherford began, "is not applying himself." The woman, in her late forties, with a subtle East Coast accent, was looking over Virgil's chart. As she read, she kept twisting her body to her left as if working a kink out of her back. "He misses a lot of classes. And when he is in class, he's not paying attention. He seems to be . . . lacking motivation."

Ms. Weatherford had been teaching at the Reserve school for going on five years now, and was very familiar with most of the kids and their families. Though not Native herself, she did claim to have a branch of Mi'kmaq growing somewhere in the family tree and was convinced it provided a window of understanding into her students. When you teach grade eight, you need all the help you can get.

"Okay, what would you suggest?"

Maggie had been expecting something like this and was wondering how serious a lack of motivation could be for a thirteen-year-old boy. When she was thirteen, the only motivation she'd needed was the threat of her mother's large wooden spoon. Still, it was her son's last year of schooling in the village. Next year Virgil would be bussed off the Reserve daily for high school.

"I don't know. All kids act and react differently. Are you having any domestic problems at home?"

A dead husband/father. A recently deceased mother/grandmother. "Nope, just the usual." She thought of John, but surely Virgil's lack of enthusiasm over their dinner guest didn't pose that serious a problem.

"I was sorry to hear about your mother. But Virgil's problem predated her passing away. I think somehow we, meaning you and I, have to find a way to focus Virgil's attention and enthusiasm. We both know he's a bright boy. We just need to let him know that. I have some ideas."

Maggie listened patiently. It was a relief for once to have somebody else come up with ideas on how to solve problems in her life. Maggie nodded as Ms. Weatherford put her BA (with a minor in Psychology) and her teaching certificate to good work. It seemed her son just needed a good kick in the pants, but Ms. Weatherford explained it in less abusive terms.

After returning home from the meeting, Maggie lay in her room for an hour. Virgil must have been out playing with Dakota or one of his other cousins, so the house was calm. She didn't have to worry about dinner; they would have the leftover chicken cacciatore. She heard the phone ring once but refused to move. Nothing short of her son being presented the Nobel Prize, by Russell Crowe, would have induced her to move.

Eventually, the headache that had been bothering her all day began to subside and she emerged from her bedroom ready to see what fresh hell the evening would bring her.

The voice on her answering machine was from Marie, her older sister. "Throw something nice on. I'll swing around your place at about seven tonight to pick you up, okay? I think we need to get you out of this village and have some fun. I won't take no for an answer."

So Marie wanted to go out. Probably to Charley's, a place about thirty minutes from the village. The last thing Maggie wanted to do was go to a loud, smelly bar and watch Marie and her friends drink and cackle.

Then the voice added, "Heard you had somebody over last night. Looking forward to hearing all about it. Talk to you later."

That was it, then. Her sister didn't really want her to have some fun. She wanted gossip, the dirt on John.

At first she felt vaguely insulted, and then flattered. In the last few years, her life lacked anything that was remotely worthy of being considered entertaining gossip. The thought of Marie and all her friends leaning over their beers with bated breath, waiting to hear about her evening with the sexy, mysterious young guy on the motorcycle, suddenly appealed to her. Maybe she *would* go. And though her sister did have ulterior motives, perhaps Maggie shouldn't pass up a chance to get out of town and leave all her chiefly responsibilities hanging in her closet.

"It will be good for you," agreed Virgil when he got home, though the truth was, he knew his mother had just come from a meeting with his teacher. This was as good an excuse as any to put off the inevitable deluge of concerned words about his education. Even better, a night out of the house with his aunt might help get his mother's mind off work. Virgil always looked forward to spending what precious time he could with his mom, when her schedule allowed it. But he knew these were difficult times for the Band Office and could see the need for this outing.

But more than getting her mind off work, Virgil hoped the outing would get his mother's mind off that guy with the motorcycle.

Everything about the man warned of danger. To the boy, John seemed like some sort of flu or cold infecting his community. The longer he was around, the deeper the infection. His mother seemed to be coming down with a bad case of the Johns. So Virgil reasoned a little time with her girlfriends might help his mother build up some resistance. Because if there was one thing he knew about women on these outings, it was that they tended to make fun of most of the men they knew. He could only hope John's name would be front and centre.

So when Marie showed up, right on time, Maggie was ready for an evening with the girls, and Virgil genuinely meant it when he said, "Goodbye, and have fun." He would find something amusing to do. And he'd be okay by himself. He was, after all, thirteen.

Virgil was watching television when he first heard it. His mother had left twenty minutes ago and he was deep into some generic cop drama when the sound filtered through the window. It took a moment to register, and then Virgil muted the television and listened. It sounded like music. There were four other houses in the immediate neighbourhood, but this music sounded like it came from someplace far off, like down near the bay.

The Second house was located about twenty metres up the road from what was affectionately called Beer Bay. Its real name was Burning Bay, named after a long-time resident George Burning. It had acquired the nickname in the sixties and seventies when it was a prime hangout for the village's youth. It was said that during those two decades, more beer was drunk down in Beer Bay per week than at most Oktoberfests. In the early eighties, things changed. Houses were built and the area cleaned up its act. But nicknames die hard in Indian country.

Virgil and Maggie's house was near the western part of the bay and, to him, the music sounded like it was coming from the east end. Everybody knew there was nothing over there except a dock where kids would go to swim and fish. The more he listened to the music, the more unusual it seemed. There was the rhythmic beat of what sounded like traditional Anishnawbe drum music, mixed in with guitars and synthesizers. And there was something else. It was hard to tell, what with the sound bouncing over water and being muffled by the trees. But somewhere under that music, Virgil was almost sure, practically positive, he could hear the rumble of a motorcycle.

Was that him? John whatever-his-last-name-is? He listened harder. "What is he up to now?" he thought. The more he listened, the more he wanted to find out. It was like the music was taunting him.

Desperate, Virgil pumped up the volume on the television in an effort to free himself from the sound. He even turned to MuchMusic, but that was no good. Dr. Dre was no match for the music coming through the window. He could feel the thumping of the traditional drum. The sound seemed to beckon to him.

Five minutes later he had his shoes and jacket on and was running to the beach. Following the natural curve of the bay, he made his way toward the music, which was growing louder and louder as he approached. Virgil had spent time at about two or three powwows a year, as well as at all the formal ceremonies at which his mother officiated, and he'd heard his share of traditional drum music. But this was different. In no time at all, he had found the source of the music. And it *was* coming from near the dock where kids swam and fished. But tonight there were no kids. Virgil crept along slowly, keeping hidden behind a row of bushes and goldenrods until he had a clear view of the dock area.

Just a short distance away, on the shore, was the motorcycle. Beside it was a huge portable CD player. On the dock was the motorcyclist, and he was in motion. He was dancing! He was a blur of movement one minute, and almost still the next. At times John was silhouetted against the almost-full moon. Virgil was mesmerized. This wasn't any type of dancing he'd seen on television, or at powwows. It had an ancient, tribal quality. And yet at the same time, a modern, innovative style. And just about everything in between.

There was something about the dance, and the way John moved, that tugged at Virgil's memory. Something had been told to him a long time ago. Was it from a television show or a movie? He couldn't be sure. Perhaps in one of the books his grandmother had given him. That's all he could remember. Occasionally the clouds rolled past the moon, obscuring it, and John would slow down, even stop in mid-pose, as the land was bathed in black. But once the moon revealed itself again, John would resume moving, as if the moon were his own personal spotlight. Eventually the man began to slow down. Finally he stopped, resting his hands on his knees and bending over slightly, panting. Yet he seemed empowered by what he'd been doing.

"Oh, that felt good," Virgil heard him say.

Perplexed, the boy continued to watch, his opinion of the stranger growing ever more confused.

Not wanting to be caught, he slowly stole away, staying as low as possible to keep out of sight. Once he got to the treeline, he began to run. Though he was no expert on the art of dance, he knew what he'd just seen had been unusual, amazing and special. Downright bizarre, too. But what did it mean?

After he returned home, he spent the rest of the night lying in bed, remembering the dancing form on the dock in the moonlight.

This had all started somehow with Grandma. Where did she fit in? What was the man's interest in his mother? John had plans to take his mother away, at the very least, and Virgil would find a way to stop him. On top of everything, the stranger had an attitude that suggested his mother was a means to an end. Exactly what means and what end the boy did not know—and this worried him. He had to put a stop to this. His mother had too many stars in her eyes right now to see clearly. It was up to him to protect her. But how?

Virgil had so many questions, all of them over his adolescent head. He needed help. His father use to say, "It takes a thief to catch a thief." Then logically, if he wanted to figure out some strange guy with unusual talents, he'd need the advice of another strange guy with unusual talents. Virgil knew only one guy who fit the description. He'd have to visit his uncle Wayne. That thought alone made him pull the blankets in closer.

He'd seen Wayne maybe half a dozen times since his uncle had moved to the island. People said he was practising to be a mystic or medicine man or monk or something else starting with the letter *m*. Maybe Wayne would know something about this John guy and what to do. It sure wouldn't hurt to ask, especially now that Virgil remembered what he had been struggling to recall. The dancing . . . A light as bright as the moon outside his window went on as he finally made the connection.

Virgil had not been alone that night in appreciating John's dancing skills. A certain Otter Lake girl whose name was the same as two large but sparsely populated American states saw him do his thing too. But she watched from across the bay, on her family dock, through her father's binoculars. They were very good binoculars and John was clearly visible along the far shore, lit by the full moon.

Sound usually travels excellently over still water. So Dakota too had heard the thumping sound of the music and had decided to investigate. And there was John, on the dock, dancing. She had taken some dance classes and was familiar with the basic moves of modern jazz and tap. This was different, however. This was . . . like what she had seen at those powwows Virgil had dragged her to. She watched the stranger for almost half an hour, marvelling at his endurance, talent and inspiration. Dakota could have watched all night, but John eventually slowed and then stopped.

She didn't see Virgil hiding in the bushes. She had eyes only for the stranger with the motorcycle. While her cousin was slinking back home, worried and confused, Dakota continued to watch, comfortably perched on the dock's edge. She saw the stranger take his clothes off and dive into the water. She knew that watching him do this was yet another thing her parents would have been upset about, but she saw it as no different than looking at that big statue of a naked man they had over in Italy.

Several times John disappeared beneath the dark water for long periods, and the last time, she was sure she'd lost him. Dakota was dangerously close to calling 911 when she saw him haul himself quickly out of the water onto the dock. Breathing a sigh of relief, she continued to watch as he stretched, dried and dressed himself. Slowly. It was a cool spring night but she didn't feel the temperature going down.

"Dakota? What are you doing out there?" her father called from the house.

Her heart in her throat, Dakota put the binoculars back in their case, albeit reluctantly, and got to her feet. "Nothing, Dad, I'll be right in."

Across the water came the sound of the motorcycle starting up. Dakota wondered if John Clayton did this dancing every night. Virgil had been right about one thing: this sure was one interesting guy—though in reality Virgil had used the word "weird." Dakota felt justified in substituting her own variation of the word.

Tonight the music travelled over the still water all the way to Wayne's Island, several kilometres away. He was doing upside-down push-ups at the time. He recognized the traditional drum sound instantly, as its bass sound travelled better. He had to strain harder to pick up the guitar and organ. At first, he thought it was coming from one of those pesky houseboats that always tried to moor near his island at night. Those houseboaters played the most god-awful selection of music, everything from Britney Spears to Brahms.

But this music was different. Landing on his feet, Wayne made his way to the shore, curious and eager to investigate. Thank god for the bright moon. The music seemed to be coming from near where one of his sisters lived. Maybe it was that son of hers, what's-his-name . . . Vinnie . . . Virgin . . . Virgil, that was it.

He didn't wear his watch anymore—there was little point to it out here—but he would have guessed it was close to ten o'clock, too late for that volume. He hoped the police would throw the little bugger in jail or something. Meanwhile, he needed his sleep. You never know what tomorrow might bring, and part of his training was always to be prepared. Like a Boy Scout, but with attitude.

The music, still reverberating in his mind, followed him up to his cabin. And by the time it stopped, Wayne was fast asleep.

— THIRTEEN —

Charley's Bar was pretty quiet that night, what with it being mid-week and all. There were maybe a dozen people scattered about the bar. The only ruckus was coming from four vivacious and loud Native women sitting near the back. Maggie was having a great time, as were Marie, Theresa and Elvira.

"Geez, he's good looking," said Elvira, after Maggie finished telling the story of the dinner. Everybody agreed with Elvira's description of John. Whether at the funeral, or just driving around the village, he'd been spotted by each of them. Consensus had been reached.

"And he just up and left? Just like that?" Marie was trying to decipher the meaning of John's sudden departure from her sister's home.

"Just like that." Maggie snapped her fingers.

All four sat in silence for a few seconds, pondering, before Elvira offered her theory. "Maybe your cooking gave him the runs."

They all burst into laughter. Aside from the sound of vintage Guns 'n' Roses pouring forth from the jukebox, their talk and laughter were the only sounds in the place. The other patrons were busy staring into their beers, trying to find inspiration or explanation for their lives.

"It had something to do with his giving the impression he could understand Anishnawbe. That's what set him off," Maggie explained. They contemplated that possibility. Then she added, "Or maybe I caught him in a lie."

"A man who lies? I didn't know they existed," Elvira said, raising her beer. Theresa and Marie joined the toast, laughing. "But what a strange thing to lie about," she added.

Theresa emptied her beer. "Men don't need a reason. They just need an opportunity. Maggie, don't tell me we have to retrain you. They're just like politicians . . ."

An awkward silence followed, as Marie and Elvira glanced back and forth between Theresa and Maggie. Then Theresa clued in.

"Oh fuck, Maggie. I'm sorry. I didn't mean anything . . . I didn't mean you. I really didn't. Okay, I'm cut off." She slid her half-filled beer glass over to Elvira.

"Why?" said Maggie. "You are absolutely right. And male politicians . . . a lot of talk, very little action. Sound familiar?"

Once more the room was filled with raucous laughter. Several of the regular customers glanced over at the women, who seemed to be having far too much fun.

"Ladies, I am telling you this here and now. I have an announcement," Maggie said.

Elvira was first. "You're marrying John."

Marie was next. "You're pregnant with John's baby."

This earned a scolding look from Maggie. "After one night? And we didn't even kiss. He ran out, remember? No wonder your grandparents had fourteen kids, if it's that easy to get pregnant in your family."

"Ah, but I think the more important question is . . . if he'd asked, would you have?" Theresa said.

Maggie looked confused. "Would I have . . . what? I don't understand."

The others found this deliriously funny. And since all three of them only laughed at such a high decibel when discussing sex, Maggie quickly got the inference.

"Oh god, on a first date? And it wasn't even a date. I *told* you, it was a thank-you dinner."

"Well, that's one way of saying thank you." More laughter.

"If I may finish," said a slightly embarrassed Maggie. "My announcement is that this, I think, is my last term as chief. I am out of here, as of next June."

"But . . . come on, Maggie. Why?" asked Elvira.

"I'm tired of it all. Of the bureaucracy. The paperwork. This stupid land thing. Of not being there for Virgil. Of not having a personal life anymore. I could go on. I think I've done my bit for Otter Lake. Time for somebody else to step up to bat." She hoisted her beer high above the table. "I rediscovered the other night that I like cooking. To cooking again!"

The others raised their beer in a toast, though not nearly as enthusiastically.

"Oh, Maggie, it's been so nice to have a woman in office up there."

Elvira seconded Marie's opinion. "Yeah, it really has been. Cooking's overrated. I know. I do it every day."

"My mom wasn't happy with me taking this job anyway," Maggie said, her decisive tone fading.

"Mom wasn't happy with me dying my hair, Maggie," said Marie. "She had her ways, and we have ours. I loved her deeply, but the world she was raised in is long gone. Maggie, you got in with a 137-vote lead over Michael. That's pretty substantial."

"But everybody keeps grumbling about the land appropriation and what we should do with it. Nobody seems to be happy with what I'm doing."

Theresa put her hand on Maggie's wrist. "But what *are* you doing? Anyway, you know Otter Lake. Grumbling is our third language. Hell, I grumble about my husband more than his first wife did, but I wouldn't change him for the world."

They were all silent for a moment. Then Maggie spoke. "You know, I had the rest of my life figured out before I came here. Thanks, guys. Now I'm back where I began. I think I need another beer. Yo, Karl, another round for me and my ladies."

Karl, the bartender, nodded, thinking to himself, *Oh good, another buck in my pocket. I left the Czech Republic for* this?

"Hey, Maggie, what was it like, riding on his bike? In his lap?"

"Oh, come on, Elvira, you seem more obsessed with him than I could be. You've ridden on a motorcycle before."

"Not like that one, with somebody like that. Andy, who owned that Honda 750, did *not* look like your John. My compliments."

"First of all, he's not *my* John. It was just dinner. How many times do I have to say that? Second, who knows if I'll ever see him again? If any of us will. Anybody who shows up out of nowhere could disappear just as quickly."

Theresa leaned forward. "But the important question is, do you *want* to see him again?" The other three nodded conspiratorially. "Maybe he wants to be thanked again, hold the food."

"If you don't want a guy like that, one who's obviously interested in you, Maggie, then maybe there is something seriously wrong with you. Possible lie or not. I'd accept a few lies if they came from a face and body like that. God, you could forgive a man like that a few mistakes." Elvira seemed to be speaking from experience.

"Listen to you all. You are terrible. Ladies, I do believe you are infatuated with the man more than I am. If he shows up again, I will deal with it. Is that understood?" Maggie took a defiant drink from her beer.

Marie eyed her sister. "Sounds like the chief in you coming out."

"I'm sure I'm not the first chief to sit in a bar, surrounded by nosy women."

"Does that include strippers?" Theresa asked. More giggles.

"Uh, Maggie . . ." Elvira seemed distracted by something behind Maggie. "What you were saying about dealing with it later if he shows up . . ."

"Yes?"

"Well, you'd better get the cards out and start dealing stud, because I do believe that's your motorcycle man coming through the front door. If it's not, somebody out there is having a sale on them."

Her heart suddenly pounding, Maggie turned around to see John standing near the front door, once more in his leathers, the blue bandana tied around his neck this time, scouting the place. Then he saw her, and the ladies.

"What the hell is he doing here?" she asked.

"Who gives a fuck," whispered Marie, "as long as he's here." Then louder, "Hey, you with the big hog, we're over here."

"Marie!" Maggie was mortified.

"What? We want to meet him."

"Oh yeah," Maggie's other two friends echoed.

They watched as John negotiated the mostly deserted tables and made his way over to them.

"Ladies. How are we tonight?"

Theresa answered for them all. "Better now. A lot better."

"What are you doing here?" asked Maggie.

"Just out seeing the town, stretching my legs. If you can do that on a motorcycle. And lo and behold, here you are."

All four checked out his leather-clad legs.

"I thought you didn't drink," said Maggie.

"I don't, but that doesn't mean anything. I'm not a woman but I could still wear a bra and panties if I wanted. I suppose." He followed this with a smile.

"Okay." Marie got her laughter in check and cleared her throat. "Uh, why don't you . . . join us?"

"Yes. Do. Please." Elvira pulled up a cigarette-burned chair for the man.

"Thank you. Don't mind if I do. My name's John."

One by one, each of the ladies introduced themselves, extending their hand to shake and, for however brief a period, touch the young man's warm, strong hand. And one by one, each of the ladies felt sure John had given her a special little squeeze and slight caress he hadn't given to the other women at the table.

As he sat down, he was aware that four sets of eyes were watching him closely, three with a fresh eagerness. He had theorized Maggie would be here. It was the local "Indian" bar, and he'd seen the car full of ladies driving along the Beer Bay Road as he was setting up for his evening dance on the dock. With the car rocking with laughter, they were definitely hard to miss. He had put two and two together, and had decided to investigate after dancing. Knowing Virgil wouldn't be at the bar, it had seemed like a good idea.

"What are the odds of me running into you here, huh? So, what's up, ladies? What's the conversation du jour?"

Marie cut to the chase. "So, did you enjoy dinner with my sister?"

"You must be Marie." John nodded, licking his lips. "It was delicious. Chickens are such ugly animals, yet so tasty. I'm sure Maggie was Italian in another life. Just the right amount of oregano and garlic. I like that in a woman."

The women laughed. Maggie chuckled nervously, not knowing whether to be offended or amused.

John continued. "Now I guess it's my turn ... Would you like me to make dinner tomorrow night?"

Maggie's friends looked at one another. This evening was getting juicier by the minute.

"Tomorrow night?" Maggie struggled for words. "You ..."

"Yes, me. I mean, it's only fair, right?"

The three women nodded.

"Very fair."

"Incredibly fair."

"Really fair."

"And," he added, "I can cook. I've been doing it all my life. Maybe not as well as you, but I can hold my own."

"Hold your own ... what?" asked Elvira.

Maggie closed her eyes at her friend's audacity.

John smiled innocently. "If it's what you're thinking, I'd need both hands."

All three women lost it, and as laughter rang around the table, John casually leaned in Maggie's direction. "So, is that a yes?" he managed to say into her ear.

In all honesty, Maggie had never expected to see the man again. Now he was offering to cook for her. She had witnesses!

"Uh, sure, that would be great, but I thought after the way you left last night, so quickly, that maybe something was wrong."

"Oh, that," he said, looking at the ground. "Sorry about that. I didn't mean to be rude but sometimes I panic in situations like that. I felt so bad after I left."

They were all thinking it but it was Marie who voiced the question. "Situations like what?"

John looked off toward the window, suddenly sombre "There's a reason I knew your mother. A long time ago I fell in love with a woman. She was a Native woman, like you four. Anishnawbe to be exact. Oh, I loved her so much. So much it . . . it hurt to blink my eyes and see her disappear for even a moment. And that fabulous Anishnawbe woman taught me her language. It's been said the best way to learn a language is across a pillow. They got that right. That woman was so precious to me. In the end, she went away. Left me. Got herself another man to love. A White man too. It hurt. It really hurt. It was then I really began to understand country music, what it was trying to say about heartbreak. In a special way, she's still part of me. But . . . oh, I'm just being silly."

Elvira and Theresa weren't sure but they could have sworn they heard a tremor in his voice. Instinctively, all the women wanted to reach over and hold his hand. It was a well-known fact that the best way to a man's heart was through his stomach, and John had long ago figured out that the best way to a woman's . . . whatever . . . had something to do with being "sensitive." He'd even looked up the word in the dictionary.

"And your mother, Lillian, helped me through those tough times. She really did. Anyway, the other night when you got me thinking about speaking Anishnawbe, it all came flooding back.

The memories, the pain . . . you know how painful it can be, to lose somebody you really love. The memory never really goes away. You just try to carry on."

He fell silent then, still looking out the bar window.

"That's so sad," whispered Theresa, herself on the verge of tears.

"Yeah," added an emotional Elvira. "Sad."

They saw a small tear run down John's cheek. He wiped it away self-consciously. All thoughts of this man telling untruths evaporated. He was so nice, and kind and . . . sensitive.

"Yeah," concluded John, seeming to pull himself together and turning back to the women. "Oh well, that's all in the past. No need to bore you with all my emotional baggage. I know women hate that."

He seemed to reach up to scratch the bridge of his nose, but Marie was sure he was wiping away another tear.

"My mother never told me anything about his. Where did you meet her and when was all this?" Maggie was about to drink from her beer but realized the bottle was empty.

"Oh, I asked her to keep everything quiet. It's kind of embarrassing, you know. But that was a long time ago and I think I'm over it now. On to new things and new adventures. Speaking of which, dinner tomorrow. Are we on or are we off?"

Maggie felt that if she turned the man down she'd have a rebellion on her hands.

"Dinner, tomorrow. Sounds like fun. When and where?"

"I'll pick you up. I'll make it a picnic. Bet you haven't had one of those in a long time. I will see you at six." The man stood up, and light from an overhead lamp flooded his face and turned his blond hair golden. "Well, I've probably overstayed my welcome.

Besides, it looks like girls' night out, and I do believe I am lacking the proper equipment. Though, you're free to check."

Marie opened her mouth to answer that offer but Maggie cut her off.

"Okay," she said. "See you tomorrow."

John leaned over and kissed her cheek. It was then she noticed something.

"John . . . ?"

"Yeah?"

"Your eyes." Maggie peered up into his face. It was dim in the bar but she was sure there was something different. "Didn't they . . . I thought they were green . . ."

Laughing, he shook his head. "No. You must have me confused with another incredibly handsome motorcyclist who knew your mother. My eyes have always been hazel. As long as I can remember. You can't change something like that. I know you mentioned green the other night and I was going to correct you, but I long ago learned never to correct a beautiful woman. Ladies, 'til next time."

And with a chivalrous nod of his head, he turned and left the bar, leaving behind four women in various states of infatuation. A common thought among the women was how leather pants can appear so smooth on a man's behind as he walks away.

Ed, thirty kilograms overweight with a severely receding hairline, a snarly disposition and a missing index finger, showed up to replace him, as best he could. The good thing was he had beer with him, and all four of the women felt the need for something cool.

"Wow." That was Marie's comment. "That's, uh . . . that's an interesting guy."

"I don't normally like White guys, for both aesthetic and political reasons, but damn . . ." contributed Theresa.

"Maggie, if you, like, get sick or break your leg, or are captured by aliens, can I take your place? Please? I like picnics. Oh yeah, love them."

"Elvira, you're married."

"That happened eight years ago, Maggie. Gotta move on. Live in the now. And I so-o-o like hazel eyes."

As the women settled back into their seats, Theresa reached over and placed her hand on John's now-empty seat. "It's still warm from his ass." She sighed.

Elvira pushed her chair back and opened the top button on her shirt. "Christ, I need this cold beer!"

All agreed and took hearty sips.

This would be Maggie's third beer of the night—unusual for her, but these were unusual times. The first dinner had been a thank-you. What was this one? Was it a date? What else could it be? Could this improbable, impossible situation actually be leading somewhere? And what about Virgil? She was sure she had noticed a bit of tension between him and John, but she supposed that was only to be expected. New man in the house and all that alpha male stuff. Still, if this did go anywhere (was she actually thinking this?), Virgil would have to be her number one concern.

For a moment, she saw the two of them, John and Virgil, building birdhouses and fishing off the dock together. It was picturesque and heart-warming.

Though something was secretly bothering her. His eyes. She was almost positive they had been green . . . hadn't they?

FOURTEEN

It had taken Virgil almost two hours in the morning sun to paddle his uncle Tim's canoe across the lake to Wayne's Island. That was not including the time it took to work up his courage. Crossing the lake on his own in just a canoe was an understandable challenge—the motorized boats and their tumultuous wakes were a hazard to most small boats, but also, going to Wayne's by himself required a little self-encouragement. His uncle's island, easily observable across the water, looked like all the other islands. But this one was where Wayne did his thing . . . whatever that was.

Actually, Wayne's Island was a glorified spit of the Canadian Shield rising out of the water. Wayne had been the island's sole resident for going on four years now. Everybody knew that and kept their distance. Virgil would have much preferred taking a motorboat there, but Uncle Tim didn't trust him on his own with his ten-horse-power motor. Still, however he had to get there, it was worth it. Wayne would know what to do—or so Virgil hoped.

Of course Virgil didn't tell Tim where he was headed. Or that he was supposed to be in school like all the other kids . . . adults had such a problem with that. But his grandmother had always told him there was far more to knowledge than just chalk, pens and Bunsen burners. Virgil almost believed that. As for Tim, he'd been placated by a simple story about Virgil doing a report on water samples for biology class. Virgil would deal with the ramifications of that lie later. Luckily Tim was such a bachelor and workaholic that he seldom noticed the difference between weekday and weekend. There just seemed to be more people around his shop on weekends.

Up ahead, Virgil could see the island. The current, channelling the water from Otter Lake to Mud Lake, was weak in this part, so he was making good time. Virgil got the chance to canoe only rarely, and he found, much to his surprise, that he was enjoying it. It was a beautiful day, and a pleasant spring breeze was coming out of the west. The lake wasn't choked with the weekend recreational boaters that seemed to be breeding with viral frequency. He knew the canoes of his forefathers had been birch bark, not aluminum like the one he was in, but he found himself enjoying the rhythm of the paddling. An hour or so off shore, he saw a loon floating placidly in his path. One quick glance over its shoulder at the boy and suddenly the bird was gone, leaving several expanding ringlets of waves where it had been moments before.

The boy instinctively stopped paddling, waiting to see where the loon would resurface. Playing a game with himself, he guessed possibly to his right, at maybe three o'clock. Instead, as if in defiance of the boy, the bird reappeared at eleven o'clock, shook the beads of water off its back and leisurely paddled away. Virgil watched him for a while before picking up the paddle and continuing his own journey.

Wayne's Island was a low hill, covered on the south side by cedar, pine, poplar and maple trees. From the sky it was said the island looked like a teardrop. On the north side, it was open and rockier, with a shallow stone bed that discouraged motorboats and houseboats. That was one of the reasons Wayne had chosen this small, three-square-kilometre island.

On average, Virgil saw his uncle once or maybe twice a year. He had heard rumours about his uncle ever since he could remember. The stories tended to revolve around Wayne being some mysterious religious hermit seeking direction. Or possibly a Buddhist monk of some sort meditating all the time. Others thought he was over there worshipping the Devil. A few thought he was trying to practise the ways of their ancient ancestors, living off the land and all that. Only, it was a pretty small island, way too small to live off for more than a week or two. But most didn't really care. It was just Weird Wayne and he was there doing what Weird Wayne did.

Regardless, here Virgil was, looking for his crazy uncle because of a bizarre stranger who had come to town. He landed on the western side of the island and pulled his canoe up onto the forest carpet made of pine needles and cedar boughs. He'd only ever been here three times before, always with his mother, usually delivering food or just giving Wayne an update on family issues. The last time had been about two months ago, when his grandmother first fell ill.

"Hello? Uncle Wayne?" Virgil's voice was hardly above a whisper. Some small part of him was afraid at what he might find on this island, and how his uncle would react when they met, and Maggie wasn't there. At the moment, that small part of him consisted of his vocal cords. Realizing this wasn't very effective, Virgil started moving toward the centre of the island. He wasn't exactly sure where the camp was but he knew it was in this direction.

The boy could see several paths worn into the fallen vegetation, and decided to follow the widest. Along the way, he saw broken branches hanging off trees in every direction. They were all snapped in the same manner, either to the right, or to the left, in a small spot near the base. No long pressure fractures as if an axe had done it.

"Uncle Wayne? Are you here?" he'd called out, but surrounded by this many trees, he wouldn't be heard by anyone who wasn't within spitting distance. He trudged forward, hoping to find his uncle's camp. Small island or not, he didn't want to be wandering around its interior for too long. As luck would have it, he didn't have to.

"I know you. Virgil, right?" came a voice from directly above.

His heart pounding, Virgil looked in the direction of the voice. There, amid the cedar branches, sat his mother's brother, Wayne Benojee.

"Yeah, Virgil . . . Maggie's son."

Wayne regarded the boy for a second before dropping down to the ground without even a grunt.

For somebody who led such a weird life, Wayne looked remarkably average. He was thirty-two years old, and had long black hair tied back into a ponytail. He wore a grey T-shirt and a worn jean jacket, worn jean pants and worn sneakers—in fact everything he was wearing seemed worn. But he was muscular in a wiry kind of way. His body said there was more to being danger-ous than sheer physical strength. To his nephew, Wayne's hands looked oddly callused. So this was his uncle Wayne. Virgil swal-lowed hard. This was what he had wanted, after all—to talk to his uncle. But the man was looking at him like he was an intruder.

"Well, what are you doing here?" Wayne sounded like some-body who rarely spoke in English. In the family, it was well known that Wayne had been the favourite. Unlike with the rest of her children, Lillian had spent long hours teaching the boy the intrica-cies of the Anishnawbe, so that now he spoke it better than most seventy-year-olds. Even his years in local schools had not cracked his command of the language. But here he was speaking in English, knowing Virgil was of the generation whose knowledge of Anishnawbe was weak or non-existent.

Virgil tried to talk but his vocal cords let him down, and he managed little more than a gurgle. Trying to gain control, he swallowed hard. Wayne studied the boy as Virgil sought desperately to say something coherent. Again it was Wayne's voice that ended the silence.

"Oh, for Christ's sake! You're scared of me, aren't you! I don't . . . people . . . they don't . . ." Wayne seemed frustrated, and swung his head angrily, his ponytail doing a three-sixty. "Why is it that everybody's afraid of me? I just don't get it. I'm a nice guy. I know a couple of jokes. But for some reason, everybody seems afraid of me—even my own family. It's 'cause I live here alone, isn't it? Can't a guy get some privacy without being branded a weirdo? Geez! It's high school all over again." Still frustrated, Wayne kicked a tree. "Your mother's the only one who gives me the time of day, barely. What, do I have tentacles? Am I rabid? Do I smell? What? Huh? What?"

A tantrum was not what Virgil had expected from his uncle. But that's what he was observing. "Uncle Wayne?"

"Finally! He talks to me. What?"

"I need your help. It's about Mom."

"Maggie?" Wayne's face had become stoic. "Okay. You got my attention. What's up with Maggie?"

Virgil took a deep breath and stepped closer to his uncle. Time to pitch his case. "Well, you see, there's this guy . . ."

———

Sometime later, back at Wayne's camp, they were sharing a cup of tea brewed over an open fire as Virgil finished telling the tale of the mysterious motorcyclist, and his blushing mother.

" . . . and she was telling me this morning, they're going out again tonight. A picnic, I think. I think she likes him. There's something weird about him, Uncle Wayne. Really weird." He almost said "weirder than you" but stopped himself. Instead, Virgil added more evaporated milk to his tea. Relieved that he could share his concerns with someone, the boy waited, sipping his sweetened tea.

A puzzled look darkened his uncle's face. "So what do you want me to do about it? Your mother's a grown woman. She's older than me. And you actually think she'd listen to me? She'd listen to you more than she'd listen to me. You know she used to beat me up when we were young? All the time . . . the little . . . Want more tea?"

"Please. She did?" Virgil shook the question out of his head. He'd get to that later, once the more immediate crisis was dealt with. "But, Uncle Wayne, there's something really not right about him. He can do strange things. Like animal calls. He sounds like the animals. I mean *really* sounds like the animals. Trains too . . ."

Wayne raised his face to the sky and let loose a spot-on imitation of a loon call. "Like that?" Somewhere off in the distance, a loon responded, eager for companionship.

"Better."

For the second time, Wayne's stoic demeanour seemed rattled. "Better? Better than that?"

Virgil nodded vigorously. "Way better. And he can do a bunch of others too that sound more real than the animals that do them.

I've heard him. It's scary. That's the kind of weird I mean. It's not normal. He's not normal."

"Better than me?" Wayne muttered, swirling his tea. "Anyway, what do you want me to do about it? I'm just out here living my life. Doing my thing. Am I my sister's keeper?"

"Please, Uncle Wayne . . ."

Tossing the last drops of his tea to the cedar-covered ground, Wayne dismissed Virgil's worries with a shrug that looked oddly familiar. "Stop with the 'please, Uncle Wayne.' You're the son of a single mother. You'd consider any guy showing any interest in your mother a threat. Basic psychology, I think. In my opinion, you're worrying over nothing. Now go home and play baseball or something."

"Oh, give me some credit. I thought of that too. I *am* thirteen, you know. But you don't know everything, Uncle Wayne. *He kissed Grandma.* And it was a *real* kiss, I mean, tongue and *everything.* The kind you see in movies. I don't think it was normal. Now he's hanging around Mom all the time."

This got Wayne's attention. "My mother? He kissed my mother . . . that way? Why? And when? When did he do that? Huh? And why?"

"I don't know, Uncle Wayne, but if you cared about my mother, your sister, it would be worth just an hour of your time, wouldn't it?"

Wayne contemplated his tea for a few seconds. Virgil was conscious of time passing and hoped he could sway his uncle quickly. It would be getting dark soon.

"Still, I don't understand why you came to get me. You've got Tim and Willie right there, and all the rest. You paddle all the way over here to find me. Not that I'm not glad for the visit, sometimes

I get kinda lonely and can use the company, but I barely know you. You barely know me. I still don't get it." With that, Wayne poured himself another cup of tea.

Virgil took a deep breath and decided to play his trump card. "You know things."

"What do I know?"

"Stuff."

"Everybody knows stuff. You know stuff. Your mother knows stuff. Most of it's boring but it's still classified as stuff."

"Uncle Wayne, he dances."

On a small island in the middle of a central Ontario lake, Wayne Benojee rolled his eyes, annoyed at the logic, or lack of it, presented by his thirteen-year-old nephew. "Virgil, everybody dances, most just not very well. I say this with the utmost respect to you, but so?"

"He dances at night. By himself. On the dock down by Beer Bay. Under the moon. And it's like no other dancing I've ever seen. It's not right. It . . . he's different."

This prompted a raised eyebrow from Wayne. "Not human? See, this is one of the reasons why I left the mainland. Too much of this television stuff screwing up minds. I don't think you would even know what's weird. And incidentally, weird can be good too."

Now Virgil was angry. "You're one to talk! You and . . . and whatever it is you're doing over here. *That's* weird. Everybody knows that. Do you know what they say about you?"

"That I'm Weird Wayne. Yeah, I know. Tell me something new."

"What the hell are you doing out here anyways? Sacrificing goats or something?"

"Who said I was sacrificing goats? I've never even seen a goat in real life. Why would somebody say that? That's so unfair. People can be cruel." Wayne sat down on a cut-in-half cedar bench, clearly hurt, tea dripping from his tilted cup.

Seeing his uncle's wounded response, Virgil realized he'd said a little too much. "Nobody. I'm sorry. Really. But people do wonder what you're doing out here. All by yourself. Are you a monk or something?"

Wayne watched the last third of the tea pour out of his cup onto the ground. "I am a martial artist. That's all."

"Like karate or kung fu?" asked the boy.

"Something like that. It's a long story. Maybe I'll tell you sometime." Another call of the loon could be heard coming off the lake. This one sounding a little more frustrated. "Anyway, you were saying about this John Tanner . . ."

"Richardson. Or so he says. That's another thing, out of nowhere he has two last names. And then there's his eyes . . ."

"I'm confused. How did we get from him dancing to his eyes?"

"It's all part of the whole thing, I guess. I think they changed colour. I'm almost sure of that. But I *am* sure about the dancing. The way he was dancing that night, it reminded me of a story Grandma once told me. It took me forever to remember it. Come on, Uncle Wayne, you gotta know it. About how Nanabush thought he was the best dancer in the world? And the grass disagreed. Ever heard it?"

Wayne nodded. "Oh yeah. I know that story. It was one of her favourites. Yeah, the grass issued a challenge, and Nanabush, being the arrogant kind of guy he was, accepted." Remembering the cadence of his mother's storytelling voice, he mimicked it as the memory came to him. "So, one hot summer day, Nanbush and the grass decided to settle the issue. At dawn, they began, and they danced, and danced, and danced some more . . ."

Virgil picked up the story. "They danced all day and night, and the next day, forever it seemed, until they both fell down on the ground, exhausted. Because neither won. It was a stalemate. It was a contest neither could ever win. It's been so long since I heard that one, it used to be one of my favourite stories, but she told it so much better."

"I know," acknowledged Wayne. "It was almost like she knew Nanabush. She had so many Nanabush stories."

"Yeah, the way she told them, you could see everything that happened to him. And that's exactly how I saw him dance, on that dock. I could hear Grandma's voice in my head telling that story."

Wayne and Virgil were both silent as they remembered their mother and grandmother respectively. Once more Wayne regretted not going to his mother's funeral. But that was in the past.

Now he had a nephew on his hands, with unusual expectations of him, and an even more crazy reason for expecting them.

"So he can dance pretty good. I think the bizarre thing about that is you don't find that in a White boy very often," Wayne postulated.

"It's not that, it's *how* he dances. I'm telling you it has something to do with the moon. Clouds would come across the moon and he would stop dancing. I need you to see it for yourself. And . . . and . . . not only that!"

"Oh god, there's more?"

"Oh yes. Then there's the petroglyphs."

"The what?"

"He carves pictures into rocks. But that's not the weird part. On my favourite rock . . ."

"You have a favourite . . . rock? That's so sad."

"Listen please, Uncle Wayne. He carved this image of what I think is a woman and a man, on a motorcycle. Together. That's gotta be him and Mom. I think he plans to ride off with her. Away. I really do."

"Virgil . . ."

"And I think they're going to be heading west, for some reason."

Wayne's face froze as he gazed at his nephew. "What makes you say west?"

"To the left of the motorcycle, there was a setting sun."

"How do you know it was setting?"

"First of all, as I said, the petroglyph on the rock was on the west side. And secondly, who picks up women and goes for motor-cycle rides at dawn?"

"Good point," said Wayne. "You said he visited my mother too, before she passed away. How long before?"

"That day. That afternoon, in fact. She, um, died that night."

Now Wayne's mind seemed somewhere off in the distance.

"Is something wrong, Uncle Wayne? Are you going to help?"

Wayne kept looking to his left, toward the west, as his eyes betrayed puzzled thoughts. Virgil didn't have to be a genius to figure out he'd hit some kind of nerve with the comment about heading west, though what exactly he couldn't say.

Virgil decided to just charge forward, hoping his uncle would be swept along with his enthusiasm. "Look, Uncle Wayne, I know how this sounds. I've been wrestling with how to tell you all night and all the way over here. I need help in figuring this out. I wouldn't be here if it wasn't . . . I don't know . . . necessary. Please!"

Wayne silently weighed all the information the boy had given him, and how this little adventure to the mainland might interrupt his training. But there was another matter to take into consideration. He had not yet made a visit to his mother's grave. He'd been putting it off because he was a private mourner, not a public one. Wayne knew his family was mad at him for not coming to the funeral, and whether they were right or wrong was irrelevant. This was still something he should do. He knew that much. And, he surmised, this was as good a time as any.

Wayne nodded. "Do we have to take your canoe or can we take my motorboat? It's faster."

"Thank god," said Virgil, on both counts.

As they walked to the boat, Virgil noticed several more branches along the way that were snapped in a strange manner. "Uncle Wayne, I've noticed these all over the island. What's with all these broken branches?"

"Training," Wayne said simply.

"Your martial artist thing? What is that anyway?"

Wayne stopped at a sizable cedar tree that leaned slightly away from the path. Reaching up with his right hand, he carefully grabbed a branch, one about four or five centimetres thick. Turning his head to Virgil, he said, "Pay attention!" Instantly, he twisted his wrist to the right, and Virgil heard a sharp crack. The branch was now attached to the tree only by the bark. Wayne let go and the branch flopped down, hanging parallel to the tree.

"Training," Wayne said once more, and continued walking toward his motorboat.

Virgil reached out and touched the broken branch. He gave it a slight yank, and it came off the tree completely. The boy was sure it would have taken all his weight and quite a bit of man-oeuvring to have snapped the branch so effectively. He could only imagine what effect a similar move would have on someone's wrist. "Wow" was his reaction.

After tying the canoe to the motorboat, they began their jour-ney to Otter Lake. On the way across the water, Virgil spoke again. "Oh, and Uncle Wayne, what does *tikwamshin* mean?"

"*Tikwamshin?* Let's see. The way you're saying it is a little off but basically, it means 'bite me.' Why?"

The glum Virgil sank to a new level of glumness.

— FIFTEEN —

The sun was an hour from setting when Maggie showed up at Sammy Aandeg's house. As she pulled into the driveway, a small raccoon scuttled across the driveway and Maggie had to swerve to avoid hitting it. She'd never actually been to the Aandeg place before. Oh, she'd driven by it all of her life, but most village members tended to give the place a wide berth. Sammy Aandeg was more than strange, definitely on the crazy side, not to mention a raging alcoholic. Her brother Wayne might be considered weird but Sammy was definitely textbook crazy in most local people's opinion. Luckily, he was not violent, but just different enough to grant him the peace and serenity that allowed him to live in his own reality, his own universe.

For some reason, John Richardson had decided to stay here.

The house itself had long since passed its days of glory. The paint seemed to have been applied a thousand years ago, possibly just after it had been invented. Dried brown paint was scattered on the ground surrounding the house, where it had fallen or been blown off by the unforgiving elements. Several windowpanes were broken and stuffed with either newspaper or rags. Emerging from the roof was a stovepipe, indicating Sammy still heated his house and cooked with an old-fashioned wood stove. It was probably older than Maggie was.

As she got out of her car, she wondered what to do. Should she go and knock on the door and risk running into Sammy? Or should she wait patiently in her car? With the doors locked. She could see the parked Indian Chief motorcycle nestled in the shade near the back shed. So he was likely here. She stood there, her fingers drumming on the hood of her car, weighing her options. Luckily Sammy Aandeg had no dogs, or that would have been an added difficulty. One of the few concessions Maggie had made to the dominant culture was her obsessive reliance on time. As chief she had to play ball in the White man's court and by their rules. Now she found herself repeatedly glancing at her watch as the minutes ticked by.

A little nervous, she fiddled with her right front windshield wiper, working up the nerve to knock on the bogeyman's (and John's) door. She also unconsciously surveyed the land, just for something to occupy her mind. To her right was a fringe of trees hiding the house and land from the highway she'd just driven in on. It no doubt provided a sound barrier against traffic. Running alongside it was a row of telephone and hydro poles, carrying communications and electricity to Otter Lake. One particular pole caught her attention, and she approached it, walking over a bed of wood chips. The closer Maggie got, the more obvious it became. Somebody had carved a totem pole out of the telephone pole. It appeared to be an authentic West Coast totem pole, possibly of the Haida variety, facing the Aandeg house. She could see all the intricate designs expertly carved into the surface of the wood. She'd been to British Columbia many times for various conferences, and had seen the real deal. She was amazed at the authenticity and talent staring her in the face.

Who would do such a thing, and why? She was quite positive, too, that it was illegal. Defacing public property or something like that. Still, it was amazing. She could make out elaborate images of a frog, a bear, and a large raven at the very top, near the telephone wires. She doubted this was Sammy's work. But John . . . would *he* do something like this? she wondered.

Just then, her chief suspect came walking out from behind the house. John, stripped to the waist. My goodness, she thought, he was indeed a fine specimen of a man, almost like those models on the covers of novels she'd seen in bookstores. Those historical romances where incredibly good-looking Indian men with chiselled (though oddly European-looking) features, washboard stomachs and long black hair blowing in the wind would sweep beautiful, defenceless-but-plucky White women off their feet and into their bearskin-covered beds.

That was it, she realized! That was what he reminded her of. It was like he'd walked off the cover of one of those books. Except he had blond hair, a fair complexion and green . . . no, hazel eyes.

He smiled as he got closer to her. "Hey, you! What are you doing here? I thought I was going to pick you up." He was sweaty, with little bits of sawdust stuck to his lean body. "Sorry for the way I look. I was out back chopping some wood for Sammy."

"You know how to chop wood?"

"Yep. Lift axe. Drop axe. Don't exactly need a master's degree to manage that. Sammy still tries to do it but he's getting kind of up there. Elder and all. Thought I'd help out. Sort of like paying rent."

Maggie was impressed. "Wow. How nice. Chopping wood is a vanishing art."

"You caught me before I could wash up. I must smell horrible."

"Uh, no, not really. John, do you know anything about this?" She pointed to the telephone-totem pole. He glanced at it quickly.

"Yeah, I got bored. I don't think I captured the frog just right."

"Really? It's amazing. I didn't know you were an artist."

"I do whatever needs to be done. It's not my best work anyway. Don't tell me you're here to cancel?"

"Uh, no. No problem. I was . . . I mean . . . I was looking over some of the property that we've just bought. It runs parallel to Sammy's place and I thought I'd drop in. Save you the trouble of driving all the way over to my place. If I'm too early, I can leave."

"Absolutely no problem. Smart thinking. Well, come on in. I think Sammy made some coffee earlier. I can fix you a cup before I get cleaned up."

"Are you sure it's okay?"

John had already turned and was heading into the house. "I wouldn't invite you if it wasn't. Come along now. Sammy might even be waiting for us."

She followed close behind, taking one last peek over her shoulder at the totem pole. John led Maggie around the side of the house to the back entrance. It was there she saw something else—something almost as interesting as the pole out front. She wasn't sure but . . .

"Is . . . is that an inukshuk?"

John nodded. "Yeah, but a more modernist version. It makes a bold statement, don't you think?"

It was indeed an inukshuk of sorts, but made from cases of beer. Piled one atop the other, it towered over Maggie, standing at least four metres high. Cases of Labatt 50 stacked in the rudimentary shape of a human body, very reminiscent of the well-known Inuit stone figure.

It was certainly creative, thought Maggie.

"In case you're wondering, those belong to Sammy. Again, just fooling around, killing time. Making do with what was at hand."

"Wow, you're pretty good. I didn't think it was possible to make an ordinary telephone pole or cases of beer look so . . . imposing."

"One thing I have always believed: Anything is possible. After you, young lady." John opened the door and politely held it, waiting for Maggie to enter the domicile of Mr. Sammy Aandeg. The invitation had been issued and Maggie thought it would be rude to decline.

As kids they'd had contests about who had enough courage to run up and actually lay a hand on Sammy Aandeg's house. But she'd never been brave enough to do it, preferring to watch the other kids from the bushes.

And now she was inside. The furniture looked older than her, and well worn. The ceiling consisted of pressed tin with a sort of starburst pattern, similar to the one her grandmother had had years ago. Still, all the plates were stacked neatly in the doorless cupboards. The ancient refrigerator hummed loudly and the wood stove looked polished. Curtains hid the cracked or chipped windows, and the floor looked freshly swept. She was shocked to realize Sammy's place was almost cleaner than her house. She wasn't sure what she had been expecting but this wasn't it. Maybe Sammy wasn't as crazy as everybody thought.

"Is Sammy around?" she asked nervously.

"Nah, it's still a little early. I guess he's out wandering the woods looking for Puck and Ariel. He does that every day about this time."

"Who?"

"That, my dear, is a very long and interesting tale. I'll tell you later. How do you like your coffee?" asked the attractive, shirtless, sweaty man.

"Um, just milk, please."

Maggie watched John move around the kitchen, preparing her coffee, and noticed the light from the kitchen window highlighting the definition of his muscles in his arms, shoulders and across his back. Everything about the man was impressive, she thought, whether it was his motorcycle or his muscles. Maybe a little too impressive. Maggie had seen her husband sweaty many times, but for some reason it had never had this effect on her. If she were of a more cynical nature, she would be sure God was somewhere up above, laughing at her schoolgirl infatuation. At some point, John opened the refrigerator looking for milk, and Maggie was shocked to see all the shelves in the door lined with dark bottles of beer.

"I take it that's all Sammy's?"

John nodded. "Well, you can't be much of an alcoholic unless you have some alcohol to drink. It's one of the rules." Then he changed the subject. "I understand that the newly purchased land you spoke of is becoming quite the bother." John placed the coffee down in front of her on a coaster. "Giving you a headache?"

Maggie nodded as she sipped her coffee. It wasn't bad at all. "Oh yeah, I'm almost sorry we bought the land. You would not believe the bizarre suggestions I've been getting for the last five months. Outrageous stuff. Who says Native people don't have any imagination. Some days I think 'the hell with it, it would make an excellent depository for nuclear waste.' Hey, they've got to put it somewhere. And I bet they've even thought of Indian land. We'll just charge them more."

Laughing, John turned on the tap. "Do you mind if I clean up a bit while we talk? Sammy doesn't have a shower so I have to do it manually in the sink."

"Okay . . ."

John wet the washcloth, then began to wash the sweat and sawdust off his body. Maggie watched.

"Anyway, you were saying? About the land?"

"Yes, the land. It's bothering me. Don't really know what to do. But I . . ." She knew she was looking at him much too intently as he washed. It was then she noticed there were a lot of scars on his body.

"Oh my God, what happened to you?"

He looked down at himself, then traced a two-inch scar on his left shoulder. "In my younger days, I used to get into the odd fight. Nothing serious. Just fun stuff. Well, sometimes fun can leave a mark. But that was a long time ago. I'm all grown up now." Again he changed the subject. "So, what do you think would be the best alternative for the land?"

Maggie was finding it hard to focus. Regardless of the scars, this man had way too many muscles, and in all the right places. If anything, the scars added to his appeal. "Me? Um, I think it should just be left there in its natural state. It's beautiful back there. Like creation intended. Be a shame to tear it up. I guess eventually, down the road, we'll need the land for housing or something. But we'll cross that bridge when we get to it. That's . . . that's what I think. Yeah, that's what I think all right. What . . . what do you think?" She winced at her own awkwardness.

"Leave it in its natural state, huh? Sounds good to me. Au naturel, you could say. There, done." And with that he began drying himself with a worn, peach towel. "Oh, that feels so much better. I probably smell a lot better too. Anyway, I think you should go with your instincts. Down the road a good home usually beats a casino or a theme park."

Casino? Theme park? How did John know about those? Submissions to the chief and council weren't discussed outside of the council meetings. It was possible that somebody in the community had told him, but most kept their thoughts to themselves, for fear of somebody stealing the idea or taking the credit.

"John, how did you hear about the casino and theme park?"

John turned around and smiled at her. He always seemed to be smiling, like it was his most dangerous weapon. Granted, it was a beautiful, glowing smile, but he seemed to use it a little too frequently, like it was a get-out-of-jail-free card. Though Maggie supposed there were worst things a man could do than smile a lot.

"Those ideas aren't open to the general public," Maggie emphasized.

"I am not the general public."

"Don't try to smile your way out of this, John. That stuff is supposed to be confidential. So where—"

"Relax. It's surprising what you can learn at Betty Lou's Take-Out. You can pick up more than food poisoning there. You're a politician, Maggie. You more than anybody else should know people like to talk. Especially when they think they have the best idea in the world. I don't spend all my time chopping wood or riding my bike."

Or working out, Maggie added to herself. Then the kitchen door opened with a crash and the infamous Sammy Aandeg entered. He stood there, a man over seventy with a shock of white hair and a wrinkled face that included two suspicious eyes, holding in his left hand a worn plastic bag. Maggie thought he was skinnier than she remembered and oddly smaller. The old man caught sight of Maggie and scowled, his whole face melting into a frown.

John looked genuinely happy to see him. "Hey, Sammy, what've you got there?"

The man answered gruffly with one word in Anishnawbe.

John responded in English. "Sure they're not toadstools? Might kill you."

Sammy scowled again and swore at John, again in Anishnawbe. He waddled through the kitchen, heading to the living room, his thumb and two fingers on his free hand constantly rubbing against each other. As he shuffled by, he glanced at Maggie and started speaking at length. But not to her. To himself. The words poured out of him.

Laughing, John got out of the man's way. "Okay, okay, just asking. You don't have to get mean."

Sammy continued talking to himself as he left the room. Maggie's command of the language was good, not great, so she understood enough to know he was talking about her. His Anishnawbe was excellent, but his syntax and phrasing sounded strange, even to her.

"I told you he was funny. Didn't I say he was better than TV? I'll be back in just a second." John walked out of the room, leaving her alone in the kitchen.

She could still hear Sammy muttering to himself, his Anishnawbe practically indecipherable unless she paid seriously close attention.

Over the next minute or so, Maggie quickly put together enough Anishnawbe words to properly introduce herself from the doorway to the living room. "Hi, Sammy Aandeg. I don't know if you know me, but my mother and father were . . ." She didn't get very far because the man sitting on the couch threw a mushroom at her. It bounced off her shoulder and landed on the table, where it rolled around." ... Lillian and Leonard Benojee ..." she managed to finish, unsure if she should continue.

At the mention of Lillian's name, Sammy looked up at her. She could almost see him struggling to surface through decades of alcohol, like her mother's name was some sort of lifesaver he was grasping to reach. Evidently he managed to grab it with a couple of fingers, because he got up from the couch, still talking in his peculiar Anishnawbe, and wandered by Maggie into the kitchen. He nodded once at her. Not moving, Maggie watched as he shuffled around, apparently making something to eat. After a few minutes, he presented Maggie with a piece of toast with some jam on it. The way he held it out, it seemed to Maggie to be more than just toast and jam, like the gluten, sugar and strawberries all contained precious memories. She took it, and he gave her a weak smile before the more familiar Sammy came rushing back.

Mumbling once more to himself, he ignored Maggie as he passed her and left the room, his three fingers never stopping their friction.

Again there was something oddly familiar about what Sammy was saying. He had stopped talking about her and had started reciting something. She cursed herself for not being more fluent in her mother's language. The mystery began to annoy her, so she put down the toast and ran over some of the words she had recognized, then translated them back to English to establish a pattern.

John re-entered the room and interrupted her thought process. He was dressed for their evening together. He wore his black pants, denim instead of leather, but he still had his boots on. And his shirt was a lovely shade of green to bring out those magnificent hazel eyes.

"Wow," she said. "You clean up nice."

"Thank you, madam," he said, giving an exaggerated bow. "Clean underwear too. Ironed shirt. They do make a difference. I do believe I am presentable to the public now. You sure are lucky I made our dinner already. I was not expecting you to show up here."

The shirt looked like it had been cut to accent his build. Maggie immediately regretted not having put on something a little more . . . attractive. He almost looked prettier than she did, and that was never a good thing.

"Where are we going on this little picnic?"

From out of the refrigerator, John removed a medium-sized cardboard box. "Our dinner. Judge it by the contents, not the cardboard. I thought we'd go to a place that's near where you live. Down by Beer Bay, I think it's called. There's a lovely spot by the dock. What do you say?"

Maggie stood up. "I'm game. What about Sammy?"

"Sammy? He'll be okay. He's looked after himself here for almost sixty years."

"John, did you understand what he was saying? I mean, his Anishnawbe?"

While they talked, John was in the kitchen, grabbing cutlery, salt, pepper, napkins and such. "Yeah. He's been helping me bone up on it. I'm actually getting quite good now. Pretty soon you'll think I've been speaking it all my life. Where did I put the matches? Can't have an evening picnic without a campfire. Oh, here they are. Ready?"

Somewhere upstairs Sammy was talking to himself. "John, have you ever noticed that the way he talks is kind of strange? I mean, he obviously speaks it very well but he speaks it really differently too. Do you know why?"

John opened the door and waited for Maggie to join him outside. "Of course. Took me a while to figure it out but the answer finally occurred to me. Well, are you coming? Or did you suddenly have an attack of good judgment?"

They both exited the house and Maggie instinctively walked toward her car as John walked toward his bike. They were both at their vehicles before they noticed they were standing separately.

"Um, Maggie, it might be more fun if we took my bike. Something tells me a 1953 Indian Chief motorcycle has got to be more kicks than a 2002 Chrysler. What do you say?"

A chance to ride on that fabulous machine once more? To snuggle against tall, White and handsome again? Sure, she convinced herself, why the hell not? Maggie locked her car doors. She didn't normally do that out here but Sammy had unnerved her.

"What was that you were saying about something occurring to you, regarding Sammy?"

John pushed his bike out from the protection of the shed. "Oh, that. He speaks in iambic pentameter."

Maggie stopped halfway to John's bike, trying to understand. "Iambic what?"

"Pentameter. You know, like Shakespeare."

It sounded so . . . everyday, the way John put it. "'To be or not to be . . .'—that kind of thing?"

"Yep, only in Anishnawbe. Same structure, weak, strong, weak, strong. Ten syllables. All the usual rules. Took me a while to figure it out. I'm not exactly a Shakespearean scholar, you know. You look surprised. There are more things in heaven and earth, Maggie. Here—" John held out her crash helmet, which was now painted similarly to his. His still had the raven on the side, but hers bore a different image.

"Is that a beaver?" she asked.

"Yep. Good eye. Hard working. Industrious. Beautiful. Loving to its children. Nice tail. When I thought of you, I instantly thought of a beaver."

Maggie wasn't exactly sure how to take that, or the innocent smile that came with the explanation.

"I . . . I . . . okay." She held the helmet in her hands, looking it over. It was indeed a good representation of a beaver, allowing for some artistic licence. But for some reason, she felt vaguely insulted. "Um, you were saying about Sammy . . ."

"Right," he said as he swung his leg over the motorcycle. "From what I can make out by what he says between soliloquies, he went to residential school."

"Yeah, I know that much. My mother was there with him, as well as a few others. Told me some pretty horrible things happened to him. She was so lucky she was there only two years."

"I find you make your own luck. But back to Sammy. Unfortunately there was some bastard there named Father McKenzie, directly from England, who thought the sun rose and set on Her Majesty's mighty empire. To him, there was the Bible and Shakespeare. Everything else was bargain-basement literature, not really worth studying. So, he was here to civilize the Native people."

Maggie took her position on the bike in front of John, carefully placing the picnic basket on her lap. Part of her was disappointed there would be no in-transit cuddling as the picnic basket required dual hand restraint. She was also engrossed in what John was telling her.

"Evidently when he was younger, Sammy was a bit of a rebel. As you probably know, they forbade the students from speaking their language, but God bless him, he refused to give it up. Even as a kid he was scrappy. They beat him practically every day. I think to the point it made him kinda crazy. That can happen after a decade of abuse. He spoke English, but every once in a while when they thought they'd won, he'd let loose some Anishnawbe just to piss them off."

"What does that have to do with Shakespeare?"

"That's the real clever part. The teacher who so loved the Bard would get incensed that this young Indian boy would dare to corrupt what he considered the most beautiful words ever written, by speaking them in a filthy bastard language. He considered that a personal insult. So the man took it upon himself to dish out all Sammy's corporal punishment. Somewhere in Sammy's mind, he's made the decision to speak just Anishnawbe. I don't think he has spoken a word of English since. And he only speaks Anishnawbe in iambic pentameter. It was sort of his revenge on the guy. Can you imagine the kind of self-discipline and intelligence that it would take to do that day after day? His mind is kind of stuck on it now. Sort of in a mental loop. Everybody just thinks he's crazy old Sammy Aandeg, but there's method to his madness. You should hear his Lear monologue. Quite moving and amazing. Stratford could make a fortune off him."

"That's . . . original. I never knew any of that. How amazing."

John nodded. "I'll say. And if you read between the lines, I also think the guy was abusing him, in more ways than one. You don't get to be like Sammy, screaming in the night the way he does, unless the Father was doing a little more of 'do as I say, not as I do' than was proper. Oh well, I think Sammy's got the last laugh. I bet to this day that guy's cursing Sammy in . . . what's that place called? Hell. What a great story, huh? Took me forever to get it out of him."

"That's horrible."

"Yes it is, but hey, it's kept him strong in his own way, and given him a purpose. How many people out there have either? Okay, put your helmet on, it's dinner time!"

Maggie donned her helmet just in time, because John gunned the machine. It took off with a lurch.

Sitting at the very top of the telephone-totem pole, on the raven's head, was a lone raccoon, watching the motorcycle as it receded into the distance. Its little fingers twitched occasionally.

All the way to Beer Bay, the Indian chief was nestled atop the gas tank of the Indian Chief, and very conscious of her proximity to the personable young man. Still, Maggie found her thoughts returning to her encounter with Sammy Aandeg, and what happened in his youth. As they made their way through the streets of Otter Lake, her hands protectively held the box across the gas tank. Absentmindedly, she wondered what a man like John had made them to eat. She would know soon enough.

Less than fifteen minutes later, they arrived at a secluded part of the bay. Turning off the ignition, John waited for her to get off before getting off himself and removing his helmet. "I love this place," he said.

"You do? Why?"

"It brings back so many memories. Maybe I'll tell you some of them someday. Hey, let's go out to the dock to eat. It's perfect there." Grabbing the box and tucking it under his arm, he extended his hand for Maggie to take.

Together, they walked toward the water. The sun was still fairly high above the horizon, casting light on this lazy spring evening. John pulled a blanket from his saddlebags and spread it on the planks. "Dinner has begun."

Slowly he unpacked all the goodies he had prepared. From the box he pulled out a bottle of Chilean Syrah.

"You keep telling me you don't drink!" said Maggie.

"I don't. That doesn't mean I can't get *you* drunk. And for me, some apple juice."

Next came a salad. "Greek salad. Love the stuff. We never had any cheese when I was young. Can't get enough of it now," said John. This was followed by a large, green plastic container.

"What's in here?" As she opened it, Maggie was hit by the most amazing aroma. "Hmm, I love chili. Smells wonderful."

"I doubt you've had chili like this. It's moose chili with a couple of unique touches thrown in. I think you'll like it."

"John, I am impressed. Where did you learn to cook?"

John gave her some cutlery wrapped in a napkin. "I spend a lot of time on my own. So I have to amuse myself. Buns! I forgot the buns!" He retrieved the bread from the box. "There, does everything look right?"

"Everything looks great," said Maggie.

"Now for the wine." John grabbed the bottle and wrestled with the cork. "I seem to be opening a lot of wine for you."

"I hope it doesn't give you any bad ideas about me."

"Oh, all the ideas I have about you are very bad," he said with a smirk.

He was flirting with her. It had been a very long time since anybody had flirted with her. And somewhere in the back of her mind was the ancient floppy disk with all her flirting programming on it. It was obvious that she would have to update it to a thumb drive pretty soon. After all, this was a full-fledged date. Maggie Second was on a date. A widowed mother of one, out here for a romantic evening with a stunningly attractive, younger, White man.

She was the chief. He rode a motorcycle. Somewhere in all this, she was sure, were the makings of a made-for-TV-movie.

After opening the bottle, she watched him ladle out the chili. Not your typical first-date meal, but what was? she wondered. Her first date with Clifford had consisted of two Whopper combos. So she was hardly an expert. She accepted the full bowl.

"Enjoy," he said.

And she did.

SIXTEEN

The sun was dangling near the horizon, saying farewell to this part of the continent. Meanwhile, on the other side of John and Maggie's world, the impatient moon was already fighting its way above the distant shore. Nobody else was around, though the odd boat skimmed by on the far side of the bay. On the dock in front of them were the remnants of their dinner. John and Maggie were sitting side by side, the past hour having drawn them closer.

"No kidding. I have been all across this country. A couple of times. From ocean, to ocean, to ocean, to way past that thing called the border. Both the American and the Mexican. I have seen mountains, prairies, oceans, trees, lakes, everything. This is a big country but I like to think I'm bigger." John filled her wineglass again from the three-quarters-empty bottle. There was no reason for her to drink fast. They had all the time in the world.

"Have you been to the Arctic? Nunavut?"

"Once. That's where I saw the inukshuk. But I don't care for the Arctic. I try never to go above the treeline. Not my kind of place."

"But aren't the prairies pretty treeless?"

"That's different."

"How is that different?" asked Maggie. Her cheeks were unusually flushed in the failing light.

"Do you really want to know? Okay, there are trees in the prairies. You just have to know where to look for them."

"There are so many places I would want to go. I envy you. Why did you stop travelling?"

John's mood seemed to shift slightly, like wispy clouds crossing in front of the moon. "I developed what could be called a drinking problem."

"I know. You mentioned something about it the other day. You don't have to talk about it if you don't want to."

"No, that's okay. It's good therapy. It's called sharing. Anyway, it was a pretty bad problem. It lasted for a while. Hard to travel when you're passed out."

"You? Really?"

"Yep. But, as they say, I'm much better now. I did learn one good thing from all those years of drinking, though. I can say 'Southern Comfort' in fourteen different Aboriginal languages. Seriously. Want to hear some?" She nodded eagerly. "Keep in mind there's no actual word for *alcohol* in most Indigenous languages, but the term *Southern Comfort* is a different story. Let's see, there's entiene aon'wesenhtshera."

Maggie was perplexed. She shook her head, not understanding the language.

"That's Mohawk. From our friends to the south. How about . . . let's see . . . sow-wee-nook a-stee-si-ni."

Maggie couldn't identify that language either.

"That's Cree," he explained. "Then there's ahhh klup-ee-huh!"

"I think you just spit on me."

"Sorry, it's a very guttural language. It's Nuu-Chah-nulth. Okay, I'll give you an easy one. Zhaawnong Minodewin. Recognize that?"

Maggie thought for a moment, trying to deconstruct the various prefixes and suffixes. "That's Anishnawbe!"

John smiled. "Very good."

"Not bad, for a White guy."

John noticed she was slurring her words slightly. Gently, Maggie lay back on the dock, looking up at the skies. She seemed to be studying them.

"You're not falling asleep, are you?" he said.

"Me? Nope. Wide awake. Just looking up there, at the stars. God, I haven't been down here having so much fun in years." She took a deep breath. "You are a very interesting man, Mr. Richardson. Very interesting. I'm having a great time. Very great." She smiled as a distant meteor burned up in the earth's atmosphere. She pointed at it. "A something . . . star!"

He looked amused. Then, after putting the dinner remains back in the box, he got to his feet. "Chief Second, I think it's time for a fire. Don't you?"

Maggie sat up. "Fire. Yes, fire. Bonfire! Big one."

"How about we start with a campfire. That might be fun." John helped her move off the dock to the shore, near a circle of blackened rocks. "This looks like a good spot."

He rapidly gathered the materials necessary for a decent fire. Maggie, feeling she had no worries in the world anymore, watched him. In no time he had built a moderate-sized fire, just as the sun finally dipped behind the distant trees.

"There, isn't that lovely?" he said, sitting down beside her.

She snuggled up to him. "I'm surprised the mosquitoes aren't out already, eating and biting us. Hate those little things. Make me scratch."

John tossed some more wood on the fire. "Oh, don't worry

about that. I had a talk with them earlier and we made a deal. If they don't bother us tonight, I'll leave Sammy's window open later. He's a very sound sleeper. They'll have a feast."

Giggling, Maggie threw a twig at him. "That's mean. You're evil."

"So I've been told. But a deal's a deal."

The fire gradually grew brighter and hotter. They watched the flames dance and glow.

"Mr. Richardson?"

"Yes, Chief Second?"

Maggie pursed her lips, trying to come up with the right way to phrase her question. "What exactly are you doing here?"

"Here at Otter Lake, or here on the beach with you?"

"Either or."

She saw him looking at her, plumbing her eyes like a spelunker examining an unexplored cave. For a moment, she was expecting him to say something deep and intimate.

"I do believe you are drunk, Ms. Second. After just three glasses of wine." Not as romantic a line as she had expected but it did show he was paying attention.

"I bet you've had a lot of girlfriends. Haven't you?" She wasn't sure where exactly that question came from but it had been hiding somewhere.

"My share" was all he'd say.

"Okay. I've had three boyfriends in my life. Tonto Stone— don't ask about his name, it's a long story. William Williams, and my husband, Clifford. That's all. But you, with your leather, your motorcycle, and green eyes . . ."

"Hazel."

" . . . hazel eyes. How many? Dozens?"

"Like I said, I've had my share." He poked the fire a few times with a stick he'd found, and the flames sprang higher.

"Your share. Okay, and what has having your share taught you?"

"That some women shouldn't drink."

"No, seriously. I'm curious. In case you haven't noticed, I'm a mother with a son. I dated a bit before I got married but I get the feeling that I missed out on the good dating stories. I figure a guy like you probably knows the score. So, come on, dish. I'm in a dishing mood. Tell me." She ended her demand with a good strong poke at his shoulder.

"Okay, what exactly would you like to know?"

Her brow furrowed. "Okay, what have all your travels taught you . . . about women? That's a good one. Answer that!"

"That there's no one answer. Some are good. Some are bad. And some . . ."

"Yes?"

"And some are good at being bad, and bad at being good. To guys like me, women are like a rainbow, you pick the colour that best suits you and wear it proudly."

Maggie looked confused. "What . . . what does that mean?"

"I'll tell you later, when you're sober. Why do you want to know anyway?"

Maggie threw a branch at the fire, missing it completely. "Because I want to figure women out, that's why. I'm a woman and I don't know anything about what they do or why."

"Are you talking about your mother?"

"Let me tell you about my mother . . ."

"Why don't you tell me about your mother."

"My mother . . . I loved her so much." Her voice trembled.

"But she could be the most infuriating, stubborn, pain-in-the-ass ever born."

"Uh-huh."

"She was a walking contradiction. Like . . . like . . . I have a brother . . . actually I have a lot of brothers, but Wayne, she spoiled him rotten. So rotten he's nuts, yet she wasn't upset when he didn't come see her when she was sick. I was mad as hell but she wasn't. Other times she'd burn sweetgrass before going to church. Stuff like that." She took another sip of her wine. "I don't know if you know this but Mom went to one of those residential schools, saw horrible things that happened there I'm sure . . . Maybe that had something to do with it. Look at Sammy . . . you know . . . we've all tried to help Sammy. Some of our health workers have gone up to see him, my husband even arranged for a psychiatrist to visit him, but nothing. He'll only talk in Anishnawbe, and not many psychiatrists are that fluent in it. Sammy doesn't want to be helped. He lives in his own little universe . . . and yet he let you in. I wonder why?"

"If you want to know a secret . . ." he said, and Maggie leaned in closer, "I'm a little crazy too. We speak a very similar language, without the iambic pentameter. If your brother's nuts as well, maybe we could start a club."

Maggie let out a short laugh. "That would be funny. My mother would love that. Sweetgrass and holy water. That was my mother. You know, she was as devout as any old Italian lady. She told me I shouldn't be chief. She thinks there should be more magic in this world. She . . ."

"Yes?"

She fell silent, looking deep into the fire. "I don't understand her."

"And you think I can help you?"

Maggie shook her head. "No. Probably not." She paused. "I don't like my job either."

"Then why are you in your second term as chief if you hate it?"

"I'm the lesser of two evils."

"I don't think you're evil."

"Thanks." Once more she looked at the handsome young man beside her. "And you never answered my question."

"And what question would that be again?

"What have you, John Richardson-Tanner, learned about women? Tell me."

"Fun, huh? Okay, I will give you a fun answer. Where to start? Let's talk about breasts."

"Breasts . . . like boobs?"

"Yep, that's as good a place as any to begin."

Maggie nodded vigorously. "Okay, let's." Then she realized what he'd just said, and what she'd agreed to. "Huh?"

"After considerable field research, did you know breasts, boobs, hooters, knockers, whatever you wish to call them, are unique, individual, like fingerprints?"

"For your information," Maggie told John in her firmest voice, "in Anishnawbe, we call them . . ."

"Doodooshug. I know. But seriously, I don't think I've seen two that were the same, even on the same woman. Other than the obvious difference in sizes and cups, there are the subtler, more unique distinctions. The shape of the nipple, the size of it, the curvature, the colour, the smell, the firmness, the size and colour of the areola, the texture, even the temperature. They're like . . . snowflakes. Each one is special, a world unto itself, deserving of its own worship. They are each a thing of life, of pleasure, of dreams, be they used for practical or aesthetic purposes. Call me a fan but I have a memory of every single one I've touched, that I've tasted, and those memories will stay with me until the day I no longer travel this country. That is one of the most important things that I've learned from all those women I've been lucky enough to know."

Maggie wasn't sure how to respond. "I've never heard a man talk so passionately about breasts like that. That's . . . quite unusual."

"I thought, in respect to the Anishnawbe language, they were called doodooshims, if you are talking plural, because I have noticed they usually travel in pairs. So I do believe that calling them breasts proves they've been colonized, young lady. Any other questions?"

"I'm still trying to digest that one. I take it you like breasts."

"Call it a hobby. Beats collecting baseball cards."

"Now that sounds like a man!" she said, laughing.

Noticing a stone sticking out of the ground, John pulled it out. Though Maggie hadn't heard anything, John had detected the sounds of raccoons somewhere nearby. Trying to be as discreet as possible, he tossed the rock into the darkness of the woods. He heard it hit something soft, and that something—he assumed it was a raccoon—scrambled away. Satisfied, he turned his attentions back to the lovely Maggie.

"I am what I am." He paused. "I don't know if you're aware of this, but your mother used to come down here and go swimming a lot. At least that's what she told me. It used be quite different down here when she was younger. More trees, right down to the shore, more privacy, and I think the water was probably cleaner. She used to love swimming here. Even brought some boyfriends to go skinny-dipping, I believe. Bet you didn't know that."

Shocked at the idea, Maggie pushed John's shoulder. "My mother! Virgil's grandmother. I don't think so."

"It's true. She was a very passionate young woman. Grandmothers aren't born grandmothers. Wise men and women aren't born wise—wisdom is something achieved over years of experience. And for some, that experience includes . . . skinny-dipping."

The fire was doing strange things to John's face. His eyes reflected the light differently. They seemed to change colour randomly. Suddenly, she felt his hand on the back of her neck, caressing the nape and playing with her hair.

"So, want to swim naked in the same water your mother did?"

It took a moment for the meaning of his words to sink into her gradually sobering mind. Was he asking what she thought he was asking her?

"Now?"

"Would you rather book it a week next Thursday, after my dentist appointment and before I have my nails done? Yes, now. The water is fairly warm. We'll have a nice fire to come back to. Nobody's around. It's just us."

John was looking at her expectantly, a slight smile on his lips. Skinny-dipping. In the footsteps of her mother. She still had enough wine in her to take the proposition seriously, but she was also sober enough to realize what was involved. He continued to play with her hair, making it difficult for her to think.

"Take your time. We've got all night," he whispered into her ear.

Virgil wasn't expected home for a few more hours. He'd been off doing his own thing today anyway. Boys could be so mysterious. But . . . this was only a second date—or was it their first date, since their meal together had been merely a thank-you?

Maggie decided not to go down that road again. A dozen other thoughts came and went as the motorcyclist sat there, patiently waiting, playing with the hair at the nape of her neck.

"You know, with global warming, they say this lake might not be here in a couple of decades." His voice sounded so teasing and melodic.

Maggie made her decision. Why the fuck not? she thought. She leaned forward and kissed the man who had so mysteriously ridden into her life. And she put everything she could into it. Three years' worth of stored-up kissing and passion were waiting to be accessed and she wanted to drain the reservoir.

And for somebody out of practice, the man decided later, she didn't do half bad.

On the other side of Beer Bay the young Dakota sat on the dock, her eyes glued to her binoculars. There were so many conflicting emotions swirling around inside her—some embarrassment, a touch of excitement, guilt at watching other people and perhaps, just perhaps, a tinge of jealously. That was Virgil's mother, their chief, kissing and doing stuff by the fire with John Clayton.

Biting her lower lip, Dakota watched some more, knowing she probably shouldn't. Though she tried not to think about it, she couldn't help wondering if this was the kind of stuff her parents did . . . and she felt a bit nauseated.

Dakota wondered where Virgil was, and if he knew John and his mother were down by the dock, together.

SEVENTEEN

Virgil and Wayne had made it back to shore just before sunset. First they returned the canoe, which they had towed behind the motorboat, to Tim, who greeted his younger brother with little more than a grunt and a nod. Worried about his mother, Virgil was eager to get started, but Wayne had a different agenda. There was something else to be dealt with first. The cemetery.

Now Wayne stood beside the final resting place of his mother, with Virgil just behind him, staring at her headstone. Underneath her name and her dates, carved into the marble, were the words LOVING WIFE AND MOTHER. Below were three more words: TRUST IN HIM. Under his breath, Wayne whispered an ancient Anishnawbe farewell. And then he was silent.

Virgil hadn't been back here since the funeral, and with everything that had happened, he hadn't really come to grips with the loss of his grandmother.

"I wished I'd gone in and seen you," he said, lost in his own little world. "I'm sorry."

The sun had long since disappeared by the time they left. Wayne walked along the path between the tombstones to the street, Virgil following.

"Are you okay?" asked Virgil.

"It's the circle of life, that's all. You shouldn't be happy or sad.

It simply is what it is. You can cry all you want, it ain't gonna change anything."

"That's a bit . . . cold," said Virgil.

"You're right. It is. I think maybe I've been on my island a little too long. Sometimes the nuances of communicating get lost when you don't talk a lot. It's kind of like the difference between playing by yourself and playing with yourself. Virgil, I loved my mother more than anybody else could possibly know. But she died. She had to die. We all do. And while it is sad that I will never see her again, I know that she was contributing to what we call the circle of life. She passed on so that somewhere out there, a baby could be born in her place. You know how much she loved her grandkids, all kids. This was not a great sacrifice for her."

Virgil wasn't sure he understood, but he nodded.

"So, where to now?" said Wayne.

They made their way to Virgil's house, but Maggie was not home. "She must be off with him," said the boy, noting it was half past ten, much too late for mothers to still be out, in his opinion. They found a note from her saying she'd be home before his bedtime. "I told you," said Virgil, dropping the note on the table. He scribbled something on the back of it.

"What's that?" asked Wayne, searching the pantry. It was well past dinner and he was hungry.

"Just a note to Mom," the boy replied.

While Virgil wrote, Wayne made a sandwich. Thank god Maggie still ate baloney, he thought to himself as he laid three slices on the whole-wheat bread. "Please have mustard. Please have mustard," he whispered to the condiment gods, and lo, they blessed and bestowed upon him Dijon.

The next stop, Virgil told his uncle, who was deep into his baloney sandwich, was Sammy Aandeg's place.

"The stranger lives there?" said Wayne.

"That's what he said."

The cool night air greeted them as they set forth on their adventure.

"Maybe this guy is strange," said Wayne. "Even when I was your age, we all knew Sammy was a crazy drunk. Nobody in their right mind would want to stay there. But I still think this whole thing is a waste of time. I think you're just having mother–son insecurities of some kind. But regardless of what I believe, you asked me for help. An uncle doesn't turn his back on his nephew, or his sister. That's family. That's obligation." Wayne picked up a small rock in his right hand and whipped it at a large cedar tree. It hit the right side, chipping off some bark, then bounced off a nearby poplar, and returned to land directly between his feet. Smiling at his own ability, Wayne disappeared ahead into the darkness of the country road, finishing the last of his sandwich. Virgil, amazed, examined the scratched cedar before running off after him.

"Wow."

"Training," came Wayne's voice from the darkness.

"Uncle Wayne? This circle-of-life thing you mentioned, is that why you didn't come to the funeral? The family was kind of pissed off."

"I'm sure they were. Virgil, be happy you're an only child. Some European guy once said, 'What does not destroy me, makes me stronger.' You can bet the world he had brothers and sisters. My relationship with my mother was different from theirs. And folks do not often like people who are different, especially people they love very much. Especially when it involves something they can't change. How I mourn our mother was and is my business. And that's why I came over here, to explain to you why I didn't go to my mother's funeral?" he asked.

"No. I was just curious."

"Curiosity is a two-edge axe. I had a very curious dog when I was your age. I spent most of my time pulling porcupine quills out of its face, and washing away skunk smells. Curiosity is highly overrated."

When they reached the Aandeg driveway, they saw Maggie's car parked off to the side, barely visible in the darkness. Virgil had mixed emotions about catching his mother in the act.

They knocked on the front door of the house several times before Sammy Aandeg came waddling out, smelling of beer.

"Excuse me, but is . . . ?"

Virgil had barely begun to speak when Sammy angrily let loose with an Anishnawbe tirade and beer-scented spit, making the boy take a step backward.

"Let me handle this," said Wayne, who moved forward and promptly began his own tirade in the language.

For a moment, Sammy was surprised, but having a comprehending audience seemed to make him relish the opportunity to speak his language with full gusto.

Virgil watched them yell back and forth at each other, catching only the odd word here and there. Suddenly, Sammy slammed the door. They could hear locks on the other side being clicked into place.

"Well, that was interesting," said Wayne.

"What did he say?"

"I'm not sure yet. First of all, there was something about it being wintertime and some people were discontented. I kind of lost track after a while. He sure talks in a funny way. But after some prodding, I found out that your mother isn't here. She went off with some guy named Caliban."

"Caliban? Who's Caliban? His name is John Tanner. Sammy is nuts."

"It was hard to make out entirely. This guy of yours told Sammy his name was John Matus, not Tanner, but Sammy decided to call him Caliban. Suited him better, he says. So what do we do now, genius nephew of mine? Where else would they be?"

Virgil had an idea. "I know. I bet you it's where I saw him dancing. He seems drawn to that place. It's down by Beer Bay."

"Beer Bay? All the way back down there? We just came from there." Now it was Wayne's turn to let loose with a flurry of Anishnawbe epithets, because from the moment they had left Wayne's Island, they had been on foot. Wayne lived most of the time on the small island and therefore didn't need a car. Virgil was thirteen and had only toy cars. So they had had no choice but to hike to Virgil's house, then over to Sammy's, which altogether was over four kilometres. Now they had to walk back to Beer Bay, which was another good two and a half kilometres. Wayne was not a happy uncle. And the night was growing very dark.

"I should have stayed home, nephew or no nephew," he muttered.

On the way to Beer Bay, they didn't talk much. At one point, in the sheer darkness, Virgil slipped off the gravel shoulder and fell into the ditch. Luckily it had not rained recently so the only thing to suffer was his pride. Wayne was the one who broke the silence. "All this because John 'Caliban' Matus can make good animal calls. I must be crazy."

"Don't forget he also goes by Tanner and Richardson. That should tell you something is wrong. But it's more than that," Virgil said.

"Uh-huh."

"I know he's been carving pictures on my rock. And there's that thing with his eye colour. And I—"

"Enough," said Wayne. "You're not on drugs, are you? Have you listened to yourself?"

"Just wait 'til you meet him. You'll see." Now grumpy, Virgil crossed his arms over his chest and walked faster. Silence hovered over them like a bad smell.

It would be about another fifteen minutes before they came upon the first house in this part of the village, and Virgil decided to start a conversation if possible. "Uncle Wayne? Back on the island. How did you break that branch?"

Wayne was walking a couple of metres ahead of Virgil, and they couldn't really see each other clearly in the night; they were just black lumps moving against other black lumps. Most of the light from the moon was hidden by the tall trees that lined the road.

"Focus. Training. And belief. With that, you can do anything," answered the voice in the darkness.

"Focus, training and belief. Okay. I'll try and remember that," said the boy.

They walked a little farther until Wayne suddenly stopped.

"What?" said Virgil. Then he heard it too. There was the distinctive sound of an approaching motorcycle. "It's gotta be him . . ." Virgil looked up and saw one of the community's few street lamps almost directly overhead. "Shit, they'll see us."

"Into the bushes," commanded Wayne, and they both dove into the undergrowth.

Peering through some tall grass, they first saw the headlight turning the corner, and then could make out the motorcycle Virgil knew so well emerging into the light and whizzing by. Maggie was a passenger. She seemed very comfortable sitting atop the man's gas tank.

"I do believe that's your mother?"

Virgil nodded, not realizing that head movements went practically unseen in tall grass, but Wayne wasn't really expecting an answer.

"Nice bike," commented Wayne.

"Everybody says that!"

"Well, it is," said Wayne. "So, what do we do now, since you seem to know everything?"

Virgil thought for a moment. "Let's go see him. He's the one who I think you should really see. So, I guess back to Sammy's place."

Once more, Wayne muttered unspeakable words under his breath. "Fine," he said finally, turning and walking in the opposite direction. "You do realize that on my island, there's only so far I can walk. Ten minutes side to side and you're in water."

"What happened to all that training you were talking about? You should be in great shape," said Virgil.

"It's like asking a champion volleyball player to run a marathon. I'm in great shape, but my feet aren't used to walking. I'm getting blisters. At least hurry up!"

Virgil ran up to catch him.

They had walked about ten minutes when they saw, in the distance, a car approaching from the direction of Sammy's house.

"That's Mom! Those are her headlights. He must have just taken her back to Sammy's to pick up her car!"

Again they dove into the underbrush, hiding as the car passed. This time, they were at the edge of a large marsh full of cattails, and their feet sank to just above ankle level. More unspeakable words issued forth, this time from both Virgil and Wayne.

"This is ridiculous, you realize!" Wayne growled. "You're positive you're not on drugs?"

"No, I'm not. And this is good. It's what we want. He's alone now. We can confront him without my mother being there. It's perfect." Virgil's voice betrayed his excitement.

"Confront him? Confront him about what? Virgil, I don't like all this skulking around." Wayne's voice betrayed a noticeable *lack* of excitement. Wet feet did that to him. Granted, the man having three different names did strike him as being unusual, as did the dancing, but Wayne was pretty sure Virgil was just going through some puberty/protective/Oedipus-complex thing. At some point in the future Wayne would have to rethink his familial obligations.

This time, Virgil emerged first from the ditch and started walking ahead of his uncle, his feet making squishy noises. They had been trudging for another five minutes when they heard, yet again, the sound of an approaching two-wheeled motorized vehicle.

"What now!" said Wayne, as they plunged into hiding for the third time that night, into the thicket that bordered the road. Luckily there was no marsh this time, only thorn bushes.

While they huddled there, Wayne whispered, "You know, the more time I spend with you, the more I really appreciate having never really spent much time with you."

Virgil ignored him. "He must be heading back to my mother's. Or maybe to Beer Bay."

"Back to Beer Bay?"

Reluctantly, Virgil nodded, for even he was getting tired, and mosquito bitten, and his feet were wet and hurting, and his uncle was slowly beginning to hate him. "Back to Beer Bay," he said.

Feeling that this night would never end, they started walking toward Beer Bay, hoping against hope that they might actually make it this time.

"It's all coming back to me, why I live alone and don't have kids; though, the two might be related."

They continued on in the darkness, leaving a trail of muddy footprints.

The moon finally peeked over the stand of trees ahead of them, lighting their way.

"Hey, Virgil, cool, look. A raccoon in the middle of the road! Two!"

It had truly been an interesting night. The motorcyclist was happy and he naturally assumed Maggie was contented. Their first kiss of the night had been quite wonderful, and the goodbye kiss when he dropped her off at her car had been even better. Everything in between had been equally stupendous. He was quite proud of himself.

It had been a long time since he had enjoyed the physical pleasure of a woman. His most recent existence had not made him the most attractive bundle of male flesh. Often women's reaction to such a proposal had been a physical one, though not of the pleasurable kind. John had worried that perhaps he had lost the touch, forgotten what goes where, and when. But like riding a bike, it all came back to him. He could still smell her hair, her scent, even the perfume she wore that they had quickly sweated off.

Maggie herself had mentioned how out of practice she was, but he hadn't complained. The only thing that had put a damper on the night was the knowledge that those damn raccoons were probably watching them.

Maggie had a lot of her mother in her, John had to admit. Maybe there was something about that particular lineage. In any case, he was just happy to reap the benefits.

Once she'd left, John sneaked into Sammy's room and opened the window like he'd promised the mosquitoes, while the man snored away. Luckily the old guy was a fiercely sound sleeper. The case of beer a day helped. Ever since those days at residential school, there was something in him that was afraid to wake up. Except for those crying fits that would occur deep in the night, but even those Sammy managed to sleep through.

With that done, John retired to his bedroom. There he lay back on his bed, his feet crossed and his arms outstretched, his head to the side, trying to figure things out. The mission had been accomplished. Now what was his next step going to be? After much restlessness, he decided to go back down to Beer Bay. It was a place of wonderful memories for him, and who knows, maybe the moon would grace him with its presence. There could be dancing tonight, on top of everything, he thought, though that might be stretching his luck. He knew people had heard him the last time at Beer Bay, and if he tried it there again people, or more specifically the police, might investigate. A new location might have to be scouted first. But that would take time, and he had the urge now. Besides, he had his iPod with him. That would surely work. It wasn't as dramatic as a big-ass ghetto blaster, but it was much more versatile.

Even the sound of the motorcycle outside his window failed to wake Sammy Aandeg. He merely rolled over, hugging his pillow close. Already the waiting mosquitoes were flying into the room, though Sammy's personal aroma was as pungent as any can of mosquito repellent. John roared down the highway at top speed, unafraid of police or obstacles, for he was deep in thought.

Before long, he was back where the evening had begun.

He went to the end of the dock, looking expectantly up at the sky. But the moon tonight, though it had been playing hide-and-seek all evening, was hidden for the moment. So John just stood there, listening, thinking, breathing and waiting. Time came and went, and the man still stood there. Being from a different time and place, he had the patience of an ice age. Time had taught him that.

It was well after midnight when Wayne and Virgil hobbled down the hill to the dock area. Neither of them was in a good mood, or in good condition. They had put in almost ten kilometres of walking that night. They had stopped talking entirely a good twenty minutes ago.

It was Wayne who first saw John standing on the dock. Painfully, they hobbled toward the water, trying to be stealthy and using what foliage they could for camouflage.

"What's he doing?" asked Wayne.

"I never know" was the boy's answer. "That is why you are here."

They took refuge near a sumac bush, close to the water. "Do you think . . ." began Virgil, but Wayne put his hand over the boy's mouth.

Wayne had noticed that they and the motorcyclist weren't the only visitors to the lake this night. One by one, raccoons began to emerge from the surrounding forest, approaching the dock. Before long, there were over a dozen masked, furry bodies standing around the man's Indian Chief, with more emerging every second.

"I can hear you. I know you're there." The man on the dock turned.

Both Virgil and Wayne thought at first that he was talking to them. But it soon became apparent that the raccoons had his full attention. John's boots making a distinctive clicking sound on the wooden planks, as he approached the furred audience.

"What the hell do you want?" he asked angrily.

One of the raccoons climbed atop a stump, stood on its hind legs, its paws outstretched, and began to chatter away. Occasionally one or several of the other animals would contribute something, but basically, this one raccoon was doing all the talking. Though it was dark and the moon was stubbornly refusing to reappear to witness this interchange, there was still enough secondary lighting from the stars, the houses on the far shore and a lone streetlight halfway up the hill for the hidden duo to see what was happening. John's face registered his annoyance at being bothered here.

"Will you guys stop obsessing over this? It's old news, and leave me alone!" This garnered a substantial reaction from several of the raccoons, resulting in a chattering chorus of disagreement. John rolled his eyes as he listened to their protest, obviously not impressed. "Yeah, so what do you want me to do about it?"

He seemed to be ... talking to the raccoons. The rider's stance, the eye contact, his attitude, the very tone of his voice conveyed a sense of familiar contempt for the miniature army that surrounded his vehicle.

The one raccoon, still standing on the stump, continued to chatter, bark and make raccoonlike noises.

Casually, the man crossed his arms and nodded in a patronizing manner. "Yeah, uh-huh, I've heard this all before. Get over it. That was a long time ago. I've moved on."

The raccoons were not mollified by such an attitude.

"What the heck is going on?" asked Virgil.

"I . . . I think they're arguing. Maybe *I'm* on drugs," commented Wayne.

John yelled at the stump raccoon. "How do you know it was me? It could have been anybody. You have no proof. You know better than to listen to rumours."

Virgil turned and looked at his uncle. "Arguing. Him and the raccoons. Do you know how that sounds?"

Wayne pointed at two parties. "Well, you tell me what's going on, then."

The raccoons' chattering had grown louder and increasingly heated. More and more of the subordinate raccoons were contributing to the argument, and others were appearing out of the dark forest, ready to support their brothers.

"Fuck you" was John's response to most of their remarks. Just a series of repeated *fuck you*'s to each individual raccoon.

"Fuck you. Fuck you. Fuck you. And especially, fuck you!" That particular piece of nastiness was aimed directly at the stump animal. "I invented roadkill, remember that."

For Virgil, it was like a scene from Narnia, *The Wizard of Oz* or the *Road Warrior* being acted out in some creepy play in his backyard. "Are we actually watching what we're watching?"

Another raccoon, a smaller one, jumped up on the stump beside the other, and began chattering animatedly at the motorcycle man. It had an oddly shaped tail—seemingly shorter than the other raccoons' tails, with a bald patch on its tip.

Wayne, his eyes never leaving the mysterious drama in front of them, nodded. "I do believe so."

John rolled his eyes at what the second raccoon was implying.

"Do you have witnesses? This is slander, I tell you. Libel too."
Pretty soon, that raccoon finished and jumped down, and the
other, larger animal continued its diatribe.

"Give it a break! I never even knew your great-great-great-
great-grandfather. How do I know what he said was true? These
are all lies. Lies, I tell you. I'm being framed." John gestured wildly
at the small raccoon, which was angrily gesturing back.

Realizing they were in another world, and completely over
their heads, Wayne gently touched Virgil's arm and gave a quick
nod indicating they should go.

"Come on. Let's get out of here. This isn't our fight," whispered Wayne.

Built with a boy's curiosity, Virgil shook his head. This was
definitely where he wanted to be. "Are you crazy? That's . . ."

More insistently, Wayne took his arm and led him forcefully
back through the woods and away from John and the raccoons.
"No, we don't know what's going on here. We're outnumbered . . ."

"By raccoons."

"Have you ever come up against an irate raccoon? Trust me,
I'd rather face a professional wrestler than a pissed-off raccoon.
They know nothing of the Marquess of Queensberry rules. And
their balls are hard to kick."

"The what rules?"

"It's a long story. I'll tell you later." So once more, they hobbled
painfully through the sparse brush until they were safely away.
Wayne seemed to be deep in thought.

"What the heck *was* that?" Virgil blurted when they were out
of earshot. "I *told* you he was strange."

Looking cautiously over his shoulder, Wayne urged Virgil to
walk faster, but he didn't answer.

Hopped up on adrenaline, Virgil was all questions. "He was arguing with those raccoons, wasn't he? I mean it couldn't have been anything else. Who argues with raccoons?"

"I guess he does. Come on."

They made their way farther up the road. Soon they came to a small footpath, which Wayne indicated to Virgil they should take. Virgil knew immediately where he was going. Though it was dark, the path was pretty well marked and broad. Soon they came to a grouping of cedar trees that had grown out of a single set of seeds, making the trunk look like a hand extending upward. And between these wooden fingers somebody had long ago placed wooden boards, providing seats. The tree trunks had grown around the edges of the boards in some cases. This little oasis must have been in existence for some time, due to the fact that two different generations, Wayne's and Virgil's, knew of it.

"Uncle Wayne, I'm afraid, for my mother," Virgil said once they were sitting. "This raccoon shit isn't normal, and I think she likes him . . . Doctor Doolittle back there. What should we do?"

Wayne didn't respond. He started to count something on his fingers, his lips moving, pushing down one finger after another. He had just started on his second hand when he reached the end of whatever he was counting.

"Wayne?" said Virgil hesitantly.

Wayne's expression was one of disbelief. "I hear you. Just thinking. It can't be. He's been gone a long time. If you believe in him, I mean."

"What? What is it? You know something, Wayne. What's happening here? Tell me."

It was almost like Wayne was afraid to say what he was thinking. But, upon reflection, he did anyway.

"Momma always talked of him like he really existed. That's what made her storytelling so special. Virgil, that . . . that guy just might . . . I know this sounds crazy . . . but he could be Nanabush." As if realizing what he was actually saying, he looked away, his face becoming lost in the shadow of the trees. "Nah, couldn't be. Could it?" Both were silent for a second as the words sunk in. "Virgil, did you hear what I said?" he asked.

Virgil had indeed heard his uncle, but he was still trying to understand the implications. "Nanabush . . . the one and only Nanabush . . . the one grandma would tell me about. That Nanabush?"

"That's the only Nanabush I know. Well, I guess he could also be called Nanabouzoo, and generically, the Trickster. He's known by a lot of different names by different people."

"Jesus, Uncle Wayne! You're crazier than he is. Nanabush doesn't exist. He's a made-up guy, from Native stories. Like Merlin the magician or Tarzan of the Apes or Santa Claus. Actually, I would believe you more if you said he was Santa Claus. I mean, besides the fact that Nanabush is make-believe, John is White. I know it's dark out here but at least you should have noticed that. I assume Nanabush would at least look a little Indian."

"Tricksters have the ability to change their shape, Virgil. Or didn't you listen to your grandmother's stories? It's all right there. He can talk to the animals. You saw him. He's riding a motorcycle, one that's named after us. Tricksters love irony!"

"So, the Ministry of Transportation gives out vehicle and driver's licences to tricksters? That's just one of those . . . coincidence things."

"Coincidences don't exist. That's exactly the kind of thing he would do. I think it's called irony. And . . . he keeps changing his last name. Tanner, Matus, Richardson . . . Depending on where you are in Canada, he also goes by different names. Weesageechak, Coyote, Napi, Glooscap, Raven . . ."

"You're . . . I don't believe this! I said he was strange but there's strange and there's strange. You are crazy, Uncle Wayne!"

"Yeah, it's a definite possibility, according to local opinion. But if I'm right, your mother is in more danger than you thought. So are a lot of other people. He's very, very dangerous."

"Wait a minute, dangerous? I thought Nanabush was this goofy guy that always got himself into trouble, did stupid and silly things like tripping on shit and stuff. That doesn't sound so dangerous."

"Those are the children's stories Grandma told you. She told me others. Darker ones. Ones with monsters. Yes, Nanabush teaches us the silliness of human nature, but don't forget he has special powers. And people with powers tend to act differently from you and me. And I'm not talking in a Superman or Spider-Man way. They have their own set of rules. According to some who really studied those stories, he is a creature of appetites, of emotions, of desires. That is not a good thing to be. That's what usually got him into trouble. He would often do whatever he wanted to get what he wanted, whenever he wanted it. And if what you say is right, he wants . . ."

Virgil took a deep breath. "My mother!" They both sat quietly in the darkness for several moments. "So, you're saying Grandma knew Nanabush? That can't be true." Then he remembered. "When I looked in her window that day he showed up, I saw them kissing. I mean, really kissing. Him and Grandma. What do you think that meant?"

Reaching behind his head, Wayne undid the leather thong tied around his ponytail. In all their bush-hopping and peeping, his hair had come loose. "That explains a lot, actually. Mom . . . Your grandma always told those stories in such a way that you believed she had been there. There was so much love in the way she told them. In my travels I've listened to other storytellers, and her way of telling tales was always different. Special. Maybe now we know why."

Virgil shook his head. "Nanabush?"

"Yep, Nanabush. It was those petroglyphs you mentioned that got me thinking. I thought it was impossible but still . . . you see, Virgil, many cultures, ours included, believe the west is the land of the dead."

Things clicked for Virgil. "The setting sun!"

"Exactly. He arrived, and your grandma, my mother, went west. Nanabush knows how to get there, and back. And now, maybe, he has developed an infatuation with your mom."

"Oh my god! I just thought he wanted to move to Vancouver with her. Mom . . . in the land of the dead. Uncle Wayne, I don't want her to die." A nervous and wide-eyed Virgil asked the obvious. "So . . . what do we do? If this is Nanabush, we gotta do something. We can't let him take Mom!"

Just above Virgil's head was a tree branch about the size of a child's wrist. In the gloom of the forest, he could barely make out his uncle reaching above him and grabbing the branch with his left hand. There was a loud cracking sound and the boy felt bits of bark and cedar falling on him. Wayne held the snapped branch in front of his nephew's face.

"If this is Nanabush in the flesh, as outrageous as that may sound, and I think he is, he's not a person you want to have around your mother. Around anybody. In the last couple of generations, his stories have been domesticated and gentrified. Remember,

Virgil, where he goes, mischief follows. Luckily he's half human, and we can deal with that part. Knowing that, we must try to convince him to move on."

Virgil took the branch and felt the broken end. Since this whole thing began, he had felt something small but uncomfortable lodged in the pit of his stomach. Over the last ten minutes it had grown to be quite substantial, grown to about the size of a motorcycle.

Nestled in her bed with most of the twigs and grass removed from her hair, and just a slight headache from the wine, Maggie thought about the evening's events, and as a result, her mind was doing more back flips than most high-school cheerleaders. It had been a life-altering night for sure. Well, maybe that was a bit exaggerated. It certainly had been a year-altering night. It couldn't have been the wine. Though she did have a fairly low tolerance for alcohol, her personality didn't radically change, like some people's. Even when she was young, and guys were always after her, the offering of gifts of Labatt and Molson had had little effect. But what had happened tonight? Now that was the question.

Maybe it was the combination of the wine, the moon and the man. That was a definite possibility because she couldn't tell where one began and the other left off. She had gone from first base to a home run, covering all of the bases along the way. Furthermore, she had enjoyed it all under a blanket of stars. This was very un-Maggie-like behaviour. She blamed her own innate shyness for thinking all the animals of the forest were watching them together on the blanket on the dock, wrapped up in each other.

She still wasn't sure how she felt about the whole thing. It had been a while since she'd felt the things she'd felt tonight, both physically and emotionally. Hell, even intellectually and spiritually too. It would take some time to figure this all out. Meanwhile, she was content to let her body tingle magnificently.

When John had dropped her off at the house, she'd wondered if Virgil would be able to tell what had happened, but luckily he wasn't home. There was a note on the table saying he'd gone out with one of her brothers but he had neglected to say which one. It wasn't like him to be out so late by himself, but she was pleased he was making an effort to socialize more. It seemed to be a night for socializing for both of them. In the dark, Maggie blushed and pulled the blanket over her face. A small giggle escaped.

And they never did take that swim.

Outside her window, perched high in a tree, a raccoon was watching her.

With her parents at their weekly bowling excursion in town, and her brother and sister off at a local high-school dance, Dakota had gone down to the dock again. She'd been spending more and more time out there, with her dad's binoculars. She'd told her parents she was doing a project on the moon and was making notes on what she could see. Little did she know her parents were now planning to buy her a telescope next Christmas.

So much had been happening over at Beer Bay lately, she could barely keep track of it. And it all seemed to revolve around John Clayton. It had grown late, and John and what she was fairly positive were several raccoons, had left. But they might be back, and so she had waited. And waited. And waited. She had not wanted to miss a thing. She'd waited until her body could wait no more.

Now she was sound asleep, her head resting on the binoculars case, dreaming the dreams of a thirteen-year-old girl.

Life with two teenage siblings had taught her to sleep soundly, so she didn't hear the sound of the motorcycle approaching the front of her house, or the engine being shut off. Or the sound of boots walking the planks of her dock and stopping so close. She was also unaware of the man standing over her, watching her sleep. Now it was her turn to be observed. She shivered a bit in the spring night, but did not waken.

EIGHTEEN

The next morning a refreshed and still-tingly Maggie rose, ready to face what fresh hell the day might throw at her. Automatically, she checked Virgil's room and saw him safely tucked in his bed. She hadn't heard him come in. Wow, Maggie thought, she must have been really tired. Virgil rolled over, still fully dressed in yesterday's clothes, grumbling discontentedly in his sleep.

Closing his door she decided that today would be a day for full-blown caffeinated coffee, none of that half-decaf stuff she'd been drinking since her husband died. She knew she had a can packed away in the back of the cupboard for just such emergencies—or hangovers.

Or so she thought. She was on her second search of the cupboard, moving cans and packages around, when she heard a voice behind her. A man's irritated voice.

"Christ, you're noisy in the morning!"

Startled, she turned, dropping a can of peas on the floor. Coming toward her from the living room was her brother Wayne, in his underwear and a T-shirt, scratching an armpit. It took a moment for the image to register. He rubbed his eyes and yawned.

"Wayne?"

"That's my name. What is so damn important in that cupboard?" He yawned again.

"Coffee. I was looking for coffee."

He turned around and went into the living room, where apparently he'd been sleeping on the couch. "It's already in the coffee maker. Just turn it on. That's one thing about living with no electricity. You have to boil your coffee. Not the same. Luckily I remember how Momma's worked. Do you remember how I like mine?"

Still having difficulty believing her recluse brother was here, in her house, half naked at that, Maggie peeked around the doorway to see him folding the blankets on the couch. Then he started to get dressed. It all seemed so normal.

"Two sugars," she answered. "Wayne, don't get me wrong, but what are you doing here? It's been almost a year since you came to visit any of the family, outside of Mom."

"Things have changed. I should have brought my laundry. Washing machines: one of the three greatest inventions of White people. Big sister, we have to talk." He started rubbing his feet. "But first, you gonna turn the coffee on or what? Man, my feet hurt."

"Your feet? What?"

Behind her, Maggie heard Virgil's door open, and saw her sleepy son walk out.

"Hey, Mom. Hey, Uncle Wayne. What's up?"

Maggie looked at the both of them, sensing something was amiss. "I'd like to know that myself."

The early part of the morning passed quickly. Maggie made breakfast for her son and brother, grabbed a shower and went about getting ready for work. All the time, though, she had a nagging suspicion the two males in the house knew what she'd been up to the night before.

Eventually, just before she was to leave for the Band Office, Virgil excused himself, saying he was going to get ready for school. That seemed to Maggie more of a strategic manoeuvre than a statement of intent, because how often do thirteen-year-olds say, "Well, school's calling. Don't want to be late"? Especially Virgil.

"Wayne, what's going on here?" she asked after Virgil had left the room.

Wayne took a sip from his third cup of coffee, carefully choosing his words. "Maggie, it's good to see you. I really should visit more. I'm seriously going to try. And, uh, Virgil's been telling me things. And we've found out other things. Events are happening around here that I think you need to know about."

"What things?"

"This guy, the one that calls himself John . . ."

"John? Has Virgil told you about John?" Suddenly it dawned on Maggie. "Oh my God, it's my son, isn't it? He's upset, thinking I'm replacing his father. He's jealous. Oh, my poor boy. This has all happened so fast. This is all new to me too."

"Oh, Maggie, take a breath. That's what I thought at first, but it has nothing to do with Virgil. Actually, it has everything to do with this situation, but not in the way you think. Uh, this is kind of awkward, but . . . John's not what he seems to be. You need to be careful."

"John? And just who is John, then, other than a man that you've never met? And by the way, why are you here, really?" It seemed to Maggie that the more her brother talked, the less sense he was making. And why was everybody obsessed with John? Was it just family concern, or something more?

"Maggie, listen carefully." And Wayne began to explain.

———

"Get out!" yelled Maggie, visibly shaking. The calm of breakfast had ended.

"Maggie . . ."

"Wayne, I swear, I will knock your head off if you talk like that around Virgil. Do you know how insane this sounds?"

Wayne hesitated before confessing. "Yes, I do, and he knows already. We've been discussing the possibility since yesterday."

"What do you mean since yesterday? Did he go over to your island by himself?"

"Well, he was worried about you and that guy and, yes, he canoed over to my island. He thought maybe I could talk some sense into either you or 'John' . . ."

Maggie's eyes practically burned a hole through Wayne. "Yesterday was a school day. What was he doing canoeing across the lake? Alone."

"Maggie, I don't think you're seeing the bigger picture here . . ."

Maggie was indeed not seeing Wayne's bigger picture. At the moment, she was seeing only red, and not the red usually associated with Native people.

"Virgil Second!" she yelled as she threw open the door to Virgil's bedroom.

Startled, he scurried over the bed and into the far corner. He knew he was in deep trouble, on a number of different fronts. He wondered if his uncle could use an apprentice.

"Your uncle was just telling me that you canoed across the lake yesterday. Alone. Is that true?"

That would be the first nail in his coffin. "Yes, Mom."

"Yesterday was a school day. Weren't you supposed to be at

school? Didn't you promise me you would start spending more time at school and not doing this kind of thing?"

Virgil could hear the hammer hitting the next nail. "Yes, Mom."

"And you did all this to talk . . . to gossip behind my back, and to come up with the idea that John is, in fact, Nanabush, a fictional character from Native mythology. Am I understanding this all correctly?"

"Yes, Mom."

Then the silence fell. No more questions or nail-hammering, just a long piercing stare of an angry and pissed-off mother. In retrospect, Virgil would rather have faced a few more nails than the passing seconds (actually more like an eternity) of silence.

Finally: "Get to school."

Nodding vigorously to the point of almost hurting his neck, Virgil grabbed his knapsack and ran out the door. It seemed his uncle had been of no help in dealing with his angry mother, and now Virgil was quite happy to leave him behind to deal with her alone. Getting an education, at the moment, definitely seemed preferable to facing his mom's wrath. It had been a long time since he'd run full out to his class. Seething, Maggie watched her son leave, though *bolt* seemed the more correct word. She had never been the sort of person to get unduly angry. She was, in fact, the calm one of the family, and her job practically demanded it. But today was an unusual day. So Wayne was to witness a rare treat.

"And as for you . . ." she said as she turned to face him.

"Uh, Maggie, I didn't know yesterday was a school day. Sorry . . . not that I had anything to do with it."

"Everybody knows Wednesday is usually a school day."

"Today's Wednesday?"

"No, today is Thursday. Yesterday was Wednesday." Maggie struggled to keep her voice calm. "Most people also know what day of the week it is."

"Well, there's no need to get so snippy. I don't have a calendar on the island. Geez, Maggie, you know, you've always been bossy. Now, about John . . ."

Unable to deal with her lunatic brother, Maggie opted to push him toward the door. All the way across the living room from the kitchen and to the front door, she shoved him, and then she shoved him through it.

All the while, Wayne tried to reason with her, but he never got past uttering, "Maggie . . ." before she would push him again, almost knocking him over. One chair and a lamp fell to the ground along the way.

"I want you out of here. Go back to your island. Leave me and Virgil alone. John too."

Wayne fought the impulse to defend himself, which he easily could have done. Rarely do circumstances arise, however, where the use of a deadly martial art is permissible on an irate sister. Instead, he let himself be pushed, struggling at least to maintain his balance, which luckily was an integral part of his training.

Once he was out the door, Maggie stopped, breathing hard.

"If you'd just listen to me, we . . ." he pleaded.

She pushed him one more time, almost causing him to tumble down the cement steps. "Wayne, you are my brother, and because of that, I love you. But I will pound your face in if you continue with this ludicrous line of thought."

"What is it with you and violence? Were you always like this?"

"Me and violence? Mr. Indian Kung Fu? I am not violent!"

Now it was Wayne's turn to display his temper. "Are you kidding! You used to beat me up. All the time. I still have nightmares of you coming into my room with a bucket of cold water. Of hip-checking me into the lake. Of kicking me in the shins, all the time. Taking my boots away on the way home from school, in winter! You were a vicious, mean sister!"

"Oh, shut up. I wasn't that bad. All sisters do that kind of stuff. Besides, you were Mom's favourite, we all knew that, and maybe I was a bit jealous. She spoiled you. Why do you think none of us liked you much? You never seemed right to the rest of us. Now I am convinced of it. But that was then, Wayne, a long time ago. So grow up and listen to me. I don't want to see you in this house again until you smarten up. I mean it. Or I will do worse than take your boots away."

The little boy in Wayne also made an appearance. "Oh yeah, I can defend myself pretty good now. So you better watch it with those threats, Maggie. Or else."

"Oh yeah?" Maggie stepped onto the front steps, hands on her hips, facing her brother. "Show me. I dare you."

For a moment, time seemed locked as they faced off. But there are a few things in the world that are almost impossible to challenge, one of them being a younger brother's fear, respect and love (though he wouldn't have used that last word in this particular situation) of an older sister. Wayne could have done damage to the slender woman standing a metre in front of him without breaking a sweat, but the thought never entered his mind. Instead, he folded, and literally backed down the stairs.

Wayne made one last attempt to make his point, but a steely glare from Maggie ended that effort. Instead, he watched her lock the house, get in her car and drive away. She didn't look back.

As he stood there breathing in the car exhaust, Wayne ran through the last twenty-four hours in his head. How do you train for all or any of this? he thought to himself. More to the point, why had he let himself be dragged across the water from the safety, security and sanity of his secluded island to this place, where he had no control over anything?

On her way to work, Maggie fought the impulse to speed. She also resisted the desire to turn around and chase her stupid younger brother down and run him over with her car.

Her knuckles turning white with the force of gripping the steering wheel, she pointed the car toward work and hoped somehow she would arrive there without killing someone.

Her brother, a major freak job for sure, who basically abandoned the family to live on an island to devise some sort of Aboriginal martial art, had come into her home and essentially confessed his insanity. Nanabush. Maggie didn't believe those stories when she was a kid, and there was less chance she'd believe them today. Those stories were fun, for little kids. She remembered how devastated Wayne had been when he had discovered there was indeed no Santa Claus—and maybe this was all tied up in the same neurosis. To her, Nanabush was a charming and inventive character from Ojibway mythology. A symbol. A teaching tool. That was all. And John was John. Yes there was something different and special about him, but she was sure all people falling in love felt this about the object of their affection (had she actually just admitted that to herself?). And Virgil was in on this too, somehow. Perhaps she would have a little chat with him during lunch.

Maggie didn't remember dating being this difficult.

———

The day had started quite badly and Virgil had an inkling that things were probably not going to get much better. As he waited outside for the school bell to ring, he noticed Dakota sitting on the lawn, by herself. Normally a sociable cousin, Dakota was idly pulling grass out of the ground, lost in her own thoughts. Needing a distraction, Virgil trotted over to her, playfully knocking her baseball cap off.

"Hey, what's up, cousin?"

"Nothing."

Virgil sat down beside her. "Yeah, you seem in a nothing mood. Why so serious-looking?"

"I got reasons."

"That's awfully mysterious. What kind of reasons?"

Something seemed to be seriously affecting Dakota, and Virgil was being drawn in. Feeling concerned and admittedly uncomfortable, he tried some small talk. "My mother caught me skipping. Boy, was I in trouble. I hope . . ."

"That guy John came to see me last night."

"What?"

"I fell asleep on the dock, and when I woke up, there he was, standing over me."

It seems Virgil couldn't do anything or go anywhere without John somehow coming into the picture. And now, somehow, he was involved in Dakota's life. And if what his uncle had said was true, John/Nanabush wasn't always a nice guy.

"What . . . what happened? And why were you sleeping on your dock?"

Dakota just kept pulling at the grass.

"Dakota?"

"I'd been watching him. I don't know if you know this but he likes to dance. And talk to animals . . . raccoons at least. He's really amazing to watch. I could see all this across Beer Bay with my father's new binoculars. And I think he somehow knew I'd been watching. That's why he came over last night. I didn't even hear him or his motorcycle."

Though only thirteen, Virgil was aware of some of the horrible people who existed out there in the world. The kind who did nasty things to people, especially young girls. And young boys. Unfortunately, Otter Lake had not been spared this experience over the years. Swallowing a lump in his throat, he slid a little closer to his cousin, afraid of where the conversation was going.

"So, what happened?"

Dakota seemed preoccupied with a ball of grass in her hands, and kept rubbing it between her palms until it became smaller and smaller.

"Dakota?"

She looked up at Virgil, and suddenly, the most beautiful smile lit her face. "Oh my God, Virgil, he is so amazing. So fantastic. I can't believe there are people like that in the world. He wasn't angry with me at all for watching him. In fact John said he was flattered. And he's so considerate. At first I think I was a little jealous, watching him with your mother . . ."

Virgil became even more concerned at the mention of his mother, but Dakota was so excited, he couldn't get a word in edgewise. "But he said he was teaching her all about the constellations, that's why they were lying there. He knows so much. And he says he saw me out here when he was taking her home, man he must have great eyesight, especially at night, like an owl, 'cause he was worried and came over to see what I was doing out on the dock so late, and he found me sleeping there. Man, if my parents had found me, oh boy, I'd really be in for it. So anyway, he woke me up, told me to go to bed, but before that, we talked. He's a really good talker. He told me a little about the constellations too, the Native names, and so much more. We talked and talked and talked. You're so lucky he likes your mother."

Lucky wasn't the word that immediately came to Virgil's mind.

"So why were you so sad looking, just now?"

"I think I'm in love. There's only, like, ten or fifteen years' difference between us. Think that matters?"

If Virgil had wondered whether it was possible for his life to get more complicated, he now had the answer. The other horrible thing he realized was that it wasn't even nine o'clock yet, and there was so much more day left for things to go wrong.

"Virgil Second!" Ms. Weatherford, standing at the front doors, bellowed in the kind of voice only teachers who have been in the educational system for over twenty years can manage. She had spotted him through the classroom window. "Perhaps we should have a little word or two before class starts. I do believe you were not in attendance yesterday. Do you have a proper note explaining that?"

"No, ma'am." Somehow his coffin, and some additional nails, had found him here at school too.

"Then, my office, Mr. Second, and we'll discuss it."

The school bell rang then, signalling the beginning of the day. Only another twelve or fourteen hours more to go.

NINETEEN

John was having his morning coffee at Betty Lou's, taking in the sun and fresh air through an open window, and listening to the conversations as people came and went. He'd flirted innocently with Elvira but was keeping pretty much to himself. Coffee, more than alcohol, tended to loosen the tongues of most people, especially in environments such as this—the local diner. All the knowledge of the community was eventually passed around those cigarette-burned Formica tables. John knew this, so like a snake out hunting, he sat there, waiting for someone to say something of interest.

The man had something on his agenda. His evening with the lovely Maggie had put familiar thoughts in his head. He wanted to help—to help Maggie, and Otter Lake, and do something positive like he used to in the old days. That was the kind of guy he was. He could be incredibly selfish and vain at certain times, but at others, he could be very community oriented and conscientious. Especially when there was a lovely and striking woman involved. Plus, Lillian would have been very pleased, his promises to her still fresh in his mind. So he sat and thought. And listened . . .

It was a slow Friday morning, so breakfast traffic was a little light. But Elvira hovered over and around John like a hawk watching an exposed chipmunk. Ever since that night at the bar, she had viewed him the way a dieter might an ice-cream cake at a

Weight Watchers' meeting. "More coffee?" she'd ask him after every sip. John had to move to the far side of the room to make it more difficult for her to reach him. Eventually three more customers entered, dressed for a hard day of manual labour judging by the amount of dirt and dust on their work clothes.

"Ahneen, Elvira," greeted the biggest one, a man named Roger. The other two men with him, Dan and Joshua, were cousins and they worked for the village, currently clearing a plot of land near the eastern border of the community. Otter Lake was getting a youth centre. Dan's glance lingered a little too long on him for John's taste, like he was sizing him up. Dan definitely looked rougher than the other two, with most of his arms covered in a multitude of tattoos, most of them homemade. John knew that people who didn't respect their bodies tended not to respect others much. John took another sip of his coffee and looked the other way.

"You guys are late," commented Elvira, still keeping one eye on the handsome stranger in the back corner.

"*Late* is a White man's term," countered Dan.

"Tell that to the Band Office when your cheque is late. The usual, guys?"

Roger and Dan nodded, but Joshua shook his head. "Elvira . . . ?"

"No eggs Benedict," pre-empted Elvira. "I've told you that a dozen times, Joshua."

"But . . ."

"I tried making that . . . that . . . holiday sauce or whatever it's called once, for you, Joshua, and it just turned into a pot of yellow gunk. Nothing fancy here. Just the basics. House rules."

"*Gunk?* Is that the proper Anishnawbe word for it?"

"It is for today. Tell you what, Joshua. I will put some poached eggs on a piece of toast piled with bacon. I'll even pour some mustard on the top. It will look identical. That's the best I can do, boys. What do you say?"

Joshua thought about his options for a moment before nodding ruefully. "I guess. I hate having to go to town for it. It looks easy."

"Then you cook it." With that, Elvira disappeared into the back, and soon, the satisfying sound of bacon hitting the griddle could be heard. And smelled.

After a second, Joshua yelled to Elvira, "Uh, but you can hold the mustard. Please."

Left to their own devices, the three men grabbed coffees and two took seats near the large window. Dan, instead, took a long time stirring the milk into his coffee, his attention occasionally wandering to the stranger. Absentmindedly, Roger stared out through the glass, his eyes once again lovingly tracing the shape of the motorcycle sitting seductively in the shade. He could never get tired of looking at it. Joshua, on the other hand, had issues of his own to discuss.

"So, can you pick up my kid on Friday?"

Roger finished dumping three small bags of non-sugar into his coffee before answering. "Yeah, I guess so. I hate museums. I don't know if it's because I'm Ojibway and they might lock me up in some display or . . ."

" . . . or what?"

Roger hesitated. " . . . or, I don't know. I thought I had another reason but I guess I don't. I thought they had teachers and people for these school trips. Why do I have to go with them? I work for a living. I don't have to learn anything."

"Hey, buddy, that your bike out front?" said Dan.

John nodded, still not looking at the tattooed man.

"Kind of old, isn't it?"

"It's as old as it is. No more, no less. Just like me."

"You're just a kid."

"I have an old soul."

Managing to tear his eyes away from the motorcycle, Roger drank his coffee, black.

Joshua continued. "Christ, it's one of those education policy things. Some kind of 'trying to rebuild the nuclear family' program. Get parents involved in their kid's education. I had to take my two girls to a play. Hated it. Had no idea what was going on. No character development whatsoever."

Incensed, Roger raised his voice, catching the distant John's attention. "There you go again. Dan's right. Nuclear. What do we know about nuclear? That's a White man's term. We never had anything nuclear. We had the extended family, not the nuclear family."

"So what? You want your second cousin and brother to go instead?"

"Hell yeah! I mean, here we are, taking it up the ass because the White man wants to make us a nuclear family."

"I didn't realize taking your son to a museum was 'taking it up the ass.'"

Dan took a small sip of his coffee. "You're the guy with the motorbike aren't you?"

"That would be me."

"I've got a 2007 Harley-Davidson. Bet it could eat your little bike up."

"Bikes don't eat each other. Only animals do."

Roger and Joshua were deep in their own discussion. "Bones. That's what they are showing at that museum. Some kind of archaeological thing. Bones from a thousand . . . million . . . years ago. That kind of thing."

Joshua nodded. "Kids love that kind of stuff. Especially dinosaur bones."

"But I don't. The only bones I like make soup."

Bones, thought John. That could be interesting, very interesting. Maybe that was what he had been looking for. It could be the stock for the soup he was planning to cook up. A soup of mischief and fun. But he'd have to think it through . . .

"Where you from, guy with the old motorcycle?"

Dan was now next to John's table, practically standing over him. John could see on the man's forearms, printed in grey-blue and wedged between various tattoos, a set of capital letters. On the left arm he read *D.G.A.F.*, and on the right, he was sure it said *D.G.A.S.*

"Everywhere, I guess."

"Homeless, I guess?"

"You got a problem with me?"

"Yeah, blondie, I do."

"Is it the fact I like to shower?"

"That snotty attitude. You and other guys like you. I met a lot of guys like you in jail. Leather pants like that, fancy bike, attitude, think you're hot shit. Tough shit. Mostly, though, guys like you are all packaging with nothing inside. I bet you're some rich kid spending Daddy's money. People like you are a waste of time. And I hear you've been riding around this village like you own it. Come to impress the Natives?"

"Dan, is it? Well, you don't know anything about me. And the less you know, the better. Now why don't you go join your friends."

"Or what?"

"You really want to know what, buddy?"

Dan leaned over the table, smiling. "Yeah, what?"

"Well, it will have to wait. Your breakfast is ready," he said, as Elvira came out of the kitchen with three fully loaded plates in her arms, including the Otter Lake version of eggs Benedict.

"Hey, Dan, come and get your eggs before they get cold," she said, putting the plates down in front of the men.

John smiled a mysterious smile at Dan. "You heard the lady. Nothing worse than cold eggs."

Dan smiled back. "Okay. Bye, for now. And you know, a museum might want that thing of yours. Try and join the new century."

Dan rejoined his two friends, and other than one quick look over his shoulder, seemed engrossed in their conversation. Much like a car stuck in a snowdrift, the discussion went on and on, grinding up the same snow repeatedly and not making any progress. The talk continued to centre on museums, bones and the disgusting lack of ambition among certain Otter Lake breakfast makers. They were so absorbed in their conversation that they never heard the only other occupant of the restaurant open the door and leave.

Elvira was busy bussing the nearby table as she watched the handsome young man straddle his bike, and then freeze. He seemed rooted to the spot, thinking. Once he looked up, at the very window where Elvira was standing, and his hand rubbed the Indian logo on his gas tank. Then, seeming to have made a decision, John dismounted and briskly re-entered the restaurant.

"One more thing, buddy," he said to Dan as he approached their table. Without warning, John punched Dan, a short, powerful right jab to the side of his face. Hard. So hard his head went flying back and, as the laws of physics demand, when it reached its limit, lashed forward onto the table, splattering eggs everywhere. Elvira stepped back in shock. No one else moved.

"Rule number one. Don't fuck with the Indian. Never ever disrespect the Indian. They were here long, long before Harley-Davidson and the others, and they will still be roaring down the highways long after all the rest are gone. Not everything new is better than what came before it. I know . . . Gentlemen." John nodded and turned to leave, then spotted Elvira standing behind him, still looking startled.

"Sorry, Elvira. It just needed to be said. And, uh, sorry about the eggs."

As he opened the door to exit for the second time in three minutes, John turned to the still-stunned patrons, and now-moaning Dan. "By the way, those letters on his arms. What do they mean?"

It took Joshua a few seconds to find his voice. "Uh, they're initials for *Don't Give A Fuck*, and *Don't Give A Shit*. At least, that's what he told us."

John nodded. "That explains a lot."

Thirty seconds later, he tore out of the driveway on his Indian Chief. But the story he left behind would be told for years.

It was lunchtime and Maggie was just leaving the Band Office, trying to decide whether to raid her own kitchen cupboards to feed herself and her son or to save herself the trouble and head over to Betty Lou's Take-Out. The phone call from Ms. Weatherford had added another straw to the camel's back. And she did not relish the thought of another blowout with her brother, if he was still lurking about her place. How had life gotten so difficult all of a sudden?

"Hey," said a familiar voice.

Parked right beside her car was a familiar motorcycle and an even more familiar man, smiling broadly. This was the morning after and Maggie smiled back, radiating a combination of delight, embarrassment, awkwardness and a certain amount of anticipation. God, he had a nice smile, she couldn't help thinking.

"Holy shit, you look good." There was a definite lack of romanticism about his compliment, but Maggie decided to accept it nonetheless.

"So do you. Bonfires and late-night swims seem to agree with you."

Instinctively he could tell there were people in the windows of the Band Office watching her. Once more her cheeks flushed. Lately they'd been flushing far too frequently for an approaching-middle-age chief, but she seemed unable to do anything about it.

"What are you doing here?" That seemed like a safe question.

"Do you have to ask?"

Even through two panes of glass, Maggie could hear the girls, and Arthur the accountant, in the office laughing and cooing.

"Wanted to know if I could buy you lunch. I know a great restaurant in town. A Thai restaurant. You know, I have had Thai only twice in my life! Can you believe it? All in the last couple of weeks. Great stuff. I know Otter Lake has more sweetgrass than lemongrass, but you gotta try it. Have you ever?"

"Yeah, though not in a while. But right now, John? It'll take a good hour and a half to get into town, have lunch, then the drive back. I have an important phone conference at one-fifteen. Maybe dinner instead?"

The man sitting on the motorcycle shook his head. "I want you to see something. And I'm hungry for Thai now. Come on, Maggie, blow it off. We'll have a lot more fun. I promise. There's something I want to show you."

"I can't blow it off, John. I love Thai but this is rather important. It's with the local MP about the land acquisition deal and a press conference we're holding tomorrow. You don't just blow off an MP. And what do you want me to see?"

John took her hand. "I don't want to tell you, I want to show you. You see, I have a plan but I can't tell you about it. Not yet. It's a surprise. And sure you can blow your meeting off. I blow things off all the time. If you want, I'll even write you a note. You are always so stressed out about these things. Let me . . . de-stress you. I'm a great de-stressor. Been doing it for years." He smiled in anticipation.

"I am sure you are, but sorry, can't do it. Priorities." Maggie could see the disappointment in his face. It was almost childlike. "The world doesn't wait for me, John."

"But you want me to wait for you . . ."

"No. This lunch was your suggestion and I appreciate it. Really I do. I can still do dinner, even lunch tomorrow. Just not today. That's not the end of the world."

John had trouble reconciling the simple fact that not everyone shared his willingness to drop everything to do anything anytime. Now he wrestled over what to do. He was a man of conflicting passions. Like a good hunter, he had the focus to lie in wait for as long as it took to catch whatever he was hunting. But if he wanted to eat then and there and nobody could present him with a logical reason why he shouldn't—then screw them and damn the consequences. The woman standing in front of him would rather spend the day in an office, talking with politicians about some theoretical land issue, instead of riding the highways with him, dodging bugs and responsibilities. That would take him a while to figure out.

"Okay," he said. "I respect that. Another time, then. I just thought it would be nice to spend some more time together. I guess you could say I've sort of become hooked. And it's such a beautiful day, Maggie. I'm sorry. However, I still have a hankering for some tom yum goong. With lots of shrimp. Another new favourite discovery of mine. Have fun at your meeting." Clearly unhappy, he pivoted his bike around, almost hitting Maggie's knee.

"John . . ."

It was too late, for John had put his helmet on and had throttled open his Indian. The only response Maggie got was gasoline exhaust farted in her direction as the bike pulled out of the parking lot.

A pretty immature response, thought Maggie. She too was conflicted. She was puzzled at his oddly emotional response, but also regretful that she'd disappointed him. Though, she couldn't help thinking that if he acted like this all the time, maybe it was a good thing she was learning it now. She was already raising one moody child; she didn't need another. Maybe Wayne was right, she thought to herself jokingly. John was indeed acting like a petulant, self-obsessed man-child, like Nanabush in many of the legends she'd heard growing up.

Still faced with the dilemma of lunch, Maggie decided to go home and open up a big can of soup for Virgil and herself. It might not be tom yum goong, in fact she remembered only having a can of chicken-noodle in the cupboard, but at least she wouldn't have to deal with all the other people hanging out at Betty Lou's Take-Out. And screw the people in the window still watching her.

Without looking back, Maggie jumped into her aging car and drove home.

John Tanner, or Richardson, or Prestor, or Matus or whoever he was at the moment had a plan—or at least the beginnings of one. He had wanted to share it with Maggie, even enlist her aid in putting the plan into effect, because nothing bonds a couple like intrigue and mischief. But alas, she had other plans: plans that didn't include him, plans in fact that openly excluded him. Briefly, the man debated pulling up stakes and saying goodbye to Lillian's daughter and Otter Lake in general. It was a big country with lots of other adventures out there. But one thing his years of existence had taught him was patience. When necessary, he had patience born of the very land. And he had promises to keep.

And now, at least, he had a direction. A road map of sorts to follow—one that would give the lovely Maggie what she wanted, and cement his place in her heart . . . for however long he felt it necessary. He would just have to do it alone. He'd done so much alone in his life; this would be no different. So as quickly as the disappointment had encased him, it fell away as he roared down the highway, his Indian Chief at full throttle, announcing to other denizens of the road that he had a purpose and they should get out of his way. He hadn't smiled with this much purpose in a long time. He would show them, especially Maggie, how smart and useful he could be, whether they wanted to know or not. Times may have changed but he hadn't. The fight in the restaurant this morning had proved it. No matter where you are, or when, jerks like Dan always popped up to disprove Darwin's theory. There was an overabundance of them in the general population, more than willing to annoy you. They came in all cultures and races.

Luckily, the Creator had also seen fit to populate the world with the likes of that pretty young girl Dakota. Such girls helped prove that whoever does watch over existence in whatever form, under whatever name, knows about the concept of yin and yang, complementary opposites. You must have the sweet with the sour. The other night, he had seen the glint of the moon coming off her binoculars, and knew somebody was watching. For how long, he wasn't sure, and what they saw he didn't quite know. He was just lucky it was only her. She fairly gushed when John woke her, and he immediately thought he should keep her as a friend. You can never have too many friends when you're on a plan, and she might come in handy someday. Besides, the man knew she was a friend of Virgil's, and maintaining a relationship with her just might annoy the boy. Again, a win-win situation.

The wheels beneath him ate up kilometre after kilometre. He had a lot to do, and he wanted to do it as quickly as possible. He had both a plan and a purpose, which made him doubly dangerous. The plan had many levels; his main purpose, solving the lovely Maggie's dilemma regarding the land. Step one was a visit to the museum. Plan and purpose are good but so is flexibility, he believed. He had suffered a minor defeat today, with Maggie and lunch, and he was eager to avoid all such possible defeats happening in the future. So, he needed a moral boost. Last night had shown him he was back in fine form. That was good. He could use that. There were some old scores to settle.

That was even better. And he had all afternoon to do it because the museum didn't close 'til eight. If he hurried, and if traffic and the dry-cleaning gods were with him, he could get everything accomplished.

John pointed his motorcycle south, in the direction of the big city. He just hoped nothing would get in his way.

Two and a half hours later, John was standing in front of a certain big-city dry cleaner in a rundown part of town. Over his left shoulder was a window to a room in which an old Indian drunk had once lived. He didn't turn around. He didn't look at it. That was yesterday. This was today. Today offered better options than yesterday had.

Inside the store, more than likely, was the address of a certain Native woman he was determined to find. But first, how? It proved to be surprisingly easy. At the back of the building was a large Dumpster, conveniently half full of flammable objects. Some gasoline from his motorcycle, a match and he'd managed to start a good-sized but safely insulated blaze.

"Hey, buddy," said John, out of breath from racing around the block and in through the front door, to the Asian gentleman manning the counter. "I think something out back of your store is on fire." He saw a dusty fire extinguisher nestled near the cash. Even better. "Take your fire extinguisher, see if you can put it out. I'll call the fire department."

"Fire? Fire?" the man screamed, doing exactly what the Good Samaritan had suggested, leaving John alone in the front office. Quickly, John grabbed all the receipts, which listed names, phone numbers and addresses, from the ledge beneath the cash register and raced out the door. As he left, he could hear the man out back swearing in some foreign language, accompanied by the hissing of the extinguisher. A minute later, John was gone.

In a nearby park, the man went through the pink receipts, hoping against all odds he would find something. Admittedly, he didn't know the woman's name, and today many Native families across the country had adopted English names, and also French, Scottish, Irish and a host of others from across the world. The chances of her being one of the minority who still had a readily identifiable Aboriginal name were slim, if not non-existent. But most of his life had been built on slim chances. Why should this be any different?

Angela Metawabin ... sounds Cree, he thought, examining the pink sheet and the list of clothes she'd dropped off. Definitely she'd been dressed like a professional woman. Could be the same person. With any luck, it was. John decided to find out. Looking up the address, he threw all the others to the wind, then put this one with Angela's name in his pocket. He was his old self again. This almost felt like he was tracking deer or moose.

Fourteen city blocks later, he found her. Parking his vehicle, he surveyed the territory. It was a house, a very nice two-storey house. The large dreamcatcher in the window, and the one hanging from the rear-view mirror of the car in the driveway gave Angela Metawabin away. Inside, he discovered by peeking, the car was a mess. She may dress sophisticated, but her Kia Spectra indicated she was a very messy young lady. The area behind the passenger seat was filled with empty coffee cups and plastic water bottles, where the driver had tossed them. The front passenger seat had about a half-a-foot-high pile of papers and files that showed signs of having slid back and forth. This indicated nobody usually sat there. So she was probably single. Signs kept looking better and better.

Time was ticking by. It was now or never. He pressed the doorbell and heard the muffled chimes announce his presence. The door opened and the very attractive Ms. Metawabin stood before him. It was indeed the same woman. He smiled.

"Yes?" she said.

She worked from home. John could see a small office in the corner of the living room.

John cleared his throat. "Hi, my name's John Savage. You don't know me but . . ."

Two hours later he was back on the road, heading north. Mission accomplished. Using every fibre of charm and eloquence all his years of experience had given him, he had swept the young Cree woman off her feet. Literally. He had amazed even himself. Of course the blond hair and hazel eyes had helped. Native people were suckers for that. There was a tiny corner of his conscience that felt bad for sneaking out while she was in the washroom, but why hang around for long goodbyes? So, after quickly making himself a sandwich—unfortunately Angela seemed to be a vegetarian but there was nothing he could do about that—John quietly closed the door behind him and left.

He'd enacted his revenge, and had had his morale boost. Now he had things to do. It would get dark soon and he was already running behind schedule.

Back to the plan.

TWENTY

Wayne was in a funk, a deep one in fact. So was Virgil. They were sitting side by side, in two lawn chairs, in the Second backyard, shaded by a large flowered patio umbrella. Between them was a small garden table on which sat two half-empty glasses of iced tea. Deep funks don't have to be uncomfortable ones.

It had been a long hard day for both. On top of the conversation with Dakota being so unsettling, a twenty-minute meeting with Ms. Weatherford had resulted in the threat of Virgil having to repeat a year of school. If he hated going to class in the grade he was in, it would be a dozen times worse if he had to be in the same grade two years in a row, surrounded by all those sucky thirteen-year-olds. And all his friends would be bussed off the Reserve to begin their first year of high school. Virgil had truly painted himself into a corner.

How does one get oneself out of a huge corner? One takes a huge friggin' leap.

"Ms. Weatherford, is there anything I can do so I won't fail this year?"

"Like what?" The glasses on her nose had slid down to near the tip.

"I don't know. What are my options? My mother, the chief, she always tells me there are options." In reality, she never had but

Virgil felt in times like this it never hurt to casually mention the fact his mother was indeed the chief.

"Yes, I already talked to your mother, the chief. She knows the situation. I'm sure Chief Second will want to have a chat with you herself when you both get home."

So much for that. "Ms. Weatherford, I really don't want to fail. It might scar me for life. Both you and I don't want that. There's gotta be a way we can meet somewhere in the middle. So I missed a few classes. People in jail get diplomas and degrees all the time, having done a lot worse things."

Virgil's teacher looked thoughtful as she assessed the young man's argument. He was indeed a bright boy, he just needed to focus his energy. Maybe she'd give him something to focus on. That had often worked in the past.

"Very well. I have a proposition for you, Mr. Second."

The way she smiled was not exactly reassuring to him.

Wayne's day was not all strawberries and cream either. First thing was to deal with the blisters on his feet from all the walking he and his nephew had done the night before. Second, he wanted to keep tabs on John, so he made the pilgrimage to Sammy's house. You can never have too much information about an adversary, especially one as unusual as this one. Since it was daylight, he took a small shortcut, trimming about ten minutes off the trip. Once there, however, he was annoyed to see that the motorcycle was gone and all was quiet.

On his way home along the shortcut, he bumped into Sammy, wandering the trees. It was difficult to say who was more surprised at their sudden woody meeting but it was Sammy who shook his head, dismissively. As he passed Wayne, he could hear the old man mumbling to himself in his peculiarly accented

Anishnawbe, something about what fools mortals are. Then, without turning around he yelled to the young man to get out of the woods or he'd be chased by a bear. Wayne thanked him respectfully, as was the Anishnawbe custom toward Elders, then continued along the path. The thought of how close his mother had come to ending up like Sammy always sent a shiver down Wayne's spine.

Halfway home, Wayne bumped into an old classmate near a construction site, a big guy named Dan. They'd been best buds all through grades nine and ten, before their differing tastes led them in different directions. It had been a few years since they'd last had a conversation.

"Hey, Dan, I heard you were in jail?"

"Nah, not for a while. I thought you were living across the lake on Western Island."

"Yeah, still am. Just running some errands. Hey, what happened to your cheek?"

"Some jerk sucker-punched me, right into my eggs."

"Sorry to hear that. Well, take care."

"Thanks, you too."

And Wayne continued walking, all the time wondering about destiny. Dan, who had once had an unnatural ability to mimic the accents of people on every Reserve in a six-hour radius, and could unerringly imitate all the characters on *Star Trek: The Next Generation*, now had arms covered with tattoos and worked on a construction site. He himself was no better, concluded Wayne. I live by myself on an island, working on something nobody cares about, chasing after a mythical man, on the outs with my family, when all I really wanted was to sing with AC/DC. Ah, he thought wistfully, the dreams of adolescents, and the realities of adults.

It was just after lunch when Wayne approached the Band Office. He dreaded what he was about to do, but it needed to be done. And he needed to do it. Marching past the receptionist, he knocked on Maggie's door and opened it.

"Yes?" came the answer, then Maggie saw her brother. This could be good or bad, she thought.

"Maggie, I need to talk to you." He entered and closed the door behind him.

During the next half hour, he became the little brother and Maggie the older sister, a relationship that had been very spottily embraced over the years. He apologized and grovelled, saying that much of his silliness was a reaction to Lillian's death. He didn't want to lose his favourite sister.

At first, Maggie didn't know how to react. This was not the brother Wayne she knew. But gradually, she softened, and a few minutes later they hugged, tears in their eyes.

"Can I stay a little longer? Please?" Wayne asked. "At your place. I don't want to go yet."

"Of course," his big sister answered. "But none of that silly talk. Okay?"

"Okay." For the second time, they hugged. Most of what Wayne had said to his sister had been the truth, but only he and Virgil truly knew the score. They had only each other to talk this out with. So that last promise had been a little tarnished. Still, they were brother and sister again, and they were speaking, and that was always a good thing.

So now Virgil and Wayne sat, late into the afternoon, taking stock of their lives.

"What should we do now?" the boy asked.

"About John? Your mother doesn't believe it. That's a problem.

She's so stuck in the White man's world, this whole possibility is inconceivable. Momma, your grandmother, always told me magic was possible."

"I didn't believe you either, until I saw him do those things. I'm still not so sure. Hey . . . maybe we should show her?" Virgil was excited about the idea.

Wayne, however, wasn't. "Right, make her wait in the bushes until he decides to dance under the moon? Or maybe we'll be lucky enough to catch him arguing with the raccoons again. I can't see her willingly doing that. We just lucked out. I doubt he will be that accommodating again."

"So what now?"

"I don't know" was his only response.

They watched a butterfly flutter by.

"Uncle Wayne?"

"Yeah?"

Virgil seemed to choose his words carefully before speaking. "If he does exist, I mean Nanabush, if it is him, doesn't that kinda open the door for a lot of questions? Scary ones."

"What kind of questions?" asked Wayne as he sipped his iced tea, another one of the three great inventions of White people. "Well, if Nanabush does actually exist, who else from stories and legends might also exist? I mean, you know that whole argument about, is there life on other planets? There's like a billion other planets out there in this galaxy alone, and it would seem kind of silly to think that if life . . . like us Ojibways . . . popped up here on Earth, that they or other similar kinds of beings couldn't pop up somewhere out there. I was told that rarely do things happen just once."

"Where are you going with this, Virgil?"

His iced tea forgotten, Virgil was lost in the possibilities of his argument. "Well, if he really is Nanabush . . . what if there really is a Santa Claus? Or a Tooth Fairy. Or Dracula. Or the Bogeyman. Or the Devil. Or . . ."

"Virgil, I get your point. You're right. That is one scary question."

"I mean, I doubt if our people were the only ones to have a magical being. It wasn't guaranteed in any treaty or anything, I don't think."

Now, that truly formidable thought hadn't entered Wayne's mind. He had been too nearsighted. But his nephew was right. To borrow another culture's metaphor, Nanabush's possible existence did open a veritable Pandora's Box of possibilities. His mind became flooded with a host of other exotic Anishnawbe tales told to him by his mother and grandparents, all peopled by a bizarre assortment of less-than-charitable characters, such as the Wendigo and the Elbow Sisters to name just two. Immediately the world became a much more interesting place, and, at the same time, a substantially less safe one.

"Virgil," Wayne said, draining the last of the iced tea, "I realize you're my nephew and that I love you as such, but sometimes . . . sometimes, I really hate you."

"Is that your plan? Hating me?"

"No, but it's as good a beginning as any. Virgil, this is a complicated issue for sure, and I am contemplating a more direct approach with our friend. But for the moment, if you'll excuse me, I must use the bathroom for it is definitely one of the three greatest inventions of White people. I'll get us some more iced tea too." Grabbing both cups, Wayne disappeared into the house.

Things in Virgil's life seemed to be careening out of control. His mother's present ill nature, his less-than-stellar academic situation (it was official, Virgil really hated Ms. Weatherford), Maggie's growing infatuation with the man called John, as well as Dakota's, added to the sense of chaos that permeated his mind. That wasn't even factoring in the whole land issue that had everybody on tenterhooks to begin with, not that he really understood it. Adults were very complicated, Virgil thought. He couldn't quite comprehend why so many of his cousins were in such a hurry to grow up and achieve that level of complication.

Virgil just wanted this man John out of his and his mother's life, and for things to get back to what could pass for normal. He didn't think that was too much to ask. And all that stood in its way was him, a thirteen-year-old boy, and his unusual uncle Wayne. He wished he knew what Wayne planned to do.

The museum was immense and well funded for such an average-sized town. Just recently a special archaeology exhibit had opened in the left wing, showcasing burial rights down through the ages, encompassing several thousand years of different civilizations. There were Egyptian sarcophagi, Incan mummies, bones from the catacombs of Rome, Jewish ossuaries and a dozen other unique examples of ways to dispose of human bodies. It was one of the finest collections of remains in that part of the province. Evidently, thought John, all those poor people who thought their spirits and bodies would be crossing over into the next world, Heaven, Paradise, the hereafter, would never have surmised that the Happy Hunting grounds, eternity, Nirvana, Kingdom Come, was a county museum in an economically depressed Ontario city. The Creator surely did have a sense of humour.

John had raced back from the city, aware that his little detour was placing his big plan in jeopardy. He needed to see the museum from the inside, and he needed time to coordinate things from the inside. So he sped along on his Indian Chief, weaving in and out of traffic. Lucky for him, the police were busy elsewhere, and he arrived back at the museum just in time for a quick tour of the building.

John had walked from exhibit to exhibit, reading, looking, assessing and plotting. He was finding his afternoon very informative. In fact it was far more than he had expected. He had planned to be in and out of the building quickly after surveying the layout. But the exhibit and what it had to offer had generated in him a legitimate interest, and he took his time reading all the little display cards. John was nothing if not curious.

The first exhibit he came to was about local history. Life in the mid-1800s. Lots of plows, spinning wheels and butter churns. Nothing about Native people in that time period. Evidently they didn't exist until the Department of Indian Affairs was created after Confederation. John wondered how those poor White women could get anything done wearing all those heavy cotton dresses. He could never understand why Native women so readily switched over to them. Still, it brought back memories.

It took an hour and a half for him to make his way through all the exhibits. As was often the case, John decided to see where his curiosity would take him today. He soon found himself in a different exhibit, this one showcasing canoes from across Canada, boats of varying lengths and designs. Some of which he recognized. Like a kid in a candy store, John studied each and every boat, sometimes making comments to others around him.

"Look at that stitching! That's not Algonquin! That's Odawa. Who curated this exhibit anyway? And look at the shade of the pitch on that boat, what does the label say? Woodland Cree! Like hell, the colour's too dark. I've seen that colour pitch on canoes myself. That is one hundred percent Saulteaux. In fact, look at that distinctive stitching design. I think I knew that guy!" A lady with her ten-year-old daughter pointed out that the canoe was supposedly one hundred and fifty years old. John just shrugged, saying, "Well, he did say he built his canoes to last!"

Next he came to the more elaborate West Coast canoes, and he became even more vocal. It was "Haida this" and "Bella Coola that!" There was something wrong, according to him, with practically every single canoe or the information posted. "Look at the dorsal fin on that killer whale, no self-respecting Salish would draw it that way! They'd run him out of the village. Jesus, that's a Tlingit dorsal fin if ever there was a Tlingit born! I want to talk to the guy who runs things around here!"

Eventually security was called, and even though John protested and ranted about his expertise on the subject of canoe recognition and on the rampant mistakes being perpetrated on the public, the museum staff were not inclined to believe him. He was asked to leave the building and never return, taking his so-called expertise with him.

John stood on the front steps of the building, yelling at the doors closing behind him. "You don't educate. You mis-educate! If I had the time . . . !" By now, however, nobody was listening, the doors were closed and he was alone on the steps. Though still agitated, he decided he'd made his point, and crossed the street to a bench, where he patiently sat and waited for the building to close.

As he sat there quietly fuming, an errant memory, stimu-
lated by the day's adventures, tap-danced across his frontal cor-
tex. Somewhere, a long time ago, he dimly recalled telling
somebody, an English collector of some sort, that this genuine
authentic Naskapi canoe was in fact Abanaki, and he should
buy it and take it back with him to Europe to impress all his
friends. In fact, now that he took the time to concentrate on the
issue, he realized that he may have done that quite frequently
over time. With a lot of canoes, and a lot of academics, among
other things. Maybe some of the mistakes in that building across
the street were his fault.

"Well, fuck them if they can't take a joke," he said aloud, to
nobody in particular.

Inside the museum, in the security logbook, a name was written. It was the last name entered on the page. It was the name
given to the security guards by a man who had caused a small
disturbance in one of the galleries and had been ejected. The
guards had laughed as they wrote it down: *John Smith.*

"Uncle Wayne, what exactly do you do over on your island?"
Virgil had been wanting to ask this question for a while now.
He knew how testy his uncle could be, but there seemed to be
no better time than now. The sun was setting, Maggie was
inside whipping up some mashed potatoes, corn and Shake 'n
Bake pork chops. The boy sat in a lawn chair, finishing his second glass of iced tea, watching his uncle warm up. But warm
up for what? Whatever it was, it required him to be barefoot,
and shirtless.

"Train."

"I know. You told me that, but train for what?"

"Not for what. For whom. I train for myself. Push myself. Develop myself. Practise for myself. It's a personal, self-motivated, some unenlightened people might say narcissistic, way of life— to see what I can do, and how good I can get at doing it. I do it to honour our culture. Some people think everything we are is rooted in the past. It is, partially. But like evolution tells us, if things don't develop, change, evolve, adapt, they die. I believe that. So I and what I do are part of that evolution. My heart and spirit are with our grandfathers and grandmothers, but my hands and feet are in the now. I do what I do to honour our ancestors, knowing that if they lived today they would probably be doing the same thing I am. I may never use what I've developed, but it's better to have it and not need it, than to need it and not have it."

Virgil wasn't quite sure what *narcissistic* was. Wayne had only a basic understanding of what it meant, based on some parting comments made to him by his last girlfriend, who didn't share his enthusiasm for the direction he wanted to take his life. "You're crazy!" was the other half of her comment.

Virgil pondered what *narcissistic* might mean as he watched his uncle take a running leap at the side of the brick house and, using only his toes, run up the side of the building, grab the eaves and swing up to the roof, all in less than two seconds. Virgil was impressed.

"That's training?" he asked.

"That's what training can train you for."

"Climbing brick houses?"

"Being prepared for everything. That's what all martial arts teach you."

"I've never heard of a Native martial art."

From high atop the house, Wayne smiled. "You have now."

Maggie's voice boomed from the window directly underneath her brother. "Wayne! Are you on the roof again? Get down before you damage the shingles. I've told you this before. I don't want you doing that stuff around here."

Suppressing a groan, Wayne leaped to a nearby tree, grabbed the strongest limb with his right hand, braced his feet against the trunk, and did a cartwheel in mid-air, landing directly where he had been stretching earlier.

"At least your mother's over being mad at us. You see, Virgil, like most true martial artists, I don't think of it as a way of fighting. I think of it instead as a way of *not* fighting. I have just adapted many of the same principles used in the development of karate and kung fu, and given them an Indigenous flavour. Wild rice instead of white rice. Get it?" Wayne did the splits, tearing up grass with both feet. As his torso hit the ground, in the blink of an eye he thrust the four fingers on each hand deeply into the ground to anchor his body for his next move.

"Did you know, Virgil, that kung fu was based on the movements of animals? A long time ago, these Chinese monks with nothing better to do would watch how animals moved, and they gradually developed these four schools of kung fu. There was the Monkey, the Tiger, the Snake and the Dragon. There were a few other variations, but essentially those four became the basis for some, if not all, Asian martial arts."

Still watching Virgil, he leaned on his anchored hands and lifted his legs into an L-shaped position, then straight up, his muscles tight with exertion. In one supple move with blinding speed—he turned in mid-air so that he was sitting cross-legged in the exact same spot, before the grass from his feet had fallen. Gradually, the grass settled on his head and shoulders.

"It's amazing the things you teach yourself to do when you live alone on an island."

"I guess. Is any of this practical?"

"How practical is a video game? And it's better cardio."

Virgil couldn't argue that point. "So that's what you do all the time? Just hang around your island, learning how to fight people who aren't there?"

"It's a lot easier than fighting people who are there. Come here. I want to show you something."

Virgil got up off his lawn chair and approached his uncle, who by now was standing tall, his toes embedded in the grass. "Take a swing at me," said Wayne.

"You want me to punch you?"

"If you can. Show me what you got."

Instinctively, Virgil crouched into a fighting position and threw a punch. The boy had been in two fights his entire life, and one was with a girl, but if pressed, Virgil was sure he could be dangerous. He'd seen enough Rocky and Rambo movies to know something. But evidently not enough to take on Wayne. By the time his arm was fully extended, his uncle was no longer standing in front of him. Wayne was standing on the side of his now-outstretched arm, and he gently bumped him with his shoulder, knocking him off balance. "Again," Wayne said.

"Okay." A little embarrassed and a lot intrigued, Virgil scrambled to his feet and took another swing.

This was even easier for Wayne, who pivoted, deflecting the punch with his shoulder, at the same time backing into Virgil and knocking him down again. During neither encounter had Wayne used his arms or legs as weapons. Just his upper body.

This time, Virgil stayed on the ground, assessing his uncle in a new light. "Cool. Very cool. But I'm sure I've seen moves like that in a dozen different martial arts movies. What's so Aboriginal about all that?"

Wayne helped his nephew to his feet, nervously looking over his shoulder to make sure his older sister hadn't seen him man-handling her son. "What I just used was called the Marten method, or the Otter Method. Same clan. You see, Virgil, there're only so many ways to punch, kick, knee or elbow. So there is bound to be a certain amount of similarity in movements. As the saying goes, there's no particularly Native way to boil an egg. Where it differs is in its origins, and its execution. Everybody can throw a ball. But not everybody can throw it fast, or with a curve, or very hard."

"Why is it called the Marten method?"

"It's based on the movements of the marten."

It took a moment for this to sink in. "The animal. Just like what those Chinese monks did, except you did it with animals around here. I get it. That's how a marten would move."

"If it was five foot ten, one hundred and sixty pounds. The martin is a very quick animal. Just when you grab it, it's gone. And when you get close, it becomes twice as dangerous. The style is geared toward very close fighting, too close for two sets of arms. Do you understand?"

Virgil nodded. He was developing a whole new respect for his uncle. Everything Wayne was saying kinda made sense. "Why marten?"

"It's one of the seven clans of the Ojibway, the Anishnawbe. It took me a while but I have based a style of fighting on each of the clans: the crane, loon, fish, bear, hoof or deer, bird and, of course, the marten. A unique style of combat completely influenced by the animals themselves, their strengths, abilities, their particular defences and so on. Do you think your uncle is so crazy now?"

That was a question Virgil still wasn't willing to answer just yet. "A fish? A fish-based martial art? I'm sorry, but fish aren't exactly known as powerful or dangerous animals. How do they fight?"

"Ah, a smart-though-naive question, my young nephew," he said, briefly adopting an elderly Chinese accent. "The entire focus of the Fish method is geared toward escape. Toward getting away. To prevent being captured or hurt." Wayne put his jean jacket on and once more stood in front of him. "Okay, let's have some more fun. Grab me."

Rushing in, he grabbed his uncle's arms and started wrestling, but before he had a chance to do anything substantially offensive, Wayne had slipped out of his jacket by bending forward and letting it slide up his body, still in the boy's grip, and somehow had wrapped it around Virgil's arms several times, incapacitating him.

Once more, Virgil was surprised and impressed. "The Fish method," he said, with a trace of awe.

Wayne unwrapped his jacket from around Virgil.

"And all those broken branches on the island? That thing you do by snapping your wrist?" Virgil asked.

"Hoof method. Quick, short movements. Incredibly powerful and effective. Like being hit with a hoof. I also try to incorporate the roles of each clan into their style. For instance, both the Crane and Loon clans are responsible for chieftainship and government. Therefore, their movements have to be respectful, decisive and considerate of both parties. The Marten clan, on the other hand, are hunters, warriors, master strategists in planning the defence of their people, so their actions are more aggressive, thought-out and effective. Like karate and kung fu, it's more defensive than offensive. I call the whole thing Aangwaamzih."

"What does Ang ... aang ... ?"

Wayne shook his head in disappointment. "Kids and their knowledge of Anishnawbe. You should be ashamed of yourself. Aangwaamzih. It means 'watching out for yourself.' That's what all martial arts pretty much try to teach you. Aangwaamzih included."

They both heard the patio door opening and saw Maggie come out onto the deck, drying her hands.

"Okay, boys, hope you worked up an appetite. Dinner's ready."

Wayne sniffed the air. "Ah yes, Shake 'n Bake. One of the three greatest inventions of White people. And I have indeed worked up quite the appetite." Before entering the house, Wayne put his T-shirt back on and cleaned his feet of all grass and dirt. Maggie stepped aside as he entered the house.

"Virgil?"

"Be there in a second, Mom."

Nodding, Maggie returned to her kitchen duties, leaving Virgil alone on the back lawn, wondering about all he had just observed. He looked down and could see where his uncle's feet had ripped up the grass, where his fingers had dug into the hard ground with surprising ease. Under the tree he saw the dislodged bark from Wayne's dismount from the roof.

"Aangwaamzih," he whispered to himself. "Watching out for yourself."

For a little while, all worries about a certain blond man of mysterious origins were no longer at the forefront of his mind.

———

Toward the end of the meal, Wayne was halfway through saying, again, "Ah, Shake 'n Bake, one of the three greatest . . ." before a dishtowel hit him flush in the face. Once he removed it, he found he couldn't tell which of his relatives had tossed it; both had extremely innocent "wasn't me" expressions on their faces. In retaliation, under the table he slipped off his shoes and pinched both mother and child with his toes, making them yelp and scurry away from the table.

"No fair!" yelled Virgil.

"Fairness is a relative concept, especially when it comes to relatives."

After dinner, the dishes were washed and put away, and the television turned on as Wayne indulged a seldom-enjoyed treat. Maggie, however, had other plans for her and Virgil.

"Virgil, my son, let's chat."

Words of such a nature, spoken by a mother he knew was angry with him, were enough to make Virgil's recently descended testicles want to rise back up into his body. He took a seat next to her at the kitchen table.

"Well?" she said.

"Well, what?"

"You know what. Skipping school yesterday? Canoeing alone across the lake. Do you know how dangerous that is? Ms. Weatherford and I had a very long chat today."

"It's okay, Mom, really it is. Ms. Weatherford and I worked it out. No problem."

"No problem that you might be failing? I think that's a problem."

Virgil, eager to placate his mother, shook his head vigorously. "Really. I have to do an essay for her. That's all."

Maggie eyed her son with suspicion. "An essay. One essay. That doesn't sound so difficult."

"Mom, it has to be three thousand words. I don't even know if I know three thousand words. That's going to be tough."

"Uh-huh, and what does it have to be on?"

"I don't know. Something to do with being Native. I can pick my topic, but it has to be . . . What was the word she used . . . ? In depth."

"When do you have to have it done?"

"By the end of the school year."

"You do realize that's in three weeks? Less than three weeks. Do you even have any idea what it might be about?"

"No, not yet. But I'm thinking. I really am."

In fact he was. The whole conversation with Wayne had whetted his appetite. Wayne's fancy martial art might just be the thing to get him out of repeating grade eight. But three thousand words . . . he'd have to use a lot of adjectives. "I'll do it, Mom. I promise."

Maggie did not look overly convinced.

TWENTY-ONE

The night was dark, with the moon, just beginning to wane, hidden behind distant trees. In the last hour, out of nowhere, rain clouds had materialized along the opposite horizon. Within half an hour, the storm clouds had swallowed the moon. This was a good thing, because mischief is best done in the dark. In the deeper darkness of a nearby tree, John sat amid the branches, waiting for the city to go to sleep.

He waited as people wound their day down and hurried home for the night. Silently, he watched a group of teenagers walk right under him, talking about an action movie they had just seen. A few minutes later, a couple, still reeking of garlic from an Italian dinner, held hands and planned for the future. At one point a stray dog approached the tree, interested in relieving himself. For no reason in particular, John growled his best wolf growl, sending the dog running and yelping into the nearby park. A little while later, he noticed a police car cruise by, and one of the officers seemed to glance directly into John's eyes, but he was well hidden behind leaves and branches.

Finally, the street was calm. Except for the figure of a man jumping down from the limb of a tree. Purposefully, he crossed the street, ignoring the do not cross sign, and stood in front of the museum. First, he tested the front doors, which, of course, were locked. But he had expected that. Anything else would have been too easy.

Stepping back, he surveyed the whole exterior surface of the museum, his eyes tracing the structure and making note of where everything was. He repeated that with the other three sides, until he knew the building as well as the architect who had designed it. Barely above a whisper, the man said to himself, "Now, to work." And with that, he smiled what some would call a mischievous smile, for he knew something most people didn't. Museums were like icebergs. What you saw was only about ten percent of what existed.

Somewhere in the cavernous vaults of this museum was at least ten times what was on display. That's what he was after, because if he took something that was on display, it would be missed immediately and things could get dicey and potentially screw up his plans. But if he took something that was buried deep in a box, among a hundred other boxes, in some climate-controlled room or from the back of tray #38763-A-88C, it could be days, weeks, months, even years before somebody took inventory and noticed it missing. Yes, he'd thought this all out. It was like old times. In fact, it was like olden times. Once more, he felt he was back in the game.

For a moment, the moon peaked out from between the clouds, as if it were signalling its approval. Then the rain clouds opened up, and rain began to pour, almost as if it were signalling its disapproval. Regardless, the man knew the rain would muffle sounds and wash away evidence. All was good. The elements were with him for sure.

———

Maggie listened to the rain falling. Normally she loved the sound of drops hitting the roof and the trees. It was calming and peaceful. But tonight, she was distressed. Her afternoon encounter with John had left her uneasy. She had been out of the dating scene so long that she hoped and prayed it was just a normal dip in a growing relationship—if that's what this could be called—and that it didn't foreshadow anything more ominous. Add to that the fact her brother was once more sleeping on the couch. Why was he still here? She didn't believe his casual answers, let alone that business about Nanabush. Smartly, they had not said anything about the topic tonight at dinner. Something was up with him and her son. So here she lay, a woman in political power but apparently having absolutely no control over what was going on in her life.

Tomorrow afternoon there was to be a press conference about the official handing over of land. The local MP, MPP, the reeve and a few other local dignitaries were to be there, smiling and placating Native and non-Native people alike about the land issue. Many felt three hundred acres was a lot of taxable land to lose to an Indian Reserve that didn't pay any taxes. More money out of their pocket was the common people-of-pallor consensus. She hated appearing on television, felt she looked too haggard and worn, like a character from a Margaret Laurence novel. But there was no way to get out of it. Thy chief's job will be done.

As a result, she was hoping for a good night's sleep to limit the size of the bags under her eyes. After all, there were bound to be cameras of all sorts. But once more, for the hundredth time, she glanced at the clock on her night table. It read 2:33 a.m., and she wasn't the slightest bit tired.

Idly, she cradled a pillow and wondered if John was over at Sammy's, lying in his bed, listening to the rain like she was. In a

way, it was romantic. But just as she thought that, there was a loud
crash of thunder that shook the house, and made her digital clock
blink out, leaving the room in total blackness. A power failure.
Wonderful. Now, in more ways than one, she was in the dark.
Hopefully, things would be better in the morning.

The loud crashing of the thunder didn't completely wake Sammy
from his usual fitful sleep. As on every other night he tossed and
turned, locked in a bygone era, unable to process or cage the memories. The thunder made things worse. It reminded him of the
sharp crack of a yardstick hitting a desk, then soon afterward
hitting flesh. Each peel of thunder reawakened not-so-dormant
memories and shoved them mercilessly into his mind. And no
amount of bottles and their contents could drive away the demons;
it could merely mute them for short periods of time.

He would sweat and mumble, his fingers gripping the sheets,
and he would roll over, as if trying to escape something. But he
never could. Occasionally, the word "gawiin" would escape his
mouth, "no" in Anishnawbe. Every night it was the same, sometimes a little better or a little worse. Sammy was a true survivor,
in every sense of the word.

For over a hundred years, scientists and science-fiction writers all over the world had debated the possibility of time travel,
the ability to instantly place oneself in a different decade or
century. All they had to do was come to this small house, located
along a quiet country road, on an obscure Native Reserve in
Ontario, and they would find evidence it was possible. It existed
in the mind of a seventy-three-year-old man who, every night,
was once again barely seven, or twelve, or fifteen, trying to

survive in a place that had once been several hundred kilometres away and a long time ago, but now was as close as his pillow. He cried now as he had cried then.

Time travel was not a thing of wonder, of amazement and opportunity. It was an inescapable and soul-wrenching reality: a curse. Luckily, every morning when he woke up, it was rare that he'd remember the images of the preceding night. The only evidence of his time travel were the sweat-soaked sheets, occasionally wet with urine, and his sore gums from grinding non-existent teeth. For decades those nights had caused him to grind his teeth, until there was little left and they had to be removed.

Tonight, as the thunder and lightning tore across the spring skies, Sammy Aandeg mumbled in his sleep, "Jinibaayaan. Kanamaa ndaabiwaajigeh. Enh, kaawiin goyaksenoon sa iwh." Loosely in English, it went something like "To sleep: perchance to dream: ay, there's the rub," but there was nothing lost in the translation.

It was done.

All things considered, it had gone smoothly enough. No alarms had gone off, no security guards had noticed him. It has been said that in a different time and different place, John was so stealthy he could dye the quills on the back of a porcupine without the animal even knowing. On both sides of John Tanner's Indian Chief, above the rear wheel, his saddlebags were laden with treasure of an unusual sort. Beneath his visor, he was smiling. Even the tenacity of the spring storm did little to dampen his mood. Somewhere high above him hot and cold air masses were fighting it out. Ions raced through the atmosphere. Rain poured down on the highway ahead of him.

He throttled back on the gas, aware that the rain was impairing his vision and the water-soaked pavement might not afford his motorcycle the texture necessary to remain upright at an accelerated speed. Now, barely doing sixty kilometres an hour, he took the time to watch the lightning stretch across the morose sky. As with Sammy, the volatile elements brought back distant memories for John. Anishnawbe legends told of ancient and immense thunderbirds, their actions responsible for the kind of storm he currently found himself driving through.

The thunderbirds, like dinosaurs, were now creatures of the past: lost long ago, with the coming of disease and famine brought by hairy strangers. Except, in today's world dinosaurs were celebrated by palaeontologists and thunderbirds by cultural anthropologists. But John still remembered them, those magnificent creatures. Some had been his friends, others he'd battled, others he'd avoided due to personal disagreements.

They, like the man on the motorcycle, had been born in an age when gods, monsters, humans and animals ate at the same table. Now man ate alone, while animals begged for scraps. The others were unable to survive in the new times and had disappeared into the folds of time. Who knew gods and monsters could and did fall victim to evolution?

Again thunder boomed and lightning made the sky crackle. In the shadow of a particularly dark and large cloud, for just a moment, John could almost see the outline of a thunderbird against the sky. Then, just as quickly, it was gone. Nostalgia knotted in his belly.

As he passed the WELCOME TO OTTER LAKE sign, John tried to pop a wheelie in the community's honour. Because of the nature of Indian motorcycles—being a very heavy machine low to the ground with high gearing—popping a wheelie was notoriously difficult. For John, the impossible was always in reach, but not today.

He increased his speed above eighty kilometres an hour. He didn't want to miss all the fun, and there was still a lot to do.

Fifteen minutes later, the rain was still falling, this time on the community graveyard. Tiny rivulets of water ran down the elevated mound of dirt that was Lillian Benojee's final resting place. The bare earth had barely settled from the funeral a week ago. Surrounding her was a plethora of headstones, detailing the life and death in this community. Names like Aandeg, Kakina, Stone, Noah, Pierce, Hunter and Kokoko crowded the gently sloped field.

The wind picked up, sending the rain slashing diagonally. Nearby, a tree rustled and bent in the wind, losing a small portion of leaves and a fair-sized branch. A rabbit, caught in the maelstrom, ran through the graveyard's cut grass, desperately seeking shelter of some sort from the wind, rain and lightning that were playing havoc.

Barely heard above the commotion, a motorcycle pulled up. The light at the front of the machine went dark, and the kickstand came down. The man slid down into the ditch that ran between the road and the graveyard. Climbing up the far side, he reached out his right gloved hand, and then his left, and grabbed the wire fence. Then he stood there, helmet still on, not moving. The rain pelted him, and leaves, twigs and unfortunate insects eager to find shelter whizzed by or into him.

The skies continued to open up and it seemed like the very forces of nature were fighting atop this tiny plot of land. A scant ten metres away a bolt of lightning hit a hydro pole, showering the area in sparks that were quickly doused by the torrent of rain. Wires fell, and more sparks erupted. The storm was building.

At one point, a small chickadee, buffeted by the storm, fell to the ground, stunned. At first the man just looked at the small, still bird, lying motionless in the grass. The man knew that death was as much a part of nature as the storm he was witnessing. The potential death of such a tiny creature meant little in the overall scheme of the world. This miniature creature would die and it would not be missed. For reasons of his own, the man thought maybe this was a little unfair. Life was always preferable to an unnecessary death. He too was worried about not being missed, should he be forced to move on.

After opening the zipper on his jacket a few inches, he gently picked up the minuscule bird in his gloved hand and placed him inside his jacket, where it was warm and dry. He zipped the jacket shut again, as the storm around him raged. Once more he gripped the fence. This storm was as good as any he'd seen in his many years. It was the earth reminding its citizens it was still the boss in the end.

John remembered the story of it raining for forty days and forty nights, and wondered if the Ark had started off in Vancouver. Forty days of rain was nothing out in B.C. And that other guy, Jesus, who had been born and raised in the desert, John was mystified by his appeal here. To truly understand how Turtle Island and its people thought and lived, John thought, you had to know the emotions of its land. The snowstorms of the Arctic, the wind of the Prairies, the humid summers of southern Ontario were all reflected in the people. Desert was desert and there wasn't much of it in Canada, other then two small patches in lower British

Columbia and the Alberta Badlands. And of course, he'd left his mark in all three.

Gradually, as dawn approached, the storm weakened. The lightning flashed less and less frequently, and the thunder crashed less. The wind died down, and the trees stopped protesting. Eventually, even the rain had other places to go, and peace returned to the land, and especially this land of internment. The ground smelled of renewal. Rain was life, even amid death.

"For you," said the man quietly. "That was for you, Lillian."

Once all was quiet, the figure by the fence loosened his grip on the wire and undid his leather jacket. The chickadee stuck his head out, aware the troubles had passed. Without even a thank-you, it flew off and disappeared into the night. The man shook his head, marvelling at some animals' rudeness. Once more he crossed through the ditch and up to his waiting bike. One long-ago promise to Lillian had been fulfilled. He had brought her the thunderstorm, finally. Off in the distance, fighting against the dark rain clouds, the first hint of dawn could be seen peeking up from the horizon in the east. It was time to go.

John had still much to do, and little time to do it. Full dawn would be in a few hours and he wanted to be done by then. The rain had softened the ground, perfect for what he must do. Afterward, he would bring a little of the rain back to wash away any evidence. Granted, he would get wet and dirty by the end of it. But leather is so easy to clean, and he'd survived a lot worse. Besides, Maggie was definitely worth it.

He started his motorcycle and headed for the controversial three hundred acres, his headlight illuminating the way.

TWENTY-TWO

The morning air had the clean feel to it that only comes after a night of rain. Wayne, Virgil and Maggie were having breakfast. The clinking of spoon against cereal bowl, the sipping of coffee and orange juice and the shifting in wooden chairs were all that was heard. All three were lost in thought, though coincidentally, their thoughts all centred on the same thing, or more correctly, the same man. Even though John wasn't there, he was.

"Did you hear the storm last night?" garbled Wayne, his mouth full of cereal.

Virgil's mouth was equally packed with cereal, but he nodded and said, "I think it went over twice."

Maggie, who was anxious to get John and his abs out of her head, decided to start a real conversation. "Hey, Virgil, want to come to the press conference with me? There's going to be a bunch of TV cameras and reporters and fancy-dressed people. You might find it fun."

"I've been to your press conferences before. They're boring. I think I'll just hang with Uncle Wayne." Virgil drained the last of his milk from his bowl. In truth, he'd barely tasted the Shreddies because he'd been so distracted thinking about John and his motorcycle.

Wayne barely heard the mother–son conversation, because in his mind he was revisiting the encounter between John and the raccoons. As a nervous habit, but one conducive to his constant training, Wayne was clenching and unclenching his toes under the table.

"Oh, really. And just what does Uncle Wayne have planned for today?"

Realizing he had been plunged unwillingly into the table discussion, Wayne tried to formulate a constructive and believable lie. "Nothing really. Just hanging out. Maybe some visiting. Supplies, that kind of thing." He added a smile for good effect.

Maggie surveyed the two, not quite believing the supposed innocence of the men sitting around the table. "Are you two up to something?"

Both males looked at each other with a passable expression of confusion. Then, in unison, they shook their heads.

"Right. Well, Wayne, you are welcome here as long as you like and don't get me wrong about my next question but how long do you plan to stay? I have to go grocery shopping at some point and I need to know how many people to buy for."

Spreading jam on the last piece of toast on his plate, Wayne thought for a moment. "No, I understand. Well, if all goes well, maybe tomorrow I'll head back to the island."

"If what goes well?" Now Maggie *knew* he was up to something.

"I . . . I have some business to attend to."

While Wayne talked, Virgil found his glass of orange juice suddenly very interesting.

"Wayne, you have no business to speak of. That I know about!"

"I might! I might have business," responded an increasingly irate Wayne. "You don't know! You don't know me at all."

"Okay, like what business? Teaching a course on how to be a hermit?"

"You never believed in me! You never did. Mom did, but you . . ."

"Mom had to believe in you. You were the youngest, the baby. It comes with being a mother. Geez, Wayne, we all worry about you, over on that stupid island, doing whatever it is you do." Maggie's big-sister complex was never far below the surface.

"You know what I do over there. I've told you lots of times. You just don't care."

"Wayne, it's not that we don't care, in fact, we do care. It's just that it's . . . kinda silly. A Native martial art . . . really? You might as well be writing a Native opera or something. That's all I'm saying."

"Well, don't worry about me. I am perfectly able to look after myself. Better than you!"

Virgil drained the last of his suddenly interesting orange juice and looked across the table for something equally distracting. He tried to force the ongoing argument from his mind.

"Yeah, right, you and your precious Indian martial art. My brother, the monk. I mean really, Wayne, I think you need a girlfriend. I know that might interfere with being a monk and all that, but . . ."

"I am not a monk. And I will not talk to my big sister about getting a girlfriend. And you should talk, what with you being a motorcycle mama!" Wayne screamed, regretting the words immediately after they left his mouth.

Virgil winced. The subject matter of the fight was getting uncomfortably close to the issues that they were all trying to avoid.

Maggie's eyes narrowed. "What are you talking about?"

"You know what I'm talking about," replied a sullen Wayne.

"John. You're talking about John, aren't you?"

"Maybe."

"Or should I call him Nanabush? The blond, blue-eyed . . . I mean green-eyed . . ." said Maggie.

"I thought they were hazel . . ."

"Shut up, Virgil. What colour his eyes are is irrelevant. Wayne, you have been on that island way too long. The family's been talking . . ."

"Oh God. Not the family!"

" . . . and we think, maybe you should consider moving back to the mainland. At the moment Willie is looking after Mom's house. Since you were her favourite . . ."

"Quit saying that. I was not her favourite."

"Just think about it. Okay?"

Now the whole table became quiet again. Maggie was staring at Wayne, who was trying not to look at her. Virgil sat between them, like Poland between the Soviet Union and Germany. If history was correct, that was not a good place to be. It seemed to Virgil that this was up to him.

"Press conference, huh, Mom? Sure. Actually, that might be fun. What time do you want me to be there?" Tension was still thick in the air and Maggie was defiantly staring at her brother. "Mom? What time do you want me there?"

Almost reluctantly, Maggie turned her attention to her son. "Um, around three-thirty. Do you need a ride from school?"

"No, that's okay. I'll be fine. Three-thirty. I'll be there. Holy! Mom, look at the time. Shouldn't you be at work? I've got to go to school!"

Maggie glanced at the clock and, indeed, she was running late. Barely uttering a word, she grabbed her car keys and exited the house, this time not bothering to glance at her brother.

As the sound of her car faded in the distance, Virgil let out a sizable breath. "That was close."

"I am not wasting my life. What I'm doing is important, damn it. So what if I don't have a girlfriend right now. It's no business of hers. Sisters, man. Sometimes they just make you want to . . ."

"Uncle Wayne, chill. And focus." Once more, Virgil appreciated the fact he was an only child.

Back at Sammy Aandeg's place, John was fast asleep. It had been a long night/early morning and he was exhausted. Normally he slept only a few hours a night, if that. Most nights his sleep was uncomplicated by dreams. He had long ago taught himself not to dream because dreams had a nasty way of interfering in his life. Though he remembered a time when strange and marvellous things had sprung from dreams, and it had been a good thing. But creation had long ago ended. Nowadays, dreams were usually messages from a higher being. Other times, they were directions in life. And still other times, they were warnings about disasters or signs that something needed to be done. None of which interested him anymore, principally because he preferred his own company most of the time, so higher beings be damned. And of course, he hated being told what to do with his life by whatever spirit might tickle his subconscious. Everything else didn't interest him. So, at the end of the day, he had chosen to dream no longer. It suited him well, especially when he saw what it did to people like Sammy. Late into the night John would stay awake, reading what few books the man had, and he would hear Sammy moaning and crying in the other room, a prisoner of his dreams.

Most of the world was unaware of the power of dreams, or simply didn't care. So people just dreamed willy-nilly and damn the consequences. It didn't matter where or what they dreamed, they just dreamed and dreamed and dreamed, confident in the belief that dreams had no meaning. A lot of problems in the world had sprung from the widespread disrespect of dreams and the power within them. Much like being a pharmacologist with a store full of drugs, a little knowledge was usually a good pre-requisite or bad things could happen. Essentially, he felt you should never dream unless you knew what the dreams were, where they came from, what they meant or what they do. But people had forgotten that. John was sure that explained the state of the world. Look at Sammy.

Once upon a time, dreams were the doorway to different spiritual lands and powerful beings. John remembered when parts of the world were created by dreams. That was how the Creator often talked to you, through dreams. That was how you found your guardian spirit. That was how you found answers, and sometimes questions. Nowadays people ignored what their dreams told them. It was like they were driving on a highway and ignoring road signs. Sooner or later this would get them lost or into trouble.

So, most nights, hour after hour, he would sit there in his host's living room, reading while listening to Sammy dream his unfortunate dreams. At least he had books. He'd taken out a library membership under an assumed alias in town so that he could enjoy the simple pastime of reading. Television was fine. In fact John loved the medium. However, at three in the morning, out in the "burbs" of Otter Lake, the quality of programming left a lot to be desired. He neither wanted his soul saved, nor coveted some new fabulous kitchen utensil or cosmetic.

This morning, a copy of *Black Elk Speaks* and the *Kama Sutra* by his bed, John slept, silently and dreamlessly, or so he thought at first. With all that had happened the day and night before, his resolve had weakened and a crack appeared. The normal silence of the night was slowly giving way. As he lay on his bed, his eyes began to move back and forth, slowly at first, but gradually faster. For the first time in a very long time, John dreamed.

John found himself in a wooded glade. He didn't know where he was exactly, though it looked familiar. But then, most wooded glades do. He was barefoot, but dressed in his leather pants and a thin T-shirt. There were no paths or roads into the glade. It was almost as if the woods had been constructed around him.

"Shit, I'm dreaming," he said. He had to be careful, for the world trembled when he dreamed.

"Language, John, language."

The admonishment came from someone standing behind him. Turning, John saw a man in his early thirties, with long hair and dressed in a robe. John recognized him instantly.

"Am I dreaming you or are you dreaming me?" he asked.

The other man smiled. They stared at each other across the glade, then they slowly sauntered up to each other, stopping only a metre apart.

"Well, John, maybe we're both dreaming each other."

"Nice little place you have here. Lots of trees. I thought you preferred deserts and places like that."

"I like to travel. And did you know, I have a cousin named John."

"Good for you. What are you doing here? What am I doing here?"

"Love the eyes. I just wanted to say hello."

"Hello back at you. I take it you heard me in the church?"

"Yes, you sounded . . . angry."

"Do you blame me?"

"I don't blame anybody. You forget, I forgive."

"Well, good for you. Lillian seemed happy with all your forgiveness. I guess I can't fault her for being happy. It worked for her. But I gotta say, you're shorter than I thought."

"Well, you're whiter than I thought."

"Touché. Hey, I read that book about you, your biography."

"My biography?"

"Yeah, that big black book everybody talks about."

"I think it's called the Bible."

"Yeah. Needed an editor. No offence, but it went on forever. And repeated itself. But man, you had a rough life."

"Just the last part of it. And it got better. It had a happy ending. As for you, you're looking . . . better. I heard some things about you, unpleasant things."

"I have you and your friends to thank for that. You're lucky I don't hold a grudge either. I can forgive too. But I've learned my lesson. I'm trying to stay fit these days. Unlike you, I'm going to do my best to avoid dying. For my people, the novelty wore off several generations ago."

"Your people are my people too."

"Tell that to all your priests and ministers who used to look after my people. Tell it to Sammy Aandeg."

"Yeah, I'm getting a lot of that lately. Well, blame free will and all that."

"Well, they had more free will than Sammy did. And yet, you forgive them for all the horrible things they did? I'll always have trouble figuring that one out."

"It's all part of the contract. Everybody deserves a light at the end of the tunnel."

"An escape clause, huh? So, why are you here? I heard you don't come and visit down here much anymore. Otter Lake the site of the Second Coming?"

"Not if you're Jewish. Well, my friend, we both loved Lillian. I didn't think we should be enemies. And many people seem to really want and love you, so I . . ."

"Sorry, but I am not loved like you are. I am not loved, I am beloved. There's a substantial difference."

"There is? And just what is that difference?"

"When you're beloved, you get all the same warm and fuzzies as you do when you're loved, but there's a lot less responsibility involved. I like that kind of difference. It's more bang for your buck."

"And the boy?"

"What about him?"

"Do you actually want him to grow up to be just like you, rootless, subject to every whim and desire, having no structure or roots? Boys, children in general, need to be loved, not just beloved."

"You know, every parent wants their kid to grow up like you, but most of them are actually closer to me. Perfection is boring. Flaws are interesting."

The other man chuckled.

"You've got a nice smile," said John. "You should smile more. Really."

"Thank you, but obviously, John, we're very different people with different priorities. But if a woman like Lillian can hold both of us in her heart, we can't be that far apart."

"Thanks. I appreciate that. You know, there was a time when I really envied that turning-wine-into-water trick. That would have solved a lot of problems for me then."

"And created a whole bunch of new ones too."

"Yes, it would have, no doubt about that." John paused. "How's Lillian?"

"She's fine. In fact, I have a message from her."

"What?"

"Thanks for the thunderstorm."

John laughed out loud, and it felt good. "Thanks for the laugh."

"I do what I can."

This made John think for a second, and an idea came to him. "There is one more thing you can do for me, a small request. A favour. Guy to guy. There is something you have the ability to do that I would love to master. It would sure make travelling a lot easier."

The other man raised an eyebrow. "Oh really? How can I help?"

"I'm glad you asked." John explained, and the other man, whose hair was almost as long as John's and who was just passing through the dream world, listened closely.

In his sleep, John smiled.

In another room of the house, Sammy sat fully awake, mumbling to himself, staring at the door behind which the stranger slept.

Sammy knew the man was not a man, at least not in the dictionary sense of the word. However, he didn't know what to do about that little fact. His social contacts, and his ability for social contact, had long since evaporated. So now he just sat, like he did most mornings, wishing the man would go or be gone.

Almost ten days ago the blond White man had shown up at his door, talking like an old-fashioned Indian (as his generation still called them) should. The grouchier and crazier Sammy tried to appear, the more the man laughed. There was something about the stranger that convinced the old man that he could not turn the man away, though he was the first house guest Sammy had had in decades. He felt about the man's presence the way you'd feel about a relative from some far-off country, or a branch of the family you'd never met, coming for a visit. They belonged there, somehow, and you had no right to deny them accommodation. You may not like it (and Sammy didn't) but it would be wrong to do anything but tolerate them.

And the stranger's eyes . . . Sammy kept forgetting to write down what colour they were. He was sure they changed colour. He knew the man was playing a game with him, and probably everyone else. Sammy grew up and lived in a world of brown eyes, so multi-coloured irises stood out. Last night, before the man left for whatever mischief he had planned, Sammy thought his eye colour had once more shifted. This time they were a peculiar whisky colour. They shone like deep amber.

Every morning, the man rose with a smile and spoke to Sammy in crystal-clear Anishnawbe. In fact, it was the kind spoken by his grandparents—ancient, and largely uninfluenced by the changing world. It was one of the many things about the stranger that unnerved him.

Sammy mumbled some more before rising from his chair. As crazy as people thought he was, there was still a schedule to follow, a pattern to his day. And no crazy White man was going to interfere. Sammy walked out of the house and into the woods. Maybe today he'd find Caliban, the real Caliban—not this guy. If pressed, he'd admit he was more interested in finding Ariel. Sammy had a sneaking suspicion she was probably cuter, and had boobs.

As Crystal Denise Park was fast approaching the Otter Lake First Nations, her assistant, Kait, was busy reading notes in the seat beside her. The 2009 Saturn engine could hardly be heard. Crystal had always had a fondness for Saturns, and had opened a dealership some fourteen years ago. It was phenomenally successful. In fact, it was so successful that she had ended up becoming a local titan of business, which, after much prodding, led her to run for the Liberals in a local by-election. Now she answered to the title Ms. Crystal Park, Member of Parliament for the county involved in the land issue with Otter Lake.

Most of her constituents felt the Native people had enough land already. The country doesn't need a larger Reserve. Crystal didn't care either way, but her job as MP was to piss off as few people as possible. And while the First Nations population in her riding was less than nine percent, the very fact they were First Nations, members of an oppressed minority and victims of systemic abuse at the hands of all three levels of government, gave them a substantially larger profile. Things had to be handled delicately.

Politics, Crystal discovered, was amazingly similar to running a car dealership. It consisted largely of paperwork, marketing, negotiating, budgeting and trying to figure out what people will want next, and how to give it to them. It also made for strange bedfellows. Her best friend ran the office for an NDP colleague, and she was secretly dating a Conservative pollster, though neither would publicly acknowledge it. Like any typical Liberal, Crystal travelled the middle road. She sometimes wondered if they should be called Buddhists instead.

Kait, on the other hand, was a political science graduate from Trent University, trained for little else except being an MP's assistant. Somewhere down the road, the civil service would welcome her with open arms into the soft bed known as federal, provincial or municipal bureaucracy. But right now, she was putting the final touches on Crystal's speech for today. Her pen could be heard scratching on the paper. Kait would have preferred to edit on her laptop, but unfortunately, they didn't have a portable printer in the car, so this clipboard would have to do.

"Kait?"

"Yes, Mom."

"KAIT!"

Kait looked up from her pad, startled. "Sorry. Yes?"

"I've told you not to call me Mom when we're out in public. It's not very professional."

"But, Mom ... I mean, Ms. Park, everybody knows I'm your daughter. It's no secret, and we're alone in the car."

Crystal's hands gripped the wheel tightly. "It doesn't matter. It's a matter of professionalism. We are professionals and we should act accordingly. Have you finished my speech yet?"

"Just about. Don't you think we should have cleared this with Mr. Miles?" Jonathan Miles was the local MPP, and a Tory.

"He can read about it in the papers, like everybody else."

"Geoffrey Pindera is not going to like this either. I mean, the local municipality is going to lose taxable income on over three hundred acres. They've made their point very clear. And a lot of those municipality people vote in federal elections. Mom, I—"

Crystal cut her off. "First of all, it's Ms. Park. Second, there are two Reserves in this seat. This will be a good gesture. Add the influence those two Reserves have provincially and federally, and it cancels out this particular municipality, vote wise. And, rumour has it the Department of Indian and Northern Development could be looking for a new minister. Anything is possible in politics. I like Native people, Kait. My parents used to have a lovely Algonquin lady clean our cottage once a week. I think she was Algonquin. I know she was Native. I've eaten deer. I have that leather vest. I've been to a powwow. I know the score."

Kait was not comforted by her mother's less-than-competent plans for their future. Crystal Park could be remarkably vivacious in front of a camera, and certainly knew how to turn a phrase in a way that made her seem remarkably bright and "with it." But her daughter knew that often the wrapping paper didn't represent the present in the box.

"Yes, Ms. Park." Kait went back to scribbling, wondering to herself how much it would cost her to go for that master's degree.

"Have you seen him lately? Huh, have you?" Dakota seemed awfully excited for somebody stuck at school on a beautiful June day.

"Who?" asked Virgil, annoyed. He'd had to wait fifteen minutes to get access to the school library computer, and he didn't have time for lovesick cousins. He was doing something called research and his next class was due to start.

"John! John Clayton. That's who."

Virgil thought for a moment, jumping from website to website. "Who is John Clayton?"

Rolling her eyes, Dakota feigned annoyance. "You know who. John. Motorcycle John! That guy from Grandma's."

Instantly, the Internet lost its appeal. "He told you his name was Clayton?"

"Yeah, he told me a lot of things. Haven't seen him at all in the last day or two. I was just wondering if you've seen him around, I mean because I know he likes to hang around with your mother and all. Well, have you?"

"No. Why?"

She looked disappointed. "Just wondering. If you see him, tell him I said hello."

"Dakota. If I were you, I'd stay away from him. You don't know what you're getting into here. He's not what he appears to be. Trust me. It's safer."

"What does that mean?"

"Just forget about him. Okay?"

Dakota looked annoyed. "No. He's my friend. He came over to see if I was okay. I don't think he's done that for you."

"Dakota . . ."

"I can like him if I want. You just want to keep him to yourself, don't you? You and your mother."

Virgil almost laughed at that. "Noooo. Not at all. I'd give him away if I could."

"Then why are you being so mean about him? He's a very nice guy. Better than you."

"What's that supposed to mean?"

"Oh, never mind. Just leave me alone, Virgil. I'll find him

myself later." Angrily, she turned away from her cousin and disappeared out the library door.

"Dakota . . ." Virgil started to follow her, but the school bell rang, indicating time to change classes. John's involvement in his life just kept getting deeper and deeper. And what did Dakota mean, "later"? His research forgotten, Virgil grabbed his books and dashed out the door without turning his computer off.

A few minutes later, Gregory Watson, the librarian, noticed the computer running unattended, and thought it better to shut it down. Whoever had been using it, he observed, had been doing some heavy surfing. At the bottom of the screen were five still-active websites. Curious, he opened one after another. They all revolved around traditional Native legends or myths. Specifically, the Trickster or Nanabush stories. Somebody was trying to get an "A" for sure.

TWENTY-THREE

The piercing call of a red-winged blackbird woke John with a start later that morning. He had actually slept several hours, which was unusual for him. And he had dreamed, which was even more unusual. And what a peculiar dream it was. Glancing around, he saw that nothing seemed to have changed—reality looked the same; that was a good sign. He lay there for a few minutes, assessing his nocturnal adventures, both physical and dream ones. That Jesus guy didn't seem so bad after all. Maybe he had misjudged the fellow. When he had the time, he would have to re-evaluate his perceptions, especially since they had each shared some secrets of the trade.

But now the sun was just rising above the crest of the trees. Though still half asleep, he felt good. He hadn't felt this alive in years. Decades, in fact.

Rising to face the coming hours, he left his cloistered cell and wandered out into Sammy's house. As usual the old man was gone on his quest—an Aboriginal Don Quixote, John thought. Stretching and yawning, he went out into the front yard, naked. The morning wind and sun felt good on his exposed skin. All was well in the world. Then, near the shed, he saw his motorcycle. And everything else.

"What the . . ."

John could almost smell it from the front yard, coming from a good ten metres away. He recognized it instantly.

"Those fucking raccoons . . ." he muttered through clenched teeth.

They had been there, marking his beloved and irreplaceable two-wheeled vehicle. His precious 1953 Indian Chief motorcycle had been the latest victim in their war. An innocent bystander for sure. He barely felt the grass underneath his bare feet as he approached. John stood there, staring at the collateral damage. It looked like several dozen of his sworn enemies had contributed to the desecration of the rare machine. It was literally fender deep in shit. And a substantial amount of piss too. The distinctive red of the machine was now darker, as if wet. It was like the raccoons had been saving up for weeks to do this.

It was a childish, cheap and not especially clever or creative attack. But it was effective, and very raccoony. John would have to spend most of the day tending to his precious vehicle, time he wasn't sure he had. And even then, there would probably be a lingering stench for some time. The raccoons had upped the ante, and now it was his turn.

Seriously angry for the first time in a very long while, he turned to face the woods. Somewhere in there he knew all the raccoons were hiding, more than likely laughing at him. His eyes scanned the wall of green, but they were too well hidden, and the woods too deep. He picked up a rock and threw it into the trees, not really expecting to hit anything but still needing to vent. He could hear it bouncing off a tree and falling to the forested floor with a soft thud. Then nothing. Even the red-winged blackbird had stopped its call.

"You fucking bastards!" John yelled at the forest. "You've crossed the line."

It has been said that the land does not forget; it is in fact the memory of all who live on it. In today's world, raccoons live closer to the earth than most people, so their memory too is longer.

"Well?" There was no response. By this time, John's breathing was heavy, induced by insult and rage. "For the last goddamned time, I did not eat your ancestor."

It seemed a long, long time ago, in a forest not that far away, that the man known in Otter Lake as John had been a bad boy. Though a friend and ally to most living creatures, he was known occasionally to . . . not be. He, like all animals of the forest and plains, had a strong need to eat. It had been a cold winter and spring was slow in coming. The man's stomach was empty. He had survived for a while on teas made from the bark and leaves of various trees. But the man craved something more substantial. That's when a certain raccoon, lost in an early spring blizzard, wandered into his camp. From there on, well, witnesses' descriptions varied.

"I didn't! I swear! It just looked that way when that other raccoon caught . . . I mean saw me. I was . . . trying to give it mouth-to-mouth. Yes, it . . . it can be done through the belly sometimes. And then I . . . I listened to its heart. That's how I got some blood on my face, uh . . . when I did that. And I tried to warm it up by the fire. That's why it looked like I was cooking it. Honest! I was trying to save its life. It just looked like I was eating it. All this is over nothing. Why won't you bastards believe me?"

Once the echo of his voice had disappeared, the forest was silent again. "Well? Got anything to say?" Somewhere off in the distance, a coyote howled. "Fine, next time we meet, I'll shit all over you. See how you like it. I've done it before and I'll do it again. Bunch of miserable, furry, flea-infested . . . I hope those raccoon-skin coats come back into fashion." John turned back to his motorcycle, almost shedding a tear at the defilement. High above him, on the branch of a century-old cedar tree, a single, aged raccoon appeared, the one John had seen several days ago on the stump. The creature called to the man far below him. It chattered and mocked and cursed and laughed. John fought an instinct to toss another rock, and instead just listened. The creature continued its verbal assault, and once, pointed at the bike with its little hand. Understanding, the man glanced over his shoulder at the motorcycle, then back up at the lecturing raccoon. Slowly, John's anger left him, and he stood there, naked to the world, nodding. Eventually the raccoon went silent, apparently satisfied with what he had said, and waited for a response.

It came quickly. "Promise?" asked the man.

Once more the bandit creature chattered, nodding its head.

John weighed what the animal had offered. "What does everybody else say?"

Almost at once, a chorus of raccoon chattering could be heard emanating from the trees. John couldn't see them but he could sure hear them. Every raccoon for a day's ride must have gathered today within a stone's throw of Sam's house.

"How do I know I can trust you?"

Again, it was the raccoon on the cedar that responded for the ring-tailed army. A short staccato burst ended the conversation, and then the old raccoon waddled along the branch into the protection of the forest. Gradually, the sounds of the forest returned, and John, realizing the deal he'd just made, took a deep breath.

"Okay, once I do that, it will be over then? We can end this stupid thing?"

There was no answer.

Scratching his crotch, John surveyed the damage inflicted by the raccoons to his metal mount. "I hate raccoons," he said to no one but himself. He'd have to use a lot of water and soap before he could fulfill his end of the agreement. But at least those pesky animals would finally leave him in peace.

He hoped.

In her office, Maggie looked out the window at the lake. In the distance she could see motorboats going by, the odd houseboat and the occasional Jet Ski. When she was younger, Virgil's age, the lake had been so much calmer. You could have canoed across to the other side without being broadsided by a wall of internal combustion–generated waves. The sound of the outboard motors through her open windows kept reminding her of another, similar-sounding two-wheeled vehicle.

The press conference was a little more than two hours away. Maybe things would finally calm down with the announcement that the land would be officially transferred. Otter Lake had a letter in principle saying the federal government would turn it into Reserve land, once all the assessments were completed. After that, who knew what would happen. Maggie was still getting stopped by people kindly "suggesting" things the community should do with that property. The most recent had come from Neil McNeil, who advocated letting the city of Toronto dump its garbage there. Maggie sighed the sigh of a conflicted head official and turned back to her desk.

Her phone rang. It was her cousin Pamela, the receptionist. "Maggie, Crystal Park is here."

"Send her in."

Let the dance begin, thought Maggie. Through this whole escapade, she'd worked closely with the MP, and she acknowledged that Crystal Park could get things done, though she sometimes wondered for whose benefit.

There was a knock at her door and two White women entered. "Crystal, and Kait, welcome." Maggie rose from her desk to shake their hands.

"Are we early?" asked Crystal.

"Nope, right on time. Have a seat. I suppose we should go over exactly what will happen at three."

"Right. I believe Kait has made some notes on the subject."

Both heads turned to the young woman, who now consulted her clipboard.

"Um, yes," said Kait. "Well, it's pretty straightforward. I've arranged for the press to be there on site, the local television station, radio and newspapers, all the usual suspects. I think my mother . . . Ms. Park should speak first, followed by you, Chief Second. Afterward there will be a brief question-and-answer session. Hopefully not too long. If we are lucky, this should last maybe twenty minutes or so."

"Finishing in just enough time to make the evening news. By the way, Maggie, you've kept us all in the dark about what the Reserve plans to do with the land. You do know the reporters will ask you about that. What are you going to tell them?"

"A decision hasn't been made yet. We're still . . . consulting," said Maggie.

Crystal Park leaned back in her chair and looked out a window. Not the one facing south over the lake, but the one facing east, over the parking lot. She was pleased to see at least two Saturns. She only hoped they were from her dealership. She made a mental note to check their licence plates when they left.

"I don't know, Maggie. After all the fuss this thing has caused, you know the local reeve is going to really kick up a fuss over this, worse than he's already been doing. You and your community had better have some good ideas about what to do with that land. You can't just let it be. People in the municipality won't stand for it after all these headaches."

"But they were letting it just lie there until now. It was an abandoned cottage and a practically unused woodlot. Why do we have to do something different?"

The MP smiled at the chief's naïveté. "Because, my friend, it's human nature. If I had . . . I don't know . . . say, a daughter that I ignored all the time, and I was pestered to marry her off to somebody, and I subsequently noticed that her husband was ignoring her . . . ? Well, I, as a normal person, wouldn't stand for it. Do you understand where I'm coming from?"

Slowly, Maggie nodded. She knew the MP was right. Her secret wish was to let the land remain semi-wild, but she knew few others held her hope. The others had their own dreams about it.

"If there's one thing I've learned in office it's that the press hates vague answers. Make something up if you have to. You can always change it later and blame it on a shift in policy—or climate, if you want to be trendy."

Kait, meanwhile, sat there, making notes on her clipboard, wishing her mother would stop using her in her allegories.

"I will put that in the microwave and see what bubbles up. But I suppose we should get going," Maggie said as she rose.

For such a sunny day, there seemed to be a dark cloud over her. "I'll give you a quick tour of the administration office, and then maybe we'll grab some lunch."

The sound of one of the three great inventions of White people could be heard flushing as Wayne entered the living room. Virgil, home for lunch, sat waiting on the big brown overstuffed chair his mother had bought two years ago. He seemed nervous.

"So, what are we going to do?" he asked.

"Not we—I. I will find him. Face him. Tell him to fuck off. You got that school thing to deal with and this could get dangerous. Does that sound like a plan?"

"I don't know. What can happen when you tell Nanabush to fuck off? If he is Nanabush."

Wayne put on his worn jean jacket. "You still don't believe it?"

"I heard them say on *Star Trek* that the simplest explanation is usually the correct one. Nanabush is not a simple explanation. I admit it's possible, only because anything is possible, but I . . ."

Now Wayne was putting his shoes on, tying the laces aggressively. "Well, if he isn't Nanabush, we have nothing to worry about. We just tell him to hit the road, and that's that. That would make life a lot easier."

"And if he is Nanabush?"

"Then things get more complicated. A lot more complicated." He stood up. "So I am out of here. I will let you know what happens."

Virgil nodded. "Where are you going first?"

"I am going to take the battle to him. At Sammy Aandeg's."

"And then . . ."

Wayne stretched, first up to the sky, then down to the ground, then in each of the four cardinal directions, before answering. "Virgil, I don't know. I am flying blind on this, just as you are. I do know one thing. According to everything I've ever read about him, Nanabush can be hurt. He can feel pain. And if it comes to that . . . it comes to that."

"You'd fight him? Nanabush . . . if it is Nanabush?"

"As you said, this is about your mother, my sister. Most people think Nanabush is a lovable goof, a children's character. But he is more human than most humans, he has all their nobility, and all their faults—magnified. He's a wild card, Virgil. I am going to have to be as wild as him. What that means . . . ask me tomorrow. I'll know then. And if I need help, I'll let you know."

Grimly, the boy nodded. "Okay, Uncle Wayne. But don't forget, I told my mother I would be at the press conference. That's in a little over two hours."

"Good, you'll be around people. Most of the legends of Nanabush deal with him going one on one, or one on two, with people or animals. Not a lot of crowd stories. Wish me luck."

Wayne started walking briskly in the direction of Sammy Aandeg's house, while Virgil began his journey back to academic salvation.

Salvation was short lived. As soon as he arrived, Ms. Weatherford found him putting his backpack in his locker.

"Mr. Second, have you seen Dakota?"

"No, ma'am, not since this morning. She's usually the first one here after lunch."

"It seems she didn't report to her last class. Do you have any idea where she might be?"

Suddenly his last conversation in the library with his cousin came back to him, as did thoughts of her growing fascination with John-of-a-thousand-last-names. She had said, *I'll find him myself later.* Maybe now was later. If so, then he knew where Dakota might be. But to inform Ms. Weatherford of all of this would take a long and potentially embarrassing explanation of the relationship among Virgil's grandmother, a motorcyclist, the moon, binoculars and a thirteen-year-old Anishnawbe girl. Way too unbelievable.

"Uh, no, sorry. I can't help you. Maybe she's at home sick or something." He hoped that himself.

"No, her mother hasn't seen her. Maybe she's on the playground. Thank you for your help, Virgil." Turning and walking away, Ms. Weatherford left the young man to ponder.

Dakota might be in trouble, thought Virgil. With John, since nobody really knew his game, that was a strong possibility. Virgil weighed his options and decided Dakota's situation was the most important. Looking around to be sure no one saw him, he quietly closed his locker door, locked it, and then snuck out of the school's side entrance. He knew this was practically committing suicide, with Ms. Weatherford and his mother on his case, but some things and people were worth that risk.

Running as fast as he could, he caught up with his uncle about halfway to Sammy's, and filled him in.

"Oh great, another wrinkle . . ." was Wayne's sober comment.

"This isn't like her, Uncle Wayne. She loves school."

"Well, what exactly happened between you two this morning?"

"Nothing much. I told her to stay away from John. That he was bad news."

"Virgil, you're an idiot. But then again, so am I. Remember when we told your mother the same thing? How did she react?"

"She got mad."

Wayne nodded. "She got mad. Just about pushed me out of the house and out of her life. Nobody likes to be told what to do and who they can be friends with."

"But I'm in school. They tell me what to do all the time."

"Do you like it?"

"No."

"I rest my case. I'll keep my eyes open for her. Better get back to school."

"No. I want to come."

"What about all that trouble you got into about skipping?"

"I'll write a four-thousand-word essay. Use lots of adverbs too. Let's go. I'm worried."

Virgil trotted ahead determinedly, and Wayne increased his speed. About an hour later they arrived at Sammy's secluded abode, moving clandestinely through the sumacs that lined the driveway. Unfortunately, Virgil and Wayne were disappointed.

"His motorcycle isn't here," said Virgil. "Neither is Dakota." The whole lot seemed quiet and deserted, and an odd, unpleasant odour hung in the air. "What is that smell?"

"Raccoon, I think," answered Wayne.

"How can you tell?"

Wayne shook his head. "You really have to stop watching so much *Star Trek* and get out into the woods more. You're embarrassing."

Taking refuge behind a large bush, they scanned the immediate area. "And FYI, a family of them got stuck on my island once. Took forever to get them off."

"I've seen raccoons. Josie, over near the cottages, used to have a pet one. It didn't smell like this."

Sniffing the air, Wayne said, "Yeah, this smell is real strong. There must have been a lot of them. An army of them. But why?"

Their minds flashed to the argument they'd witnessed between John and the raccoon.

Wayne whispered to the boy, "I think something is definitely up."

Virgil was about to respond when he and his uncle heard the now-familiar growl of the vintage motorcycle. Crouching down farther behind the bush, they peeked through the large tear-shaped leaves. The red-and-white machine roared into the driveway, a multitude of plastic bags hanging from each handle bar, each heavy with its contents. Once the bike stopped, the bags swayed back and forth like pendulums, almost knocking John and the bike over.

"Nanabush grocery shops?" Wayne said, more to himself than to Virgil. They watched John push the kickstand down, and gather up the six plastic bags. Carrying them, he walked over to the edge of the lawn, where the forest began, and dropped all of the bags contemptuously. The two in the bush heard John call out: "All right, you overgrown mangy rats. I'm here and I brought the stuff. Do you want it or not?" Then John started mumbling under his breath.

Suddenly they heard chattering, twigs breaking, leaves rustling . . . it sounded like the woods themselves had come alive.

"Look! Oh my God . . ." Wayne pointed at the trees. At the top of an ancient cedar, a lone raccoon sat, looking down at the blond man as if in judgment. It waved its arms around. At any other time it might have seemed cute, but today, it seemed decidedly uncute, more in the eerie category. Another raccoon appeared in a nearby tree. Then another. Then four more in the pine tree next to the cedar. The maple tree that bordered the lawn suddenly held a dozen. The trees around Virgil and Wayne were now peopled (or raccooned) with dozens and dozens of grey, masked mammals, crying out in victory. Like their leader, the rest stood up on their hind legs and waved their arms. More appeared along the ground bordering the forest.

"Holy shit!" said Virgil.

From their hiding place, they heard John grumbling as he lifted up the first grocery bag and took out six packets of bacon. Flicking out his hunting knife, John sliced open each package, grabbed handfuls of the meat and started throwing handfuls of thin strips into the forest. It was raining bacon. The forest pulsed with the rapid movement of raccoons. Bacon was hanging from branches, draped over rocks, wedged in the crooks of trees, lying on the leafed forest floor—and the raccoons feasted on it. Virgil and Wayne could smell the maple-smoked aroma.

"Enjoy the bacon. I hope you all get heart attacks and die," muttered John as he reached for more food.

From the next bag he took out five boxes of half-frozen shrimp. He grabbed handfuls of the pink seafood and tossed it as hard as he could. Again a cry of victory rose up from the furry army as they scrambled to grab the delicacies that rained down.

Wayne and Virgil knew they were witnessing something their grandchildren in the far future would never believe. At one point, an errant shrimp struck Wayne's baseball cap and bounced to the ground beside him. A raccoon darted out of nowhere and grabbed it. It looked up at Wayne briefly before popping the shrimp in its mouth and running off.

The third bag contained various fruits and nuts. Handfuls of cherries, walnuts, strawberries, cherry tomatoes, peanuts and dried banana slices were tossed to the waiting forest denizens. Like little furry vacuum cleaners, the raccoons hoovered up the treats, which lasted barely two minutes on the forest floor.

Next came the contents of bag number four, a mixture of bagged popcorn, potato chips, cheeses, Fritos and pork rinds. Once more John opened the bags and pelted the woods around him with their contents.

Virgil leaned over and whispered to his uncle, "All of this must have cost a fortune. Where does Nanabush get money?"

Wayne shook his head to indicate he had no answer.

From the next bag, John took out half a dozen cartons of eggs. Taking care not to break them, he gently let them tumble out onto the soft grassy lawn. One by one, raccoon after raccoon came waddling out of the brush, eager to grab and devour the white and brown orbs of gooey goodness. There were not nearly enough to satisfy all the creatures but it was all he had been able to hang from his handlebars.

That left one bag. The dessert bag. Inside it were bags of jujubes, Smarties, butter tarts, Maltesers, gummi bears, Twizzlers and chocolate-covered almonds—a dentist's nightmare. But raccoons didn't have dentists, so it was a moot point.

It was a food orgy of Roman proportions. But clearly it was not enough. High atop the cedar tree, the chief raccoon chattered loudly, silencing all the rest.

"More?" exclaimed John. "You want more? That's all I got."

Again, the raccoon scolded the man, and for the first time the man responded in kind, sounding exactly like a raccoon. This did not sway the aged raccoon, which scolded again.

Frustrated, John held up all the empty bags. "Do you see any more, you miserable . . . ?" He looked around him, and saw Sammy's house. Specifically, his kitchen window and all that existed behind it. With realization came a smile. He held up two fingers.

"Give me two minutes!"

The two Otter Lake residents, still well hidden, watched John run into the house, wondering what would happen next. All around them they could hear raccoon mastication and the raccoon equivalent of satisfied purring.

A few minutes later, John emerged from the house carrying an old cardboard box. Now it was John's turn to dictate terms. "Okay, this is everything in the house. Everything. It's either this, or we go back to the way things were. Now eat this, shut up and leave me alone. I got a lighter, you know. Better stick to the deal before I set fire to the forest."

He grabbed a loaf of white bread, savagely ripped the plastic bag open and threw the slices high into the forest. Next came a large jar of pickles that he didn't bother to open. Tossing it, it broke on landing, releasing its contents. Then came a sealed box of Cheerios, followed by a half-empty package of Fig Newtons and finally a box of fish sticks. All soon disappeared into the shadows of the vegetation.

"That's it. That's all I got. Looks like Sammy ain't eating for a week. So what do you want to do now? Huh? Tell me!" John yelled into the forest. "Is it over or does the cold war get hot?" To illustrate his point, John flicked his lighter and a small flame appeared.

The head raccoon surveyed the scene of his victory, happily munching on a Fig Newton. Then, with a satisfied final gulp, it turned and disappeared down the trunk of the tree. As if by magic, all the other creatures began to melt into the forest background, their hands, tummies and mouths full of man-made booty.

"It's over. Finally," they heard him say, as the man stood there on the empty lawn. It was as if a great weight had been lifted off his shoulders. No longer would he have to look over his shoulder or wonder what trouble waited just beyond the next tree. Wiping his crumb- and food-smeared hands on the grass, John walked toward the house, a look of accomplishment on his face.

"Of all the animals on this continent to be made extinct by the White man, why couldn't it have been those things? Oh well, I'll have to tell Sammy . . . Puck was hungry." That thought made the man laugh. That had gone better than he had expected. It was a good sign. Now for the next adventure.

As John entered the house, Wayne nudged his nephew, still crouched down beside him. "Still not convinced he's Nanabush?"

Virgil struggled to speak. "He . . . um . . . Uncle Wayne? Uh, what was that you said about Nanabush legends saying he only dealt with things one on one or one on two? Huh? That was a little more than one on two. I thought you knew this stuff."

"Virgil, tikwamshin."

"Well, Mr. Nanabush Fighter, what do we do now?"

"I don't know."

"Boy, you just know how to inspire confidence, don't you?"

Wayne gave him a sour look. "Virgil, you are getting on my nerves."

"And what about Dakota? Aren't we supposed to be out here looking for her?"

Wayne nodded. "Yeah, we will but the safest place in Otter Lake for her to be right now is anyplace but here. One mystery at a time, little nephew."

Virgil was not convinced. His uncle was not being as helpful as he had expected. "So what are we going to do now? Do you want to break another tree branch?"

For that, the young boy received an annoyed scowl from his uncle.

"Fine, you want me to do something, I'll do it." Wayne stood up behind the bushes and walked toward Sammy's house.

"Uncle Wayne, what are you doing?"

"Something. Don't get in the way."

He stopped near the kitchen window, then seemed to change his mind. Virgil saw him look at the motorcycle and trot over to it. Pulling a jackknife from his back pocket, his uncle leaned over the front end of the machine for a minute, then lifted the now-disconnected headlight over his head and gestured triumphantly to Virgil. He wrapped it in his jean jacket and returned to the kitchen window.

Placing the wrapped-up headlight on the ground behind him, he took a defensive pose and yelled, "Yo, you in the house. Come out now."

Hesitantly, Virgil too emerged from the bush, amazed at his uncle's confidence. He stood discreetly two metres behind Wayne. There was an uncomfortable silence as they both waited for a response. It came when John emerged from the back door, onto the lawn, locking eyes with Wayne.

"Ah, more guests. What a busy morning. Good morning, Virgil. And who is your friend? Let me guess . . . Maggie's fabled weird brother. Dwayne."

"Wayne. My name is Wayne."

John smiled. "Wayne it is. I assume you are here for a reason?"

"I . . ."

Virgil tugged on his uncle's jacket, reminding him he was there. "Uh, we want you to leave my mother alone. That's all." Virgil noticed the man's eyes. "Jesus! Your eyes ... they're yellow!"

"I prefer to call them amber. You should see them at sunset. And is that what your mother wants too, for me to leave her alone?"

"Maggie doesn't know who you are," Wayne said.

"Who am I?" John said tauntingly.

"Nanabush," said Wayne.

For a second John didn't respond; he just stared at Wayne with quiet amusement. "Nanabush. The Trickster? The central character of Anishnawbe mythology, the paramount metaphor in their cosmology? The demigod? The amazing, handsome, intelligent and fabulous Nanabush? That Nanabush?" John noticed Virgil was nodding behind Wayne.

"Well, that's a little egocentric, but essentially, yes," said Wayne.

"What about you, Virgil? What do you say?"

Virgil didn't say anything. In fact, his uncle answered for him. "He knows you're trouble. And definitely not good for his mother. We both want you to get out of town."

"Or what?"

"You are dangerous. So am I."

Virgil had never heard his uncle sound so cold.

"If I am this ... Nanabush, what makes you think you can fight me, let alone beat me? And why should I fight you? I just have to tell Maggie about this and I'm fairly sure she will take you apart herself, saving me the problem. So I see no advantage in discussing this any further. Now, if you will excuse me, I have a press conference to attend. As an Italian I once knew used to say, *Arrivederci!*"

John nodded with mock politeness and was about to stride victoriously to the press conference when Wayne pulled the headlight of a fine, familiar vintage motorcycle from underneath his jean jacket. John stopped in his tracks, his eyes widening at the sight.

Casually, Wayne tossed the headlight at John's feet. "Just to let you know, we mean business."

Carefully, John picked it up, brushing off the dirt and pine needles, and cradled it. He sighed, then gently put the headlight back down on the ground beside the injured motorcycle. "My poor, poor baby. You bastard. That motorcycle never did a thing to you."

Wayne shrugged. "It got your attention. Virgil, step back, over to that tree."

The boy did as he was told.

"You are right about something. We don't have to do this. If you just jump on that machine of yours and get the hell out of town, we can all go our separate ways. What do you say?"

"How do I even know if my Indian will run? If you did this to it, you could have done worse."

"Oh, it works. I'm not stupid. Damaging your engine would force you to remain here. So, gonna take the smart road or does this have to get messy?"

Virgil watched the two men, aware of the tension in the air. His uncle was going to fight this guy—this guy his mother really liked, who might possibly be a creature from Anishnawbe history. He wondered absurdly how the school's guidance counsellor would advise him to handle the situation.

John's face had a grim set to it. "You see, the problem is, you defiled my little bike. That machine is very important to me, so I can't allow that. It's a matter of pride. I didn't have my pride for a while, but I got it back. And now I'm not going to lose it again. You, Dwayne . . ."

"Wayne!"

" . . . kick over a beehive, and you can't expect the bees not to get angry. You run naked through poison ivy, you're going to get a little itchy. You poke a stick at a—"

"Enough with the metaphors. I get the point." Wayne took off his sneakers and socks, flexing his toes.

Looking mildly amused, John asked, "So what are you gonna do now?"

"Whatever I have to. Virgil, just stay where you are. Don't get involved."

"You should listen to your uncle, and not get involved in things that aren't your business."

"John, Nanabush, or whatever your name is . . ."

John cocked an eyebrow. "Yes?"

Wayne stepped forward, until just a metre or so separated the two men. "Normally I train purely for defensive purposes. However, the world is a complicated place and you can't always do what is planned. Sometimes you have to do what is necessary."

John's brow furrowed. "What the hell does that mean? What exactly do you consider necessary?"

"This!" Wayne fell to the ground, landing on his butt with his legs stretching directly in front of him, between John's legs. Spreading his legs, he forced John's apart a fair distance, causing him to fall backward, his hands grabbing his groin. Surprised and stunned, Virgil stepped back to relative safety behind a low-hanging pine branch.

Both men jumped to their feet, though John was a little slower. Without warning, he kicked forward and his cowboy boot went flying off and hit Wayne in the forehead, making him fall back. Taking off his other boot, John limped around, his groin still clearly troubling him.

"You wanna get tough? I'll get tough. I've fought more battles than you've had days in your stupid life. Come on, I need the cardio." He leaped toward his opponent, who was scrambling to his feet. Wayne managed to dodge John and, using his leg as a wedge, tripped him and sent him falling against a tree. But only for a second. John coiled his legs low to the ground and jumped straight backward, hitting Wayne and sending them both into the bushes. There was some rolling around, but Virgil's view was obscured by the shaking branches.

"Tag, you're it." Like a squirrel chased by a dog, Wayne broke from the bushes and ran a short distance to a tall pine tree, and with barely any effort, he raced up the trunk, his toes digging into the uneven bark and his hands skimming the branches. The blond man's eyes widened.

"Okay, so you can climb like a marten. Kid, I've been doing this kind of thing since long before anything you could possibly remember existed. You want to play games, just remember, I *invented* those games." John looked at Virgil. "This is going to be more fun than I thought." John leaped up the side of the tree just as quickly as Wayne had, and disappeared into the leafy canopy.

Virgil scanned the treetops but could see nothing in the dense foliage. The branches of a dozen different trees laced together blocked out the blue sky. Occasionally a twig or leaf would drift down, and a muffled grunt or hidden yell could be heard, indicating the fight was still going on. Virgil wondered what was happening up there in the forest top. "H-h-hello? Uncle Wayne? Uncle Wayne? John . . ."

Like a wave breaking on shore, hell descended from the trees. The first thing Virgil heard was the thud of two bodies meeting, and a flurry of noise. An avalanche of twigs, branches, leaves and ancient bird's nests pelted the boy and the forest floor, followed by last year's tent caterpillar silk. Cedar, maple, willow, elm, oak, apple, leaves of all kinds fell and blanketed the area like a green snowfall. Ancient kites, deflated balloons and the remnants of a long-forgotten tree fort were forcibly dislodged. An abandoned beehive nearly hit the boy but instead bounced off a limb of the pine tree.

The battle seemed to be moving. Just a minute ago he could have sworn it raged directly above him in the pine tree, but now it was a dozen metres north, where there stood an aged outcropping of oak. And now he was sure the damaged limbs and leaves were falling from a huge weeping willow that stood next to a clearing.

It was a matter of time before the animals that called the trees home became collateral damage. A porcupine landed not a metre away from Virgil. Confused and having notoriously poor eyesight, the porcupine thought that the young Native blob crouching next to the tree was at fault. Luckily Virgil had access to a large stick and managed to poke the disgruntled animal away.

Occasionally, the boy caught a glimpse of his uncle's denim jacket or John's black pants against the blue sky or green leaves or brown bark. As best he could, he tried to follow their progress. Virgil just followed falling things, and the sound of grunts, thuds and curses, the constant rustle of leaves and branches being shaken.

Out of nowhere, there was a movement to his left. "Virgil, what's going on?" It was Dakota, crouched a few metres away, looking dazed.

"Dakota? There you are!" Virgil grabbed her and sheltered her under the branches of a long-fallen tree. "Are you okay? I was worried."

"I . . . I came looking for John. Did you see what he did back there? John Clayton. He . . . those raccoons . . . what . . . ? Virgil, I don't understand. I just wanted to make sure he hadn't left.

John . . . he told me he was staying here. I thought I should tell him what you said about him. How . . . how mean you were." Something crashed above them. "That's your Uncle Wayne up there, with him, isn't it? Virgil, what's going on?"

So, she had seen the whole thing, raccoons and all. Virgil wasn't sure he could clarify it himself. "It's hard to explain, Dakota. I told you John wasn't who he appeared to be."

"Then who is he?"

Virgil took a deep breath. "My Uncle Wayne thinks he's Nanabush."

"Oh" was all she said.

Now Virgil was getting really worried.

"How can they do that? I mean, fighting up there? In the trees. I . . . I don't think that's possible."

Virgil didn't know how to respond to that.

"Virgil, who's Nanabush?" she asked.

Virgil remembered Dakota's parents had strongly embraced the Canadian lifestyle. They probably hadn't seen fit to fill her head with stories of Anishnawbe history or culture. Their daughter should have her feet firmly planted in the here and now, they thought. Their only nods to any form of Aboriginal history were the names of their children, primarily because they thought the names sounded cool and might jump out on a job application. Dakota knew more French than Anishnawbe, and more English history than Anishnawbe history. Her only connection to the past had been Lillian. But now wasn't exactly the time to fill her in on the details. It would have to wait.

"You remember those stories about the trickster, the ones that Grandma told us? Him," Virgil said.

Dakota tried to focus on what Virgil was saying "That's

Nanabush? That guy from those kids' stories? My parents didn't
like me listening to them."

"No," Virgil said, "Not the Nanabush from kids' stories.
Grandma's Nanabush."

Then, almost as quickly as it had begun, the war in the treetops ended. The odd leaf floated down, but peace had returned
to the forest of Otter Lake.

"I think it's over," Virgil said to Dakota. "Uncle Wayne?" he
yelled. There was no sign of Maggie's youngest brother. Or of
John, for that matter. All was oddly quiet. Virgil called louder.
"Uncle Wayne!" Only the echo of his own voice responded.

Oh shit, thought Virgil. His uncle had recommended a direct
approach to dealing with the stranger, but the boy had not expected
an old-fashioned, down-and-dirty, drag-out, bar-room fight. That
had taken him by surprise. Now Wayne was missing, and that was
not a good thing.

"Virgil, how do people fight in the trees?" Dakota still seemed
a little confused.

"I don't know . . ." Then, "Uncle Wayne!" he yelled again to the
silent woods.

Almost directly above him a supple and pliant weeping willow branch groaned softly. Virgil looked up to see Wayne floating down to the ground, both hands gripping one of the tree's
whip-like extremities. He landed not ten paces away from his
nephew. Virgil and Dakota rushed to his side.

"Well, that didn't go exactly how I'd expected," said Wayne.
"Wow. That guy's pretty good. Man, I could use some aspirin," he
said, trying to smile through a fat lip.

Neither Virgil nor Dakota had ever seen somebody who'd
been in a real knock-down, drag-out fight before. Well, now they

had, and it wasn't pleasant. Most of his hair had slipped from the neat ponytail he normally wore, and morphed into a twig-infested, leaf-inhabited shambles. Both hands and feet looked cut and bruised, as did his right cheek, and he was developing a black eye. There was also a large budding bump along his hairline. The right knee of his pants had been torn, revealing a nasty scrape. He was favouring his left leg, and one finger on his right hand looked like it might be broken. Add to that the plethora of scratches, cuts and blood spatters across most of his visible skin.

His clothes didn't look much better. His jacket was ripped along the left shoulder seam, and the sleeve was completely missing. There was a tear along the middle of the jacket's back.

"But, all in all, all things considered, when you take everything into consideration, under the circumstances, I feel great!" Wayne grinned, showing some blood on his teeth.

"Uncle Wayne, are you really okay?"

Wayne took a deep breath before answering. "You know, they always say there's a world of difference between training and the actual thing. I think I get the point now. He threw a raccoon at me. He actually threw one at me. How do you train for that? Oh, hi, Dakota . . . glad we found you. You look good. By the way, have you seen the sleeve of my jacket?"

Virgil, too stunned to reply, just shook his head.

"Hmm, I had it on this morning. It must be around here somewhere."

To the boy, Wayne's voice sounded oddly detached.

"Uncle Wayne, what happened up there? Where's . . . you know . . . John?"

Absentmindedly, Wayne looked up into the trees whence he'd just dropped.

"Did you win? Did he? What happened?" prodded Virgil.

"I think . . ." Wayne found himself sitting on the ground before he could summon the energy to finish his sentence." . . . it was a tie. I think. I'm . . . just going to take a little nap now. Okay, Virgil? Wake me up before dinner." Curling up into a fetal position amid the fallen debris, Wayne went to sleep. Almost instantly he started snoring, his right leg twitching.

"Maybe we should get some help, Virgil. He doesn't look so good."

"Uncle Wayne? Uncle Wayne, what should I do?" His uncle didn't respond. Dakota was right. He didn't look good. Now Virgil truly felt he was in a pickle. Everything was out of his control. "John!" Virgil called his name a few times before accepting that the man was no longer around. At least he wasn't here to gloat. Maybe his uncle had given as good as he got, and the man with the motorcycle was licking his wounds somewhere.

The motorcycle headlight! Virgil's head jerked toward where John had put down the light. It was gone. So John had been here on the ground too, collecting his prize. But where had he gone? And what should Virgil do now, with his unconscious uncle a few metres away?

"Come on, give me a hand." Somehow, Virgil and Dakota managed to lift the sleeping Wayne, each of his arms over their much smaller shoulders. "We'd better take him to some help. Maybe the clinic."

"Virgil, what happened to John?"

"I don't really know, Dakota." Slowly, they dragged the unconscious man through the woods.

"Can you tell me more about this Nanabush now?" asked Dakota.

———

If there was one thing history had taught the stranger, it was that he should never plan for victory until it was fully achieved. Stories from many different cultures, including the Anishnawbe, told of fools who anticipated one thing, and through their own hubris, achieved the exact opposite. Now here he was, hiding on top of Sammy's roof with a detached headlight in one hand, and cradling a sore, perhaps cracked, rib in the other. His nose was bleeding, and his elbow was swelling up. Whoever that Dwayne guy was, he was tougher than he had anticipated. The Indian fought like an animal. Regrouping, John opted to hide from the two kids and his unconscious opponent on the other side of the roof until things settled. He couldn't hide, though, from the pain in his left shoulder. Somehow, he thought, fighting a great battle used to be a lot easier. And less painful. Maybe he was getting old.

But at the moment he had more important things to worry about than this little tussle. Besides, he was a fast healer. At least he used to be. John knew the press conference would be starting any minute. He wanted to be there when all the fun began and, internal injuries or no internal injuries, he couldn't miss it for the world. Luckily, all three of his uninvited guests were leaving. The two youngest seemed to be supporting Dwayne as they half carried him away. And there, just below the sore and impatient John, waited his precious Indian Chief.

A few minutes after the sound of the Chief faded into the distance, Sammy came running into his house, out of breath and in a panic. As always, the first thing he did was grab a beer. This time it was two, then he hustled his aging and damaged body into his room, slamming the door behind him. Huddled in the corner, on the floor, he drained the first beer without tasting it. Things were happening. If the teachings of the residential school had stuck in him, he would have called it the End of Days—for just half an hour ago, he was sure, positive, one hundred percent convinced that he'd seen the marching of Birnam Wood. What else could it have been?

Out wandering, he'd been up on a grassy rise when Sammy saw what he saw. There, down below him, the trees were moving. Bushes were waving, leaves were scattering, the forest (a small part of it anyway) was swaying, no doubt getting ready to march. He could even hear the trees shout out in anger, scream in rage and yell in pain.

He stood there, wondering if after all these years the gods had indeed intended to destroy him by making him mad. After twenty seconds Sammy could take it no more, and with a small scream, he went running back to the relative sanctuary of his home. The night before had been the tempest.

What was happening? The only answers Sammy knew involved five-percent alcohol, and he planned to ask a lot of questions that day.

TWENTY-FOUR

It was showtime. The media, which consisted of one local television station and one cable station, the official city newspaper, the weekly supermarket coupon paper and two radio stations, were ready and waiting. Some were thinking, *This is what my career has come to, covering a minor Native land shuffle in the middle of nowhere.* They had been milling about for half an hour, waiting for the show to begin and carefully avoiding the water-filled potholes that dotted the landscape.

Crystal and Maggie were off by the MP's Saturn, discussing this afternoon's protocol and the need for arranging a meeting with the local reeve and MPP once the dust settled. Kait was busy handing out the official press release to all interested members of the fifth estate. All in all, it was a boring, typical press conference that would be lucky to make the tail end of tonight's newscast.

Already in town that day there had been an attempted bank robbery by a meth addict that had been foiled easily by the local police—the man had locked himself out of his car. In the north end, a pine tree had been blown over by last night's thunderstorm, trashing the mayor's brother's RV. So the line-up for tonight's news was pretty much already set, and a news story about Native land claims just didn't compare in excitement. Still, everybody had to go through the motions.

Maggie whispered into Crystal's ear, "I've been thinking. I know you were going to speak first but maybe I should say a few words of introduction, just to set things up, and then you can speak. Is that okay?"

"Perfect," responded Crystal, with her professional smile on full wattage, though she preferred being the opening act.

Maggie stepped up to the mike. "Excuse me, I suppose we should get started before all these trees die of old age," she said. She had managed to get somebody from Otter Lake's community centre to set up a mike and loudspeaker system, attached to a small portable generator. Though there were scarcely a dozen people there, this made things look more official. "I want everybody here to take a good look around them, at the trees, at the land beneath them. This is why we are here."

Under normal circumstances, Maggie hated public speaking, detested it in fact. She considered it the least enjoyable, or perhaps a better expression was the *most unenjoyable*, part of the job of being chief. But today, before everything took place, she wanted these people standing before and beside her, and hopefully the people watching and listening later that night and reading the newspaper the next morning, to know what all the fuss was about.

"This is the land of our ancestors. We have been here anywhere from ten thousand years ago to time immemorial, depending on whose calendar you are using. We have always considered ourselves a part of the land, so you will have to excuse us if we get a little ornery when it comes to deciding what to do with that land. Our legends say the ground is Mother Earth's skin, the trees and grass her hair, the water her blood. It's hard to bargain away or discuss appropriating land when you think of it in that way. Otter Lake was originally founded almost two hundred years ago when . . ."

Crystal whispered to her daughter, "This is what you call a few words?"

Behind her, leaning hidden against a tree, stood John, listening. Even in this time, Native people still knew how to talk and think like the Native people he remembered. He nodded in agreement, and privately wondered how long it would take for these people to do what Maggie had suggested. Specifically they needed to take a good look around them, at the trees and, more important, at the land beneath them. Because unless somebody did that, he would have wasted an awful lot of time and energy.

"There's been a lot of discussion over what to do with this land, both inside our community and outside. The issue has been controversial, and caused some disagreements. But remember, we are neighbours, and whatever happens, this land, this ground you stand upon, will be here long after you and I and everyone we know will have passed on."

Terry Nash, radio reporter for CNDN, unconsciously glanced down when Maggie mentioned "this ground you stand upon." He was off to the left, his mike held high, trying to catch cleaner sound as he had been taught in community college the year before. Arriving late, he hadn't been able to leave his tape recorder on the lectern where Maggie was speaking.

At his feet, Terry saw something sticking out of the ground. It appeared odd, and very unlike a rock or root. He tried to ignore his growing curiosity; after all, he was a professional reporter here to do a job. But the more Terry looked at the strange, knobby thing near his right foot, the more suspicious he became. After all, he was a professional reporter. He nudged it with his foot, slightly loosening it from the packed dirt. Terry then kicked it, and the object came free and rolled over onto the surface of the land. Though unskilled in forensics, the young reporter was fairly sure, almost positive, that it was a human bone. A leg bone, if all those episodes of crime-scene investigation dramas he watched were correct.

Dropping his recording equipment, Terry screamed and backed away, knocking over a cameraman, whose training fortunately included knowing how to throw his body between the ground and his camera.

"What the hell's wrong with you?" said the prostrate cameraman.

Pointing, Terry backed away even farther. "Over there! On the ground. A bone. A leg bone. A human leg bone. I know it is. There's a body under the dirt. Somebody should do something."

Hungry for a more interesting story, all the reporters rushed to where the young reporter had been standing and, as he maintained, there was indeed what appeared to be a human leg bone lying half exposed in the dirt. Immediately the newspaper photographers and cameramen fought for space, desperate to take the first images back to their editors.

Maggie and Crystal, with Kait in tow, ran toward the disruption.

"What's going on here?" asked Maggie.

The reporter from the local paper, *The Leader*, was kneeling down, looking at the exposed bone. "That kid over there found this. It looks human. I think maybe you got a skeleton down here." Using a pen, he moved a few small chunks of dirt, and looked closely into the hole left by the disturbed bone. "Yep, there are definitely more bones down there. Now *this* is a story!"

At once, both officials were surrounded and harassed by the press, eager to get a quote on this mysterious happening.

"No comment! No comment!" said Crystal, as Kait vainly tried to shoo the reporters away.

Maggie, however, had no such assistant. Confused by what had just happened, she tried to find a way through the turmoil of media smelling the fresh blood of a potential exposé.

"Hey, look!" It was the cameraman from CDRW. "I think I found some more. Over here." Indeed, he was recording a dark brown human skull, partially covered by leaves. "Somebody should call the police. We could have a killing field here!"

If the reporters had been excited before, now they were ecstatic. The sound of electronic and print reporters in full frenzy flooded the clearing. Somehow, through the confusion, Kait had managed to get her mother to their car and was manoeuvring the Saturn through the scrum, if nine could be called a scrum, of journalists. Finally, she found the exit to the road, and floored it.

Maggie's last glimpse of Crystal Park was of her sitting in the passenger seat and pulling out her cell phone. A few seconds later, Maggie's cell rang. It was Crystal.

"Maggie, you sure know how to throw a press conference. Call me when you figure out what's going on. And also, if you ever want to consider turning that Chrysler in for a Saturn, at cost, give me a call. I'm sure we could work something out. Good luck." Then, *click*.

Maggie was alone with the media. Like sharks circling a hemorrhaging tuna, the reporters gathered around her, asking questions far too quickly for her to comprehend. Recording instruments were thrust at her.

"Is this why your people wanted the land back? Because of the bodies?"

"I grew up in this area and I always heard of campers mysteriously disappearing in the woods. Do you know anything about this, Chief Second?"

"Didn't the federal government and several Churches try to ban First Nations religions? Do you think it had anything to do with these newly discovered human remains?"

"Chief Second, is this an ancient Indian burial ground, or perhaps the dumping ground of the first Aboriginal serial killer?"

Maggie struggled to be heard above the din of the excited journalists. "I . . . please keep in mind that we have just taken possession of this land today. These bones were obviously here prior to our interest. I can't comment on something I don't know anything about."

It was as if they didn't hear her. She kept trying to get away but everywhere she turned there was another microphone. Nearby, she could hear one reporter calling his bureau chief, telling him to send more reinforcements! The noise was overwhelming. Almost too loud for her to hear the sound of a motorcycle revving up.

The helmeted John roared through the story-hungry crowd to Maggie. Journalists and photographers and cameramen jumped left and right, out of the way, and suddenly John was at Maggie's side.

She heard the muffled words "Hop on!" as he tossed her his spare helmet.

Grateful, she did as she was told.

"Here, hold this," he added, giving her a detached headlight. "Now, hold on tight!"

As he fed the carburetor all the gas it could take, the crowd parted like the Red Sea to let him and the ear-splitting machine through. Two seconds later, all that was left of them was the exhaust that the milling media was breathing in.

As they barrelled down the road at a dangerous speed, Maggie held on tight to John's forearms. She had never been so happy to see anybody in her life. But where had all those bones come from? She'd walked through that area many times. A lot of people had hunted deer and pheasant in those woods, or gone camping. While the land was fairly wild in nature, it wasn't exactly unexplored. What the hell was going on?

The man driving, however, smiled under his helmet, content in the effectiveness of his plan, and the pleasant feeling of having Maggie close to him once again. The WELCOME TO OTTER LAKE sign flashed by them. He was taking her home. It was time Maggie learned the truth, and he was just the man to tell her.

Fifteen minutes later, they arrived at the Second house. Maggie was almost afraid to let go of John, but he gently helped her off his machine and onto the porch step. As she sat there removing her helmet, she smiled. And once again, he couldn't help thinking it was the best smile in the world. Almost as pretty as her mother's.

There was something different about him, she thought, but for the moment, she didn't care. "Thank you. Thank you. Thank you," she said, jumping up and hugging him.

"You politicians, always doing everything in triplicate."

"What the hell happened back there? Those people were pulling bones out of the ground! Did you see that! I saw a skull, half buried in the . . ." She couldn't finish her sentence.

"Pretty cool, huh? Maggie, let's chat."

Calmly, John led her to the back of the house and sat her down in her lawn chair, making sure she was comfortable.

She barely noticed. Her mind was still on the press conference, trying to reason things out.

"An ancient Indian burial ground, one of them said. Couldn't be. We know where that is. Could we really have a serial killer here? Oh God, that's all we need. But nobody's missing. John, something is all fucked up. This was supposed to be a simple press conference about us taking possession of the land and . . ."

Then she noticed that John, who was sitting beside her, was smiling. Not a supporting "I'm here for you" kind of smile, but more like a "I know something you don't know" kind.

"John," she asked hesitantly, "why are you smiling?"

"Well, your problem is solved."

Maggie knew problems were seldom solved by mayhem, and even less seldom by the discovery of human bones. "It is? My problem? And what is my problem and how is it now solved?" Just a few minutes ago she had been so happy to see this man. Now, her rising pulse rate was telling her something different.

"You were wondering what to do with the new land. You were getting all these silly suggestions, and . . ."

She swallowed once, quite audibly. "And . . . ?"

"You told me you didn't want anything done with the land. Just leave it the way it was, as it was created. A smart and, in a very special way, a long-range plan. It is something your ancestors would agree with. I certainly agreed, and wanted to help." There was that maddening smile again. "So I did."

For the second time in half an hour, she could feel her world beginning to shake and crumble. This man was smiling much too broadly, speaking much too calmly, with much too much confidence for this confession to bode well.

"John, what did you do?"

Practically beaming, he took her hand. "What I did, I did for you," he said with what seemed to be genuine caring. Seven words that have started more fights and caused more divorces than "I was drunk," "She meant nothing to me" and "If you'd just calm down"—all put together.

"John, those were human bones in the ground. At least they looked like it. Human! What do you have to do with that? Tell me before I start screaming."

"You're right. They are human bones. I know. I put them there. Thankfully the ground was soft and muddy after the rain last night or it would have taken me forever."

Now would be a good time for screaming, Maggie thought, but she found she didn't have the energy.

"Relax, Maggie. Those bones are quite old. Ancient, in fact. You are getting stressed out over nothing."

Now he was laughing, apparently finding the whole situation quite amusing.

Maggie grabbed her chest. "I'm having trouble breathing. Why did you bury bones, ancient or otherwise, in our woods? What possible logic would explain that? And where did you get bones?" Then it hit her, about John. "And . . . what the fuck's up with your eyes? I know for certain they weren't that colour when I last saw you. The part that isn't bloodshot is amber." In all the excitement, she only now noticed the dried blood and dirt on him. "And why do you look all beaten up? You look like you've been in a brawl. John, what the hell have you been doing?"

"That's a long, unimportant story, except for the fact I won. I'm sure of it. Listen, Maggie, those bones I seeded will guarantee the independence of those woods for a very long time. First of all the police will close off the area for a criminal investigation.

And trust me, I've buried enough bones all through the three hundred acres to keep them busy for a very long time. Two big saddlebags full. They'll be digging up knee caps, and humeri and ribs and stuff forever. Cool, huh?"

Maggie took a deep breath, the kind she often took before lecturing Virgil. "If it's a crime scene for several years, then we won't have access to it. So what's the point in appropriating it if we can't use it?"

For a second, John's victorious smile flickered. Then he smiled more brightly. "A minor detail I will deal with later. Now here's the beauty of the plan."

"This plan has beauty?" One of her throbbing headaches was beginning.

"Definitely. Once those bones are properly analyzed, they'll realize how old and ancient they are. Like they belong to an ancient . . ."

" . . . Indian burial ground."

"Bingo! Exactly. And every organization, governmental or private, has their hands tied with ancient Indian burial grounds. Nobody will want to build there, even your own people, even if you begged them. Too much bad karma. You've seen all the movies. Get it?"

Somewhere in her future, Maggie was already anticipating a lot of awkward and embarrassing questions being asked. And she, being the chief, would have to answer them. For a long time, if she decided to run for the next election, and managed to survive the democratic process. And she thought she hated her job before.

"John, they have scientists that can tell the difference between a fake burial ground and an authentic one. People have spent their lives studying this stuff. Oh, John, what have you done?"

"Maggie, trust me. I know a few things about how the Anishnawbe used to live. More than a few things. Believe me, I know what I'm doing. They won't know anything I don't want them to know."

Maggie wasn't responding in the manner John had been expecting. She was not thrilled. She was not happy. She was not smothering him with kisses of gratitude.

"Um, I can't help but notice a certain lack of enthusiasm here. I thought you'd be overjoyed."

"John," she said wearily, "in a couple hours, the entire country will know the Otter Lake First Nations has a forest full of human remains. I bet the phone in my office is ringing off the hook right now. I can't see how you possibly could think this was a good idea."

Just then, the phone in her house started to ring. It seemed unusually loud and incessant, but that could have been Maggie's imagination. For the sake of her sanity, she decided to ignore it for the moment.

"Maggie, I think you're lacking a little imagination. Perhaps if you . . ."

"Where did you get those bones anyway?"

"The museum in town. They have lots. Boxes and boxes full. They won't miss a few. Like I said, I know what I'm doing."

"You just grabbed a handful of bones, just like that?"

"More or less."

"How do you know they're Native bones?"

Now John was becoming angry. "Give me some credit. I can read. Ojibway remains, pre-contact. Circa thirteen hundred to fifteen hundred. All collected within six hundred and fifty kilometres of here, so the soil traces should be roughly compatible. Smart, huh?"

Maggie's headache seemed to be getting worse.

"Of course, just to keep things interesting, I did throw in some ... variables, just to make sure those scientists are on their toes and don't doze off."

"Variables?"

He nodded, once more eager to share his brilliance. "Yep. I wanted to make sure this caught their attention. Ninety percent of everything I buried out there is pure Anishnawbe."

"And the other ten percent?"

"A more, shall we say, eclectic mixture."

Maggie knew immediately that she did not like anything described as "eclectic" in her life. "And what exactly does that mean?"

"Once they gather up everything they can find hidden out there, and once they get around to analyzing and testing and categorizing all them bones, there are a few surprises." John stopped, as if playing a game, making Maggie wait for every little nugget of revelation.

"Oh, John, you're killing me. What fucking surprises?" Her loud voice startled a nest of crows in a nearby tree.

"The other ten percent ..."

"Yes, John, yes."

"A mixture of other bones I found in the museum. A little of this, a little of that. Kind of like a skeletal potpourri. Those scientists will find a wrist bone from an Eighteenth Dynasty Egyptian nobleman, a fragment of pelvis from a three-thousand-year-old Australian Aboriginal woman, the bottom jaw of a pre-Columbian Mayan warrior and a couple of toes from somebody called *Homo erectus*. That should keep them guessing for a while, huh? I mean those scientists and forensics people must have lives that are so boring, they probably would welcome a little mystery into their lives." Once more, the man smiled proudly. "Just one of my little jokes."

In a bizarre kind of way, Maggie could see the humour in what he'd just done. Unfortunately, she wasn't in much of a mood to laugh. And to think she thought her life was complicated before! She found herself breathing heavily, panting almost.

"I take it you aren't in a mood to thank me." John looked puzzled.

Maggie started panting harder. Her chest . . . no, her entire body hurt. Was thirty-five too young to have a heart attack? But somehow, she managed to find the resolve to utter what she thought might be her last words.

"You . . . you . . . did WHAT? You . . . son of a bitch . . ." She panted some more. "You planted caveman bones in my forest!"

"Caveman!" He snapped his fingers recalling the connection. "That's what a *Homo erectus* is. I knew I recognized the name." Then, John noticed Maggie's clenched teeth and narrowed eyes. "I don't get it. You should be happy. I'm happy. Goodbye, problem. Yeah, we still got some loose ends to figure out but all in good time. Maggie, are you okay? You look like you are going to pass out or something."

Using what little strength her hyperventilating body had left, she curled up her right fist and, with little hesitation, sent it directly into John's solar plexus. Her brother had tried that move earlier in the day high atop the forest but the blond man had been prepared, and had blocked it easily. This time, the punch was completely unexpected, and Maggie's fist went deep into his body. A loud whoosh of air escaped his lungs, and his knees buckled beneath him. He fell to the ground, one hand grasping his mid-torso, the other reaching for her pant leg.

"Why?" he whispered harshly.

Maggie knocked his hand away and put her hands on her knees, trying to catch her own breath. She took a wobbly step toward the kneeling man. John tried to scramble away from her and her lethal anger.

"Don't," he managed to say, barely above a whisper, before he fell over.

He had been hit by a lot of women in his time but for some reason, he had never managed to get used to it. He couldn't understand their logic. John always had their best interests in mind, surely.

"I don't . . . believe . . . you did this. This is so stupid. How could you?"

"Give . . . the plan . . . time," John said, trying to convince his diaphragm to function normally.

Using all his strength, he climbed back to his feet, though still a bit unsteady. Then Maggie Second, chief of Otter Lake, completed this impromptu meeting with John Tanner/Richardson/Clayton/Prestor/Frum/Smith by kicking him squarely in the crotch. Again, though with less of a verbal response, the man hit the grass, facedown this time.

Feeling confident that her point had been made, Maggie found the strength to walk shakily to her front steps. She turned back to him. "Get off my Reserve," she snarled.

By now, John was on his back, hands protectively cradling his vital areas. "What?" he managed to grunt.

"Get off MY FUCKING RESERVE!" Leaning against her house, Maggie's strength and voice returned. "You have half an hour to get your White ass out of here. Or I am going to call the Res cops and make sure they escort you as far away from here as they are allowed. Maybe farther." She seemed to be reconsidering her demand. "Or maybe I'll have them just shoot you."

Now on his hands and knees, John was realizing that his brilliant plan wasn't as sure-fire as he had anticipated. "Maggie, you don't mean that. There's so much we can do together. This is ..." The rest of what he had to say was lost in a coughing spasm.

By now, Maggie had made it up the concrete steps to her front door. "I am so tempted to just tell the police everything and let them do whatever they want to you, but that might somehow implicate me, my family and possibly Otter Lake in your idiocy. I will figure the rest of this out later, but just get the fuck off our land before I replace what you took from the museum with *your* bones. Do I make myself clear?"

There was no mistaking the tone of Maggie's voice, and John, though still racked with pain, understood this was not the time to engage in a debate. Nodding, he struggled to climb up onto his motorcycle, trying to fight off another coughing attack as he gingerly adjusted his privates on the seat.

Feeling stronger already, Maggie opened her front door. "Like I said, you have half an hour before I send the police to Sammy's and have them patrol this entire community looking for you and your *classic* motorcycle. Go. Now."

"I don't suppose we could ..."

"No, we can't." Maggie reached just inside the open door, and her hand materialized with a phone. She began dialling. "I'd start moving if I were you. My cousins, the constables, would love the opportunity to work over a White boy on a motorcycle. They've heard it's good exercise."

Across her front lawn, John could just barely hear the sound of a phone ringing through Maggie's receiver. As with his first encounter with the raccoons in Otter Lake, he saw the wisdom and knowledge of fighting this battle another time.

Seconds later, he had departed the chief of Otter Lake's driveway and was already disappearing down the road, feverishly avoiding all the potholes.

TWENTY-FIVE

What a day it had been. Virgil didn't know if he was coming or going or not moving at all. He had witnessed an epic battle. Sure, the leaves and branches had hidden most of it from him, but he'd seen the repercussions.

Dutifully, he and Dakota had walked his uncle to the clinic. At first Wayne hadn't wanted to go, insisting he was fine, but after he'd walked into three outcroppings of rock and repeatedly tripped, and even tumbled down one embankment, Virgil managed to convince him a quick medical checkup wouldn't be a bad thing.

Along the way, Virgil had managed to inform Dakota as much as he could about the Nanabush legend. He told her of the stories his grandmother would tell, and of the information he'd found on the Internet at school and of his conversations with Uncle Wayne. At first Dakota didn't say much, just listened as Virgil poured out everything he knew.

Finally, twenty minutes later as they approached the health clinic, she commented, "Wow, you sure know a lot about Nanabush. Wish my parents had told me more about him."

Virgil left Dakota with Wayne at the clinic. His cousin was definitely not the type to deal with Nanabush and the kind of things Virgil had been seeing lately. The little she'd seen had already shaken her world. He told her he'd call her later to explain things further.

Wayne, on the other hand, thanked his young nephew for helping him. As the nurse practitioner was cleaning the wound on his head, he added, "Boy, sometimes magic can really hurt."

As Virgil left the building, he could tell something was up. People were running around, phones were ringing repeatedly and staff kept talking excitedly about mysterious bones and bodies somewhere on the Reserve. Normally the boy would have been overcome by curiosity, but today, he just shrugged and kept his eyes on the floor ahead of him. He could always get excited about whatever it was tomorrow.

Now he was alone. Really alone. His grandmother was dead, his bruised and battered uncle was being cared for, Dakota was busy wrestling with the concept of reality, and his mother—if not packing to run off with the guy who just might be Nanabush—was probably off doing chiefly things at the press conference ... which he suddenly realized he had in all probability missed. He had been way too preoccupied with certain motorcycle-man issues to keep track of anything more. It was late afternoon but already Virgil felt tired. He just wanted some time to collect his thoughts. He needed to figure out what to do. Nothing had been solved, and he was no closer to understanding things. So he bought a large bottle of water to fight the hot sun and dehydration from all the running around he'd been doing, and headed for his flat-topped rock ...

... which, he discovered upon his arrival, was again occupied. John was sitting there, seemingly deep in thought, head in his hands. Virgil could see his torn clothes and some cuts, but he'd managed to take back the headlight without being spotted, and end up here, so he couldn't be too badly injured.

Virgil was confused. Part of him wanted to walk right up to the man and hit him as hard as he could. Another part wanted to run away and hide, and hope that the man would just disappear. Still another part wanted to ask why the man had decided to torment Virgil and his mother. Having so many questions paralyzed him.

John spoke first, his head still in his hands. "Why do you like this place so much?"

At first, Virgil didn't even know for sure that the man was talking to him. But the forest was otherwise deserted. Still, he opted to not respond.

"Don't get me wrong. It's a good place. I was just curious, why?"

"I don't know. I just do."

"'I don't know. I just do.' That sounds a lot like me, and pretty much how I justify just about everything I do. You must have a better reason. There are a thousand big rocks like this scattered all over the area. Why here?"

He sounded tired, almost defeated. Virgil could see now that John was massaging his temples.

Still standing on the tracks, Virgil kicked an iron rail. "I like watching the trains go by."

"You like watching the trains go by."

"Yeah."

John took a deep breath, and Virgil could tell it hurt.

"Why do you like watching trains go by? Most people usually require a reason to repeatedly do stuff."

Virgil shrugged, unsure how much to share. "They're going places. People look out the windows at me. I look at them. Each one of them is coming from someplace and going to some other place."

"Meanwhile, you stay here. As they go by."

"Something like that."

"Maybe someday you'd like to hop on that train yourself, and see a little more than what Otter Lake has to offer?"

"Maybe."

Finally, John raised his head and looked at the boy. "Maybe."

His whisky-coloured eyes were now severely bloodshot. He was no longer the handsome young man who'd ridden into the community just over a week ago, setting all the female hearts aflutter. He looked . . . worn, beaten and exhausted.

"Where's my mother?"

"Your mother . . . is safe. Very safe. She's at home, I would imagine. Trust me, little man, she doesn't need any protection from you. She's quite capable of defending herself. And I don't think she wants to see me anymore. So, your problems are solved."

Virgil's mood lifted when he heard that. Was there light at the end of this tunnel? But there were still other issues to be dealt with, relating to this man.

"You hurt my uncle."

"I hurt your uncle. Well, he started it." John lay down flat on the rock, groaning.

"You don't look so good. Did my uncle hurt you?"

"Well, same family, wrong member. Virgil, a word of advice from someone who's been around for a very long time. I have been everywhere, done just about everything, and everyone, and to tell you the truth, I don't know if I've learned a goddamned thing in all that time. That's kind of scary, now that I think about it. Your grandmother once told me I wouldn't be me if I actually learned from what I did. That kind of hurt."

Virgil noticed a pile of freshly braided sweetgrass beside the man.

"Anyway, trains come and go all over the world, just like people. You know, there are probably people sitting on that train looking at you sitting on this rock, thinking, 'Sure wish I could be out in the woods, watching the world go by, instead of sitting in here beside somebody who's snoring and farting, and going somewhere I'd rather not be going.'"

Virgil watched the man put down the sweetgrass, watched his fingers trace the carvings Virgil had discovered a few days ago in the rock.

"Did you carve those?"

Still lying on his back, the man nodded. "I suppose I did. Are you angry? I mean, it's your rock and all."

Virgil shook his head. "No. They're kind of cool, I guess. Even though . . ."

"Yes?"

He was quiet for a moment before working up the nerve to speak. "I have a question."

"Maybe I have an answer."

"Were you going to take my mother away? Maybe to the land of the dead or something?"

For the first time that afternoon, John gave Virgil a puzzled look. "Now why would I do that? You mean take your mother to the land of the dead? What would be the point of . . . Are you on drugs or something?"

"Why do people ask me that all the time? The petroglyph. Right there. You're riding west, toward the setting sun. I heard that's where the land of the dead is."

John snickered, and it seemed to cause him some pain. "Yeah, that's true, but there's also a cute little motel on the west side of the Reserve, Virgil, called the Setting Sun Motel."

For a moment, Virgil struggled to deal with the simplicity of John's statement. Virgil knew the motel, in Roadside. He had been driven by it several times a week ever since he could remember.

"Sometimes, Virgil, a pipe is just a pipe."

Virgil didn't get the exact meaning of John's pipe comment but on some level he understood. Both were quiet for a moment. Then John started laughing, and again it was clearly painful. The more it hurt, the more he seemed to laugh, so his laughter grew. And suddenly, Virgil too started giggling. He was fairly sure the land of the dead was not located in some rundown, cheap motel. The conversations he'd had with his uncle about what the carvings could mean, his own personal fears—it was all too ridiculous. And the stress of the last few days added fuel to the outburst. And so the laughter kept pouring out of them.

Now John was on his back, struggling to take in air, and Virgil was leaning against an oak sapling, using one hand to keep himself upright.

"Oh, that felt good," said John. "That felt really good. I needed that."

"Me too," acknowledged Virgil, and he had. It seemed the weight of the world had been lifted off him, and he felt better than he had in days. Virgil managed to stifle his giggles, then he took a deep breath.

"John, are you really Nanabush?"

"What's in a name, Virgil? I am who I am. Aren't you who you are?"

"Maybe, but that's not an answer."

"Let me ask you a question first, Virgil. Who is Nanabush, to you? You tell me."

Virgil mentally went through all the stories his grandmother had told him over the years, and also through what he'd read recently. "He's a hero, a fool, a teacher, someone silly, someone clever—my grandmother would say he's us."

The man on the rock chuckled wearily to himself. "He's us, huh? I guess that's as good an explanation as any. I think we're all Nanabush, Virgil."

Not that long ago, the boy had wanted this man to disappear from his life, the Reserve, the world. Now he was curious about John's future. What was this Nanabush fellow going to do next? "What are you going to do now?"

"Me? That's a good question, a very good question." Again his fingers traced the markings in the limestone.

"Do you have an answer?"

His fingers stopped. "Hey, want to see something interesting?"

Curious, Virgil nodded, though cautiously.

John climbed off the rock and searched the immediate area. Moments later, he grabbed a thick, stout log, over two metres in length. "Come here, I'm going to need your help." For a second Virgil didn't move, until John yelled, "Will you get your ass over here! I can't do this by myself. You wanted to see this. You wanted answers."

Strangely, the animosity Virgil had felt toward John just a few hours ago was rapidly evaporating. Virgil ran to him, where he was busy thrusting the log under the big rock.

"Here, hold this." Handing the end of the log to Virgil, John once more began hunting around.

"What are we doing, exactly?" asked Virgil.

"Ah, found one."

Virgil saw the man bend over a mid-sized rock that was half embedded in the earth. John started digging around the edges, attempting to free it.

"Um, John . . . ?" It felt odd, talking to the man in such a familiar manner.

Ignoring the boy, John dug his fingers under the rock and heaved with all his might. It took a few seconds of effort but the small boulder eventually came loose, and flipped over. John repeated his efforts and turned it over again, a metre or so closer to the boy.

"What are you *doing?*"

"You'll see."

Finally, after much rolling, he managed to get the rock right next to the larger boulder bearing the petroglyphs. John was sweating. He took the log from Virgil and placed the end that was not under the big rock on top of the smaller one.

"Man, this is harder than I thought."

"It's a lever of some sort. Why?"

"Help me flip over the boulder and you'll find out why."

Together, they heaved and pushed and grunted until finally, after much manoeuvring and repositioning of the fulcrum and lever, they succeeded in flipping the large boulder over onto its side. Though a few hours ago they had been sworn enemies, now they both let out a cheer of success.

"That's the first thing that's gone right for me today," said the man.

Virgil took a long drink from his sizable bottle of water. "So why did we spend all that time and effort to turn this thing over?"

"That is a question I can answer." Grabbing the bottled water, he began to squirt it at the underside of the mud-encrusted rock, washing away layers of earth.

"Hey, that's my water!"

"You know, I never thought I'd see the day when Native people would be paying good money for something as available as water. White people I understand. They like to buy and own everything, but, man, Native people too? That's when you know something is wrong. Now look. What do you see?"

The water had revealed what lay hidden under the big boulder. "Hey, are those more . . . petroglyphs?"

"Yep. I thought you might like to see them."

Virgil took back his bottle and poured the final drops onto the carved images, furiously rubbing away the remaining dirt. "How old are these, do you think?"

Virgil traced the carved indentations with his hand. Already he could make out what seemed to be a moose, a dog, or more likely a wolf. A group of people holding hands in a circle. To the boy, one petroglyph looked like a fire. And some other images he couldn't make out yet. It was quite a thrill, knowing he was probably the first person in a very long time, maybe since they were carved, to see and touch them.

"Don't remember. Maybe a couple of hundred years, maybe a thousand. I forget."

"How did you know they were here?"

"I carved them myself."

It took a few seconds for the words to register on Virgil, whose attention was focused on the petroglyphs. He dropped the empty water bottle.

"What?"

"That was so long ago, I barely remember carving them. And you have to keep in mind, I've carved a lot of petroglyphs in my life, and painted pictographs too. It all depended on how I felt that day."

"You did this? But you said they were hundreds, maybe a thousand years old!"

"Yeah. So?"

"That would mean . . ."

"Come on, Virgil, you can make the leap."

Virgil could not talk.

"Geez, the ice age came and went in less time."

Finally the boy caught his breath. "Nana . . ."

"Like I said earlier, what's in a name? They're as common as the leaves in a forest. I am who I am. Simple as that."

"You can't be!"

"Excuse me? A second ago you were ready to believe. You even asked. But now . . . So what's changed?"

Virgil slipped to the other side of the overturned boulder, giving himself space from the man who had just said he was Nanabush. True, Virgil and his uncle had been discussing that possibility. But for him to actually claim it—that was a different matter. A very big and stupendously different matter.

John picked up the discarded bottle, hoping there were some remaining droplets of water, but it was empty.

"You can't be! There is no such person. I . . . I was joking. My uncle's weird and . . ."

The man shrugged. "Okay. Makes no difference to me."

"Prove it to me. My grandmother said you could change into animals."

"Yeah, when I have to. It's actually really painful. You try not to do it if you can avoid it." The man winced at the memory.

"I remember my grandmother telling me this story about you coming upon a wigwam in the forest one night where these three beautiful women were sleeping and you changed yourself into a bear and entered . . ."

John flung the empty bottle at the boulder, sending it bouncing off into the undergrowth. "Fuck I hate that story. Sure, you boff a couple of women who are asleep when you're a bear, and over the years the story gets blown completely out of proportion. I've done other things too, you know! More productive things."

Realizing he was alone in the woods with this man and that no one knew he was here, Virgil thought he'd better change the subject quickly.

"What do they mean? The petroglyphs?"

Almost as quickly as it had flared, the man's temper abated. "Oh, that. Nothing much. I was just bored. When I get bored I petroglyph, if that can be a verb. It's just something to do when you're on the road." John quickly scanned the carved images, as if reading. "Ah, let's see. Something like, I hunted a moose. Had a party with some friends. Changed into a wolf. And that"—he pointed to a stick figure of a man—"just means 'I was here.' That kind of thing."

"That's it? That's all? Nothing mystical or spiritual? Just a diary of some kind?"

"I guess it is. As I said, it gets boring on the road."

"But there are petroglyphs and pictographs all across the country, all over North America."

"Yep, I know. I've been on the road a long, long time. Places to go, things to see."

"But they're all different kinds of symbols and markings. Not like these."

"Different languages and different dialects. When you're in Okanagan country, you don't write and speak Anishnawbe. Don't they teach you anything in that school you go to? When you decide to go."

"All those . . . they're all nothing but . . . graffiti? That's all? Just graffiti? Left by you . . ."

"Yeah, what did you think they were? I mean, who knew people would think they were important? People crack me up."

Virgil was quickly becoming disillusioned. "I don't believe this. This is not what I expected."

The man shrugged, indicating he didn't really give a shit. "That's your choice. But you should realize that if you don't want to know the answer to a question, you shouldn't ask it. It's always amazed me how the simplest concepts are often the hardest for people to follow."

John stood to his full height, still looking a bit worse for wear from his visit to Otter Lake. "Virgil, I think it's time for me to go. I've exhausted my stay around here. And if I were you I wouldn't tell your mother that you met me here." He sighed. "After all this time, I still don't know how to impress and keep a woman. Isn't that kind of sad?"

"I . . . I don't know."

"Count yourself lucky, young man. Before long, in another year or so, I bet, you too will begin that long road to hell. And heaven."

Two dragonflies briefly danced in and around the two figures.

"John, why did you come here?"

Virgil was almost sure he saw a flicker of something . . . something he couldn't describe . . . play across John's eyes.

"Why did I come here? Well, the simplest answer is your grandmother was very special to me, Virgil. More special than you could understand. Simply put, she was the last person to really believe in me, not as a legend but as a real flesh-and-blood person. She saw me, touched me, loved me. You don't forget a person like that. This is a changing world, Virgil, but your grandmother didn't change. Okay, maybe a little, but she was still Lillian. She got new friends but I think I always held a special place in her heart. And she in mine. When she was dying, I couldn't let her go without saying goodbye. I owed her that. Old friends are the best friends. Always remember that."

"You said something about a promise to her. What was that?"

"Well, that's between me and Lillian. Whatever promises you had between you and your grandmother are yours. Of course . . . I could give you a hint. Interested?"

Virgil nodded eagerly.

"It was a big promise. And part of it involved you. Because she really cared for you. She thought you needed a little magic in your life. Everybody does occasionally."

John slumped over and Virgil felt a lump in his chest for his grandmother. Both stood quietly in the forest, each remembering the woman who had passed away.

John broke the silence. "Virgil?"

"Yeah?"

"Do you want a ride home? It's a pretty long walk."

The boy thought for a moment. "I shouldn't." Ever since he could remember, he'd been taught not to accept rides from strangers, and there was nobody stranger than the guy standing next to him.

"I gave your mother a couple of rides. She loved it. I don't think she'd mind. It's your last chance."

That was true: both his mother and Dakota had been given rides. Virgil finally nodded. "Yeah, I could handle a ride home. That would be cool."

John smiled his perfect smile, though one tooth seemed to be loose. "Okay but we will have to take the back roads 'cause I think the cops are looking for me."

"Why?"

"It's a long story. I will drop you off near your house. Your mother and I have already said our goodbyes. Is it a deal?"

"It's a deal."

The boy and the man shook hands.

"I left my bike by the road down that way. Let's go."

Side by side they walked through the woods. And they talked. They talked about life, about being Native, about being young and about being old, about Lillian and about the need to be silly occasionally.

"Never underestimate the need for some sheer silliness," said John. "That's why some people drink. That's why some people take drugs. Of course that's the cheap way out. A good bout of complete nonsense now and again would keep everybody sane. You can quote me on that."

Virgil found the thought itself quite silly. "Yeah, I plan to go around directly quoting Nanabush."

"Ah, now you believe me?"

"I believe nothing."

"Now *that's* silly, and I like it."

"John, Nanabush, or whatever you want to call yourself, what's next?"

"Whatever I want. That's what I do."

"I mean more specifically."

"Virgil, half the fun is not knowing, but I'll send you a postcard when I do."

Before long, they emerged from the forest near the spot where he'd parked his motorcycle. John could tell the boy was eager to sit atop the machine.

"Go ahead. Just don't scratch anything."

Slowly, as if he were in a dream and the bike might disappear in a heartbeat, Virgil approached it. He threw his leg across the fabled 1953 Indian Chief motorcycle, admiring its ageless beauty. Yeah, he'd seen Harleys and Hondas and Kawasakis in magazines and on television, but he had to admit, there was something very different about this machine. He could understand why John would choose to ride it.

The Indian Chief was big for the boy physically but not too big for his imagination. Sitting atop the bike, hands stretching forward to grasp the handlebars, he could almost feel the wind blowing past him. He imitated the sound of the motorcycle as he pretended to shift gears. At one point, deep into his fantasy, he was trying to avoid the police as he raced down a highway. Up ahead, the cops had thrown "sticks," with their tire-piercing prongs, across the blacktop. Desperate to avoid them, bad boy Virgil lurched to the right—only to find himself and the motorcycle falling over onto an obscure dirt road in Otter Lake.

He found himself on his back, John standing over him with an amused look on his face.

"You scratch it, you buy it."

Scrambling to his feet, Virgil helped John lift the bike up and onto the kickstand. "Just having some fun."

"That's what I like to hear. Ready to go home now? The helmet's a bit big but it should be fine."

Virgil put on the oversized helmet and sat across the gas tank, while John donned his own headgear. Virgil's heart thrilled at the vibrations when John turned the ignition and kick-started the beast. To please the boy, he revved the engine a few times, making it growl, then joyously gunned it and sped down the road, leaving behind a trail of dust.

For the last time, the 1953 Indian Chief cruised through the streets and roads of Otter Lake, though avoiding the well-travelled routes where the Res cops might be lurking. Virgil enjoyed every kilometre of it. He waved to the Otter Lake Debating Society as they roared past, momentarily disturbing today's topic of discussion: who was sexier, Charlotte or Emily Brontë?

John weaved in and out of side roads until he ended up down by Beer Bay, near the Second house. There he stopped the vehicle with a skidding flourish.

His heart still beating a mile a minute, and his butt tingling from the engine's humming, Virgil ripped his helmet off, smiling ear to ear. "That was so incredible! I want one!" He slid off the bike and turned around.

Slowly, John removed the screaming-raven helmet from his head. For a moment, Virgil's heart almost stopped. The blond White man he'd known for over a week was not the man before him. In his place sat a strikingly handsome Native man, still lean, but with a dusky skin colour, high cheekbones and long black hair that danced in the slight wind. Still in John's clothes. And for a second, Virgil could see the last traces of amber in his eyes, before they filled in with brown.

Through gritted teeth, John managed to say, "Christ that stings. I told you it hurt."

"J—John . . . ?"

"Not quite, but close enough." The pain seemed to subside, and the Native man who was dressed like John now sat tall in the saddle.

Virgil felt his eyes widen. "Then who . . . ?"

"Yes, Virgil, there is a Nanabush."

"Oh my God . . ."

"Well, that's a bit presumptuous, Virgil, but thank you for the compliment. You know, through these brown eyes, the world does look a little different. Curious, huh?"

Nanabush took a deep breath. "Just smell that. Anishnawbe. Otter Lake. It never really changes, you know. You could say the more things change, the more they stay the same."

"Wow."

"You really have to work on your vocabulary."

"You *are* Nanabush!"

"And you are Virgil. I thought we established that already." The now-Native-looking man surveyed the surrounding land. "Virgil, this road here, where does it lead? Down to the water?"

Virgil nodded, finding it an effort to answer. "Yeah. That's where they take the boat trailers in the spring, to put boats into the water. And in the fall to take them out again."

"Good. That's what I needed to know. Well, this is goodbye, Virgil. I am quite confident I've overstayed my welcome."

"You're leaving! But you can't! I want—"

"Sure I can." He began tying his hair back into a ponytail, similar to Wayne's. "I've been away for a while, Virgil, and now I'm back. It's a whole new country, a whole new adventure now. Lots of new people. I've been negligent lately. Got things to do now. I didn't before. I hear Ottawa's a fun town. Might go into politics. Never know. I'll be around."

"Goodbye, then, I guess."

"No, Virgil. There is no word for goodbye in the Anishnawbe language. Only . . ."

"I'll be seeing you. Ga-waabamin."

"There is hope for you after all. Ga-waabamin, my friend." Grunting, he turned his bike toward the weed-infested road.

"But I told you, you can't leave that way. That's a dead end. It ends at the water."

Smiling his trademark smile, albeit a more tanned, high-cheekboned version of it, the man formerly known as John shook his head. "Haven't you figured it out yet, Virgil? There are no such things as dead ends. Only people who find dead ends. I sometimes wonder if that's the only thing I have to teach."

"Before you go . . ."

"Yes?"

Virgil took a braided strand of sweetgrass out of his pocket and held it up for the man to take. "I took one of these from the pile you made. I think you should keep it. A little something from Otter Lake. My mother and a lot of my relatives with cars have dreamcatchers or these hanging from their rear-view mirrors for good luck. You don't have a rear-view mirror but still, I . . ."

Reaching out, the stranger took the gift and smelled it. "That is truly the smell of the Anishnawbe. I accept your gift. Even though I made it." He attached it to the mirror on the left handle-bar. "Thanks."

"That's so . . . White. I think you're suppose to say 'meegwetch.'"

"Meegwetch, then."

He put on the helmet and, with a nod to the boy, Nanabush kicked the bike into gear. The wheels spun and shot vehicle and rider down the road.

There are no such things as dead ends. Only people who find dead ends. Virgil stood, pondering the meaning of that. It would make a great title for an essay. He had planned to write about his uncle's martial art, until Dakota, a much smarter kid than him,

told him she was amazed at what he now knew about Nanabush.
It would mean a lot less research too. And maybe he wouldn't
have to use so many adverbs and adjectives.

TWENTY-SIX

Dinner was almost over and Virgil, Maggie, Wayne and Dakota were finishing off the final crumbs of their apple pie.

"Oh my God, that was tasty," Wayne said. "I could almost get used to this kind of cooking. That pie was almost as good as Mom's."

"Keep complimenting women like that and you'll have a girlfriend in no time," Maggie said with a smile.

"Hell, I wouldn't know what to do with one anymore." Mildly amused, the three other dinner mates all looked directly at him. "I mean . . . I would know . . . I mean . . . it's just been a long time since I dated . . . and I . . . geez, leave me alone, guys." Sheepishly, he licked his plate, trying to hide behind it.

At this, as in the other recent suppers, nobody mentioned the elephant—or in this case, the White man—in the room. It had been almost two weeks since John had left. Most of Wayne's bruises had healed and he was walking with only a slight limp. More importantly, he had used the time he was laid up to devise a usable defense against a raccoon being thrown at him, at least in theory. He was, understandably, in no hurry to test it. Besides, he was safely ensconced at his sister's, feeling oddly comfortable there.

Dakota was studying up on Nanabush. Though her parents tended to dismiss "all those old stories," she was enthralled.

Especially by the more adult, bawdy ones that many teachers and social workers might find inappropriate for a girl of Dakota's age. Every time she found a new Trickster story, she would mumble under her breath, "Yeah, he'd do that" or "Nah, not in a million years," almost as if she were reading a biography.

Maggie tried hard not to think of he who must not be named, who had entered and left her life so suddenly. But John was a hard man to forget. Like the dust from the meteor that had wiped out the dinosaurs, it would take quite a while for things to settle. At that very moment, as it had been since the press conference, that particular patch of woods was crawling with police, forensic teams, archaeologists, anthropologists, media and, for some reason, a lot of fat raccoons. Bones were still being found and there was a rumour that some ancient Mayan artifacts had been uncovered.

In the meantime, Maggie was trying a more Zen approach to her work and her life. She could not control the things that happened in her community; she merely had to react. That, in itself, lowered her blood pressure. John, if nothing else, had taught her chaos was to be expected and nobody can really plan for it. Just prepare as best you can and deal with it when it arises. No more late nights worrying about "what if . . . ?" Instead, more television or fishing with Virgil, thinking "whatever." She was sleeping better.

And then there was Virgil. Essentially life had not changed much for him. He still went to his rock by the railroad tracks, though less often, and the last time he took Dakota, to show her the petroglyphs. He was still waiting to find out if he'd managed to salvage his year, but he had handed in his essay. One of the most significant changes, if it could be called that, was the knowing smile he shared with his uncle and cousin.

Perhaps most importantly, it was the phrase uttered by John-of-a-thousand-last-names before he disappeared that caused Virgil to think and ponder.

"There are no such things as dead ends. Only people who find dead ends."

That was almost T-shirt worthy, the boy thought. How to apply its wisdom to his own life . . . well, that would take a bit more thinking. He was only thirteen, after all; he had a few years ahead of him to ponder it.

"Do you want us to clean up, Mom?" Without waiting for an answer, Virgil began to stack the plates while Dakota gathered the cutlery.

"No, don't worry about it. We can look after this later. I'm too full to even think about washing them now. Why don't you two go outside. Show Dakota some of that stuff your uncle has been teaching you." She stacked the plates from around the table and looked at her brother. "I could go for a coffee, how about you?" Wayne nodded, pushing himself back from the table. In his scant two weeks on the mainland, his pants had gotten unusually tight. Might have to start training again, soon and a lot. Nothing more embarrassing than a fat martial artist.

"Okay, we'll be outside." Almost instantly, Maggie and Wayne were alone in the kitchen. Wayne picked the last pickle from the bowl in the centre of the table, somehow finding room for it.

"Wayne, they're putting in Mom's headstone this afternoon."

"Already? I thought that took two or three months or something like that to carve."

Maggie smiled. "Well, when you're chief, you can pull a few strings. Put a rush order on things. I told them she was a matriarch of the community . . ."

For a moment, Wayne lowered his eyes. "Well, she was," he answered softly.

"Yeah." A silence rose up between them. "Wanna come with me? Make sure everything's fine?"

"Yeah, you know, I would like that. Sounds good."

They shared a sibling smile. "Hey, what about that coffee?"

"Ah yes, coffee. Coming up." Rising from the table, Maggie got out her can of ground coffee and began to spoon half a dozen helpings into the machine.

"Maggie . . . ?"

"Yes?" She now filled the pot with water.

"That nurse at the clinic. Do you know her?"

"Colleen. Kinda, why?"

"I've been saving up my compliments. I might want to try a few on her. Think I should?"

She looked at her brother and raised an eyebrow. "She's heard the stories. She knows you're weird, you know."

"Not weird. Eccentric."

"You're not rich or White enough to be eccentric."

"Then I'll have to settle for 'peculiar.'"

"Feel free to use me as a reference. By the way, on Thursday nights, she teaches a beginner class in tae kwon do at the Health Centre."

Now it was Wayne's turn to raise an eyebrow.

Outside, the two kids were wrestling on the grass. Dakota seemed to be getting the better of Virgil, pushing him backwards until, with a little flip, she went flying over her cousin's hip in a very ungirlish manner.

"Ow!"

"I'm sorry. Did I hurt you?" Virgil rushed up to her.

"This is supposed to be fun? When do I start having a fun time?" Helping her up, Virgil flicked some grass off his cousin's back. "There better not be grass stains!"

"Nope, you're okay," Virgil lied.

Off in the distance, the telltale sound of a motor, gradually getting closer, made them freeze. Their eyes locked. For a moment, they shared a joint sense of excitement, concern and delight, touched with a flavouring of apprehension. Then, as the sound grew louder, they began to relax, albeit with some disappointment, for like anybody who lived by a sizable river or lake, they knew the unmistakable growl of an outboard motor. Somebody was boating in Beer Bay.

"Where do you think he—" Before he could finish, Virgil went flying over Dakota's hip, also landing in a very ungirlish manner.

"Is that how you do it?" she asked innocently.

Staring up at the sky, Virgil had to laugh in spite of himself.

Seventeen years, three months and four days later, Michael
Mukwa, the last remaining member of the once-famed Otter
Lake Debating Society, passed away quietly. On his deathbed, as
on every single day since it had happened, he swore up and down,
by every god that was worshipped, that the story was true.

On a certain summer day so many years earlier, he had been
travelling home by boat across the lake after a busy day of fishing.
Three bass and two pickerel lay at the bottom of his boat, and he
was content. Though this wasn't nearly the number of fish he'd
have caught when he was young, it was still a good day's catch by
any standard.

So there he was, steering his boat, propelled by a Johnson
ten-horse-power motor, through slightly choppy water when
something caught his eye, and casually he looked over to his right,
and to the back. That's where he saw what he saw. A familiar, large
red-and-white motorcycle was barrelling along behind him, riding
the wake from his boat like a surfboard.

At first the image failed to register in Michael's brain, it was so
ridiculous and impossible. It was like an Apple computer receiving
a PC command. Then the man on the motorcycle waved a hand,
and automatically, without thinking, Michael waved back.

After a few minutes, the rider, with what appeared to be great difficulty, managed to pop a sizable wheelie in the middle of the lake. Then, waving his hand in victory, he sped up and pulled ahead of the boat.

Michael caught glimpses of an Indian headdress on the gas tank, some sort of bird on the crash helmet and a braid of what appeared to be sweetgrass wrapped around a handlebar. The last he saw of motorcycle and rider, they were moving farther and farther ahead of the boat, riding the waves like speed bumps, until they disappeared around a spit of land.

Michael Mukwa swore this really happened. Yet nobody in the village believed him. Well, almost nobody. There were three who did.

And that's how it happened to a cousin of mine. I told you it was a long story. They're the best 'cause you can wrap one around you like a nice warm blanket.

— ACKNOWLEDGMENTS —

In many ways a novel is like a pyramid, with several people lay-ing stones to build up the story. The writer is merely the architect, or perhaps foreman. With that in mind, there are many people to thank who have provided this humble architect/foreman with the raw materials and expertise to construct the story you have just read.

I had the opportunity to work with such people as Alan Collins, James Cullingham and Larry E. Lewis in hammering out the original story, back when I thought it might make a cool movie. Then others joined the bandwagon, showing their support for my storytelling: Kateri Akiwenzie-Damm in the guise of Kegedonce Press, and the Ontario Arts Council, which financially believed in me. Also, the Leighton Artists' Colony at The Banff Centre. What a place to create!

Then of course, there's Tom King and Basil Johnston, whose writings about the Trickster helped lay the groundwork for this and countless other books.

A special thanks goes to Helen Hoy, who gave me the clue on how to get to the "bones" of the issue.

The following people provided technical or moral support as I feverishly laboured away: Dan David, Linda Cree, Anita Knott, Kennetch Charlette, Umeek of Ahousaht, the mysterious

T. L. Corell, Tom Wilcock—and Michael Schellenberg and Amanda Lewis of Knopf Canada.

And finally, a special thanks goes to the lovely Janine, whose efforts, faith and understanding almost mirrored my own. This is as much her book as mine.

Thomas King

DREW HAYDEN TAYLOR was born and raised on the Curve Lake First Nation (Anishnawbe) in Central Ontario. A writer for over twenty years, he has done everything from performing stand-up at the Kennedy Centre in Washington, D.C., to a proud stint as Artistic Director of Canada's premiere Native theatre company, Native Earth Performing Arts. Drew has written in practically every medium available, including television, documentaries, theatre, short stories and essays. He enjoys spreading the gospel of Native literature. *Motorcycles & Sweetgrass* is Drew's first novel for adults. Currently he is juggling two new plays, a television series and a collection of essays.

www.drewhaydentaylor.com